WARRIOR QUEEN

The Story of Boudica, Celtic Queen

Alan Gold

 NEW AMERICAN LIBRARY

New American Library
Published by New American Library, a division of
Penguin Group (USA) Inc., 375 Hudson Street,
New York, New York 10014, USA
Penguin Group (Canada), 10 Alcorn Avenue, Toronto,
Ontario M4V 3B2, Canada (a division of Pearson Penguin Canada Inc.)
Penguin Books Ltd., 80 Strand, London WC2R 0RL, England
Penguin Ireland, 25 St. Stephen's Green, Dublin 2,
Ireland (a division of Penguin Books, Ltd.)
Penguin Group (Australia), 250 Camberwell Road, Camberwell, Victoria 3124,
Australia (a division of Pearson Australia Group Pty. Ltd.)
Penguin Books India Pvt. Ltd., 11 Community Centre, Panchsheel Park,
New Delhi—110 017, India
Penguin Group (NZ), cnr Airborne and Rosedale Roads, Albany,
Auckland 1310, New Zealand (a division of Pearson New Zealand Ltd.)
Penguin Books (South Africa) (Pty.) Ltd., 24 Sturdee Avenue,
Rosebank, Johannesburg 2196, South Africa

Penguin Books Ltd., Registered Offices:
80 Strand, London WC2R 0RL, England

First published by New American Library,
a division of Penguin Group (USA) Inc.

First Printing, June 2005
10 9 8 7 6 5 4 3 2 1

Copyright © Alan Gold, 2005
Map copyright © Jeffrey L. Ward, 2005
Readers Guide copyright © Penguin Group (USA) Inc., 2005
All rights reserved.

NEW AMERICAN LIBRARY and logo are trademarks of Penguin Group (USA) Inc.

LIBRARY OF CONGRESS CATALOGING-IN-PUBLICATION DATA
Gold, Alan.
Warrior queen : the story of Boudica, Celtic Queen / Alan Gold.
p. cm.
ISBN 0-451-21525-7 (trade pbk.)
1. Boadicea, Queen, d. 62—Fiction. 2. Great Britain—History—Roman period, 55 B.C.–449 A.D.—Fiction. 3. Great
Britain—History, Military—55 B.C.–449 A.D.—Fiction. 4. Romans—Great Britain—Fiction. 5. Women soldiers—
Fiction. 6. Britons—Fiction. 7. Queens—Fiction. 8. Iceni—Fiction. I. Title.
PR9619.4.G65W37 2005
823'.914—dc22   2004029210

Set in Centaur
Designed by Ginger Legato

Printed in the United States of America

WARRIOR QUEEN

For Jonathan Gold,
who helped me re-create every moment of Boadicea's life

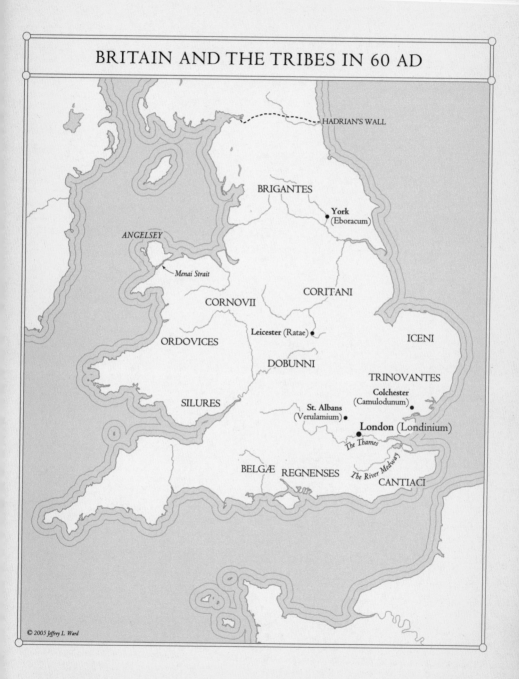

BRITAIN AND THE TRIBES IN 60 AD

HADRIAN'S WALL

BRIGANTES

York
(Eboracum)

ANGELSEY

Menai Strait

CORITANI

CORNOVII

ORDOVICES

Leicester (Ratae)

ICENI

DOBUNNI

TRINOVANTES

SILURES

Colchester
(Camulodunum)

St. Albans
(Verulamium)

London (Londinium)

The Thames

BELGÆ   REGNENSES   *The River Medway*

CANTIACI

© 2005 Jeffrey L. Ward

CHAPTER ONE

Spring, 43 AD—The Land of the Iceni in Eastern Britain

To his ears, it was little more than a rustle in the leaves, a disturbance in the riverbank's undergrowth; but her ears were the ears of a warrior. She was a young woman whose eyes were sharper than needles and whose sense of animals was so finely honed that it was said of her that she had an animal spirit in her body.

He held his breath to concentrate his mind, but try as he might he couldn't focus as acutely as could his daughter. He listened but heard no sound of the animal; yet he knew Boudica heard and saw that to which he was deaf and blind. She crouched on the spot like a wolf, not moving a muscle.

Boudica's muscles suddenly tensed and slowly drew her spear arm back to be ready for the boar's attack, while her right hand firmed its grasp on her sword's handle.

She looked to her father, and used only her eyes to indicate that the boar was ready to make its run. Would it home in on her, slighter and less muscular than her father? Or would it attack Gadrin? Suddenly the undergrowth came to life; an outlying branch snapped, a twig yielded and a bird in the distance flew noisily away.

With terrifying suddenness and squeals of fury, the huge boar began its run for freedom. Gadrin and Boudica had driven it into the copse and it had lain in wait long enough. Now it would attack whatever stood between it and liberty.

The huge beast, half the height of a man and with evil tusks which could skewer a victim to death, burst out of the undergrowth, head lowered, little pink eyes narrowed in hatred, and hurled itself at the place where Gadrin and Boudica were crouching. Before it had even cleared the copse to charge into the open ground where they stood, Boudica suddenly stood and hurled her spear at the frantic beast. She threw it as hard as she could and aimed it to fly between the copse and where her father stood. As the boar reached its full speed, the spear thudded into its rib cage. The animal screamed again, but its fury and momentum kept it charging. Instantly, Boudica leapt forward, sword raised, and closed the short distance between her and her father. She screamed a bloodcurdling oath and brought the sword slicing down on the boar's neck, almost severing the head from the rest of the body. It pitched forward at her feet, shuddering in death throes.

And in the time that Boudica had speared and killed the beast, Gadrin had barely been able to raise his sword, let alone defend himself.

Delighted with her kill, her long red hair cascading down her back, Boudica stood with one foot on the quivering beast and one on the ground. "By the gods, that's a big animal," she said, panting in excitement. "Imagine what would have happened had it reached you."

Gadrin looked at the boar, which was still shuddering as the spirits continued to leave its tortured body, and asked his daughter, "How did you know it was coming at me? Your spear seemed to fly from you before the beast had left the clearing."

She smiled, and said softly, "The boar spoke to me."

Mystified, her father looked at her, and asked, "Its spirits? They talked to you?"

She nodded slowly, her eyes narrowed. Breathing deeply, she stared at the sky as though transfixed. He had long known that Boudica was a strange girl, the most unusual of all his children. She was often seen alone in the fields, as though talking to herself or communing with the spirits of the ground or the sky, maybe even the gods themselves. But this was the first time she had intimated that she had a connection with animals.

"What did the boar say to you, Boudica? Did it tell you that it was going to attack me?"

"Yes, Father," Boudica said, her voice deepening in seriousness. "The boar spoke to me from the riverbank. It said, 'I think I'll attack Gadrin because he's as mean and ugly as I am.'"

She looked at him in all seriousness, and then burst out laughing. Gadrin shouted, "You cheeky little sprite child," and playfully tried to spank her on the bottom. She jumped away and was halfway across the field, laughing and shouting, by the time he'd picked up his weapons and begun to walk back to his home. He shook his head in wonder at his daughter. So mischievous, so beautiful, such an amazing hunter; she was the joy of his life. More than his sons, who were good boys, but plodding; more than his other daughters, who were gentle and nurturing like their mother, it was Boudica who sought him out and begged him to allow her to go hunting with him. Sometimes they went hunting as a family, even his wife Annika joining in a couple of times a year; but the moments he enjoyed most, the real satisfaction he gained as headman of the village and surrounding land, was when he was hunting alone with Boudica.

And hunting the wild boar which had killed his lambs and was menacing villagers along the river was a perfect event for father and daughter to set out on a mission together. He had made the decision to hunt the beast, but it was Boudica who had planned the strategy, instinctively knowing where the boar's lair might be and the hunting paths it would be taking; and it was Boudica who had tracked the animal down to where it lived, to drive it into a place from which there was no escape. And it was Boudica who would instruct the slaves to carry the boar to their nearby village so that the entire tribe could feast for days on its flesh.

Boudica! He smiled and shook his head as he saw her tall and lithe figure running tirelessly across the fields, her long straight legs leaping over the fallen logs. Boudica! Still a child, yet more woman than many who were already married and full with children. Soon she must marry and start her own family. Annika had been pressing him for some time to find a suitable husband. And he'd tried; but everybody who initially looked suitable failed his test. And it was a simple enough test: Were they sufficient and man enough to share their lives with one such as Boudica? With her strength of mind, her willfulness and her strange ways? What sort of a man would be capable of marrying her . . . and surviving more than a year?

He shook his head with love and exasperation, and followed her on the long way back to their house. The air was warm, the crops were ripening and there would be plenty to eat this summer. And if the gods were particularly kind, and accepted the sacrifices, then there would be an abundance of food, and the villages of his domain would be able to store enough to last through the depths of winter and into spring, when the growth would again ensure life.

Life? It was good. He and his family were rich, and he and Annika had been fortunate to lose only two of their children to the gods. They lived well, and even though they collected food, clothes and other taxes from the villages under his command, they were liked by his people. And best loved of all was Boudica, whose open smile and easy manner had endeared her to many of the tribe. She was at her happiest when she was hunting, but she also loved visiting the ironworkers, the jewelers and the herdsmen and watching how they performed their work. Sometimes, when she found a knob of oak, she would whittle it into a god or goddess which she'd give to an elderly tribesperson for their protection.

But good as she was, Boudica was also the most playful of his children. Only thirteen years old, she already had the body of a woman and the strength of many a man. Yet she still had the mind of an impish child, always trying to trick her brothers and sisters, her mother and father, as a paean to Lugh, the god of laughter and mischief. Even though she was younger than either of her brothers, it was becoming plain that on his and his wife's death, it should be Boudica rather than his sons who should be made ruler of their lands. By ancient Celtic tradition, the hetship passed down to the oldest of his children, boy or girl; but Boudica had such a instinct for leadership that in the interests of his family fortune and his people, he might not have a choice. He sighed. It would be so simple if Boudica could be found a husband; then she would leave the family home, leadership of the tribes would devolve on his sons, and his problem about succession would be over.

As he was trailing after her, he saw that she had suddenly stopped running and was standing starkly still. He, too, stopped, knowing that Boudica was acutely aware of potential danger. She turned and signaled to him to approach her, but as quietly as possible. She crouched down in the undergrowth, her spear level with her head. As he walked softly toward her, Gadrin looked around for what could have caused his daughter concern. There were no birds in the air, and no animals visible in the field or the nearby forest. But in deference to Boudica's senses, he approached her quietly.

When he was beside her, she whispered, "Men. Running."

He raised his head above the level of the grasses, but could see nothing. Boudica pointed to a distant road, which to him looked empty.

"How many?" he asked.

"Many."

They continued to look, and then he, too, could hear the sound of feet on the earthen road. Around a bend and over the brow of the hill, three, then five, and then nearly twenty men came running, each carrying a sack of provisions; some were armed with swords and spears and shields. They looked more like a war party than a raiding party of robbers.

"It's all right, Boudica, these men aren't dangerous to us," said Gadrin, who stood and walked quickly to join the road. As the men reached him, they stopped and engaged him in conversation. Then they ran on. He returned to where Boudica was standing.

"Well?" she asked, "where are they going?"

"To the south. There's talk that the Romans are massing in Gaul, across the water."

"Is that bad?" Boudica asked.

"For some, it's bad."

"Is it bad for us?" she asked.

He smiled. "That depends on whether we fight against the Romans, like the men of Germania, or whether we learn to live with them like the Gauls."

She waited for her father to tell her whether her family was going to be like the Germans or the Gauls; but he remained silent.

She followed him home.

43 AD—Gesoriacum, Shores of Northern Gaul in the Reign of the Emperor Claudius

"Madness. Bloody simpleminded madness."

Titus Flavius Vespasianus listened to the legate and remained silent. Others in the commander's tent stopped examining their maps, and listened.

In the silence, the legate continued. "I'm sorry, Commander, but this crossing is insane. Why would we risk our men's lives and sanity to fight in Britain, and against these . . . these . . . barbarians, when there's no need. This shouldn't be a part of the Roman world," he said, pointing north. "You know it as well as I do! This is a land of demons and devils and evil spirits from Hades; it isn't where our men should be. Remember what happened to Varus and his men when the barbarians from the German armies got hold of them!"

Vespasian continued to remain silent. As subordinate general, he had the right to order the man's arrest as a traitor. But Vespasian realized that this interview presaged the beginning of a rebellion in his army, for no legate would have dared to enter the commander's tent and make such statements unless he and the eight other legates who commanded the gathered legions had severe reservations about the course of action the emperor had commanded; and if the legions weren't committed to the task ahead, then despite the forty thousand men gathered, there was the strong prospect of failure.

But just as much as the men under his command, Vespasian knew that they all had good reason to be afraid. The Druids were a terrifying prospect. Tall, blond-haired men with drooping mustaches, their long hair was stiffened with lime into spikes which made them look as though they were wearing the quills of a porcupine on their heads. Were they not so fearsome, they could have been characters in some bacchanal, especially with their skin colored bright blue from a lifetime of painting themselves with woad.

But it wasn't the outward appearance which frightened the Romans as much as what the Druids did. Sacrificing humans to use their intestines and entrails for the purposes of divination was only the beginning of the nightmare which was the land of Britain. According to the travelers and escapees who knew Britain and had been given permission to address the Roman Senate about conditions in that foul country, when the Druids captured and tortured their prisoners, they would roast them alive and eat their sizzling flesh. This, Vespasian understood, was what terrified his men. And Vespasian himself was just as horrified at the prospect of leaving Gaul and bidding what might be a last farewell to his wife Drusilla and son Titus, and entering the lands of the unknown.

But any nightmares they might face when they crossed the waters weren't as dangerous as the present moment, because Vespasian knew that this interview with the legate signaled huge risks for the Roman army. It wasn't the first time the Roman army had rebelled when forced to cross this narrow sea to attack Britain. Only three years earlier, in the reign of the madman Caligula, the hapless emperor had been humiliated by his legions when they refused to board the boats and sail north. In fury, he ordered them to pick up seashells as a sign of the only victory of which the cowards were capable; they marched back to ignominy and ridicule in Rome. And that was something which neither Vespasian, nor his general Aulus Plautius, would tolerate.

"I'll tell you why we're crossing the seas to Britain," Vespasian said softly, in order to show that he and the commanders of the Roman army controlled the moment, and neither the legates nor their men. "Since the Emperor Julius landed on British soil a hundred years ago, the trade with us has become increasingly important. Roman merchants are growing rich and fat on the wheat, gold, silver, hunting dogs, cattle and slaves which this land produces in abundance. And the money the emperor receives in taxes from these merchants goes to pay your wages. In return, we supply these Britons with wine, jewelry, glass and olive oil, which gives the emperor even more tax."

"Then why . . . ?"

"Because, Legate, the Britons are fighting among themselves and the land is about to burst into the flames of tribal warfare. It needs the calming hand of Rome to settle things down. More and more British chieftains are seeking refuge in Rome as they escape their tormentors. These men tell us what's happening, and the emperor doesn't like it."

"The emperor just wants a victory so his reputation—"

"That's enough!" shouted Vespasian. "How dare you impugn the Emperor's name! Retract that remark, or I'll have you arrested and punished for insubordination and treason."

Humbled, the legate said, "I withdraw. But I will not apologize, Commander, because everybody knows that Messalina is making a mockery of the emperor. Even some of my own friends have been forced into the palace to join in her orgies. All they were doing was drinking in a tavern nearby and they were picked out by the empress' guards as though they were common prostitutes. And these are good soldiers, loyal Romans, and family men."

Vespasian, the son of a Sabine banker and tax collector, had heard all of the rumors and was equally disgusted. But as commander of the II Legion Augusta, he had a duty and a sworn oath to uphold the good name of the emperor and the empire, even if the emperor was blind to the way in which his wife was bringing that good name into disrepute.

"I'm not privy to the workings of Claudius' inner circle. But I'm informed that once we've established a beachhead and quelled the immediate problems— and forty thousand trained legionaries is force enough to quell any gathering of blue-faced Britons—the Emperor Claudius himself will be traveling to Britain in order to lead us into victory."

"Victory?" The legate laughed. "So the old man will arrive just in time to see the battle won! Come on, sir, you know that he's no Augustus, and he's certainly no Julius," the legate sneered.

"Back to your men, Legate, and enough of this insubordination. I've tolerated it because I know the men are frightened of the Druids. But be assured that I'll endure no more. Any insubordination, any refusal of orders, and the man or men will be whipped and sent back to Rome in a cage. Tell your fellow legates that!"

As the soldier saluted and began to leave the tent, Vespasian said, "And tell them one other thing—that Druids are no more and no less than men. Brutal and barbaric men, but men nonetheless. To fear them is to give them the first part of a victory. They might invoke their gods, but we fight under the banner of Rome and the protection of Mars. They might paint their faces blue, but their armies wear no armor to protect themselves. They have no machinery of war. They still use chariots, which gives us an advantage over their terrain. Yes, they sacrifice human beings, but first they have to win, and neither General Plautius nor I will allow that to happen. Go and tell that to your men."

Southern Britain, the Land of the Belgae

Once, when she was a young child, Boudica had defied her parents' instructions and had left her house to creep into a sacred grove in the woods beyond her village, to witness the secret rites of the Druid priests. Their look terrified her. Their hair, full of dried mud, was white with stiffened lime; their faces, painted blue and red, and their cloaks which were embroidered with symbols of awesome mystery, made her whimper, too terrified to breathe. She had seen them enter a knot of villagers pulling a struggling goat, bleating and straining against the ropes which bound it. In horror and fascination, she watched as the Druids intoned prayers she couldn't understand; she'd heard the villagers, including her parents, repeat and amplify what the Druid priest was saying. And when he had raised the knife and slit the throat of the hysterical animal, she had come close to exposing her position by screaming.

Yet she watched in awe as the priest slit the goat's stomach and cut out its entrails to examine them. After anxious moments, he'd declared that the omens were good, and the people had laughed and clapped and hugged each other. In the silence of her hiding place, Boudica had also laughed and clapped, though she didn't know why. She continued to watch as the villagers drank and said more prayers until Boudica grew bored and returned to her home.

But she was seen by another village child, who had told his father; the father told the head priest, who then took the petrified Boudica for a walk by the river which ran into the fens and marshes below their village before draining into the sea. The priest had explained why their religion could only be witnessed by adults and not children. Since then she had waited patiently to become an adult, and now that she was thirteen, her parents and the priests believed that her time had come.

For her first true experience of the worship which would take place to mark the end of spring and the beginning of summer—a sacred time in a sacred land which presaged the coming of the solstice, the day when the sun stands still—she had been given the male and female gods Arawn and Brigid to protect her. They were lovers in the sky, according to her mother Annika, and their passion made the sun hot, yet the motion of their bodies coupling wildly in the sky made the cooling summer breezes blow. In order to be eligible for the journey, Boudica had to study the old traditions long and hard. They were taught to her by one of the priests, and once she could repeat the narrative and liturgy, she was judged ready.

What she hadn't realized as a child, but now knew as a young adult, was that each blade of grass, each rock, each leaf on a tree, every stream and lake and river, was the domain of a god or a sacred spirit. Boudica realized that she couldn't be anywhere without being observed by the gods, and so she must be able to account for her every action, her every thought. And because the spirits were everywhere, she was protected wherever she went. It gave her at the same time a profound sense of responsibility for her actions, and also a great sense of comfort, knowing that she was never alone.

Gadrin had administered the oaths before the entire village; she remembered the pride in his eyes when she repeated the Celtic virtues of loyalty, hospitality, honesty, honor, justice and courage. Her mother had broken through the cordon of men and hugged her daughter in front of the entire community, much to the chagrin of the priests.

As a woman, Boudica was now entitled to travel across the country, outside of the land of her tribe, and with her family and peoples, gain special right of passage even from warring tribes to the sacred places in which the Druids held their ceremonies. Leaving their land of the Iceni in the far east of Britain, those who set out to walk to the sacred meeting places of the Druids traveled southwest to the cliffs of the southern coast, and after twenty exhausting days, the people of the Iceni arrived at their destination.

Boudica felt a sense of humility as a full member of her tribe, walking deeper and deeper into the sacred woods toward the renowned, blessed grove of oak trees which the gods had created in the shape of a horseshoe.

Some of the oaks were entwined in the clasping embrace of hallowed mistletoe. She felt overcome with the awe of the forest as she entered the dark wood; its dim green light filtered through the dense canopy, and she became part of the thick ancient smells of the forest. She shuddered in the growing coolness of the air as she and her people walked deeper and farther into the ever more silent wood. Her silence told her father and mother that this passage, this transition between Boudica's childhood and adulthood, was the turning point in her young life. Even the excitement, the gaiety of the tribe, died down, and everybody became silent as their journey ended and their spiritual crossing began.

Suddenly the woodland, which grew to the edge of the cliffs overlooking the southern sea, cleared, and a brilliant patch of summer sky illuminated a large area which looked as though it had been felled by the hand of some gigantic farmer; yet there were no tree stumps, no sign of an axe having taken down these majestic oaks. The great gods Danu and Herne and Lugh had refused to allow trees to grow in the area so that the people could enter the grove and there see before them the awesome and terrifying horseshoe of oaks which was the place of ritual.

As she entered the clearing, Boudica came close to fainting. Nothing her mother or father had told her prepared her for the mystery. In this vast clearing in the dense wood was the semicircle of oaks, their canopies joined at the top to shroud the altar at the center in shade, and all of the trees faced the edge of the cliff toward the vastness of the sea beyond.

"What did I tell you?" whispered Gadrin. "Isn't it a wondrous place?"

Normally the god Lugh would have entered her and Boudica would have made some quip to make her parents laugh; but she was overwhelmed by the awesome power of the grove, and simply nodded. Suddenly, she felt herself to be a child again.

The Druid priest who was the teacher, judge and guide of her village started to mumble and chant. In the swirl of her mind, Boudica barely heard what he was saying. As he became louder, his chants were joined by the many other Druids who had traveled from other parts of Britain. The people stopped to allow all the Druids through into the inner sanctum of the shrine. The huge host stood on the periphery of the semicircle surrounding the outside of the grove, silent and enthralled. Only the priests walked forward, protectors and initiates of the sacred site.

Rapidly her priest's words, in concert with all of the other priests, became distinct and understandable.

> I am bowing my head before my gods. I see the eye of the lady who made me. I close my eye to the crone who hates me. I walk to the altar of the gods who create all things. I walk beneath the sky which sees all things. I pray at the altar of the gods who know all things. I give my body and mind to the true gods who are the today and the tomorrow. I close my eyes to the false gods who were the yesterday. In all things I am the servant of the gods whose breath is the wind, whose anger is the storm, and whose laughter is the rain which gives us food.

As the priests gathered around the mistletoe-strewn altar in the center of the sacred grove, the people at last began to walk forward and approach the altar. Thousands of Celts had come from the different tribal lands to participate in the ceremony. Many had camped for days until the auspicious moment arrived.

All who attended the ceremony wore the finest cloaks of their tribal colors, blue and red and green. Their cloaks were studded with dazzling gold clasps and jewelry that flashed in the brilliant sunlight of the clearing, as though fireflies had suddenly descended. Her own cloak and jewelry, specially made for this journey, and which she'd proudly put on that morning in preparation for the ceremony, seemed dull in comparison with those which some people from other tribes were wearing.

But Boudica didn't care, for she was lost in the overwhelming spectacle of the dozens of Druid priests removing sheep and chickens and dogs from their cages for sacrifice. This, thought Boudica, was the most exciting day she had ever known. Slowly and cautiously, every person began to approach the altar, the huge circle of people drawing closer and closer and becoming denser and denser. In the center of the vast circle were the fifty or so Druid priests who stood still now, waiting for a sign that the sacrifices should begin. The only noises came from the animals held tight by acolytes as they were readied for the slaughter. Everybody held their breath, waiting for a sign. Boudica peered through the arms and legs of the adults, trying to see what was happening in the center of the circle.

And then the chanting began again. One of the Druid priests, the one wearing the tallest helmet of fiery gold and a shimmering silver robe, turned to face the sea and raised his arms above his head. As he began to sing, the other priests joined him. Boudica strained to understand the words.

Great gods, we stand before you and the earth and the sky; great spirits of the woods and of the lakes, the rivers and the hills, we come to your sacred place to offer you food and sustenance. O ancient and great ones, for the sake of your people who love you, for the love of our soil from which we derive, for the sacrifices we make to you, spirits of fire and air and water, spirits of oak and ash and yew, spirits of sky and earth, we your people demand that you protect us from our enemies, slay those who would dare to assault our sacred land, strip our enemies bare and make the snow freeze their manhood. We will give you food and sustenance in our sacrifices. You show us the path.

His voice rose until at the end he was shouting the words at the sea. Then the chief priest turned and picked up a knife that lay on the altar. Boudica stood stock-still, not daring to move a muscle, transfixed to the spot.

An acolyte laid a chicken down on the altar, its legs kicking furiously as it squawked in fear. The priest brought down the knife and sliced through the animal's stretched neck. Blood spurted over the altar, and immediately, he turned the twitching animal onto its back and sliced open the stomach. He stuck his hand into the shuddering bird and pulled out the entrails. The crowd held its breath in a collective gasp of anticipation. The priest examined the innards, and shouted, "It is good."

A yell of relief arose from everybody's lips, and suddenly the tight circle broke ranks and began to surge toward the altar. Boudica was nearly toppled over, and had to struggle to remain upright. She paced forward with her parents and crowded into the middle of the sacred grove of oaks to see more of what was happening.

Each priest took a turn slaughtering the dozens of animals that had been brought for sacrifice. As each animal was killed, its stomach was opened, and the priest examined the entrails. Only two of the animals were rejected: a young dog whose gut was covered in white spots, and a baby lamb whose innards the priest believed were an unhealthy and unnatural dark red.

But the rest of the animals were subsequently sacrificed, and as night began to fall, a huge fire was made on the cliff top where the skinned carcasses were placed for the evening feast.

Amid the laughter and shouts of joy from the huge assembly and the noise of hysterical flies buzzing above the dried blood and offal, Boudica and her parents found a sheltered spot and cut lumps of meat from the roasted sheep and chickens, which they ate with roots her mother had cooked in the fire pit the previous night.

Exhausted, Boudica covered herself with a blanket and stared up at the brilliant stars. She wanted to sleep, but there was so much noise and laughter and running around and excitement among the people that she wondered if she would even be able to close her eyes. Propping herself up on her elbow, she saw that her father and mother were no longer eating, but were lying on top of their blanket, making love. Smiling, she looked carefully at her mother. Still handsome despite her thickening body, she was writhing beneath her thrusting husband. Annika grasped her Gadrin's long hair with one hand, his back with her other, and seemed to be pulling him closer and closer, deeper and deeper.

For some time, Boudica had enjoyed those feelings within her body which the other children in the village had told her were the feelings of desire and sex. Now she felt them again. She looked around, and saw that many men and women were lying around the roaring fire, also making love.

It was such a special day that she, too, felt like enjoying the body of a man. She'd only once experienced a man's penis within her, and it had been painful and frightening. But Annika had told her that it would be better the second time. She looked around, and couldn't see any man who was alone. And she was tired, and she didn't want such a momentous day to be spoiled by pain.

CHAPTER TWO

43 AD—The Coast of Britain, at the Mouth of the River Thames

Vespasian was certain that the traitor would try to fool the Romans as they approached the shores, but as the boats passed the southern coastline of Britain, there were no swarms of wild-eyed Britons dancing on the shoreline preparing to slaughter them. No fearsome warriors wearing animal skins and painted blue appeared on the cliff tops, threatening them with spears.

Indeed, as the flotilla of boats landed in the gentle swell, it appeared that the renegade Briton had been telling the truth. Adminius had assured them that they would meet no resistance, and as the sun rose over the sea and the boats breasted the waves of the shore, the Roman army could have been landing for a summer holiday on the beaches of Neapolis.

Amazed by the absence of fighting men, Vespasian ensured that his boat was the first to strike land. It arrived to no more resistance than the lapping of the water and the suck of the undercurrent. But being cautious, he was the first to jump out of the boat when it reached the shallows. He walked partway up the beach and looked carefully to see whether any Briton was hiding behind the tufts of sand grass. When he was convinced that he was alone on the shore, he signaled to the eighty men in the first *centuria* to jump out of the boat and assemble in the formation called the Tortoise. It was the first establishment of a beachhead, the first Roman military attack against Britain, since the time of Julius Caesar. Joined by the second and third boat, there were enough troops to ward off initial resistance. But no British response came.

Vespasian was as shocked by the unpreparedness of the British as he was by Adminius being correct in his intelligence. Yet even as the Romans were unloading the boats of their weaponry, their machines, their armor and their cooking equipment, Vespasian still refused to trust Adminius. The man's capricious behavior since he'd been in Rome told Vespasian that he must not trust the Briton's word without subsequent qualification, and neither would he allow him to wander out of his sight.

It took an entire day to land the eight legions in a thousand ships, but the maneuver had gone smoothly, perhaps even too smoothly. Not a single Briton, save for Adminius, was seen in the three waves of ships which had put ashore on the coast, close to the vast mouth and slow-moving outflow of the River Thames.

Even as the last boat was being hauled out of the water, Vespasian and his front-line assault troops remained ready for anything: armed to the teeth with short-swords and stabbing lances, spying out the nearby land in case of ambush.

They set up a supply base and stationed lookouts and guards to ensure that any sporadic assaults by guerrillas didn't interrupt the process of consolidating their toehold in the land of the Cantiaci, Britain's most southeasterly coast, the land nearest to Gaul.

Aloof and detached from the exhausting work of the legions, Adminius watched the military precision of their preparations, admiring their efficiency and skill. Britons, he thought, were a far less civilized people than those Romans with whom he had made his home since being expelled by his brothers. He would give a fortune just to see the look on their faces when they saw him return to Britain with legions of fierce Romans, determined to reclaim his kingdom.

Vespasian looked up for a moment and wondered why Adminius was standing on a hill overlooking the beach, smiling. He didn't like the man; didn't trust him in the least. Short, squat and balding, Adminius was one of three royal brothers who had been given administrative authority by their father over the land of the Cantium people during the reign of Emperor Tiberius. But Adminius had quarreled with his two brothers, Caratacus and Togodumnus, who drove him from Cantium. Since the Roman army had set out on the journey to claim Britain, Adminius had been bleating incessantly to Vespasian about how unfair his brothers were, and how he'd relish the joy of fighting them to regain his rightful place as king of Britain.

Vespasian often wondered how it was that Adminius, an exile, had managed to befriend Caligula. It was Adminius who had persuaded the mad emperor that Britain was ripe for plucking, which had led to the disastrous and aborted attempt to follow in Julius Caesar's footsteps a few years earlier. And now, for inexplicable reasons, this Briton had somehow also managed to persuade Emperor Claudius to do the same thing. The honey-tongued Briton had assured Claudius that once Rome was in control, he should be put back in charge of the eastern kingdom of the Cantiaci, and he would open the gates to anything Rome required. But all Claudius needed to secure his shaky hold on the Roman throne was military honors, and that was what Adminius had assured him he could gain.

Being a military man, Vespasian didn't trust traitors or turncoats, and greeted all of Adminius' friendship and advice with utter skepticism, trusting only Roman spies and intelligencers. So rather than spend time listening to Adminius' moaning about his evil brothers, Vespasian was frantically busy doing the bidding of his general, Aulus Plautius, and ensuring that his men could eat, defend themselves and prepare to attack any enemy they encountered.

Better than anybody, Vespasian knew that an attack army of forty thousand needed sixty tons of grain a day, as well as three thousand mules, five hundred carts to transport supplies, horses and their food, and war machines such as catapults, ballistae, onagers and scorpions. Normally, the army would use the conquered land to feed itself, but because this was the spring, Vespasian knew that the summer crops wouldn't yet be ripe and the previous year's foodstuffs would have been exhausted by the Britons or stored and hidden well out of sight of the Romans. So feeding the army after the third or fourth week of the invasion would become an increasing problem for him. The Romans had to conquer the Britons and appropriate their food supplies quickly, or they would be in trouble within the month.

Now that they had landed and secured the beachhead, Vespasian retired to his tent. Writing orders and requisitions, he didn't notice that General Aulus Plautius had entered his quarters until his orderly and other soldiers stood stiffly to attention and saluted. Vespasian immediately stood up and saluted his commander, who was followed into the tent by Adminius.

Plautius shook his head in mystery. "What's your view about why the Britons haven't yet attacked?" Vespasian remained silent, knowing that the general's question was rhetorical. "We're at our weakest when we're landing and establishing a bridgehead. Yet they haven't attacked. Why?"

Vespasian had been told the reason by Adminius, but hadn't bothered to pass the information on to his commander, doubting its veracity.

"Perhaps, General, Lord Adminius knows the tactics and strategies of the Britons better than we do."

Center stage, Adminius said, "General . . . Commander . . . you have to understand that unlike great Rome, Britain isn't one people. It is many peoples. The land is divided into tribes and kingdoms and as you know, there is often war between the groups; after all, isn't that why Emperor Claudius has sent us here? Also, many of the tribes are trading with Rome, and so they wouldn't want to raise a militia against you."

"But where are the other Britons?" demanded Plautius. "Where are the Druids and the warriors from tribes which aren't disposed to be friendly toward us? Why haven't we seen any? Surely they couldn't have failed to notice a thousand ships sailing across the sea and up the coast. Have they no guards, no lookouts, no sentries?"

"The near mutiny which you and Commander Vespasian suffered in Gaul would certainly have become known to the spies that the Britons sent over there. I can only assume, gentlemen, that they thought this Roman army, like that of the Emperor Caligula a few years ago, would not have crossed the sea, but would have retreated back to Rome," Adminius said.

Plautius laughed. "These Britons are fools. Why would their army commander trust his spies to the extent of not posting lookouts along the coast or mounting a surprise attack on the beach? What kind of fighting men are these that they leave their shores undefended?"

"Never underestimate the bravery of British fighting men, General. But it's precisely because the Britons are so divided among themselves that they will fail. It is what I've been telling the Roman Senate for some time now," said Adminius.

Exasperated by the man's arrogance, Vespasian poured three cups of wine and offered one to Plautius and the other to Adminius. "Sir, I've almost finished the security of the area. Now is the time for me to take half the men inland and establish fortifications. With your permission?"

Plautius smiled, and put his hand on his young commander's shoulder. Such an unattractive man: He looked squat and brutish, yet he had a marvelous military mind. If Plautius had a dozen Vespasians, he could conquer every remaining barbarian land beyond the borders of the empire. "Go, friend. Show these Druids and Britons that Caesar has come again, and this time, he will not leave."

The following morning, riding high in the saddle of his warhorse, Vespasian trotted slowly up and down the lines of men, all arranged in rows behind their centurions and legates. It was a vast host; yet even with so many, they still would have a difficult job quelling every single Briton before them. Merchants and spies had told them that there were only two hundred thousand souls in all of the lands of Britain, but these were such wild guesses that it could be half, or ten times, that number. Either way, a dozen Britons would be needed to subdue one highly trained and dangerous Roman soldier. He shouted out his first order of the day. "Centurions, examine your men!"

Each centurion turned and looked at his *centuria*. His first glance told him that all the men were correctly equipped for the forthcoming march and any battle they might have to fight along the way, but since the time of Augustus Caesar who had reorganized the army, a drill had to be followed every morning before the soldiers marched or went out on maneuver.

Each centurion shouted out, "Each man will mark off the armor and weaponry of each other man. Is your fellow wearing his *cassis?*"

Every soldier looked at the head of the soldier next to him to ensure that he was wearing his leather helmet.

"Is your fellow wearing his *lorica segmentata,* his *gladius,* and is he carrying his *pilium?*" the centurion asked.

Vespasian knew that checking such details with an army of this experience was largely a waste of time, because these soldiers knew how to dress, and the importance of each item of personal weaponry. Indeed, the Roman soldier could force-march twenty miles in a day, and still be ready to fight an engagement at the end of the journey. No army—not the Greeks, nor the Parthians, nor the Egyptians, nor the Carthaginians, and certainly not the barbaric Germans or Gauls or Britons—could match a Roman army.

Satisfied that each man was correctly kitted out for battle, Vespasian tugged on the reins and encouraged his horse to the middle of the field. Standing in the saddle so that he could be seen by everybody, the young commander shouted, "Centurions and soldiers of Rome. You are about to embark on an epic and heroic journey. The Roman Empire is the greatest empire that the world has ever known. Little of the world remains that does not bow its head to our glorious emperor, and that is because Rome rules not only by force of arms, not only because of the bravery of its soldiers, but because we are a good and just conqueror; fierce and merciless in battle, principled in victory and honorable in peace, Rome offers not just a strong hand of friendship, but a hand which is valued by all who grasp it.

"Men, we are about to face and do battle with the people of Britain. Their priests, the Druids, look fearsome. Their faces are blue from a lifetime of painting with woad. But your faces are red from a lifetime of wine—"

The men burst out laughing and cheering. Because of their nervousness, Vespasian allowed the laughter to continue, but at his sign, the centurions turned and ordered their men to be quiet for the commander.

"A rumor has passed among you that the Druids kill and sacrifice human beings, and use their innards for their foul religion. As you know, the Emperor Claudius has banned the Jews and these new Chrestians from Rome because they are too arrogant and refuse to worship our gods and goddesses. That, men, is what Romans do to those who live within our borders. But to barbarians, we apply the sword, the javelin, and the war machines so deadly that nobody can stand against us. Yes, it is true that the British look fearsome, but that is all— they only look fearsome! And remember that fear is in your hearts before a battle, but not once you start fighting. For once you plunge a sword into a Briton's body, you will see that he will bleed just like a slave in the gladiator's arena, and when you hack off his head, he will fall at your feet.

"There are rumors that these Britons are undefeated and undefeatable. Those were the rumors that faced our men in Carthage, in Parthia, and in other places which now bow down to Rome. Fight for the empire, and we will extinguish and crush these Druids like we crush grain when we make bread to feed the people."

A huge cheer went up from the body of men. Vespasian hoped that he had given the men courage to march into the unknown.

"Now we march to glory. You fight for your emperor, for your commanders, for your centurions and for yourselves. For in your fight you will grow in stature, and for generations to come men and women, boys and girls, throughout the empire will sing of the day when Romans conquered Britain and brought light to a dark land. March now, and fight for your gods and your emperor. Long live the Senate and the people of Rome."

As one, the men shouted out, "Long live the Senate and the people of Rome."

Vespasian wheeled his horse and followed the standard bearer up the hill and away from the sea, inland and westward toward the armies and the people of Britain. He was followed by legates and centurions and columns of men, each led by its own standard bearers. Behind the army trundled carts and wagons full of supplies, food and war machines. By the time the last one of the wagons had left the encampment just above the beach, Vespasian and his forward troops were already deep into the unknown.

The Sacred Cluster of Oaks in the Land of the Belgae

For two days and two nights, the Celtic people had been celebrating their faith. The ground of the sacred copse of oaks was awash with dried blood and the stench of entrails. The huge fire which had blazed since they arrived, illuminating the darkness of the night and turning it into the light of day, was now beginning to fade as one by one, in clusters of families and as members of the same clan, the Britons began to wander away to return to their lands and tend their crops in preparation for the bounty of summer's harvest. Fond farewells were said, promises made, assurances given that new friends and old would meet again at this spot in the following years.

Boudica felt despondent as she saw groups of people leaving. Once she had overcome the feeling of awe which had oppressed her at the very beginning of the ceremonies, she had brightened up, and amused everybody with her playfulness, her vitality and at times her irreverence. She had only just started to get to know and like the people she met from other tribes and now they were disappearing, drifting away like mists on a summer morning. She had reveled in meeting them and getting used to their ways. Some used strange words for familiar objects, some spoke in odd and unusual accents which she found difficult to understand, and some had customs or ways of doing things which she found fascinating. She was learning so much about the people of Britain, and about how different many of them were to her people of the Iceni. Yet all too soon, they would drift away and she didn't know when or whether she would see them again.

One of those leaving was the lovely boy with whom she'd spent the previous night. He had been concerned for her when she told him that her first experience had been painful. Immediately the boy threw off their blanket, searched his baggage and extracted a fragrant balm which he spread onto his penis, telling her that this way, he could enter her without causing her discomfort and distress. She'd explained to him that because she hadn't been entered frequently, it was his size which would cause her pain, and so he had been as gentle as possible, until eventually they enjoyed each other once, then a second and a third time as they woke in the morning.

Sadly, Gadrin and Annika told their family that it was time for the Iceni people to pack up their belongings and also to leave the sacred grove, assuring Boudica that they would bring her again the following year, if they made the journey.

But as they were beginning to tie their food and cooking pots and other possessions together in the blankets for the return journey, Boudica heard a commotion outside of the clearing. They were sounds of distress and apprehension, and she looked up to see what was the cause.

The people who still remained created a path for an agitated messenger who suddenly appeared in his war chariot, shattering the peace and sanctity of the grove. He was gasping for breath, and his horse was exhausted to the point of dropping by the time he'd forced his way through the remaining press of people to where the priests were lying and resting.

Concerned, Boudica watched the interchange between the messenger and the priests. She heard raised and excited voices, and several times the word "Roman" could be heard. Boudica suddenly became worried when she saw the look her parents gave each other.

"People," shouted the high priest. "Gather around. Bad news has just come to me. Gather near and listen."

Although far fewer than the previous day, the multitude gathered around the altar on which he stood so he could be properly heard.

"The enemy has dared to breach our holy Britain with his armies. Our soil has been befouled. Iron men of the Roman legions are, as I speak, marching on our sacred land. Their iniquitous feet are treading on our precious ground and making the hills and valleys thunder with their weapons of war."

There was an immediate outcry of horror and fury from the Britons.

The high priest continued. "Already Caratacus and Togodumnus, brave chieftains of the Cantiaci, are preparing for battle on the River Medway. We must arm ourselves and join them and drive this plague away and off our lands."

But to Boudica's surprise, there was a sound of dissent from within the body of people listening. It grew into a quarrel between different parts of the crowd. The priest held up his hands and demanded silence, but the noises of opposition grew more intense.

One voice was heard above the rest. It belonged to a tall blond man in a vivid blue cloak. "Wait, people. Listen to me, priest. Why should we fight the Romans? They're here precisely because we fight among each other. For twenty years, my people have been trading with the Romans. We've grown rich and prosperous from the trade. We've made friends with the Romans. Now you want us to fight them? Do you think we're mad?"

The priest screamed, "Yes, you must fight them. They are on our land—"

"Their merchants and traders have been on our land for years, and have never once caused us problems. They're our friends. They share in the bounties of what we have to offer, and we share in the bounties of the Roman Empire. We of the Atribati people will not join you in any fight. We will welcome Romans onto our land, and live in peace with them."

Boudica saw that the priest was pointing his oak staff at the leader in fury, and he began to shout in condemnation when he was interrupted by a chieftain from the green-cloaked Regnenses tribe, who said loudly, "Neither will we join in this battle. It is not our fight. We will not lose our men and women when we could live in peace. There are Roman armies in many different client lands, and the people live and prosper. All we do is fight against each other. Why shouldn't the Romans come here and bring some order and peace? We of the Regnenses have spoken long and hard about what we would do if the Roman army landed and occupied our nation. And we have made a vow that we, like the Atribati, will be their friends and trade with them. And you will find, priest, that many other British tribes will do the same."

Before the priest could intervene, there was a huge uproar. Many in the crowd from different tribes were arguing directly with the two chieftains who had spoken out against fighting. Boudica was frightened that there would be a battle there and then between the Britons, when surely they should be joining together against the Romans.

Eventually, the priest's voice overcame the din of shouting, and as they began to quieten down, he said, "Only fools and cowards will refuse to fight the invaders. Why? Because the gods are with us. Last night, I had a dream that a vast host of blue-faced men hacked down a forest of trees whose trunks and branches were covered with Roman armor. Even before this messenger arrived, I knew that the Romans had landed. A vision from the gods told me so. And it also told me that we have to propitiate our gods in order for them to gain the strength to help us to destroy the foe and push them back into the sea from whence they came.

"We must select a perfect youth, boy or girl, and sacrifice this wondrous child of Britain to the gods to ensure that they smile favorably upon our armies."

Boudica understood the words, but not the intent. Yet her mother suddenly grabbed her by the shoulder and pushed her backward to stand hidden from the priest in Gadrin's shadow. Suddenly a mother from the other side of the clearing screamed out "No!" as the priest pointed with his oaken stick into the crowd and shouted, "A boy has been selected. Bring the boy forward and let us all raise our voices to the great gods Erin and Maldoch and Issua that they receive this child and turn his youth, vigor and strength to the potency that our armies will need to fight these inhuman invaders."

Boudica heard, but couldn't properly see the commotion. She struggled free of her father's hand and was able to stare out between the people. She could vaguely make out a bevy of priests marching through the press of people, and grabbing hold of a boy who struggled to be set free. A fight began with the boy's father, who was shouting and pushing, but his neighbors and the priests held the parents firmly as others took the boy and forced his struggling young body into one of the empty animal cages.

Clasping and shaking the bars of the iron cage, the petrified boy screamed and cried for his mother. As the cage was pulled up and elevated above the altar, high into the canopy of the trees, Boudica was able to see him properly for the first time. With a shock, she realized that she knew him and had noticed him several times in the past two days. Why he had been chosen? He seemed so ordinary.

He was about her age, only much shorter and younger-looking than she was. But now his once innocent and open face was a mask of horror as he looked down through the bars and tried to find his mother and father. Yet they'd been dragged away and were being held on the periphery of the group, still screaming and begging for their son to be freed.

Priests brought lighted branches from the clifftop fire and placed them on top of the altar. More and more dry branches were heaped on the rapidly growing flames, and the higher they grew, touching the bottom of the boy's cage, the more the boy screamed and shouted, desperately trying to move his body away from the heat of the flames which licked at his skin. His screams were horrific and the look in his eyes was unbearable. Boudica blocked her ears and looked away from the ghastly sight as the boy's robe caught fire, and then his flesh began to burn. He screamed louder and louder . . . and then his screams suddenly faded as he fainted from the unbearable pain and grew silent forever. The grove was plunged into an unnatural and eerie quiet, the only noise being the crackling of the burning wood, and the sounds of the fire which had engulfed the boy roaring upward into the trees.

Softly at first, but then with increasing strength, the people began to chant and sing, holding up their hands to the boy in supplication for his young life being given for the benefit of the tribe. The sound was the sound of worship, but in Boudica's mind, she could still hear the boy's screaming and his parents' plaintive wailing. The sounds of such misery and pain touched her young mind and made her want to cry out in grief. The sounds of people nearby coughing from the smoke, and the screaming of his parents as they looked at the flames dancing higher and higher and consuming their dead son, filled her with ineffable horror. She realized that she was wailing. She looked up at her mother for consolation, but to her dismay she saw that her mother's face wore a look of ecstasy, the light of the fire and the burning flesh of the young boy reflecting in her eyes.

Boudica felt sick. Her joy in womanhood had been shattered.

The journey home was infinitely more perilous than the journey there: the landscape more hostile, the copses more threatening, the rivers faster and more hazardous; and the hills now seemed to be harboring malevolent forces. Everywhere, there was fear of the Roman army and what it would do to Britons.

When they had journeyed to the land of the Belgae, her family and the people of the Iceni had been exuberant, singing songs and offering sacrifices of rabbits and hares and birds along the way. On the way there, life had been so full of prospect for Boudica. On her return, there was just blackness.

There was no singing, no joy; animals were caught both for food and for sacrifice, and were slaughtered as offerings to the gods, but it was done in an atmosphere of fear rather than exultation. Her mother and father talked in whispers, and when they sat to rest, other members of her tribe came over to them and engaged in quiet conversation.

They saw many Britons rushing to join the army of Caratacus and Togodumnus. Even members of their own Iceni tribe decided to fight. Everybody was walking anxiously south, toward the River Medway. The images in her mind, of Roman soldiers lurking behind the trees, never eventuated. Exhausted and grateful at last to be home, Boudica slept for the best part of that night and for much of the following day.

CHAPTER THREE

43 AD—The Palace of Emperor Claudius in Rome

Short and pudgy though he was, Polybius drew himself up to his full height, and said to the Lord of the World and Master of the Roman Empire, "This decision is unworthy of you, Caesar. Indeed, it's the decision of a fool."

His colleague and coworker, Pallas, looked at his fellow Greek ex-slave in utter amazement and horror. He frowned as deeply and seriously as he could, shaking his head to shut Polybius up, but Pallas couldn't attract Polybius' attention because the philosopher refused to look at anything or anybody except for the Emperor Claudius.

"What did you say?" asked Claudius, managing to restrain himself from stuttering.

"I said, Caesar, that only a fool would have thought up this idea. You would risk your life just to gain the approbation of a Senate which holds you in contempt. Why, when you can write an edict that overnight will double the number of senators, and halve their voting power? Why bow and scrape to those arrogant fools, those nepotistic idiots, when they'd see you overthrown in an instant?"

"You just called me a fool," said Claudius. "You called the emperor of Rome a fool!"

"You are one," responded Polybius.

"Pallas," Claudius said, looking at his other freedman advisor, "Polybius called me a fool. Isn't that worthy of having him arrested and thrown into the dungeons?"

"And having him dragged behind a chariot in the Colosseum, Claudius," said the other Greek.

Claudius sighed. "You know, Polybius, you really mustn't call the emperor of Rome a fool. Others might hear you, and they'll think you're serious. Then nobody will respect me, I'll be overthrown and you'll be thrown out of the palace on your ear."

Polybius shrugged and was about to say something when Claudius continued. "And I'm not going to Britain to please the Senate, but because my reputation is very poor with the people of Rome. By conquering the savages and barbarians, I'll be a hero to my people, just like Augustus and Julius."

He began stammering again, and bunched his fists and slapped his thighs. It sometimes helped. But what really irritated Claudius was the impertinence of his advisor Polybius. After all, he was only an ex-slave, philosopher or not. "It's bad enough that the senators refuse to dine with me, and that I have to go into a self-imposed exile because of all these plots on my life, but I've elevated you and Pallas and Narcissus as my advisors well above your stations, and you more than anybody should respect me. Especially as you're all Greeks and everybody but me detests you."

"Claudius, I do respect you. I respect your intelligence and your imagination and the fact that you've somehow survived the most murderous family in the entire history of the world; but where would your respect for me stand if all I did was to say 'Yes, Caesar' and 'No, Caesar' to all of your wild schemes? And this plan of yours to go off in Narcissus' footsteps after he's only just managed to quell a huge rebellion in your army in Gaul is insane. It's not as if your health will allow you to travel far from Rome.

"But that's not all. Your plan to cross the water to Britain of all places, where men and women wear animal skins and paint their faces blue, is sheer folly. Ye gods, do you realize the unworthiness of an emperor of Rome traipsing all the way to the boundaries of civilization and setting foot there! And worst of all, to leave that drunken sycophant Lucius Vitellius in charge of the empire while you are gone . . . why, it's sheer madness."

"That's enough," shouted Claudius. "I'll tolerate your criticism of me and your being rude if it's in my interests, but you have absolutely no right to criticize Lucius Vitellius. He's a dear friend, and a great companion."

"A drinking companion, Caesar," said Polybius. "And a man who licked the arses of Tiberius and Caligula. He was the very first Roman to bow down and kiss the ground when Caligula declared himself to be a god. Why, even the damned Senate delayed for a couple of days to show its disapproval. But not Lucius! He was in the palace and shouting out 'O Great and Mighty God Caligula' down every corridor."

"He was an excellent governor of Syria," said Claudius. "Look at the way he quelled the trouble in Judea by removing that violent madman Pontius Pilate and his coruler Caiaphas. The Jews and that new sect, the Chrestians, could have spread their fury as far as Egypt if he hadn't acted with resolve and intelligence. It was a very dangerous situation for the empire, but he handled the problem magnificently."

"Yes, that he did. But he also created a huge problem for us here with the Jews and the Chrestians. He was noble when he was in the provinces, but the moment he returned here, things seemed to change. It was as if he was happy to be infected by the corruption which afflicts all of Rome when he entered the city gates. And now he's here in the palace every single night and you and he go to the inns and the brothels in the worst parts of the city and drink and gamble and play until all hours of the morning. What kind of an example is that for Caesar to offer to his people?" The Emperor Claudius sighed, and sat at the table. He didn't like quarreling with his freedmen advisors, the only people in the palace whom he trusted completely. And none more so than Polybius, the Greek-born genius on whose advice he had come to rely since the emperorship was forced upon him the day that Caligula was murdered. One thing which he particularly liked was that occasionally they called him Caesar, which none of the senators was willing to do.

The Senate still considered him a usurper to the throne because he'd been elected by the soldiers immediately after they'd slaughtered Caligula and his family two years earlier, and although they paid lip service to his position, any one of the senators would have stabbed him in the back if he could get away with it. But for reasons which he still didn't quite understand, Claudius had the overwhelming support of the Praetorian Guard and the rest of the army, and despite his physical infirmities, that made him by far the strongest person in Rome. Except, of course, for his wife Messalina, for whom he would have done anything.

"Nonetheless, Polybius, it's necessary for me to achieve a major military victory in order to establish my authority with the people, as well as with the Senate. And with my physical impediments I don't exactly cut the figure of a Julius or an Octavian or even a Tiberius. The people laugh at me when I stumble through the streets. They mock me. I need the military prowess which comes from a famous battle and victory to ensure the love and respect of the people."

"Rubbish, Claudius," hissed Polybius. "To ensure their love and respect, all you need do is to give the people good, responsible, stable government. Bread and work, not bread and circuses. You need to lower the cost of grain and improve the city's housing shortage, and make Ostia safer from attacks by pirates, and increase the number of gates in the city walls now that Rome is spilling outward toward Neapolis. And you need to clean up the Tiber, which is nothing these days but a pestilential sewer full of the bodies of animals and drunken Romans floating downstream toward the sea. You should also reduce the burden of taxation, for as I've been trying to explain to you for years now, increased taxation makes people work less, not harder. And you need—"

"Enough, Polybius, enough!" shouted Pallas.

Both Polybius and the emperor turned and looked at the Greek in shock. Rarely did Pallas speak unless spoken to. Never, ever, did he shout. He was a man who considered every word, a man incapable of being roused to anger by insult or excitement. Criticize him, and he'd present a reasoned argument why you were right, followed by an equally correct and reasoned argument why you were wrong. Yet even the gentle Pallas had had too much.

"Let Caesar think for a minute. Don't give him a list of problems which date back to the time of the Republic. He can't be expected to overcome in a day every problem he's inherited from a succession of dreadful emperors. Where will the money come from to do all the things you want done? Who will do the work if there aren't enough slaves? That's why Britain is so important to us. More and more, we rely on their—"

"Of course conquering Britain is important to us, Pallas," said Polybius, "and that's why we've sent General Aulus Plautius to ensure our constant supplies are safe from all the squabbling of the barbarian tribes. But why does the emperor himself have to go? For what reason will the people of Rome go out into the streets and cheer him on, just because he comes back with the name Britannicus? What a name! Tiberius Claudius Caesar Augustus Germanicus Britannicus! You've already got a name which takes most Romans a lifetime to remember, and adding Britannicus to it will strain their poor minds to the breaking point. I say again, Caesar, that it's not necessary for you to go. The sea voyage, the journey through Gaul, the crossing to that dismal land of clouds and rain, and the dangers of the Druids are completely unnecessary things for you to face, especially when there's so much administration to do in Rome."

"But that's why I'm leaving Lucius Vitellius in charge—"

Polybius shouted his fury and frustrations to the ceiling. "A city of fools in the hands of an idiot," he hissed before bowing and leaving the library in a state of agitation. Both men watched the Greek go, and Pallas said softly, "I think I ought to follow him, Caesar, to ensure that he doesn't say anything untoward outside these walls. When he's angry . . ."

Claudius nodded. "Yes, go and ensure that he says nothing. But also ensure that he's alright. Sometimes he gets so unhappy with me; I can't seem to do anything to please him."

Pallas smiled and said, "Claudius, it's our job to please you."

Alone, Claudius pondered whether perhaps Polybius was right. After he'd dispatched Narcissus to quell the unrest in Aulus Plautius' army on the northern shores of Gaul before it left to cross over to Britain, he'd been doubtful of the wisdom of the journey. Somehow Narcissus, another of his Greek freedmen, had managed to quell the fears and unrest which the soldiers were exhibiting. But how long would that last once they came face-to-face with the Druids, a race of priests more terrifying even than the Germans?

Yet it looked as though things were going particularly well in Britain. Since the army had landed, early dispatch riders had brought the news of Plautius' victory at the River Medway and the defeat of the British forces. One of the rebel leaders, Togodumnus, the brother of Claudius' friend Adminius, had been killed, and now the remaining leader of the Britons, Caratacus, was fleeing for his life toward the west where the Druids were apparently gathering in great strength. Vespasian was currently chasing the rebels up the hills and into the valleys of Britain. From the intelligence brought to him, it seemed that they were being forced to live in caves like wild beasts. Yet with all the good news came reports that rebel groups were mounting raids on the army encampments, and the whole of Britain was still considered dangerous territory.

But a big military victory would do wonders for Claudius' reputation. The empire hadn't increased in size since the time of Augustus, and if he could absorb Britain with its fantastic resources of wood and silver and lead and grain and slaves, then his name would resound throughout the annals of history—just like the names of Julius and Augustus.

Claudius smiled as he thought of his illustrious predecessors. Never for one moment, from the time of his birth until he was caught quivering behind a curtain after the murder of Caligula, did he consider himself worthy of being emperor. Tiberius and Caligula had brought the office into such disrepute that Claudius had written long and detailed—and very secret—letters to friends about the urgent need to bring back the Republic and return Rome to the hands of the people.

But the gods had decreed that he would become the emperor, and he couldn't resign or the Praetorian Guard would murder him within moments. So he determined that he would be the best emperor Rome could possibly want. And for that reason, he needed the people to support him. He had to do something for which he would be respected. The conquest of Britain was the most obvious move. For that, he would gain respect.

Unlike his predecessors. For what reason would Tiberius be revered, let alone remembered? For being a brutal and capricious tyrant who schemed and plotted and entertained himself with little boys and girls on his island of Capri? And worse—ten thousand times worse than Tiberius and his dreadful assassin Sejanus—was Claudius' nephew, Caligula. So young, yet so unutterably evil. A man who ripped babies out of the stomachs of pregnant women and ate them; a man who seduced his own sisters as though he were an Egyptian pharaoh; a man who took pleasure in making senators bark like dogs whenever he ordered it. He'd even made his horse, Incitatus, a senator. And all those wives of the ruling men of Rome he'd slept with; and the children; and the grandmothers! He even ran a brothel for profit in the palace.

Well, thought Claudius, it was time for Julius' family to have another Octavian. Augustus had expanded the empire, and so would Claudius. And maybe on his death, he would be called Augustus as Octavian had been called. Yes, he thought, Claudius Augustus; much better than Britannicus.

Messalina read the scroll for a second time. The first time she'd read it, she had shaken her head in amazement, and without commenting immediately read it again.

"Elephants?"

"Yes, elephants. Big war elephants like Hannibal used."

"But it's twelve hundred miles to the north of Gaul. How are you going to maintain your health on such a long journey?"

"I'll have my physicians."

She shrugged, and again glanced at the scroll. "And twenty ex-consuls? They're so old, they'll never last the distance."

"I'm selecting the younger ones. They're still in their sixties, but only those who are fit enough for the rigors of the journey will go."

Finally, she said, "And you're taking the Praetorian Guard. But they've spent the past two years drinking and whoring. There's not one man who has the strength to lift a sword, let alone use it in defense of the emperor's person. Claudius, this is a foolish thing for you to do, my dear. Your place is here, beside your wife. Little Octavia is only four and Britannicus is only two, and they'll miss their father while he's away. And the emperor's loyal and loving Messalina will miss you, too," she said.

Despite his adoration of her, Claudius replied acidly, "The children might miss me, but there's no chance of their mother being alone at night to fret for her husband."

"Oh, love, you don't believe all those rumors about me, do you? And if I am a bit playful, it's only in the service of your needs. Your relationship with the Senate has to improve if you're not to be subject to constant plotting. And if they won't talk to you and you won't acknowledge them, then surely it's up to your loyal wife to use every means at her disposal to assist," she said.

"Most wives would have contented themselves with a banquet or two to help their husband's career. I'm told that you only seem satisfied with orgies and wild parties and fetching men from the taverns to satisfy your lusts."

"That's rubbish," she insisted. "This palace is full of rumors and innuendo. If I listened to every tale told about you, I'd believe that you spend your days and nights indulging yourself with every whore who works in every brothel in this town. But do I listen to gossipmongers and tattletales? Of course I don't, because I have more faith in my Claudius than he has in his Messalina."

The emperor shuffled some papers on his table in an attempt to concentrate his mind on the plans for his visit to Britain. But Messalina walked over and put her arms around his shoulders. She bent down and started to bite his earlobe, something he particularly enjoyed.

He shuddered, and turned to kiss her. Messalina licked his lips with her tongue, and used it to pry open his mouth. She put her hand inside his tunic and was about to move it down to his lap, when the noise of a man coughing was clearly audible.

In annoyance, Messalina turned, and saw that Polybius was standing at the entryway to the library.

"Oh, for the sake of the gods, what is it? Can't you see that the emperor and I are busy?"

"Apologies, Lady, but this is a matter which won't wait."

"Then enter," she commanded. "Really, Claudius, you give these slaves too much liberty. They're Greeks, after all . . ."

Used to her insults, Polybius drew close to the emperor's table.

"I must speak with you, Caesar," he said.

"Then speak, fool," said Messalina.

The Greek stood there in silence.

"Are you deaf or dumb or both?" she said.

Still Polybius remained silent, merely standing and looking at the emperor.

"My love," said Claudius, "Polybius is unable to speak in your presence. This must be a matter of great urgency, for the emperor's ears only."

Furious, Messalina shot a vicious glare at the Greek, who bowed to her as she swept out of the room.

"Well, Polybius, what's so important that you have to interrupt the first time Messalina has been intimate with me in a year?"

"Our spies have just returned from Egypt. They tell us that there has been a terrible plague of locusts, and that more than half the country's wheat grain has been stripped off the crop. In two months, Caesar, Rome will not have enough wheat for bread, and the prices will increase to such an extent that there will be starvation unless we can buy supplies from other sources. The problem is that once the locust plague is known, prices throughout the empire will rise steeply and there'll still be problems for the citizens of Rome."

"Very well, have men go out immediately . . . tonight . . . to all the sources in the empire and buy whatever is necessary to fill the granaries. This is the fifth crop failure from Egypt in the past twenty years. That, Polybius, is why we need

Britain. It's much less wooded than Germany, and the open plains and fields are able to produce as much wheat as Rome requires. The country can sustain so much production that it could feed the entire world. I'm told that the soil is as black and as rich as that of the Tuscans. And who knows how far the land of Britain stretches?

"But better, Polybius. With the more moderate temperatures in Britain, the wheat and fruit ripen more slowly and are richer and tastier and fuller. And the best thing, of course, is that the land is too cold for locusts. Now do you understand why I'm going to Britain?"

Polybius shrugged indifferently. "The grain and the land will still be there tomorrow, whether you go or not, Caesar. Meanwhile, there was another dispatch which I must mention to you; this one comes to us from Britain. Having been defeated, the rebel chieftain Caratacus has now scattered his troops throughout the middle of the country and ordered them to fight as insurrectionists in a constant stream of assaults in order to destroy the morale of our troops. Your general, Plautius, wanted to pursue and destroy Caratacus, but much to his chagrin, he is following your orders to stay and oversee preparations for the fall of the capital which, I am informed by the messenger, is to be undertaken by yourself. Is that correct?"

Claudius nodded.

"I'm informed that the capital, Caesar, is nothing more than a village with houses made of wood and straw and mud." He searched the intelligence scroll until he found the reference, and said, "Apparently, Caesar, the British make these domestic constructions from something called wattle and daub. Yet you seem to believe that it requires the presence of an emperor to conquer this outpost."

"Oh, for once in your life, Polybius, shut up, can't you!" said Claudius.

The Greek looked at him in shock. This time, he realized that Claudius meant the censure, and that he'd gone too far. He bowed slightly in apology.

"And one other thing, Polybius. While I'm gone, I want daily reports on the behavior of my wife. Messalina does not behave like the wife of a Caesar when Caesar is in his palace. When Caesar is out of the country, only the gods know how far she'll go. I can't have my victory marred by being ridiculed as the husband of the most elevated whore in Rome, now can I?"

The Land of the Iceni in Britain

The days were now warm and sunny; the mud in the fields had long dried up, and dust was in the air: dust from the dry earth and dust from the flowers which were in abundance in the woods and fields. Dust seemed to be everywhere these days. There was grime and dirt on the clothes of the farmers as they started the long process of readying the fields to gather the crops, and dust in the house brought in by flies and moths and animals which wandered in and out of the villages.

But worse... far worse... was the dust from the battlefields, the constant stench of smoke from fields set ablaze so that the Romans couldn't follow the defeated British and which denied them food; dust on the clothes of the fleeing men and women who had managed to escape the terrifying war weapons which the Romans were now deploying throughout the land; and dust from the many dead whose bodies were returning to the earth.

The defeat of Caratacus had come as a shock to some, yet strangely as a relief to others. But the news was an unparalleled devastation for Boudica. Never had she felt as bereft as when she listened to the messenger who came to her parents' home and told of the lost battles. He was a returning Iceni soldier who had fought side by side with Caratacus at the River Medway, and who testified to the bravery of the Britons, and the invincibility of the Romans.

Since returning from the meeting of Druids and the joy of the religious ceremony, Boudica had felt increasingly morose. She had begun the journey with such enthusiasm, and had relished the long walk, the adventures, seeing new places and wondrous sights, and finally being one of thousands of people from all over Britain, all of whom were different, yet all of whom worshipped the same gods. For the first time in her young life, her world stretched beyond the lands of the Iceni, beyond the rivers and the fields and the forests she knew so well. She had come to realize that what she had been led to think of as her vast world was little more than a small part of a huge land, and that as she grew older and more independent of her parents, she would set out and explore it, find out who lived within it, how they worked and thought, what they ate, how they dressed and who they worshipped.

But then news had come of the landing of the Romans, and suddenly everything was thrown into chaos. Instead of feeling free as she wandered back from the sacred grove with her tribe, she had felt the same sense of gloom which had settled on her family.

And arriving home to everything with which she was familiar had not made her feel better. She needed to know everything that was happening, so that she could understand how to cope with the new circumstances. So she demanded of the messenger, "What was the battle at the river? Who was involved? How many Romans were there? What did they wear? What weapons—"

"Boudica," shouted Gadrin. "For the sake of the gods, one question at a time. The poor man has only just arrived."

"But how are we to deal with the Romans, Father?" she asked.

Gadrin nodded, and told her, "That's a problem which I will have to deal with. It's not a problem for children."

"I'm not a child. I'm a hunter. And I can fight the Romans as well as any other Briton."

"There'll be no fighting any Romans until we know their intention," he said sternly. "The Romans don't fight battles lightly. They fight to destroy anybody who stands against them. If we fight, then they'll destroy us for certain—"

She interrupted. "So we're not going to fight?"

"Caratacus fought, and look what's happened. How can the Iceni fight a force as mighty as the Romans?"

A sudden fury entered her eyes. "I'll fight. Even if I have to fight on my own."

"Yes," said her father. "I believe you would. And then where would I be, looking at the dying body of my beautiful Boudica, high on a cross, being crucified? No, darling, there'll be no fighting. The time for fighting is over. Now is the time to negotiate."

Later that night, she forced the man to repeat for her ears alone all the details of the battle lost by Caratacus. And the more she heard it, the less she understood why the Britons had been defeated. Caratacus was such a noble warrior, such a supreme fighter, and one who was protected by all the gods through the sacrifice of the young boy in the sacred clearing. What was the value of the sacrificed boy's pain and suffering if not to strengthen the Britons so they would win the war?

Caratacus's brother Togodumnus, a man of men, had been killed, along with thousands of brave Briton men and women. And according to the soldier, the women had fought valiantly, equaling the men in strength and perseverance. The soldier had hailed their bravery in fighting the Roman hordes. Yet it wasn't enough. Britain had lost its army.

"You should have seen them, Lady," the Briton told her. "The Romans were like a solid wall. We did everything in our power to breach their lines, but the more we attacked them, the more of them there seemed to be and the more of us they killed. The dead and dying just mounted up and up until it was like a writhing hill in front of the Roman lines. And then, when we were given orders to pull back, the Romans came after us with their short swords slashing at us, and their long spears jabbing. And the arrows . . . they were like a swarm of bees which blackened the skies, and hundreds of us fell dead or gravely wounded. There's no hope for us, Lady. We are doomed to be conquered by the Romans. Nobody can fight against an army like that."

"Doomed? How can Britain be doomed? We are so many. And we're strong!" She knew she sounded young and immature. She simply didn't understand how her land could suddenly be conquered by a nation which she only knew of from her parents' conversations. And now Rome was here, threatening her life and all that she loved.

"What about the priests? What about their sacrifices and their prayers?" she asked.

The messenger smiled. "Roman swords and shields don't seem to care much for the prayers of Britons."

Young as she was, Boudica knew that prayers must work. Why weren't the gods listening? And if Caratacus was fleeing from the Roman army, and Togo-dumnus was killed, along with thousands of Britons, then who would defend Britain against the invading Romans? She asked Annika and Gadrin later that evening, and they gave noncommittal answers, such as "Things are not as they might appear," or "You're young yet, and soon you'll understand."

But what they really meant was "Sometimes it's better to live in harmony with those who conquer you than to fight them and die."

Boudica was in a state of despair. Every aspect of her being told her to pick up a sword, march south and confront the Romans. Her land was being invaded, yet her father and mother were behaving as though it were merely a bad season for their crops. Gadrin's workers were still toiling as though nothing had happened instead of preparing for the battle of their lives. The mines were still giving up their ore, the fields their crops, the trees their fruits. Yet all around her people were in a state of panic. Why couldn't her parents understand what was happening beyond the borders of their tribe?

Why was nobody listening to the Druid priests? A priest was almost as potent as a king or the leader of a tribe. They were the sons of very important and rich people; they studied for years and memorized all of the rituals so that they had the answers to everything. Druids were the judges and wise men and men of medicine of the Celtic people, elevated above ordinary men and women who belonged to tribes. Druids had no tribe other than their own priesthood, and so, unlike ordinary men and women who belonged to the land on which they were born, Druids didn't need permission to cross another tribe's land, but were permitted by ancient laws to wander wherever in Britain they wanted. Nobody was allowed to stop them, or even to lay a hand on their sacred persons, for they knew the gods by name.

Many of the Druids had come to her home and tried to convince her parents and her people to rise up and join the rebellion against the Romans, but it hadn't resulted in anyone leaving the village. How could her parents not listen to a priest and do as he said? It didn't make sense. Nothing any longer made sense.

Nothing, that is, except for the growing conviction that if nobody in the tribe of the Iceni was willing to fight the Romans, then it was up to her to save her country. So Boudica gathered her own army from her own village and two other villages nearby. She spent days making wooden swords and shields for the young boys and girls, and outfitted all twenty-four of them with the equipment they would need to defeat the iron-heeled invaders. Then she marched them in single file down the roads which linked one village to another, and within the villages, shouting out orders and instructions until her voice was hoarse and her army was ready for any battle.

The villagers stopped what they were doing in the fields, or came out of their houses, and smiled at Boudica's antics. They offered oatmeal cakes to her army and drinks of honey water when they saw how hot the children had become with the incessant marching and fighting practice which Boudica made them undertake.

But when the harvest of fruits from the trees, and honey from the hives, and wheat and turnips and other crops were ready to be gathered, all of the children left her army to assist their parents in the essential work of survival for the coming year.

The food which was gathered in was carefully hidden in large pits in the ground, covered with a wooden lid which itself was then covered with earth and straw to blend in with the landscape in order to prevent the Romans from scavenging and appropriating everything for themselves.

And life went on.

CHAPTER FOUR

47 AD—A Village in the Lands of the Iceni, Eastern Britain

They knew to remain silent, even when all their hunting had ended and they were returning home. It wasn't like the old days, before the Romans had invaded: days when Boudica and her friends could run through the woods and the fields, laughing and shouting on their way to or from the hunt. Those days, carefree and happy days, were at an end. As was their childhood.

In the four years since Rome had conquered Britain, Boudica had remained firm in her conviction that the Britons should have banded together in order to drive the invaders out of her homeland. Yet in spite of the constant, oppressive changes to their daily life, Boudica maintained her delight in the everyday, and found new ways of making mischief. She especially delighted in the subtle, subversive tricks which she and her cohorts played against the Roman soldiers. It was Boudica who encouraged the villagers to give the Romans rotting food instead of trying to placate them with fresh; it was she who tried to fool them by weighing down a sackful of precious grain with river mud placed surreptitiously in the middle. Anything to fool the Romans, provided they only discovered the deception when they were miles away and it was too late to determine which of the villages had deceived them.

It was the fun which Boudica and her friends created for themselves as a replacement for the fun which they could have had if the invasion had never happened. Sometimes Boudica would wake early, her mind having worked out a scheme to make fools of the Romans, and at others, the opportunity presented itself.

Now was such a moment. Boudica and two of her friends from a nearby village were returning from a hunt. As usual, they walked silently through the woods in case they were noticed by a party of Roman soldiers, who seemed to be ever-present on the new roads which they were building throughout the land. The three youngsters walked quietly, as carefully as possible, avoiding sticks and twigs whose breaking would alert any Romans nearby.

They had caught twelve rabbits in distant fields, enough food for themselves and the elderly in their villages for some time. Instead of talking animatedly about the excitement of the hunt, they trod warily. And it was their silence which allowed them to hear a man's laughter from the far distance.

Alert to anything which might spell danger, Boudica instantly stopped and signaled her friends to remain absolutely still. They listened, and again, they heard the man laughing; this time, though, his laughter was joined by the noise of two other men.

She signaled for her friends to crouch on their knees, and they all listened carefully for where the sounds might be coming from. And then as the wind changed into their direction, they smelled the smoke of a fire, and the smell of food being cooked. With her hand, Boudica indicated that the sounds came from the north, toward where the new Roman road had been constructed.

She and her friends carefully threaded their way through the undergrowth, as silently as stalking wolves, until they drew close enough to the men to see them from a distance.

They were Romans. Four of them. They had a cart, and their horses were tied up to a nearby tree. They were obviously working for a tax collector, because their cart was full of burlap sacks, taken no doubt from nearby Celtic villagers as tribute.

Boudica felt anger rise in her throat, but these weren't moments for her to be brave. Her father had given her the strictest of instruction that she must avoid Roman soldiers at all costs, because in a field or on a road, they wouldn't care whether she was the daughter of Gadrin of the Iceni; they would look at her as a slave, capture her, and before her parents even knew she'd been taken, she would be trussed like an animal, manacled, and on her way by ship to Rome. And that would happen if she was lucky; many Britons died slowly and in agony by the hideous method called crucifixion.

But there was something about the Romans' arrogance, sitting there around a fire on her land, eating food stolen from her people, breathing her air, which infuriated Boudica. Her mind told her that she must turn and creep away. Her heart told her differently. And whenever she had enjoyed herself most, it was when she'd listened to the pleading of her heart instead of the logic of her brain.

A mischievous smile crept over her face. Her two companions, knowing her as well as they did, immediately knew that she was planning something naughty.

In complete silence, and with her hands alone, she indicated what she intended to do. When they understood, they nearly ruined the entire scheme by laughing, but Boudica put her hands over their mouths to ensure silence.

They moved surreptitiously closer until they were fifty paces from the Romans. Slowly, quietly, cautiously, they found what they were looking for: a young sapling twice the height of a man. It was strong, green and supple. And it had a small canopy of leaves. And there were no trees or other obstacles between where the sapling grew in the ground, and the Romans sitting beside the roadway.

Silently, two of them reached up and pulled the sapling down toward the ground. It was a hard job; the sapling resisted the strain of the two youngsters. But without breaking the supple trunk or any of the branches, they managed to bend the young tree almost in two, the leaves reaching down to the forest floor.

While her friends held the tree in place, Boudica threaded the leaves and branches so that they made a bed; then she untied one of the dead rabbits from the clutch and placed it in the bed of leaves. She maneuvered her friends so that they moved the taut sapling slightly to the right, accurately altering the aim. And then she nodded. Her friends let go of their hold on the tree, which immediately straightened up, hurling the dead rabbit up into the air, and straight toward the Romans.

As it flew silently, Boudica let out a terrifying scream, which the Romans heard at the same time as the rabbit landed out of the thin air only four paces from where they sat. The three youngsters immediately fell to the floor of the forest, smothering their laughter. The Romans yelped in fear, grabbed their weapons, and prepared for the attack. But they stood there in the sudden and enveloping silence, utterly mystified.

Boudica was close to hysterical laughter, and had to pinch herself to prevent any noise. Through the undergrowth, she could see the Romans, terrified, transfixed, looking at the rabbit which had suddenly flown through the air and landed at their feet.

One of them stepped forward, sword in hand, and picked it up. He shook his head at his companions, who were peering into the forest, trying to see whether they were about to be attacked by a Celtic war party. But the silence told them that they were alone. They looked up into the canopy of the trees, they looked around, but they stayed together for protection. Quickly dousing the fire, the Romans packed up as quickly as they could, and left the eerie forest.

When they were out of sight, the three Britons lay on the forest floor, and laughed until their sides hurt. And they knew that this was a secret which they mustn't tell anybody. What they'd done wouldn't be nearly as funny to their families as it was to them. Boudica retrieved the rabbit, and they returned home.

It was the roads which made the difference. First, parallel ditches were dug and the earth from the ditches used to build up the road surface high above the surrounding countryside. The roads were then topped with large flat rocks and gravel to ensure a smooth passage for feet and wheels.

These were long and straight roads and they traversed the countryside linking cities and towns which were busily being constructed as administration centers and places for the Romans to live. Some of the cities were built on top of existing towns; some were carved out of the naked countryside. Within four years of the arrival of Rome, the British landscape began to change. And the roads which crisscrossed the country were the most visible sign of Rome's presence. Their elevation was deliberate, so that no thief or murderer, no rebel militia or tribal army could lie in ambush without being seen from a long distance. Roads made traveling faster and safer and didn't cause the wheels of carts to break and fracture in the ruts. But most importantly, the roads enabled fruits and grains, breads and carcasses to be transported from place to place faster than they could spoil in the heat of summer or freeze and be ruined in the icy grip of winter. The construction of the roads was one of the benefits which Boudica's parents used to justify the Roman presence against their daughter's anger and concern.

"Never mind what the Druids say," her father, Gadrin insisted, placating her when the most recent news of Caratacus' latest defeat had filtered down to her village. "I know you don't like it, but look at the many advantages we're enjoying now that the Romans have brought all the benefits of their empire to Britain. Look how we're all prospering! Look at the money we're earning and the trade we're doing with them.

"Do you think you'd have your beautiful dresses if money from the Romans wasn't coming in? Do you think we'd be able to afford all these slaves and servants if I didn't trade with them? Look at the prices we're getting for the jewelry the villagers are making and the money we earn for the grain we sell. Can't you see the way we're all doing so much better now that the Romans have brought peace and order to Britain? Do you want to live through the sorts of conflicts which happened every day between the tribes before they came here?"

In anger, Boudica rounded on him and snapped, "Oh, we're doing well under the Romans, Father, but what about the slaves they're taking? What about the poor people who are dying of starvation because of Roman taxes? What about the way they're forcing our men to work deeper and faster in the mines? Men are being killed by rockfalls because the Romans demand more and more silver for their coins."

No matter how she argued against the occupation, Boudica knew that in her father's heart and mind, he believed what he was saying. But Boudica knew he was wrong, regardless of how much her family was profiting. In the four years since the Romans had landed on the nearby shores and humiliated the British forces, she'd grown skeptical of everything her parents said and resentful of the Romans who strutted around her village like roosters.

Her greatest shame was the way her father and mother gave them entry to their home. Boudica felt tainted every time one of them dined in her house, every time she heard their ugly tongue being spoken. Despite being forced to sit at the table during the meal, she would find any excuse to leave early so that she didn't have to listen to their conversation.

For Boudica, hers was a family who had diminished itself by befriending a natural enemy. She recognized, of course, that things were certainly better and richer and more peaceful today than before the Romans came. There was no longer the perennial fear of Britons that the peace they enjoyed today would turn into a nightmare tomorrow when one British tribe attacked another.

But even with the obvious benefits which the Romans had brought, this wasn't the Britain that Boudica had grown up in and known all her youth. This was a Britain where Rome ruled, where British towns were suddenly filled with the iron clatter of armed soldiers who barked out orders in a foreign language, and where tax collectors extracted vast amounts of money and produce and live-stock; where the poor men and women who wandered the countryside were suddenly pulled out of their blankets in the dark of night to become slaves, and where a herd of cows or sheep in a village pen would suddenly be divided in half and disappear into the ever-hungry jaws of the Roman empire.

This was a Britain where freedom was no longer what she woke up to, where the air wasn't hers to breathe, where the woods and waters and hills and valleys suddenly belonged to somebody else—and where everything was done in the name of a distant Emperor who had suddenly appeared one day riding a huge elephant, and the next day had disappeared forever, never showing his soft, fat and deformed body again.

✳ ✳ ✳

It was morning, and the start of a new day. Rising with the sun, Boudica combed her hair and poured water from the ewer into the new bronze bowl her parents had given her to celebrate her seventeenth birthday. After dressing in her blue tunic and fixing the bodice with the gold clasp she had been given a year earlier, she emerged from her room. Their new house was built in the style of a Roman mansion. As one of the Iceni chieftain families and clients of the Romans, on order of the local governor her family had been given a Roman house in which to live and Roman clothes to wear. And so Boudica and her family left their one-story wood and wattle home by the river's edge and moved into their new house, one made of stone and timber, with a roof covered in baked clay, with paved floors, and walls painted with scenes of men and women in togas lying on couches and eating bunches of grapes.

For the first few months she rebelled, sleeping in the barn. But by the winter, her mother had persuaded her to come into the house, and though she continued to feel uncomfortable, Boudica started to enjoy the luxuries which made life so much more pleasant. She enjoyed the additional rooms which faced the south, and which meant warmth in the cold months of the year, but somehow managed to capture the breeze which cooled them in the summer months; she enjoyed the sense of roominess and ease of flow; and she especially enjoyed the way in which shelves had somehow been built into walls so that she could keep her personal possessions tidy instead of in a bundle on the floor. Despite her contempt for everything Roman, Boudica was forced to admit that the house was a clever design. But even though she'd now lived in it for a year and a half, it still felt alien and ill-fitting and not the sort of house in which a true Briton would want to live.

Greeting her parents, she received a bowl of hot oatmeal and a slice of bread from the slave, and she sat and ate as the family talked about the tasks which they would undertake during the day. Boudica was irritated when she noticed her mother had the shells of walnuts and the pits of olives on her platter. Why she had to eat Roman food was beyond Boudica's understanding, when British food was warming and welcoming. And she said so!

Suddenly irritated, Gadrin snapped, "Why do you speak to Annika and me like that? Why do you try to make us feel guilty just because of what we're eating? And why do you assume that the food we used to eat is better than the food we're eating now?"

Surprised by her father's vehemence, Boudica said, "Because we're becoming more Roman than the Romans. Can't you see what's happening to us . . . what we've become since they arrived?" She waved her arms around the room. "Look at the gods you're worshipping. Roman gods!" she shouted, pointing to the idols of Venus and Cupid, Diana and Apollo, sitting in niches in the wall. "Look at the clothes you're wearing. Look at—"

"Silence!" said Gadrin. "Do you want to go back to those times when we were always looking in fear at the hills in case the wild men of the Trinovantes or the murderers from the Catuvellauni came marauding into our territory, stealing our men and raping our women? Have you forgotten those times, Boudica, or were you too young to remember?"

"Rather warring against Britons, than bound in slavery to Roman masters," she said. "Half of our money goes to an emperor we never see who lives in a city we've never been to. His troops are stealing our food, his—"

"You know nothing about why the Iceni have agreed to—"

Annoyed, she said, "Father, please don't treat me as though I'm still a child!"

She wanted to say more, but the look on Gadrin's face told her to remain silent. "Since the Romans arrived, not one tribe has dared to raise its hands against us. Not one! And that means that our people aren't dying in wars and aren't being ambushed when they travel from village to village.

"Your mother and I have status and wealth and slaves. We're happy with what we've got. When you go out into a cold and friendless world, you'll understand the value of being friends with Rome. Until then, remain silent, and respect those who protect us from ourselves."

Shaking her head, she stood from the table. "Please excuse me, I don't wish to stay here." She left the house and went into the fields to organize the slaves who were gathering for work, to continue with the crop harvest. As she walked, she wondered if she was right and her father was wrong. It was such a complex situation. Despite what he had said and the indignation with which he'd said it, Boudica knew in her heart that Romans didn't belong in Britain. But that was something about which she could do little.

Gadrin watched his daughter leave the house, and said to Annika, his wife, "That girl needs a husband. A man who is as strong as she is and can keep her in check. With our wealth now, we can buy her a good husband. Someone from Castuveni or another village nearby."

His wife looked at him in surprise. "But every time I've suggested we find her a husband, you've objected, saying that there was time enough, and that she was too valuable working here. Why the sudden change of mind?"

"I've seen the way the Roman soldiers look at her. Right now she's looking at them in contempt, but that seems to make them more interested. And with the way she's enjoying some of the village boys, how long do you think Roman soldiers will leave her alone, just because she's our daughter? I don't mind trading with the Romans, but it's another thing for Boudica to have a child with a soldier. If she's going to marry a Roman, it'll be a governor or a procurator, and they're not disposed to marry Britons. Understand, Annika, that I want to keep her from liaisons with men from the army. You know how many of our British girls are heavy with Roman children. Well, not Boudica!

"Until she has a husband, who knows what mischief she'll get herself into. She's a lovely-looking girl and she's tall and proud. For a husband, she needs a man who has experience of the world. You've been looking at boys for her to marry; I think she needs a man."

"And is there any particular man you have in mind, husband? From that look in your eye, I'd say that the matter is already settled."

He grinned. Gadrin couldn't hide anything from Annika. "I was selling logs to Prasutagus the other day, when he mentioned that he was no longer happy being a widower, and asked if there were any widows or lonely older women in my village that he might inspect with a view to marriage. I told him about Boudica, and although he thought she might be too young for him, I assured him that she was mature in her body, and would bear him many fine children."

"Prasutagus? Are you mad? He must be as old as you, if he's a day," said his wife.

"He's only recently turned forty, and he's as virile a man as he was when he was twenty. He's wealthy, lives in a fine big house with many slaves, and wants a child to inherit his wealth."

"But he has a son," Annika said.

Gadrin shook his head. "The boy isn't his. He came with Prasutagus' first wife, so he's only a stepson. Prasutagus wants to leave his wealth to his own blood. If he dies without blood offspring, his fortune will go to Rome. His first wife died of a pestilence when they'd been married only a year, and his second wife and the child within her died from fever in childbirth after only two years of marriage. For the past eight years, he hasn't been married. He's been with many women, mainly slaves from the north and Germania, but none of whom he'd want to marry. He needs a woman of the Iceni to make his life complete. He has a fine head of hair, he's muscular and robust and he will satisfy Boudica in her body. She'll never be hungry or cold. He's very rich, and he's the sort of man who'll keep our willful daughter in check."

Annika looked at him skeptically. "A man who'll keep Boudica in check? You said no such man had been born." Gadrin remained silent. After some thought, Annika continued. "Boudica will not want to marry a man of his age."

"She'll marry who we tell her to marry."

"And who's going to tell her? Not me, with that temper of hers."

"I'll tell her. This morning! She'll do as she's told."

"And the payment? How much will he want for her?"

"Because she's so young, he'll take her for half what he would otherwise demand. And a year's supply of wood."

His wife looked at him questioningly. It was far too modest a gift for a man of Prasutagus' stature and wealth, a man more closely connected to the ruling families of the Iceni than their own.

"Alright," said her husband, realizing from his wife's skepticism that she wanted the entire truth, "not only a year's supply of wood, but also a year's supply of grain."

"And . . ."

He sighed. "And a double measure of silver."

"What! That'll ruin us. That silver is for the Romans. I've already negotiated the supply!" she shouted. "It's for delivery next month. We can't give it to Prasutagus or we'll not have the money to pay for food for the winter."

"Stop worrying, woman. I've just begun opening up a new seam in the eastern mine, and from the looks of it, it's going to be a rich lode, as good as the best we've dug up so far. It promises to be richer in silver than other mines in the area, even those which are close by, and the lead is coming out easily from the smelting. I've not told Prasutagus when I'll deliver the silver, so we can keep our undertaking and sell the requisitioned amount to the Romans and spend the next few months producing enough for the wedding dowry. They won't be married until the spring, and so there's plenty of time."

"Fool of a man," she said. "Why didn't you leave negotiations with Prasutagus up to me? You know I drive a harder bargain than you. You're far too soft. We have other daughters to think about. What about them?"

Stung, he responded, "We have more than enough so that we don't have to belittle ourselves by negotiating too hard about any of our daughters' futures. Look at the money we're earning from all of these merchants crossing our land with their gold from Ireland. Why are you making such a fuss? It's our daughter and her wedding gift. We've never been this wealthy, so why shouldn't we show the people of the Iceni how we're benefiting from the Romans. Those who are fighting them are living in caves and suffering, while we're eating walnuts and olives. And anyway, you might criticize me for not negotiating a better bargain, but how hard are you when it comes to dealing with Boudica?" he asked.

She nodded. "Boudica is different. She's as smart as a bee sting. She has an answer to everything I raise with her. May the gods help Prasutagus if he marries our daughter, for I certainly haven't been able to calm her wayward spirits."

While her parents were discussing her future, Boudica was in the fields, instructing the slaves on how to reap the ripened wheat with the new Roman scythes. Dislike the invaders as she did, she had to admit that their iron cutting tools were far superior to those of the Celts. Their shape made it possible for the slaves to gather and cut much larger armsful of the crop, and the cutting edge was superior.

But when it came to the artistry of working with metals, her people, and many other British tribes, far excelled the Romans. The Britons produced the finest quality bronze, from copper mixed with a tiny amount of tin which came from the mines of the southwest of Britain. Once the ore was smelted, British metalworkers produced the most beautiful and intricate jewelry in the entire world. The Romans only knew how to make tools which were clever and practical. But for all their lack of subtlety, the new Romans had created a scythe which enabled her slaves to cut double the amount of stalks than they were able to with the old implements.

Satisfied that the work was going well, she decided to speak to Alvanus, her father's foreman in the galena mines which produced the argentum for the Roman coinage. Now that the silver mines of Spain were running dry, the Romans were buying as much silver as the British could mine—which was making her family, and other mine owners, very rich. And partly as a result of her father's ability to smell a new seam of ore in what looked like plain rock, and partly because the merchants trading gold in Ireland were crossing Iceni lands to get to the ports at the mouth of the Thames in order to sail to Gaul, the money which was flowing into her father's and mother's treasury was drawing them closer and closer into the Roman web.

Alvanus was a man of lands in the far north of Britain, near to the border with the wild men of Caledonia. Indeed, because of Boudica's waist-length flaming golden red hair, Alvanus often remarked that she was most likely the spawn of a union between the goddess Balthena and a Caledonian.

Boudica and Alvanus had known each other for four years; he had been one of many who had come south from the lands of the Carvetii and of the Brigantes in order to join with Caratacus to fight the invasion. But instead of continuing the fight and fleeing to the middle lands of Britain, and ultimately to Wales with the remnants of the rebels, he had sought refuge with Boudica's parents, and in return they'd put him to work in their mine.

The promise which Alvanus had shown was extraordinary, and soon he was responsible for much of the profits which the family was enjoying. Although he was still a slave, he was given the freedom of the land and often joined the family in meals.

While he was arranging the site of a new dump for the rock extracted from the recently opened mine, Alvanus saw Boudica walking across the fields to the shafts, and waved to her. When she joined him, he bowed in deference to their social positions.

"How is my lady?" he asked.

"Sad. More news came by messenger about Caratacus yesterday. He is fighting bravely in Wales, but the Romans are increasing their numbers in the west, and it's only a matter of time."

Alvanus nodded and waited for her to say more. She wouldn't have come all the way to the mine just to tell him what everybody knew, or guessed.

"And while the hero of Britain is struggling for our freedom, my family grows rich trading with the Romans."

"As do many other families in the lands of the Iceni. And other tribal lands throughout Britain, Lady." She nodded. "I know it would be a wonderful thing to see Britain free of the iron glove, but now that the Romans have brought such prosperity for men and women like your parents, it seems a little enough burden to pay them taxes and remain free of their soldiers. They don't bother us all that much, and meantime, we all prosper," Alvanus said softly.

"You're not saying . . ."

"Of course not. But while you and I can be enraged by the conqueror's presence and feel contempt for those Britons who serve them, you're not silly enough to think that they would forgo money in their pockets for freedom from Rome and a return to the old ways, are you?"

She shook her head, and remained silent. Eventually, she asked, "How is the mine? Have you begun to smelt the ore from the new lode?"

He nodded, and smiled. "It's rich, Lady. Very rich. I was with your father yesterday when we crushed some of the rock and heated it in the furnaces. We brought out the lead in the usual way, but when we extracted the silver from it, it was shining like the morning sun on water. And it's the purest we've ever extracted so far from this site. I think it's worth double or more of the other galena deposits around here. It should make your mother and father very happy when I have enough silver to show them."

Boudica picked up the pannier which her personal slave had carried and took out a flask of wine and some bread and cheese. "Here," she said to Alvanus, "let's celebrate our riches."

They sat on the ground, and took deep draughts from the bottle. Chewing on the bread, Boudica said, "Alvanus, what would you say if I told you something which would make my parents very angry, but something which I must do? Would you feel bound by your oaths to tell my parents, or would you keep my secret? If you feel you must tell them, then I would ask you to let me inform them first."

"Are you asking my advice, Lady?" She nodded. "Then what you ask is between the two of us."

Slowly, ensuring that her slave was out of hearing, she whispered, "I want to leave here and join Caratacus. I want to fight against the Romans. I don't want to be in my home and deal with them. I want to run down from the hillsides and scream battle cries and wield a battle-axe and kill them. I've had enough of trying to make them seem like idiots, of trying to fool them. Now I'm a woman, I want to kill them and free my land of their presence."

She waited in anticipation for his reaction. But his delay in responding with approbation and congratulations made her wonder if she should have told him anything, even though she was in the habit of confiding every secret thought to him.

"I did that once, Boudica. I walked from my home and my lands and traveled south to join with the rebels and fight the Romans. And I know from experience what it's like to fight them. They have skills on the battlefield which we can't begin to match. No matter how strong or determined we are, their proficiency in maneuvers, their tactics, overwhelm any advantages we have. I fought with Caratacus for months before realizing that it was a hopeless battle, and that all I would succeed in doing was getting myself killed.

"So my advice to you, Boudica, is to let others fight for this land. You are young and beautiful and precious to us all. Your future doesn't lie in fighting for Britain, but in using your mind to help us understand our circumstances and your wiles in defeating the Romans by guile rather than by force. Carrying an axe and killing a couple of Romans might give you a moment's pleasure, but it will undoubtedly see you killed, and you will be buried in some distant muddy land and forgotten except by your grieving family . . . and me. But treating with the Romans, making them understand the wonders of Britain and the importance of the Druids . . . now that will make a difference. I've seen your mind at work, Boudica. I've seen you negotiate with traders and travelers; I've seen the way you deal with the Romans, how you tie them up in knots with your words.

"We'll never beat Rome with the sword and the lance, but with our minds and our talents. And to do that, Boudica, you have to remain here, and become even more important than you already are."

47 AD—The Court of Emperor Claudius, Rome

"As the gods witness my actions, if that man touches me again, I'll poison him, emperor or not. The Empress Livia got rid of half of Emperor Augustus' family, so why shouldn't I get rid of one stuttering, limping fool of a husband whose stomach is so fat that he needs a mirror to see his manhood? Not that there's anything hanging there to see."

The naked men and women burst out laughing, and applauded. Even Messalina giggled at the sound of her own voice. The others continued to laugh uproariously, impelling her to go forward, to tell them more about what she and the emperor did at night; about his fumbling attempts to touch her breast or his begging her to fondle his manhood.

"And the way he's suddenly talking to people, and then he doubles over and cries out in pain. His slaves have to carry him out of the audience room. They lie him on a bed, and try to straighten him out, but he's in so much agony that he can't straighten his puny legs until he farts. One fart after another. Fart, fart, fart! And when his farts have filled the room and it smells like a cowshed, he stands up and says that he feels much better now, and he walks back into the audience room, as though nothing has happened."

Everybody was cackling in hysteria at her imitation of her husband's farting. Women were laughing so hard, they couldn't breathe; men were cackling, and nodding in empathy. But as they laughed, a thought struck Messalina and stopped her from continuing and saying more. Some momentary caution made her stop telling stories about Claudius and remain silent, some foreboding sense that a dark cloud was gathering in her mind.

She could no longer feel her toes, and held up her hand to see if she could feel her fingers wiggling in the steam of the bathhouse. She could see them moving, but they didn't seem to belong to her, which made her laugh even more. Her instincts told her when she'd drunk too much, and that nagging voice of caution told her that now was the time to stop drinking.

Those around her laughed at her wiggling her fingers and toes. They thought it was still part of the performance. Messalina looked around, and tried to remember their names. Some she knew. Some were her very best and closest of friends, men and women whom she'd loved for a long time; others were recent friends, mostly men whom her servants had found in the nearby tavern and who fitted her requirements of being tall and dark-haired and muscular.

The room was becoming too hot, and she shouted, "Slave! Water!"

A tall naked Nubian woman walked into the steam room and poured a bucket of water over Messalina's head, cold and shocking. She shuddered with pleasure and, as the frigid water on her skin began to warm in the heat of the room, she felt her body start to cool down and feel delicious.

But she was already beginning to tire of the steam room. She'd been in there since her breakfast, and the stench coming from the men's bodies was beginning to overpower the attar of roses which perfumed the air.

"Enough!" she said suddenly, standing from the wooden bench. She looked around, and the dozen men and women frantically grabbed their robes and towels in an attempt to do her bidding. It was a funny sight, and she giggled. "Enough! I've had enough of the steam. I want some entertainment."

She turned and walked toward the door of the steam room. As she neared, three of her slaves wrapped her in white robes and placed sandals on her feet. The others in her entourage were forced to find their clothes as best they could. Messalina walked through the door, and was joined by her closest and most trusted friend, Paulina, wife of a young senator from Illyria.

"How did Your Majesty enjoy the baths this morning?" she asked.

After the heat and cloying dampness of the steam room, the cold air of the palace suddenly made Messalina's mind more sensible. "As I enjoy it every morning, dear Paulina. I really shouldn't drink wine before the bath, because I need to get rid of the leaden feeling from the night before, but the wine makes me feel like waking up and starting the day."

Paulina nodded, and continued to walk with the empress toward her private chambers. It was a walk which the two women took almost every morning. It was a walk which had earned Paulina's husband, the young Illyrian leader Marcus Vipsanius Secundus, rapid elevation in his standing in the Senate, as well as trading rights between Rome and his province which were making him a fortune.

"I think I have a problem. I said something in there which I shouldn't have said," Messalina told Paulina. "I was drunk, and I said that I was going to poison Claudius."

Paulina looked at her friend in shock. "In front of them," she hissed, looking back toward the sycophants struggling into their clothes who were trying to follow to be in her footsteps. "Empress, why do you belittle yourself so?"

"I know," Messalina said, almost to herself. "I get drunk and then my anger erupts and I can't seem to control myself. I'll get rid of them, expel them from the palace."

"No, you won't!" said Paulina in an urgent undertone. "Lady, if you get rid of them, the first thing they'll do is to spread gossip about you and what you've said. With Pallas' and Polybius' spies in every tavern in Rome, it'll get back to the emperor's ears in no time."

Messalina's head was now clearing rapidly, although she was desperate for some cold water to quench her raging thirst. "What shall I do?"

"I'll speak with Marcus. He'll know."

"Can your husband help?"

Paulina smiled. "He'll create a mission to Judea or Parthia or somewhere, and appoint all of these so-called friends of yours to be ambassadors. Once they're in the back of beyond, their caravan might meet with a tragic accident. Maybe their wagons will be attacked by barbarians, or fall off a mountain. Or what about being swept away in some raging river, their bodies never to be recovered?"

Messalina smiled. "I'll ensure that they have a wonderful ceremony performed in the temple of Juno, and that I make a votive offering to the priestesses to say prayers for ten years."

They arrived at Messalina's private apartments. The guards opened the doors and admitted the two women. As one started to close the door, Messalina said softly, "Do not allow them inside. Instead, escort them to an antechamber, and have them wait on my pleasure. Then send to the Senate and ask the Honourable Marcus Vipsanius of Illyria if he would be pleased to attend upon his wife and his empress. Immediately!"

Later in the morning, after Marcus had assured Messalina that she would never be bothered by her friends again, she was lying upon her couch eating diced honey- and watermelons with Paulina, when she ordered her slaves away. As soon as the room was cleared, Messalina said to Paulina, "It was wrong of me to have said those things in the steam bath in front of people like them, but what I said was true. Paulina, dearest, I can't abide Claudius anymore. I can't stand to be near him. He revolts and disgusts me. His breath stinks of rotten meat, he slurs his words terribly so I only understand a quarter of what he says, he dribbles when he drinks, spills his food down his tunic when he eats, and when he touches me, my flesh crawls. And that terrible limp of his is driving me to distraction.

"If only he'd walk up to me like a real man one day, instead of hobbling and shuffling. I'm going mad, Paulina. More and more, he's insisting that he come into my bedroom. I supply him with beautiful girls all the while, but he yearns for me every night."

"What reports do you get back from the girls?" asked Paulina.

"They say he finds it difficult to rise up, and when he does manage it, he can't sustain it for more than a few moments at a time. Some of them even said that he isn't stiff enough to put it inside them, so they pleasure him with their hands and their mouths. And even then, only a bit dribbles out, as though it's a dried-up fountain in the height of a Roman summer. I swear, Paulina, if he comes into my bedchamber tonight, he'll be dead by the morning."

"Can't you stop him, Empress?"

"How can I forbid the emperor, even if it is Claudius? In the old days, the Praetorian Guard used to make fun of him; but since his conquest of Britain he's now a respected figure." She picked up another dice of sweet honey-melon, ate it, and wiped her hands on the wet towel. "Even the Praetorian Guard cheer him whenever he enters their barracks. He loves it, and goes there often."

She suddenly shuddered, as though a cold breeze had entered her room. "Oh gods, I hate and detest him so. And his stomach problems make him stink all the while. I can't bear to be in the same room with him anymore. Or even the same palace."

Paulina understood what the empress was going through. "But Lady, think where you'd be if the emperor were dead. Your children are too young and they would never allow you to be regent. There would be an immediate battle for succession, and whoever won would oust you, your children and your mother from the palace. And you'd all be dead within the week. If you did run, where would you go to be safe? Claudius' successor will never let your children live while they have a claim to the title."

A silence descended upon the two women. They lay on their couches, eating the delicacies which lay between them, pondering the future.

"Then I must let him live? And while ever he lives, it means I'll have to endure his hideous body and his pathetic stammering for the rest of my life?"

Paulina shook her head. "Not necessarily, Empress. There are ways, and there are ways." Messalina looked at her friend. Paulina continued. "For example, sleeping draughts so that he might end his working day and begin the evening intent on visiting you, but he'll fall asleep before he leaves his chambers."

"But he'll know if I—"

"Not you, Majesty. Get one of his personal slaves to do it. Bribe the man. Threaten him with castration . . . anything, but last thing at night, get him to put a draught into Claudius' wine. His taster will sip it, and won't notice a thing from a small amount. But when Claudius drinks an entire cup and gets a full draught, he'll be snoring in no time. And no one will suspect anything, because he'll wake up in the morning feeling fit after a good night's sleep."

Messalina smiled, and listened attentively. "And that's not all," Paulina continued. "When you're invited to join him in a meal, explain that you'd love to, but you have to visit some temple or other. He's a pious man, and he'll welcome your sudden interest and devotion to the gods."

"But he'll know I'm not there. He'll send a servant to my chambers, and he'll find me here. I dare not transgress on his piety."

"Then don't be here."

"Where will I go?"

"My villa. Don't tell Claudius precisely which temple you're visiting or praying in. Leave the palace dressed in white and don't take more than a couple of trusted servants with you. No doubt he'll be looking out of the windows. Instruct your litter to take you in the direction of the temple of Apollo one day, Jupiter the next, Venus the following and then Diana. As soon as the litter is out of sight of the palace, come to my home by the back roads, and a wonderful time will be waiting for you."

Messalina couldn't help but smile. "Oh, dearest Paulina. You're so clever. I can spend the entire day out of this place, have a wonderful time, and Claudius will think I'm the most holy woman in Rome. It's brilliant. And better . . . when I return to the palace, I'll be so exhausted from my piety that I'll need to lie down for the entire day and rest. Claudius will love that.

"Well, dearest friend, tell me what treats you'll have in store for me when I begin this subtle subterfuge. Who will you have for me to visit?"

Now it was Paulina's turn to smile. "As Your Majesty knows, my husband

Marcus satisfies my every need. However, I have an eye both for men and for women, and although I don't indulge myself, I do like to see what there is on offer. Some of my recent objects of delight have come with me to the palace. You had the Egyptian charioteer last week . . ." Messalina felt faint as she remembered back to her shock and delight at the sight of his huge black penis. But he had only been good for one session, and useless for the rest of the day, despite her encouragement. ". . . and some of the Judean dancing girls have delighted you.

"But when you come to my home, there are new delights which I will present to you. Has Your Majesty ever shared her body with two men at the same time?"

Messalina looked at her friend in shock. "You don't mean . . ."

Paulina nodded.

The Emperor Claudius lay back and allowed the Greek girl to massage his temples. First she put a cold compress steeped in balm of Gilead on his forehead, and then gently spread aromatic oil over his head, massaging it into his scalp. The smell of sandalwood mixed with the essence of oranges opened up his stuffy nasal passages, and for the first time since his aromatic bath in the morning, he was able to breathe properly.

The girl moved her skillful fingers from the crown of his forehead, down to the temple above his ears, and alternated between a hard and quite painful pressure, and a gentle, almost seductive insistence. And then the damnable Polybius insisted, "May I continue with the letter, Caesar?"

"Yes," Claudius said softly, lost in the embrace of the Greek girl's fingers more than in the doings of the wild men of Britain.

"Your propraetor, Publius Ostorius Scapula, who as you know replaced General Aulus Paulinus as governor of Britain—"

"Yes, yes, I know all about Publius. Get on with the intelligence."

"He informs us that he has repulsed an attack by the enemy Caratacus, and has moved the Twentieth Legion into a new fortress which he has had built. This he was able to do because before he moved them to the west of the country, he replaced the men in Camulodunum with a colony of veterans. This, says the propraetor, will defend Rome's current possessions against insurgencies and assault, and will save the empire money for the veterans' pensions. In place of money, Publius has given them land to farm. They have expelled the few Britons who used to live there, and as a result of your great military conquest, Caesar, it is now becoming our capital city in Britain."

"But the outbreak of hostilities in the lands of the Iceni and the Catuvellauni? Why have they risen up? I don't understand it, Polybius. In good faith, I signed a treaty with the eleven kings, and in return, they promised me peace. What's happened all of a sudden? Why am I being bothered with this when I thought it was all settled?" asked Claudius.

Polybius put down the intelligence scroll which had arrived from Britain that evening. "Because, Caesar, Publius Ostorius Scapula, the governor you selected to replace the excellent Aulus, is a fool and an idiot. Your decision went completely against my advice, if you'll remember. Anyway, it appears that because there was a time lag between Aulus' leaving and Publius' arrival, the wilder tribes of Britain decided to attack Roman fortifications. When he set foot in Britain, instead of using negotiations and diplomacy, Publius used massive force to quell the rebellion. This angered the docile clients of Rome who weren't, at that time, fighting, which made some of the hotheads within the Iceni fight against us. The propraetor used auxiliary troops, which cowed the Britons into submission, because they realized that if mere auxiliaries could do that much damage, they had to be wary of our regular troops.

"But then, having put the rebellion to flight, Publius went much further than he ought, and demanded the disarmament of all the Britons, even those favorable to Rome. This led to further outbreaks, and instead of discussion and conciliation with Rome's friends in Britain, the fool captured the rebels and executed them.

"Unfortunately, in certain of our friendly kingdoms in Britain, a war began between the peoples themselves. A civil war, Caesar! Those Britons who wanted to remain loyal to Rome were fighting against those who had turned against Rome because of the brutality and insensitivity of Publius. In the meantime,

Caratacus has suddenly found new life in his campaign against us, and thousands of Britons are flocking to his side. I did warn you about Publius, Claudius. If you remember, I did tell you that—"

Claudius sat up, to the surprise of the Greek slave. "I know what you told me, Polybius, but you know exactly why I had to appoint Publius."

"When Roman policy is made by Messalina, Caesar, we're in a sorry state."

Claudius stared coldly at Polybius, and propped himself up on one elbow. "You dare to speak of policy made by my wife. Don't think I'm so foolish that I didn't know what you and Pallas and Narcissus were up to with Messalina in the early days. I know you were all trying to gain power through her. I know you conspired with my wife to dupe me into taking action against senators who stood in the way of your ambitions, Polybius. How many senators did you have me kill because of your avarice and hubris? Ten, twenty . . . ?"

"Do you think that I would be so naïve as to associate my political fortunes with Messalina? Narcissus might very well have done so, but I certainly didn't. And you know that I've never trusted Narcissus. Caesar, how could you think such a thing of me? Be that as it may, and I know that I can't change your mind about my intentions, what I say about Messalina is true, Claudius. Messalina has no right to decide which official is appointed by—"

"Don't be impertinent! Messalina might not have the right, but the gods speak through her. Why do you think that I made the appointment when Aulus' term of office ended? She was informed by the god Mars while praying in his temple that I should give Publius Ostorius Scapula the governorship of Britain. I'm not one to go against the wishes of the gods, now am I?"

The Greek stood fuming in front of the emperor's couch. And then the dam holding back his self-control broke, and he said, "Caesar, there's something I must tell you about your wife. This is very difficult, because I know what you think the Lady Messalina is doing when she goes to pray, but . . ."

The look on Caesar's face made Polybius draw back, knowing he'd gone too far; knowing he mustn't say anything further for fear of his life.

"But what? She's a changed woman. Piety and godliness have descended upon her. I prayed for years to change her, and my prayers and sacrifices have been answered. She is no longer debauched, but now she is pious and holy. The change is remarkable. And do you take me for a complete fool, Polybius? I've had her followed; I ordered it just the other week, to ensure that her conversion from a life of dissolute pleasure to a life of holiness was genuine. My slave told me that she went to the temple of Minerva because she wanted to acquire knowledge from the goddess of wisdom, and that she stayed there the entire day. Why do you doubt that this is a changed woman, Polybius?"

The Greek shook his head in despair. He had been threatened by both Pallas and Narcissus not to disclose what Messalina got up to during the days. The emperor was at last content and happy, sleeping well at night, and knowing that his wife was true and faithful during the day. If he was to learn the true evil of Messalina's life, he would become suicidal again, and then where would Rome— and the Greeks who advised her—find themselves?

The Greek girl begged the emperor to lie back and relax himself so that her fingers could continue to work their magic. He did as she asked, admiring for the first time the shape of her breasts and her delicate neck. He might have her tonight, if he didn't fall asleep so early!

"Continue what you're telling me about the wars within the British tribes, Polybius. Who's fighting whom?"

"The king of the Iceni, Antedios, is our old friend. Or should I say, he was our friend, for he has now gone to wherever Britons go and sitting beside whatever gods Britons sit beside when they're dead. Surely you remember Antedios? You signed the treaty with him during the time of your glorious conquest of Britain, Caesar. He was one of the eleven kings who became our clients. More than the others, Antedios proved to be a good friend of Rome, but our new governor in Britain appears to have put aside the value of our relationship, and simply killed him. Anyway, Publius' son, Marcus Ostorius, who is a much finer man than his father, is planning to ride to the land of the Iceni with a full legion of soldiers in order to put the matter to rest. Hopefully, Marcus will have greater diplomatic instincts than his fool of a father."

47 AD—The Lands of the Iceni, Eastern Britain

After the chaos, after the madness, after the anger and the fury, came the recognition of the inevitable. Boudica reluctantly accepted that she must marry Prasutagus if she and her family were to remain safe. Being a single woman, even the daughter of a friend of the Romans such as her parents, put her in a dangerous position. Single men and women, some little more than girls and boys, had been captured by the Romans during the fighting, abducted from their homes, never to be seen again. Everyone, especially their distraught parents, knew that they'd been taken to the slave markets in Gaul and Rome.

Roman soldiers had been merciless in putting down the insurrection. King Antedios had been killed, along with hundreds of his fellow soldiers. The countryside had been ravaged by the army, the food stores stripped bare and some of the fields salted as reprisal for rising up against the might of Rome. Few were recognized by the Roman soldiers as friends; houses were broken into, people killed, possessions taken. Only those who had proven their long-term friendship with Rome and had remained out of the fighting—Britons such as Prasutagus— could be assured of Rome's protection.

The new governor, Publius Ostorius, had determined that the British not only would never be armed, but would remember who was master and who was servant in Britain.

Boudica's regret was not that she was marrying Prasutagus, but that she hadn't taken up arms against the Romans and defended her home. But the rebellion was short-lived and now in the past. The soldiers had moved on, the land of the Iceni was returning to calm, wounds were beginning to heal, and her commitment to Prasutagus, renegotiated by her mother, was brought forward by three months.

Boudica admitted that she liked Prasutagus. She'd only met him twice, but he was passably handsome, experienced in matters of the bed, and he had a winning sense of humor, all things which Boudica prized highly.

And eventually the day dawned when the marriage ceremony was scheduled to take place. With eager anticipation, Boudica looked forward to meeting her future husband for the third time in her young life. While he was much older than she, he looked as though he was a good and caring man. He was tall and strong and still had a full head of hair and all his teeth . . . and best of all, his breath smelled of apples. Boudica initially feared that there was a chance of the Romans arresting Prasutagus, as a nephew of King Antedios, but even Publius realized that of all the Iceni, Prasutagus was the one who was most friendly and accommodating of Roman ways.

Though a proud Briton, Prasutagus was wise enough to realize that in other lands, the Romans left their client peoples in peace—in return for taxes. Trade improved, and the Romans brought many advances to make the lives of the people better and richer.

Only in those provinces such as Judea and Germania, where the people rose up against the occupation, were the Roman armies merciless. Prasutagus had made his views very well known. It was better to learn to live in the new world than be destroyed trying to retain the old world—which was why Boudica's father had insisted that now was the right time for her to marry him. Protection, wealth and security were what Boudica and her family needed, and Prasutagus could provide them all . . . in abundance.

Her mother fussed with Boudica's new green dress, ensuring that the bodice exposed the shape of her breasts so that she looked fertile. Woven into the dress were leaves of mistletoe, the bark of an oak tree, needles of pine, and the preserved blossom of the apple tree, all showing the gods that this was a fertile girl who would produce many children. Annika carefully placed the garland of fragrant flowers on her daughter's head. Then, when she was certain that Boudica looked beautiful with her hair combed and sprinkled with rose water, she asked the Druid to enter the house for the priestly blessing.

With his tall head of stiffly spiked hair, the Druid was almost as high as the roof, and had to bend as he entered. He looked at Boudica and smiled. He'd known the girl since childhood, watched her grow, and delighted in her love of the old ways, even though her parents insisted on adopting Roman habits and customs.

"Child of the goddess Hedu, listen to my words. Now is your womanhood;

now is your time of joining with your ancestors and those who have lived and died before you. Soon you will leave this house and travel to the house of your husband. I have seen with my closed eyes the wonders which lie before you. In the air the spirits fly; in the brooks and beside the running waters, the spirits dance in joy; in the trees the sacred mistletoe grows and kisses the mighty oak. And just as these things occur without the intervention of man, so you, Boudica, will grow and love the man who will be your guide and lover and companion in all things. And you, Boudica, will be his guide and lover and companion until you both will die.

"Go now, child of Hedu, and join with Prasutagus, for between you there shall be love and around you will gather the sacred spirits who are messengers of the very gods themselves. Go now, Boudica, child of Hedu, and take this man Prasutagus into your heart and welcome him into your body, and within the year create between you a healthy Briton who will stride fearless across our lands and walk in the footsteps of no man. Go, child of Hedu . . ."

And with his final blessing, the priest turned and led the family from their house, through the village to the smiles and admiration of her friends, through lines of children throwing apple blossom, and then across the fields to where Prasutagus and his party were waiting.

As the procession walked, it was joined by men, women and children from nearby villages, who smiled and shouted greetings and blessings from the gods, and greeted Boudica with flowers. Farther, beyond the field and near to the wood, the large procession was joined by men, women and children from Prasutagus' village, who also showered her with flowers.

And shortly after entering the sacred wood, Boudica, her heart pounding in anticipation and fear, saw a party of men standing there in the illumined and sacred grove. Prasutagus was in the center, surrounded by his family. He looked at her, and smiled. She had seen herself in the bronze mirror and knew that she looked beautiful, but for the first time, now that his beard was trimmed and his hair combed and his clothes were new and clean, Boudica realized that her future husband was actually a tall and handsome man. Older than she'd first wanted, but handsome nonetheless.

She smiled at his brothers and sisters who bowed in respect for her status as Prasutagus' future wife. Boudica felt a sense of warmth toward them, until she saw a young man who was looking at the ground. But even with his face averted, she could see that his expression was strained in anger. He was muttering something out of the side of his mouth. She had met him only once before; it was as though he deliberately kept out of her way. He was Cassus, son of Prasutagus' first wife, a young man of fifteen years. The first time she had been in Prasutagus' house, she had tried to talk to him, but as she approached, he had refused to acknowledge her, and he had walked out of the house. Prasutagus assured her that he would talk to the young man, but obviously things hadn't changed.

Prasutagus and Boudica joined their hands, and the Druid priest called them forward by name. As they stood before him in the clearing, the Druid raised his hands to the canopy of trees, and placed leaves and the preserved berries of mistletoe into their joined hands.

In a dark and sonorous voice, the Druid said, "Harken to me, people of Iceni, and I will tell you the story of the mistletoe, which in the old language means 'the plant which heals all.' It is told that the goddess of love, Frig, had a son whom she called Balla, and that she made him the god of the summer sun. One day, the boy god Balla had a dream which presaged his death. He told his mother of his terrible dream, and she was frightened, because she realized that if Balla were to die, all life on the earth would come to an end as it does in the days of winter. Frig immediately begged the earth, the air, the fire and the water, as well as every plant and animal, and made them promise no harm would come to her son. And so Balla could not be hurt by anything on earth or in the sky. But the evil Lugh hated Balla, and realized that Frig had forgotten to gain a promise from the small and inconspicuous mistletoe, which hid from the sight of the world by growing neither on the earth nor below the earth, but grew only on the apple and the oak tree.

"So Lugh soaked an arrow tip in the juice of the mistletoe berry, and he gave it to Hod, the god of winter who hated Balla, the god of summer. Hod killed Balla with it, and his mother Frig was distraught and wept. The sky grew cold and pale, and all things cried out in pain for the sun god. For three days, each plant, animal and element attempted to restore life to Balla, but it was no use. Frig shed tears for her son. The tears turned pale as they fell from her cheeks, and the mistletoe took the tears and made them into the white berries which grow beneath the leaves. In her joy at the sight of the berries, Frig kissed everybody who passed beneath the mistletoe, and her joy warmed the cold body of her son Balla, who came back to life. In her joy, Frig said that anybody who passes beneath the mistletoe must kiss another so that no harm might befall them, only a kiss and a token of the love which she feels for all of her children.

"Hear me now, gods of the trees and the air and the sky, gods of the clouds and the waters which give us life. Hear me, for I beg you to accept the union of this man and this woman. Bless this couple with many children, curse any who wish them ill and reward with a kiss any who give them comfort and friendship.

"Now listen to me, Prasutagus and Boudica. Be faithful to the ancient ways of our people. Turn your hearts and minds from the ways which will lead you into the pathways of defeat. Trust in yourselves and in your people. And remember that the gods know, see and remember all things.

"Husband, take your wife and revere her; wife, take your husband, and revere him. Give unto him, and give unto her. And long may this union be blessed."

As they were about to hold hands and kiss, the signal that their marriage was complete, one of the crowd suddenly growled angrily and pushed his way out of the circle which had gathered around them. Surprised, Boudica looked, and saw that it was Prasutagus' stepson, Cassus. All she could see was his back, disappearing to the rear of the crowd. She hoped that Prasutagus hadn't noticed.

When the Druid had said his final words, the villagers began to sing the marriage song. Boudica and Prasutagus joined in; he had a strong and lusty voice, and she delighted in his joy. But her own happiness only lasted a moment, because the raised voices were suddenly interrupted by the noise of a distant trumpet which rang through the woods, causing birds to fly noisily from their branches. Prasutagus froze, for the occupying force always announced its arrival with the sound of trumpets. He turned to his new wife, and then to the Druid.

"Romans!"

Boudica's mother cried out in sudden fear, and the villagers began to panic.

"Silence," commanded Prasutagus, shouting above the hubbub. "This can't be an attack. The Roman armies have withdrawn from here. Nor can it be a raid. The fighting has finished. I'll go to the edge of the woods, and see what they want."

"I'll come with you," said Boudica's father. They were joined by the men of the village. The women followed immediately after, Boudica pushing her way through the throng in order to stand with her husband.

"Boudica," said Prasutagus, "go back. There might be danger."

"I stand with my husband," she said. He smiled at her.

His stepson, Cassus, pushed to the front, and drew his sword. "I'll see what they want," he said.

"Stand back, boy," commanded his father. "We wait until we see what their intent is. Put away your sword."

As the Celts stood there, waiting for the force of one hundred Romans to draw near, Prasutagus recognized the commander leading the force. It was Marcus Ostorius, son of the new governor of Britain. Now what was he doing here . . . and with a *centuria?*

The young Roman galloped up to the wedding party. Never having seen a Celtic wedding, he didn't recognize the dress or the ceremony, and assumed that the villagers had gathered near to the woods for a festival. He immediately recognized Prasutagus, though not the rest of the people.

"Marcus Ostorius, son of Publius Ostorius Scapula, greets Prasutagus of the people of the Iceni, in the name of the Senate and the emperor of Rome."

He dismounted from his horse and shook hands with the surprised Celt.

"Prasutagus, we are well met, for I have ridden here in order to find you. I am sent with authority by my father the governor of Britain to give you good news. Now that the rebel king Antedios has been slain, I am instructed, in the name of the emperor, to offer you the crown of the land of the people of Iceni. I announce you king of the Iceni. My congratulations, friend."

Prasutagus looked at him in shock. Never for a moment had he considered that he would be made king. Yes, he was friends with, and had prospered from

Rome, and had spent many weeks convincing his people that accommodation with Rome was the only way for the future. But to be made king . . .

Recovering, and realizing that the entire populations of the two villages had suddenly fallen totally silent, Prasutagus said, "Marcus Ostorius, my new wife, Boudica. May I present her to you."

Marcus Ostorius smiled as he greeted the young and beautiful bride of Prasutagus. He bowed in deference to her new rank, and said to her, "Boadicea, I congratulate you on becoming queen of the Iceni. Rome accords Your Majesty its respect."

CHAPTER FIVE

48 AD—The Emperor Claudius' Palace, Rome

Messalina looked at the horror on the face of her friend, Paulina. She'd seen that look before, on the face of runaway female slaves who were thrown into the arena to be torn apart by wild beasts. But the look on Paulina's face failed to mollify the empress. Indeed, the senator's wife had become increasingly censorious, even condemnatory, and she was forgetting who it was that elevated her to her present position as the friend of the wife of the emperor.

Her friendship with the empress appeared to have gone to her head, and now the Illyrian woman was becoming provincial, irritating . . . and presumptuous. "Paulina, dearest," said Messalina, "while I thank you for the use of your home, I find the tone in your voice to be offensive to my ears. Do I really have to remind you that you're speaking to the empress of the Roman Empire, the beloved wife of the emperor? Nobody, especially a woman from the provinces, shall tell the empress what to do."

But Paulina knew only too well that the empress' downfall would result in her own certain death as well as that of her husband and their children, and despite the rebuke, she knew that for the sake of her own life, she must make the empress open her eyes to the dangers.

"Majesty," she said, a note of despair entering her voice, "make love to Silius, chain him to a wall and ravish him; lead him around on a rope and make him bark for your pleasure. But I beg you . . . not this. I beg of you. If your husband . . ."

"My husband thinks I'm a goddess. If I raise my finger, he comes running. I shall marry Silius. It's a laugh. It's only in fun. I've invited my closest friends to the ceremony. People whom I trust. I can't retreat now, or I'll be a laughingstock. Anyway, the emperor's niece, Agrippina, will be coming. She's the sister of the Emperor Caligula and is fast becoming my dearest friend."

"Agrippina! Friend? No, Majesty, she's not your friend. She wants to replace you as Claudius' wife. Why don't you open your eyes, and see what's going on? Don't you realize what's happening? I was always your true friend, Messalina, and now you're listening to others, you're in serious danger of—"

"Enough! Your empress commands you to silence," Messalina hissed, bored now with the constant carping and faultfinding of a woman she once considered her truest supporter. "How dare you speak that way of the emperor's niece? Agrippina is a fine woman, and you are neither highborn nor important enough to comment upon her. If you don't want to come to my wedding—my pretend wedding with a man, yet a man I truly love—then stay away. There are plenty of people in Rome who will gladly lend the empress their villas for her enjoyment. Agrippina, for one. You know, Paulina, perhaps it's time for you and Marcus to return to your little village in Illyria, and raise your turnips and carrots and cabbages, or whatever you people in Illyria do for fun."

With that, she turned and left Paulina standing. The Illyrian woman was suddenly and terrifyingly alone and now friendless in Rome. Shunned by the empress, her moment was at an end. Near to tears of fear and consternation, Paulina left the emperor's palace and determined that she would beg Marcus to take a long holiday back on their estates. She wanted to be as far away from Rome as possible when Claudius learned that his wife, the empress of Rome, had gone behind his back and married another man. The repercussions for all in Messalina's circle were beyond comprehension.

The two men hobbled and hid along the corridors, like thieves trying to escape detection of their crimes.

"Now look, Narcissus, this is beyond a joke."

"Caesar, I beg of you to be quiet. Just for once, trust me and remain silent."

"Of course I trust you, but——"

"Oh, for the sake of the gods, Claudius, stop talking. Please understand what I'm trying to say to you! Your blindness killed Polybius, and it is in danger of ending your reign. If things continue as they are now, the people will rise up against you; you'll be openly ridiculed and your authority will be destroyed. Or worse, you'll be overthrown. Open your eyes for once and see what's going on around you."

"Narcissus . . ." Claudius hissed angrily, stunned by the intemperance of the normally taciturn and placid Greek.

"Please, Caesar, place your trust in me just this one time. If I'm wrong, then deal with me as you dealt with Polybius when Messalina whispered into your ear. Have me exiled or murdered or sent to the arena; but just for now, be silent."

Mention of the name of Polybius made Claudius feel guilty. He had ordered the execution of the Greek on Messalina's advice, and had regretted the loss of one of his most brilliant servants ever since. The Roman emperor looked at his advisor and was forced to acknowledge that the man had taken a considerable personal risk in being so candid, and Narcissus certainly wasn't known as a man who took risks.

They rounded another corridor, this one used only by the servants. Two doors presented themselves. The one on the right was for musicians who entered the balcony above the empress' suite of rooms to play for her. The other led to her servants' quarters. Narcissus silently opened the door to the musicians' gallery.

As they entered the room, they heard the chatter of people down below. There was laughter, and Claudius was surprised to hear Messalina's voice quite clearly within the hubbub. He had been convinced that she was out of the palace on her religious duties, and that the Greek was wrong. And as they'd neared their destination, Claudius silently prayed to himself that she was at the temple of Juno and this was all a terrible misunderstanding.

Narcissus put his finger to his lips in order to ensure the emperor's continued silence. Claudius and Narcissus crept forward, and peered over the edge of the balcony. On the floor below were gathered twenty or thirty people; he recognized many of them as Messalina's friends and the people with whom she prayed daily. They were wearing colorful togas, reds and blues and greens and yellows: the sorts of togas and tunics worn by men and women at the theater or in the amphitheater or at a feast, not the sorts of clothes people wore to pray to the gods.

Confused, Claudius looked at Narcissus, who indicated that the emperor should continue to view the scene from their hiding place below the level of the balcony.

Feeling uncomfortable and ridiculous, Claudius whispered, "I don't understand, Narcissus. So you were right. So Messalina didn't go to the temple! She took the day off from her prayers. What are we doing here, behaving like spies? It's wrong for a husband to spy on his wife, and—"

"I beg of you, Claudius, wait and watch," the Greek whispered into Claudius' ear. "My intelligencers have told me something which must be brought to your attention. For too long, Pallas and I have remained silent. Polybius tried to warn you, but you listened to Messalina and now he's dead. In all this time, we've gone against our consciences to protect you from reality, but now you must see for yourself, for if news of this gets out, your reign will quickly come to an end. The Senate will ensure that!"

Stunned, Claudius peered over the balcony at the gaiety and joy of the scene below. Messalina, wearing a somewhat immodest red tunic exposing her breasts, was surrounded by people who were kissing her and appeared to be congratulating her. She was also wearing a wedding laurel in her hair. And at the other end of the room was the young senator Silius, who was also wearing a wedding laurel. A piper and a drummer were weaving their way through the crowd, followed by naked girls who were throwing rose petals into the air. Claudius turned to ask Narcissus, but again the Greek indicated that he should remain silent.

And then, to Claudius' amazement, a man who looked like a priest, naked with the accoutrements of the god Cupid, walked into the room. Before him, a female acolyte was rubbing his penis to keep it erect. Horrified by the sacrilege, Claudius began to stand in order to put an end to the immorality, but he was firmly held down by Narcissus. "I beg you, Caesar," he hissed, "just a few moments more. Your niece, Agrippina, told me what to expect—"

"Agrippina!"

Narcissus nodded. Claudius, of course, was oblivious to the fact that Agrippina so badly wanted to replace Messalina as his wife, and she was the last person on earth whom the advisor would suggest to the emperor. While Narcissus would be well placed if Messalina were brought down, he had women other than Agrippina to place before the emperor. If Agrippina somehow became Claudius' wife . . . but it was impossible, for that was incest and the Senate would never allow it.

The man playing the part of the priest suddenly shouted out, "Silence for the great god Cupid, god of love and laughter and lots and lots of wonderful sex between men and women, and men and men, and women and women, and boys and girls, and animals and everybody."

The entire room erupted in laughter and cheered. Encouraged, the priest walked toward Messalina and beckoned for Senator Silius to come toward him. When they were standing in the center of the room, the priest took the two wedding laurels off their heads, and crossed them over.

In horror and revulsion at what was happening, Claudius now understood the full enormity of why Narcissus had insisted that he see for himself, for he would never have believed intelligence of this affair. With a sudden and awful insight into his own blindness and stupidity, Claudius understood that Messalina, behaving like a bride in the first blush of happiness, was performing a travesty of a wedding ceremony. The wife of Caesar, the wife of the emperor of Rome, was about to marry some junior senator in a sacrilegious ceremony within Claudius' very own house. It was too much. He struggled to his feet, but Narcissus held him back and whispered urgently into his ear, "The plan is for Messalina to assassinate you, and then she and Silius will rule Rome as regents for your son Britannicus."

He attempted to restrain the emperor, but Claudius shook off Narcissus' hand, and stood above the level of the balcony.

"Stop!" he shouted.

The laughter, gaiety and music down below came to a sudden end. People looked up and saw the emperor. A woman screamed. Messalina's face immediately changed from one of joyous expectation to a look of utter horror. Silius turned and began to run from the chamber. Others tried to hide their faces and escape.

Immediately Narcissus sprang to his feet and shouted out, "Guards!"

The doors suddenly burst open, and fifty Praetorian guardsmen ran into the room and blocked every exit. Nobody could leave the room for fear of being impaled on the guards' lances and spears or cut to pieces by their drawn swords.

Trapped, Messalina looked around her in terror as she realized the danger of what had suddenly happened. She looked in despair for her friend Paulina, but the Illyrian woman was nowhere to be found. She looked for Agrippina, but she, too, wasn't there.

"Claudius, my love," said Messalina, struggling to regain her composure. "You've spoiled the surprise we were planning for you. We were—"

"Silence!" screamed the emperor. "Silence! You are married to the emperor of Rome, yet you would marry? You would belittle your sacred marriage vows to me in front of these beasts . . . these traitors . . . these giggling morons. You, the wife of the emperor of Rome, would marry another man?"

Trying to make her laughter sound genuine, Messalina said, "Marriage? It was theater, my love. For you! We were planning an entertainment for the Bacchanalia. I was to be one of the Maenads, and you, my god, were to be portrayed by the noble Senator Silius. As a Maenad, I was going to give my body to you so that we might renew our love—"

Still trying to prevent himself from jumping over the balcony in his horror at what he'd witnessed, Claudius shouted out, "Fool, Messalina! Fool! My advisors have tried to warn me, but I didn't listen to them—I was too much in love, too besotted by your charms and your beauty. But they were right. You're amoral. Utterly evil. An inveterate whore. A worshipper of wrongdoing and wickedness. You had Polybius put to death and everything you told me was false—falsehoods and deceit. But now I see the truth. And these . . ." he said, pointing to everybody in the room, ". . . these things with which you surround yourself and your immoral ways—"

"Caesar," she shouted, her voice breaking with tears, "it was these people who led me astray. I was praying every day, and then Paulina and all the others forced me into doing things which I knew in my heart were repellent. I couldn't tell you, because I knew how upset you'd be. Claudius, husband, love of my life, I beg of you to listen to your Messalina, and not to believe what you see before you. I—"

"Guards!" shouted Narcissus. "Arrest everybody in the room. Take them to the dungeons to await their deaths. And you know what to do with that woman," he said, pointing to Messalina.

She looked up at the Greek standing next to her husband on the balcony, her face contorted in hatred. "How dare you give orders to the emperor's guards? You, Greek, are above yourself. Claudius, that man has been guilty of giving you wrong advice. He's—"

"Messalina, you will remain silent," said Claudius, his voice now less shrill, less taut. "Guards, you have been given your orders. Arrest everybody. Including the Empress Messalina."

Claudius turned and retreated. He heard a scream from below. He thought it was Messalina's voice. But he was on the point of weeping, and he just wanted to quit the room.

"It's been three months. He's got to recover soon, or the empire will go to the dogs," said Pallas.

"I spoke to him just this morning. He knows that he has papers to attend to, but every time he sits at his table and tries to work, he tells me that he sees the face of Messalina, contorted in a death grimace, her eyes bulging as the guards plunge the sword into her heart. He keeps calling for Polybius. He's racked by guilt. The question is, Pallas, what are we going to do?" asked Narcissus, his voice tainted by the sadness and concern for their own, and the empire's, future.

The older Greek advisor looked at Narcissus, and said softly, "I have been considering introducing a certain woman to him, to ease the strains of his life and to put a smile back onto his face."

Narcissus looked suspiciously at Pallas. "And who is this lady?"

Softly, he said, "Agrippina."

"Agrippina?"

"Caligula's sister."

Suddenly Narcissus swung around and stared at the older man. "What!"

Pallas nodded.

Narcissus burst out laughing. "You're mad. Agrippina is Claudius' niece. The relationship is against the law." But in his heart, he knew that this was no obstacle, for she had been scheming to get rid of Messalina, and now her rival was dead, she was intent on lying beside the emperor.

But even before Pallas could defend his choice, Narcissus continued. "Agrippina! She's the most devious, amoral, evil, conniving, incestuous woman in the whole of Rome. How could you even consider her as a wife for the emperor? You're truly crazed, Pallas."

"The law is no obstacle. The emperor can change the law. And am I any more crazed than you, Narcissus, who has been introducing the emperor to women like Postuma and Vipsania and Claudia? Women whom I wouldn't allow to clean my bed, let alone lie in it."

"They're all noble Roman women from fine families. Buxom like the emperor prefers, and each has shown her ability to bear children. All of them are widows . . . and none is the emperor's niece. Really, Pallas, I think you're mad. The emperor will never, ever allow the daughter of his brother into his bed. Incest!"

"Why are you so shocked? The Julian family is built on incest," said Pallas.

48 AD—The Home of Prasutagus in the Land of the Iceni

Prasutagus looked at her naked body and again felt a stirring in his groin. He'd seen her naked countless times since their wedding, yet each time he thrilled and delighted in the firmness of her breasts, now growing as her belly swelled with the child. But what attracted him most were her strong and gripping legs and her slender fawnlike neck. Or was it was her brilliant red hair, as burning as a fire, which attracted him the most? Or her amazing eyes, as alive as the dawn and as vivid as a field of grass.

She was a beauty, alright. Young and willing and yet with the experience of pleasing a man which appealed to him from the moment they first lay together that extraordinary night following the most extraordinary day of his life.

After a wedding ceremony and the wedding feast, a bride and groom were traditionally accompanied to their bedroom by parents and friends. Once the couple was in bed, flower petals were thrown, rose water and honey were smeared onto their naked bodies, and then they were left alone and in peace to consummate the marriage.

But not on Prasutagus' wedding night to Boudica. Never, to his knowledge, in the entire history of the Iceni people, had such an extraordinary scene taken place. The whole night and the following drunken morning had been full of visitors who had heard the news, of well-wishers, of sycophants who wanted to ingratiate themselves with the new king and queen, of Romans who had retired to land nearby and who wanted to offer themselves as advisors, of farmers who wanted a grant of land and of women who wanted a dispensation to divorce their husbands . . . it was a procession of applicant after applicant, supplicant after supplicant.

It wasn't until the middle of the next evening, without a moment's sleep, that an exhausted Prasutagus suddenly remembered that he was now a king, and a king could do almost anything. And so he ordered that his doors be closed to further visitors, that his house be emptied, that his relatives and friends be sent away, and that he be allowed time alone with his new wife.

When the house was nearly empty, Boudica noticed that Prasutagus' stepson, Cassus, was still seated in the reception atrium.

"Cassus," she said gently, "your father has ordered that his house be emptied, and that all leave. Why not go and stay with one of the elders, until the morning? Then you can come back and dine with us."

"This is my home," he said to her sharply. He had a high-pitched voice, and although he was tall for his age, he was unmanly, ungainly, and awkward.

"Yes, this is your home, but it is also the home of your father, and he orders all to leave."

"Then you should leave," he said, staring at the ground.

"I am his wife," said Boudica.

"I'm his son. I'm fifteen. I won't be sent from my own house."

She could call Prasutagus and allow him to handle it, or she could establish the authority which she was beginning to realize she'd have to wield. "Cassus, when you speak to me, it's as if you're speaking to your father. I'm his wife. I am as much ruler of this house as is he. He says you will leave. I say you will leave."

He stared at her in anger. Sullenly, he walked past her and left the house. She breathed deeply, trying to control her anger. How was she going to deal with a boy like him? Her own brothers had been more friends than siblings; her sisters had been loving. She had rarely experienced jealousy in her own home, yet she realized that Cassus was exhibiting all the marks of a jealous boy, feeling disposed in his father's affection. She would have to handle Cassus very carefully, or it would affect her relationship with Prasutagus.

She turned, and saw that Prasutagus had been in another room; yet he had heard the conversation. Wordlessly, he walked over and put his arms around her, affirming her actions.

But his mind wasn't on the troubles with Cassus. He was exhausted. Yet Boudica appeared to be as fresh as a morning field, and as happy as a lark ascending despite the interchange with his stepson. Prasutagus remembered looking at her in utter amazement as she greeted each person, introduced them to her new husband, offered them refreshments, removed them when their moment with the king was ended, and seemed to be everywhere and everything to all people.

Now that the house was completely empty and they were alone, they had looked at each other, and, despite the upset over Cassus, both burst out laughing.

"King," she quipped.

"Queen," he responded.

They had fallen into each other's arms and hugged. She had laid him on the bed, brought him a drink of wine, honey and spices, and prepared herself for the consummation of their wedding. But when she returned, he was already fast asleep.

He'd woken the following midday after a deep and refreshing night's sleep to find Boudica in the garden, instructing his slaves about the way in which the lettuces and carrots were to be grown; he listened to her talking to them, explaining that rather than growing them haphazardly by spreading the seeds, they were to be grown in rows to make weeding and gathering easier. She had an easy way with people, yet at the same time, it was understood that her will was to be followed.

Prasutagus had called her into the house and made love to her with the sun streaming into their room, illuminating the wedding bed.

And now, after more than a year of marriage, he realized with a flush of warmth and joy that he was beginning to fall deeply in love with her. The difference in their ages meant nothing. As he was lusty, Boudica was willing and adventurous. When he was exhausted and spent after loving her, she would allow him a short rest, and then use her mouth and her fingers and her breasts to invigorate him one more time. Not even her pregnancy had dissuaded her from pleasuring her husband, or herself.

At times, he would be attracted to another woman, and be absent for the night. Boudica assured him that she didn't mind, provided that Prasutagus had no objections to her pleasuring herself with a man who took her eye.

Their life together was vivid, exciting, and fulfilling. But between them there had arisen, and continued to grow, a dark stain which had the capacity to threaten their relationship, and it was a problem which Boudica was incapable of resolving. The Romans used trade and money to build their relationship with Prasutagus and their Iceni people. And he seemed quite content to prosper from the contact which the governor and the officials in Camulodunum were initiating, despite the fact that he was paying a fortune in taxes and tributes.

A huge stone two-story villa with mosaics on the floors and beautiful wooden furniture in every room had been speedily and specially built for Prasutagus and Boudica by the Romans as a gift from the emperor and the people to their client king. As in her parents' home, Boudica felt happy to be in such a lovely building, but guilty at accepting it. She thought of it as a traitor's tribute. Despite her misgivings, Boudica had reluctantly agreed to move from Prasutagus' home into the house built by Rome. And while she reveled in the expanse and the cleanliness and the lack of dirt and rushes on the floors, in the high ceilings and the feeling of coolness in the summer and warmth in the winter which rose from the floor, fed by underground fires, she nonetheless couldn't reconcile her feelings of guilt with her pleasures.

And what pleasures. She was constantly amazed by what the Romans had managed to achieve, the advances they brought to her home. Boudica's first joy in moving into the house was to see that there was always water somehow brought from an outside well into the kitchen. It came through pipes or tubes and when she lifted a flap of lead, the water just seemed to run into the basin like a stream. And not only that, but there was a hole in the bottom of the basin, and the water didn't fill it up, but ran away through tubes to the outside of the house, where it watered a patch of vegetables which had been planted.

Nor did she have to step outside of the house any longer to piss or shit, because the Romans had built a small room in the upper floors of their house, a room in which there was a seat, and she sat on the seat and her waste simply dropped out of her body and plunged into a pit at the bottom of which was fresh straw and lime, and which the slaves emptied every day from a trapdoor outside of the house.

Oh, she could see all the benefits of befriending Rome. But unlike her husband, she could also see the damage to her land and her people. The taxes and tributes which were regularly extracted from them were breaking their backs. And the greatest amount of tribute was taken from her husband, a fortune every year. Indeed, he'd had to borrow a fortune from the Emperor Claudius just to pay the Emperor Claudius his taxes. It was a ridiculous situation.

But the Iceni were in a far better position than many of the other tribes and kingdoms of Britain. Many of her Iceni had come to an accommodation with Rome, and were benefiting massively. The wealth of her people had never been greater, and their prosperity was a source of jealousy from other tribes who lived on the borders. Boudica knew with certainty that if ever the Romans turned their backs, these tribes would attack the Iceni, and the slaughter would be horrific.

And her discomfort was compounded when merchants who passed through her lands told her of the misery which was felt throughout Britain. In despair, and in the privacy of a walk in the woods, Boudica sometimes cried to herself that for all his good deeds, Prasutagus, like her father and mother, had willingly blinded himself to reality. Caratacus was still mounting raids against Roman towns and forts and army encampments, some of the British kingdoms were fighting Roman incursions into their realms and in many cases, Britons had formed militias to sabotage Roman supply wagons which were denuding the country of its food and livestock. Still trying to free the countryside of swords, spears, javelins and other weaponry, the governor, Publius Ostorius, continued to order his men to enter British villages and to rummage through houses, to empty grain pits, and to pull down haystacks in order to uncover caches of weapons. Many died as a result of their resistance and the resentment toward his evil and dictatorial rule continued to grow, even among those Britons who wanted to live in peace with Rome.

And the Druid priests were maintaining that same ferocious opposition which had initially impelled the furious Celts to attempt to repulse the first invasion. With the slaughter of so many followers of Caratacus and the Druids who supported him in the southeast of Britain, the army had been forced to move its sphere of operation into the west of the country. The Druids were now gathering in large numbers off the coast of Britain, on the island of Anglesea as well as throughout the hills of Wales. All this was weighing down her mind, when Boudica's servant, Issulda, approached her mistress and begged to be allowed to leave.

Boudica was in her bedchamber, about to retire. Prasutagus was in the lower floor of their villa with merchants who were traveling to the eastern ports in order to ship their precious cargo of tin, the secret ingredient of bronze, to Rome.

Prasutagus had just concluded a deal by which they would also purchase a ship-
ment of silver from his mines and transport it for a far cheaper price than he
could himself.

In the bedchamber, Boudica had finished washing herself and combing her
hair. Issulda brought her a frayed twig of elm which had been soaked in the juice
of an apple for her to cleanse her teeth and mouth. The girl, aged only thirteen
but already tall and womanlike with a proud bearing and piercing blue eyes,
helped her mistress wash her body with a woven cloth. Then, on another cloth,
Issulda spread a rare oil given to Boudica and Prasutagus as an offering of
friendship by a visiting Roman priest of the Capitoline Triad of Jupiter, Juno
and Minerva. It was made of the cedar tree from Lebanon, though Issulda had
no idea where Lebanon was. But the oil made Boudica's skin glisten, and she
smelled like a forest in the dew of the morning. Instead of bidding her mistress
a restful night, as was her usual custom, when Boudica got into her bed Issulda
stood there looking at the queen of the Iceni.

"Majesty, I have something to beg of you."

Boudica looked at the young girl. She assumed that she wanted permission
to marry one of the young men who looked after their horses; the couple had
been together for many nights, and they looked sweet and loving together.
Boudica would most certainly give her permission.

She smiled, and said, "What do you wish to ask, child?"

"I want to leave your service. I'm unable to return the money you've paid my
parents for my service, but I don't want to just run away, because you've been
very kind to me and I don't want you to think badly of me. But I can't stay here
any longer, Your Majesty."

Stunned, Boudica asked, "What's happened? Has somebody—?"

"No. I'm treated well. That's not the reason. It isn't to be found in this household. I can't any longer bear the way in which the Romans are killing our people.
I want to go to Wales and join in the fighting. The Romans are destroying my
home, and they're taking over, and I want to stop them: drive them back across the
sea; force them to take their horrible gods back with them. I want to bring back
the ways my father and mother talked about before the Romans came."

The child within Boudica's belly suddenly kicked. She so greatly loved the feeling of the life growing within her. But now she was looking at a child who would soon be dead if she were to follow her heart's path.

"Issulda, listen to me. And listen very carefully. The great Caratacus began his battle by fighting a war to stop the Roman invasion. When he was so badly defeated, when so many thousands of brave Britons died in the mud of the fens and marshes, Caratacus withdrew and began to fight other forms of warfare; but this time it wasn't to liberate our country, but to prevent the spread of Rome into all of Britain. Now, Caratacus and his men hide in caves in the distant mountains, and attack Roman supply wagons and scouting patrols. He does little more than scratch the body of Rome with the point of a spear.

"His men and women are dying by the hundreds. He is being deserted every day by Britons who realize that the fight is all but over. Kings and queens throughout Britain are trading with Rome and their people are benefiting. This is the reality with which Prasutagus and I have been forced to reach an accommodation."

She looked carefully at Issulda, and saw the look of disappointment, of disenchantment, in her eyes. She remembered back to when she was thirteen, and her parents had taken her throughout Britain to the ceremonies of the Druids . . . and of how she was filled with awe at the wonders of the country. What a tragedy that Issulda would never know the freedom of the land which Boudica had known at her age. And as she looked at the child, she suddenly had a memory of a conversation which she, herself, had had with her servant Alvanus some years earlier. She, too, had wanted to leave her home, travel to the west, and fight the Romans; and it was Alvanus who had made her see the stupidity of committing suicide.

"Child, I know better than you realize what surges through your heart. You want to strike a blow for your family and your people. You want to raise a sword and see the arrogant Romans cower in fear. But the moment you raise that sword, Issulda, a much bigger and stronger sword will plunge into your heart, and your life will be no more. You have so much to live for. You and the stable boy are beginning to understand the joys of why we were created. Soon you will have a child in your belly like I do and you will come to understand the meaning that the gods have for you."

Issulda shook her head in sorrow. "Lady, I can't say what's in my heart, for if I do so, I'll be flogged. But I beg you to open your eyes to see what the Romans are doing to our country. Our priests are fleeing to the west. Our people are dragged into slavery. The Romans are cutting down our sacred woods and forests to make their houses and ships. And you and Prasutagus . . . I can't stand it."

Issulda's face became a mask of distress. The danger was that she would spread this dissent through the household, and then Boudica would have to have her put to death.

But Issulda hadn't finished, and her frustrations suddenly erupted. "Lady, I don't want to dress like a Roman. I want to look like a Celt in a dress of green or blue. I don't want to wear togas and shifts and sandals, nor eat Roman food off metal plates. I want to go back to the way I was when I lived in my parents' house. It wasn't as grand as this, but it was honest." The girl burst into tears.

"Listen carefully to me, girl. My husband and I do what we have to do in order to rule the land of the Iceni. Do you think that I like the iron heel of the Roman soldier treading on our land? Do you think I enjoy entertaining visiting Romans who treat Prasutagus and me as though we were barbarians? But Issulda, I do what I have to do because Prasutagus is my king, and he has determined that we will live in peace and harmony with Rome in order to bring the greatest benefit to our people—"

"But you're the queen. You have as much right as does King Prasutagus. Why don't you object to what he's doing? Why don't you—"

"Enough!" said Boudica, realizing that she could show no sympathy at all to the youngster, for this sort of dissent and treason against the king and queen could spread like a summer fire, and engulf the entire lands of the Iceni. "Who's been putting ideas like these into your head?" Boudica demanded.

Suddenly terrified, Issulda shook her head and said, "Nobody. They're the thoughts I think at night."

Boudica knew she was lying. "It's Cassus, isn't it!"

Issulda's silence told Boudica that she'd guessed correctly. "Has Prince Cassus been talking to you about these things?" demanded Boudica.

Issulda refused to say yes or no. Instead, she looked in increasing fear at Boudica.

"Understand me well, girl. Cassus may be King Prasutagus' stepson, but he's a son by another wife. He's using you to hurt me and my husband. Now I'm commanding you to think no more of these thoughts, and not to listen to Cassus again. If he whispers in your ear, tell me. I must know. But you've said more than enough for me to have you put to death! One more word and I'll have you chained and sacrificed in the sacred well. You're too young to understand the dangers of what you're saying. It's only because of your age that I don't punish you. Go, and there will be no more talk of joining Caratacus and fighting the Romans. And if I find that you've left here without my permission, I'll have you followed and caught and then you will die in the wicker basket. I have spoken."

Trying to stop herself from crying, Issulda bowed and retired from the room. The baby continued to kick, but Boudica didn't find pleasure in it. She was too upset by the interchange to rejoice in her unborn child. She remembered back to the high-spirited child she had been when she was Issulda's age, a child who could see everything so clearly, understood everything which was happening, and couldn't comprehend why her parents were so incapable of seeing what she could see.

Perhaps the reason she hadn't punished Issulda for her audacity was because so much within her agreed with her servant. And because her stepson Cassus had manipulated the child.

Cassus! Why did he always cause her problems? He was like a dark cloud covering the sun of her life. Ever since Boudica had married, Cassus had shown his resentment of her. His surliness and aggression had grown to such an extent that Prasutagus had banished him from their home and forced him to live in another house. She would have words with Prasutagus in the morning, and go and see Cassus herself. She wouldn't hide behind her husband. This rudeness toward her, this underhanded manipulation of a young girl who was her servant, was something with which she would deal personally.

As queen, she would tell him how he would behave, or he would be exiled.

As the wife of his father, she would tell him what were the duties she expected of a son, and where respect should be shown. And as a Briton who had learned to live with the Romans, she would tell him the realities of politics. She would bear no more of his snide insolence, his demeaning of everything she loved behind her back. Cassus had taken on the wrong foe, and Boudica would set him on the right path, or she would expel him from the country.

But neither Cassus nor her own wealth and happiness altered what Issulda had said; it rang so very true in Boudica's mind. More than at any time since the invasion, Boudica wanted to take up arms and slay the arrogant and imperialistic Romans who treated her country as if they were the perpetual owners.

The invaders didn't behave that way to her or Prasutagus, of course, because they were clients of the Roman state, contributing vast amounts of money in taxes and keeping their Iceni people happy and content under Roman rule. But she knew how the Roman soldiers treated the citizens of the land of the Iceni when they entered the villages and wanted to eat or pleasure themselves with the women. And each time somebody whispered a story into her ear of the latest Roman atrocity, she cringed at her enforced powerlessness. Yet just as embarrassingly, she was beginning to agree with Prasutagus that the lives of her people had never been richer or more rewarded than since they had become a part of the empire of Rome.

She closed her eyes, and tried to go to sleep. She breathed in the forest perfume of the oil of cedar which made her skin and hair smell of delightful, sinful fragrance. But when she stared into the void of her night, she continued to see the furious and self-righteous face of a thirteen-year-old girl mocking her . . . not Issulda, but a young Boudica.

48 AD—Claudius' Palace, Rome

The tentative knock on the door told him that it wasn't Pallas or Narcissus. They didn't knock any longer, but merely burst into his private chambers, not waiting

for his permission, speaking as they entered and informing him of the latest cri-
sis. So the knock on the door was most likely one of the girls selected by the wily
Greeks to pleasure him. It happened every night. They said it was to fill the void
in their emperor's life, but for the past few weeks, the girls hadn't been girls, but
had been widows or older women who were obviously marriage prospects, sent to
remind Claudius of the joys of partnership.

Claudius smiled when he thought about the way in which the Greeks were ma-
neuvering to gain ascent through marrying him off to one of their choices. The
stakes, of course, were very high. Now that Messalina no longer ruled Claudius'
heart and mind and he didn't listen to her suggestions, he who advised the emperor
was more powerful than all but the most senior senators or consuls. Trying to
make Claudius fall in love, and then to rule the emperor through his wife, was their
obvious ploy, and Claudius admired the way in which they went about their duties
on his behalf.

But in truth, Claudius had no intention of remarrying. The experience of
Messalina was enough to put him off marriage for all time.

"Enter!" he commanded, his voice squeaking a bit from too much wine, although it wasn't the wine, but the cinnamon that floated on top, which his doc-
tors had put into it to overcome his problem of constipation. And for some
reason, he was no longer sleeping after the evening cup of wine, but was remaining awake until the late hours.

The door opened, and he was surprised to see his niece Agrippina the
Younger walk demurely into the room. Despite what was said about her by the
spreaders of rumors, Claudius had a soft spot for Agrippina. She was reputed to
be harsh and vicious to her enemies, but Claudius had always found her a sweet
and gentle girl, the daughter of his dead and dear brother Germanicus and his
fine wife, Vipsania Agrippina the Elder. He knew that some of his Greek freedmen didn't like her, but others did, and while she had friends and enemies in
equal number, she couldn't be all bad.

"Dear niece, come in. Sit. Have a cup of wine. What are you doing here, so
late at night?"

"Dear uncle. How are you? How are the burdens of office?" She walked over to his table and bowed in deference. But he stood, and kissed her on the forehead and the cheeks.

"As you can see, niece, I'm constantly at work. There's never an end to the problems of ruling the whole of the world. But who more than you would know that, having seen your glorious father rule the army and your brother..." Remembering her terrible fate under Caligula, he quickly recovered and asked, "And how's my favorite niece?"

She giggled. "Claudius, you continue to treat me as though I were a child, but I'm only four years younger than you. I'm thirty-four. My son is eleven years of age..."

"How is the dear child Lucius Domitius Ahenobarbus? Is his education going well? I haven't had time to see much of him...or you...because of the pressures of my office."

"Nero is doing well at his lessons, Claudius. He's very musical and he's now writing songs and odes."

They sat, Claudius behind his desk and Agrippina beside him. Claudius was somewhat surprised that she hadn't positioned herself on the opposite side of the table, but since he had brought her back from the exile imposed upon her by her brother, he had felt close to her and she had always shown her gratitude.

"Show me what you're doing, Great One," she said.

"Surely you're not interested in the affairs of the state?"

"On the contrary, Claudius. When Caligula was emperor, my advice was often sought by him. I would receive senators and visitors and was often present when the emperor was in council. Of course, you were only rarely present in the palace in those terrible days when Caligula became insane, but whenever you were there, I always admired your skill at handling my poor brother."

He smiled. "In those awful days, I played the part of the fool, and everybody was happy to believe me. When Caligula elevated me to be suffect consul, it was my first public office, and I treated it seriously, even though all Rome thought it was a joke. But enough of me. I haven't really seen you since you returned from exile. Tell me, how bad was it?"

"Being exiled is hard enough, Claudius. Being exiled by your own brother is a terrible blow. But I survived. I have many friends in Rome who told me what was going on. But now that I'm back, I'd relish the chance of returning to the center of the world. As you know, Majesty, I'm living in a villa, doing nothing but attending games and entertainments and looking after Nero, the joy of my life. But I have so much to give," she said, looking at him in a way in which nieces didn't often look at uncles.

Somewhat embarrassed by her attention and closeness, Claudius unveiled the map of Judea that he'd been scrutinizing, and said, "Well, if you're so interested, I'll tell you something about the current rash of problems which beset the emperor. The Jews are rising up against my edicts. I command, and my generals try to enforce, but they tell me a group who call themselves the Zealots are fighting in the deserts and the hills, and conducting audacious raids against the forts. I had a dear friend called Herod Agrippa who was king and while he was there, everything was alright, but he died in the arena four years ago. His son Julius Marcus Agrippa is the king now, but he's not a shadow of his father and he can't keep control."

Agrippina was about to speak, but Claudius was lost in his troubles. Pushing aside the map of Judea, he pulled another scroll from beneath his desk, and opened it out. "This is the land of the Celts. I've got problems there also, because the priests, called Druids, are encouraging the people to attack our soldiers. Some of the kings and queens of Britain are really very good—I made clients of eleven of them some years back when I conquered Britain—but some of them are now turning against their agreement, and—"

"Claudius," she interrupted. "Please, dearest friend. Stop this. I know I asked, but I didn't realize how troubled you were, or how tired you must be. It's very late at night. Your voice tells me that you're exhausted. Pallas informs me that you hardly sleep anymore. No wonder, when you go to your bedchamber with all these worries flooding around your mind. Put your maps and your papers aside for the night, and relax."

He looked at her. He suddenly realized that she had her hand on his leg, flesh touching flesh. He wasn't sure why she was so close to him, being a blood relative and the daughter of his late brother. He knew that she was devious, and was the prime coconspirator with, and latterly against, Caligula, but why was she suddenly so physical with him, her blood uncle?

"Dearest Claudius, in the privacy of your chamber, I'm going to take control and be in charge. I command you, emperor of Rome, to roll up your maps, clear your table of all the problems of the world, and let Agrippina get you some wine and food. Then I'll soothe your brow with unguents and perfumes, and sing to you so that it relaxes you for the overwhelming problems you have as the greatest emperor the world has ever known. Let all of your problems wait until they're illuminated by the light of the morning."

He sighed, and realized that much of the night had already disappeared. He was tired . . . no, exhausted . . . and the thought of lying in a woman's lap, her hands gently massaging his temples, filled him with sudden pleasure.

Claudius looked at Agrippina and accepted her open hands. She gently persuaded him from the table, and held his hand as they walked to his bed. "Lie down, great Caesar, and let your loving Agrippina make all your troubles and worries disappear."

Against his better judgment, knowing that there was some devious purpose behind what she was doing, Claudius put himself into her hands. She was his niece and he'd always considered her a little girl . . . that was probably because he was prematurely old with all the cares of the world on his shoulders. But he now saw that she was not just a full-grown woman, but a woman of great poise and charm and beauty. He lay on the bed, and Agrippina removed her tunic, standing naked before him.

Claudius' eyes widened in shock, but Agrippina put her fingers to his lips and said softly, "Do you think I want to get oils on my toga? Mighty Emperor, put your head on my lap, and I'll massage your shoulders."

And she did. Her lap was warm and soft and giving, and his manhood stirred in an uncomfortable way.

"Claudius," she said, as she gently eased her fingers over his taut neck and shoulders, "my family was very intimate when we were young. Even when my brother Caligula was emperor, we maintained our intimacy. I often used to sleep naked in his bed. He loved the feel of my breasts and my buttocks. He said that it made him stronger, and that the ruling family was so noble and high that it was almost a crime against nature for us to have sex with those who were not intimately related to us."

"What?" Claudius laughed. "Like the Egyptians?"

"Precisely like the Egyptians. Brother marries sister, uncle marries niece."

He tried to twist his head around to see her, but her fingers were gripping him too strongly. "That's incest. It's against the law," he said.

"You are the law, Caesar."

"Tell that to the Senate and the censors. Are you suggesting that you and I . . . that we . . ."

"Great and mighty Caesar," said Agrippina, "I'm merely suggesting that you allow me to ease the tensions of the day. If you like what I do, then maybe I'll come again tomorrow night, and ease your burden."

And softly, gently, Agrippina's hands worked their way from his chest downward, until she grasped the ruling staff of the empire in her hands.

CHAPTER SIX

54 AD—The Palace of Prasutagus and Boudica in the Land of the Iceni

The interference of Cassus in her household had put Boudica into a foul and adamant mood; since the moment of her marriage to Prasutagus, Cassus had been behaving like a spoiled child. And for years Boudica had tried to reason with him, cajole him to more adult behavior, and invariably she had ended up cursing him. But nothing would make him change toward her. She had hoped that the permanency of her marriage to Prasutagus would have encouraged the young man to accept the inevitable and settle down, to learn to adapt to the situation. But now, she would have to make a change, or the situation would become intolerable.

Either he would change his ways immediately, or he would leave her lands forever. His rudeness toward her was something which she had come to accept as part of his immaturity and which she hoped would disappear with time, but his attempts to manipulate her servants were too much. Now he would be told.

As Prasutagus' stepson, he was entitled to the regard and respect of the people of the Iceni; yet his behavior only served to earn him contempt from all with whom he came into contact. Prasutagus had now banned him from feasts which celebrated the conjunction of the days of Celtic and Roman gods, because his behavior had become so bad. And his treatment of Boudica was a source of embarrassment for the family.

Determining to put the matter right for all time, the following morning, Boudica conspired to walk along the banks of the river, where she knew that he would be fishing. Although a solitary occupation, it was one of the few things he seemed to enjoy in life and which made him smile, apart from drinking and chasing the women of the nearby villages.

When she set out to confront him, she had intended this to be a final warning. But as she walked across the fields and heard the song of birds in the warm air, an instinct within her told her to give him one more opportunity to come good. If she could bring reason to bear on his mind, maybe there could be a way of rescuing their turbulent seven-year relationship, and that would greatly please Prasutagus. So she forced herself to remain calm when she saw him, and walked over as though their meeting were a surprise.

"Have you caught anything yet, Cassus?"

He turned in shock at her voice. His face flushed crimson. "No."

She went and stood beside him, looking down at the river. The young man continued to stare at the ripples the line made as it entered the water of the slow-flowing river. Boudica decided to say nothing until Cassus initiated a conversation. In all the years she'd been married to Prasutagus, he only ever seemed to grunt and growl at her, or snarl like some cowardly dog.

After what seemed an interminable time, Cassus said, "Do you want something?"

"Yes. I want to know why you're hurting your father so badly."

He shrugged his shoulders, and continued to stare at the water.

"Why are you doing this to him and to me?" she demanded.

"I'm not doing anything to him," Cassus replied sternly.

Boudica laughed. "Don't treat me like a fool, Cassus, if you don't want me to treat you like a child. Your behavior since I married your father has been a disgrace. You've made me unwelcome in my own house. I want to know why. What is it that's made you so angry at me?"

The young man turned and gave her a look of contempt, his lips pressed tightly together, his eyes narrow in derision.

"Cassus, the sooner you understand that Prasutagus loves me, the sooner you'll see that nothing will divide his love from me. So why are you hurting him for marrying me? Isn't he entitled to your respect?"

"What would you know of respect?" he snapped. "My mother's body was still warm when you seduced my father and replaced her."

"Cassus, that's just not true. Your mother had been dead for a long time when Prasutagus decided to take another wife. How dare you question his right to comfort?"

"He forgot my mother and married you. It was as though she'd never existed."

"Had your mother not existed, you wouldn't be here fishing," Boudica said softly. "You're a reality, Cassus, and so am I. So is your father's marriage to me. For the sake of the gods who look down upon us, Cassus, he and I have been married for seven long years. When are you going to accept me as his wife, and stop this aggression toward me? You're behaving like a surly child, not like a grown man."

Cassus continued fishing, without saying anything.

"If I were to go away, would you forgive your father for his marriage to me?" she asked.

He didn't answer. He shook his head.

"So no matter what I do, you and I will never be friends. If you're happy with that, then so am I," she said.

Again, he remained silent.

"For seven long years, I've had to put up with your moods and aggression. So remember this: I make a good friend, but a very bad enemy. I warn you that it's not up to me to change, Cassus, but up to you. I came to this family as a young woman prepared to—"

He turned and snapped, "That's it, Boudica. That's why I hate you. Because you came to my father as a young woman, a girl not much older than me. Yet you slept with my father. You're too young for him. It's not right!"

"I heard no complaints from him on our wedding night. I was of the right age for your father."

"You're disgusting."

"Why do I disgust you? Your father finds me attractive. I have no difficulties with any of his brothers or their wives, or the people of the Iceni whom we rule. Only you find me disgusting. Am I disgusting to you as a queen, or just as a wife to your father?"

Again, Cassus remained surly and silently stared at his fishing line.

Trying to make light of the situation, Boudica asked. "What about you, Cassus? What age does a woman have to be to marry you? Young, old, fat, thin, tall, short? What sort of a woman would you want to marry?"

Cassus flushed bright red. He turned away, and stared fixedly at the water.

"Well?" she asked. But he refused to look at her.

She moved closer to the river and turned to look into his face. Rarely did his eyes meet hers. She always thought he was surly; but now she detected something else in his face. The look he gave her wasn't the same look of contempt which he always seemed to carry whenever they were in the same room; this was different. It was as though . . . and with a jolt of surprise, she looked at him more closely, trying to perceive what lay behind his eyes. And then understanding dawned on her.

Could it be? Was it possible that Cassus was . . .

He looked away, staring downstream far into the distance, anything to avoid her knowing stare.

"I see," she whispered.

And then the years of pent-up frustration burst from him. "From the first time you entered my house, you should have been mine. Yet you made eyes at my father, let him see your breasts in those dresses you wore, and you seduced him, and—"

"Silence! Be quiet. I will hear none of this. I am your father's wife. He and I—"

"You should have been mine!" Cassus shouted, whipping the line and hook out of the water and throwing them to the ground. "It's me you should be sleeping with. You're a whore who used her body to seduce a stupid old man. It's not fair! He was too old for you. I wasn't. I wanted you; he didn't."

Boudica lifted her leg, and kicked Cassus hard in the backside, pitching him forward and propelling him into the river. As he dived headlong into the water, he yelped like a wounded fox. She heard the splash, but didn't wait until he surfaced. Instead she turned and stormed off.

She was too stunned to speak, too hurt to think rationally; the question on her mind was whether to tell Prasutagus. And if so, what to say?

She didn't see Cassus for the rest of the day, or that night. Or the following day, a day when Prasutagus received important Roman visitors, accompanied by merchants, who were traveling to the settled parts of Britain to prepare a report for the Senate and to increase trade. Boudica's head was still spinning from the revelation. How could she not have realized that the boy's hatred was bound up in the lust he felt for her? How could she have been so blind, so stupid?

She would have to tell Prasutagus! Cassus would have to be removed from the land of the Iceni. And she would have to find him a wife so that he could settle down, and stop his dissolute life.

But for now, her role was to be the queen of the Iceni, and though she found it difficult to concentrate on her diplomatic role with such an enormous family problem, she knew she had no alternative. The man who sat before the king and queen of the Iceni was the tenth, or maybe the twelfth, visitor that day, and she'd already forgotten his name, despite the governor's aide having introduced him just moments earlier. Secundus? Octavian? Quintilius? Aurelius? All the names of the Romans were beginning to sound the same to her. And she knew with certainty that Prasutagus felt precisely as she did.

They joked it about it in bed at night, when their duties as king and queen had been done, and they were allowed some time to themselves. The Romans had such peculiar customs, such odd names. Even now, after ten years of Roman conquest and society in Britain, Prasutagus was still incapable of saying more than a handful of words in Latin. Boudica, on the other hand, was able to converse fluently with her Roman visitors, and didn't need the services of an interpreter.

As king and queen of the Iceni, their lives were frantic. Prasutagus had never been busier, or, he had to admit, more content. Before he'd been appointed king of the Iceni, he'd been busy doing what a wealthy landholder did. He would ensure that his grains and fruits and vegetables were being tended properly and profitably. Or he'd go to his mines and discuss the work being done, the quality of the ore and whether more slaves were needed to work the seams or whether some could be redeployed in other work. And on still other days, he'd go to his forests and hunt for partridge or ptarmigan or deer.

While he had duties to his slaves and servants and to the people of the villages who paid him tithes and dues and taxes, and while he had maintained a small but efficient militia to protect those in his villages who served him, he was the first to admit that he had too much time on his hands, and so he turned his energies to the sea and fishing in the waves, or hunting game for his table.

But now that he was king, he had almost no time to do any of the things he used to love, and much of his time was spent being little more than Rome's representative. The wealth he and Boudica had accumulated was comforting, and the prosperity which their relationship with Rome had brought to their lands made life wondrous. He and Boudica weren't the only Celts who lived in large Roman villas. Other men and women who prospered with the increase of trade in wood and silver and lead and slaves were also living in the most sumptuous houses and villas.

Of course, Prasutagus knew only too well that even though his new wealth came easily, much of it left his coffers just as quickly as it flowed in. Every year, he had to virtually denude himself of wealth through the money he was forced to pay as a client of Rome. His taxes and tributes to the emperor emptied his treasury every year. Not only that, but at the beginning of his reign, he had been forced to pay a fortune in tribute, money which he didn't have. He was so furious that he threatened to turn against Rome and raise arms against her. But Marcus Ostorius promised him that as time went by, the rewards would be far greater than the tributes and taxes, and reluctantly he had agreed.

But with his great wealth came times of great debt. Prasutagus was so often in debt at the time that tribute had to be paid, that he had been forced to borrow forty million sesterces from the Emperor Claudius himself, the interest on which absorbed much of the wealth that flowed into the land of the Iceni from its mines and forests and from the traders who traversed the land. He was trapped in a cycle of debt and income while living a luxurious life, and apart from fighting the Romans—a battle he knew he would lose—he could see no way out of his situation. Just the previous year, Prasutagus had sent an emissary to Rome to beg the emperor to reduce his tributes, and the emperor had promised to consider the situation. But so far nothing had happened.

Prasutagus lay in bed and looked at his wife in love and respect. He couldn't imagine a more suitable queen. Regal, intelligent, supremely capable, loving of her family and her people, she was equally loved by them. Prasutagus was a happy man. He had never been truly successful with women until he had met and married Boudica. His first two wives had died, and he had long ago given up hope of ever being a father and passing on his possessions to his own kin. His only child had been Cassus, but he wasn't the father, as his first wife was already pregnant from a previous husband who had died in a hunting accident. Out of pity, Prasutagus had married her and brought up Cassus as his own. But after she died and left him alone, and his second wife died in childbirth taking his hopes with her, all prospects of being a father left him—until Boudica.

But now he had two fine daughters, Camorra and Tasca, who were the pride of their lives. Beautiful, tall, proud, clever girls with fine hair the golden color of straw, girls who were as wild and willful as their mother, yet as strong and responsible in their dealings as their father. Now aged six and five, the girls had never experienced living in a Celtic house, but had known only the marble floors, the piping, the heating and the mosaics of the Roman villa in which they lived. They would grow up more Roman than Briton, but now he didn't really care. Life was good, so why shouldn't they have the benefits of a Roman upbringing?

Prasutagus' mind often wandered while he was receiving guests in his villa. Sometimes, sitting beside him, Boudica had to discreetly nudge him in his ribs to bring his mind back to the conversation. But this time, even though late in the evening, Prasutagus was listening carefully to the conversation between Boudica and a Judean merchant who had come from the other side of the world in order to visit the kingdoms of Britain, and to see what trade he could do. In Judea he was a gold merchant, but while he had been in the Celtic villages and towns of Britain, he had been stunned by the craftsmanship and beauty of Celtic gold jewelry, such as brooches and necklaces and rings and earrings and clasps for dresses. He had purchased a fortune's worth which he was now taking back to his land where he would sell it for a huge profit. His bodyguards were sleeping in Prasutagus' stables, while he was enjoying the hospitality of the house.

The man was strangely dressed, his robe being decorated by long woven stripes of alternate blues and reds and yellows and greens. On his head, he wore a twisted scarf which gave his otherwise short frame an additional height. He was brown-skinned and stocky with a black glistening beard, and his face looked as though it were made of leather which had been left on a mountaintop in the cold and rain.

Ensuring that the room was empty of Romans, Prasutagus said, "Abram, tell us more of your people's fight with Rome."

"My people are divided, Your Majesty. Some wish to live with the Romans; some wish the Romans weren't there but have learned to live with them; and yet many others are seething with rage at the obscenities which the Romans perpetrate on our nation."

"Obscenities?" asked Boudica. "Their lewd paintings? Their feasts and orgies?"

"No, their gods' statues and the head of the Roman emperor in our holy places."

Boudica sighed. "That's what they're doing to our sacred places. They cut down our sacred groves for their trees and use our holy sites for their temples."

"We only have one God, and He is a very angry and jealous God, and He is telling our people to rise up against the Romans as we rose up against the Greeks before them."

"One god?" Prasutagus was stunned. "But how does this god know everything that's happening? How does he see everything?"

Abram shrugged his shoulders. "For a thousand years, and a thousand years before that, our God has protected His people."

Boudica laughed. "But weren't you telling us that in the history of your people you've been conquered by the Egyptians and the Assyrians and the Greeks and everybody else? Your god doesn't seem to be doing very much for you."

"A strange god for a strange people, Your Majesty. And there aren't many who are stranger than the Jews of Judea-Samaria. We aren't even one people. And there are more Jews in Egypt and Greece and Rome than there are in Judea. Those who have remained in Judea have formed as many factions as there are grains of sand on the shore. We've even created a new and rapidly growing faction which follows a crucified Jew who ran afoul of the authority of one of Rome's procurators, Pontius Pilate. This man, who called himself a prophet, was executed by the Romans in the reign of the Emperor Tiberius. Yet amazingly, his popularity continues to grow with the ascendancy of his brother James and a band who has gathered around him. Although their leader died two decades ago, they now number in the thousands, and their numbers are growing. What other people would continue to follow a leader when he's been dead for twenty years? Only the Jews.

"And within our country of Judea-Samaria, there are many different groups who think that they should be running the land, with or without the help of the Romans. We have the friends of the Romans who own the temple of our God; they're priests called Sadducees. Then we have a rebellious group of men who hate the Sadducees and shun the temple; they are called the Pharisees and they're a troublesome party who spend all their time arguing and discussing and demanding. The next group of madmen who follow a long-dead leader is known as the Essenes, who worship a man called the Teacher of Righteousness who died in the time of the Hasmoneans, but they live mainly in the deserts of our country.

"And as though these groups were not enough of a dilemma for our Roman masters, there is a group, similar to those who once followed your own Caratacus of blessed memory. We in Judea call them Zealots. These are wild men who live in caves and in the hills, and who attack the Roman armies and their followers. But the more they attack, the more Romans are flooding into the nation to put down the attacks."

Prasutagus asked, "How serious is this uprising by these Zealots?"

"Very serious, Your Majesty," said the Jew. "There are thousands and thousands of people flocking to the side of the leader of the revolt, a wild man called Jonathan ben Isaac. They've been flocking to Jonathan's side ever since the Emperor Caligula, may God rot his evil bones, put his statue in our temple. We even sent a delegation to Rome to beg him not to defile our sacred place of worship, but he screamed at us. If he hadn't met his untimely death—thanks in no small part to one of our own, the blessed Herod Agrippa—he would have destroyed our temple and much of Jerusalem with it. Since that time, the Zealots have become one of the biggest groups in the land."

Boudica was riveted when he spoke of the uprising. She had never heard of the Zealots, but they interested her greatly. The Germans were fighting and damaging the Romans, but they weren't a conquered country. Some years ago, the German leader Arminius had defeated three Roman legions under General Varus in the Teutoburg Forest, a rout that was unbearable to Rome's pride and was still being felt by the emperor. The Germans would continue to fight until they either drove the Romans from their borders, or until Rome's overwhelming might destroyed their tribes and their land, and established whatever would be left of Germany as a client state.

Not so the British. Since Caratacus had been defeated by Ostorious Scapula three years earlier, the revolt of the British against the Romans had collapsed. Caratacus had tried to escape north out of Wales into the lands of Cartimandua, Queen of the Brigantes, but she had betrayed him and handed him over to the Romans. He'd been caged and sent to Rome to be paraded like some beast.

But his courage and bearing and decency to those captured with him had impressed Claudius so much that he and his wife Agrippina had given him his freedom, and allowed him to live in Rome. Unfortunately he had died only a year later, probably because of his own feelings of humiliation.

So what particularly interested Boudica was the way in which anger, uprising and rebellion within settled client nations of Rome could unsettle the empire. She knew of problems with the Parthians and with tribes in the north of

Africa, but these were minor skirmishes by handfuls of disgruntled people. Now she was hearing of the beginnings of a full-scale uprising within a long-settled client nation itself . . . and her mind was again excited.

If this intelligence spread through the Roman world, it would cause many of the clients, breaking under the rapacity of the governors and procurators, to revolt and destroy Roman rule within their borders.

"Abram, what is the strength of these Zealots; what is their god telling them to do; what arms do they have?" she asked.

But before he could answer, a runner came into the reception room, his face flushed from riding his horse hard, even during the night.

Interrupting the audience, he bowed, and walked urgently over to where Prasutagus and Boudica were sitting.

"I have urgent news from Rome, Prasutagus."

54 AD—The Palace of the Emperor Claudius

The nights were turning cold, although the days seemed to have retained their warmth despite the dimming of the summer sun. But even the unexpected warmth in the air didn't seem to please the emperor. Old now beyond his years from spending so much of his life trying to rule an empire which refused to be ruled, Claudius was aching for a rest, a holiday, a retreat from the constant barrage of problems and decisions and tensions which were his public and private lives.

How had it come to this? All he had ever wanted to be was a scholar, to lose himself in scrolls written in far-off times by the geniuses of Greece and Alexandria and even Rome herself, to think and study and ponder . . . and to write the history of the greatest civilization the world had ever known. And had it not been for the evil of Tiberius, and the insanity of Caligula, he would have lived and died in peace and serenity, unnoticed and unknown to all but his servants, close family and fellow scholars. But Caligula had unleashed more obscenities on Rome than all the previous rulers put together, and so his execution was inevitable.

And Claudius could have made a fine emperor, had it not been for those damnable women he'd married. After the disaster of his marriage to Messalina, he had truly believed that Agrippina was the answer to all of his problems. Yet within weeks of crawling into his marriage bed, she had consummated a most disreputable bond with Pallas. She'd forced Claudius into elevating her son Nero above his own son Britannicus, younger than Nero by three years, and now Claudius was afraid for his own life, certain that one day, Agrippina was going to poison him. Livia had poisoned Augustus, so why shouldn't Agrippina poison another emperor? It made the circle complete.

Alone, sick, old, tired and friendless, Claudius picked up the cup of wine and cinnamon which his slave had left beside his couch. In the old days, he would drink long into the night with friends. But these days, Agrippina had discouraged his friends from coming to the palace and nobody accepted his invitations to dine any longer, knowing that if they crossed her, eventually her fingers would reach out and crush them. Nor did he drink with his advisors, the Greeks who had been with him for so long. Narcissus, who had tried to have Claudius' natural son Britannicus elevated to be the emperor's successor against Agrippina's son Nero, had fallen afoul of the empress, and was never seen in the palace these days. And Pallas was . . . Pallas! Perhaps he was having an affair with Agrippina? Perhaps he was too smart for his own good, and was working against the interests of the government? Ha! *Senatus Populusque Romanus,* indeed! It was all for the pockets of the powerful, and to hell with Rome, its people and its empire. Well, Pallas would soon come to realize the full measure and dangers of the claws of Rome's most vicious eagle, Agrippina. But whether or not he was sleeping with her, either way, he wouldn't last long when Nero became emperor. Did he realize that? Did he know how brilliant yet ruthless the philosopher Seneca was, and how he had influenced the mind of his young pupil Nero?

Sipping his wine, Claudius lay back, and continued to see the pictures of an old, rotten and diseased carrion crow, which he knew to be the empire, being chased by a young female eagle with sharp talons and a bloody beak. Not content with destroying his life's work, his friendships, his family, his inheritance, Agrippina had now found her way into his mind, circling around in his brain like a nightmare foretold by a Sibyl. Was there no respite from this woman?

These days, the inside of his head was like the walls of a brothel, covered by frescoes of writhing bodies and contorted faces. But there was no sexual release, no joy in these faces or in their serpentine bodies—only pain and cold death. He wanted blissful sleep to overcome him but the dish of mushrooms looked too tempting. Reaching over, he took the plumpest and most glisteningly succulent fungus. They had been plucked from beneath his country home in the Tuscan hills, washed carefully in an uncontaminated mountain stream, brought to the palace by his most trusted of guards, and prepared in his kitchens by cooks to whom he gave daily a purseful of gold to ensure their loyalty. And two had been eaten by his food taster in front of him to ensure that Agrippina hadn't meddled with them.

He bit into one of the mushrooms' canopies, and allowed the divine nutty and buttery juices to slither down his throat. It was like eating meat, they were so full of flavor and substance, and as tasty as any food he'd ever eaten. These were the true joys of life . . . good food, good wine, and the memory of good company.

Too many problems to think about tonight. Tomorrow would be time enough for him to solve the problems which beset the world. He was so tired. The wine, sweeter than usual, tasted so good. He ate another mushroom, and then another. So very good. Soon, he would wake refreshed and begin again to shore up his life's work, think again about Britain and Judea and Gaul and especially Germania. Maybe he should take a trip to Germania and conquer it, as he'd conquered Britain so long ago. Elephants! Yes, he'd take elephants to the German forests. That'd terrify the barbarians . . . .

The emperor and commander of the world fell silently, alone, into a dead sleep.

Outside the emperor's chamber, the body of Claudius' food taster had been hastily carried away by Pallas' servants. The Greek philosopher wanted desperately to see what was happening, but Agrippina was guarding the gap in the door like a jealous soldier, and only reported sporadically in an infuriating whisper what the emperor was doing.

"He's lying back. He's sipping the wine. He's going to eat another mushroom now . . . no, he's put down the cup, he's picked it up again, and I think he's crying. No, he's talking to himself. No, he's crying. Now he's sipping the wine. He's mouthing something, looking around as though there's somebody else in the room. Yes, now he's taking a big draught of wine. He's spilled some of it down his tunic. Now he's rubbing the tunic with his cloth. Oh, gods! He's a filthy drunken beast. How could he have been my father's brother? He's going to eat one more . . . no, he's not . . . yes, wait, now he's reaching over for a third mushroom. The old idiot's mumbling as though he's talking to somebody. No, he's lying back, and . . . I think . . . he's fallen asleep."

At last, Agrippina allowed the Greek access to the gap in the door. He peered in, and saw the familiar sight of Claudius sprawling asleep on his couch, his deformed legs akimbo as though he were straddling an elephant, his arms splayed like a carcass in a butcher's shop. Pallas turned up his nose at the sight of the man.

From this distance, he couldn't tell whether Claudius was asleep or dead, breathing or still, his chest rising with life, or falling with the expiration of death. And he didn't dare tiptoe into the room to find out. Either way, by the morning, Pallas would know whether he was advisor to the new emperor Nero, or advisor to the old and hungover emperor Claudius—husband to the mother of the new young emperor, or still a disfavored servant to a fading star.

He could wait. But Agrippina couldn't. When a suitable time had passed in the silence of their conspiracy, she cautiously opened the door, indicating for the Greek to remain outside where he was, and walked silently over to the emperor. She felt his brow, shook him, tickled him and shouted at him. The emperor didn't move. She looked at his fat belly and his withered leg, his drooling mouth still full of mushroom and wine dripping in globules onto his neck and toga.

"Wake up, god of all things."

But the emperor was silent and unmoved.

"Awake, my hero, my god, my one and only love," she shouted. She loved ridiculing him when he was alive, but how much more enjoyable now that she was making fun of his corpse.

With a smile of triumph on her face, she turned to the Greek who now stood tentatively within the room, though Agrippina noted with contempt that he was still clinging to the door, and said, "Inform the Emperor Nero that his mother wishes to speak with him."

54 AD—The Palace of Prasutagus and Boudica in the Land of the Iceni

"Nero?" asked Prasutagus.

The messenger nodded.

"Isn't he the adopted son of Claudius?" asked Abram the Jew.

Again, the messenger nodded.

"And where did you learn of the death of the Emperor Claudius?" asked Boudica, knowing that the Roman Empire rose and fell on rumor and speculation.

"In Londinium, Boudica. A small Roman settlement on the northern shores of the River Thames."

"I know where Londinium is," she said icily. "Who gave you this news? Did the Romans believe it?" she asked.

"The embassy from Rome which told the people of Londinium of his death came to Britain with a box of coins bearing the head of the new young emperor. The coins had already been struck showing Nero as emperor even while Claudius' funeral rites were being accorded."

"Then they knew when he would die," said Prasutagus softly.

"Then they killed him," said Boudica.

Silence settled on the room. Eventually Abram the Jew said, "Not necessarily, although knowing the new emperor's mother, especially as she was the old emperor's wife, I'd say it was a very good possibility. As a mark of respect for the next in line, the Romans often mint coins for successors while the current emperor lives, though they wouldn't call the successor 'Emperor'. But in many cases, provincial governors will risk their careers and even their lives by minting their own coins of a man they believe might be the future successor. Of course, if they guess wrong, and their choice of a successor is poisoned or fails to make the grade, then they probably won't last long. As for Nero, I have been in Rome, and seen this young man. Of all the relatives of Julius, Augustus and Livia, he's the last I would have thought could have become emperor. He's of average height, big in his belly and dull, and the most unattractive of people. No," he said, "this isn't Nero's work. He's only a boy. If anything, this is the work of his mother Agrippina."

"Yes, it sounds like the work of the emperor's wife," Prasutagus said.

"A most evil lady," whispered Abram. "Like her grandmother Livia, she is a dangerous person." He smiled, as he said softly, "You could almost call her poisonous."

Prasutagus thought deeply about the implications for himself and his people. "Do you believe that there will be a difference between this new emperor and the old one, as far as we in Britain are concerned?"

Abram shrugged. "In these cases, only time will tell. The Emperor Caligula began his reign very well, but developed into a monster. Claudius started as an idiot, but ended up wise and beneficial, at least for those he didn't put to death when he listened to his wives. This one is little more than a boy, so we have to consider not what he will do, but what his advisors—and more especially his mother—will advise him."

"Who are his advisors?" asked Boudica.

"One is very clever, and very rich since he returned from exile with Agrippina. His name is Seneca. He's a philosopher, and is Nero's tutor. The other is called Burrus, and was the commander of the Praetorian Guard, a most virtuous and upstanding man. I met them both last time I was in Rome. While Seneca is tricky and you have to be careful of every word you say, Burrus is the very opposite. He's a soldier and doesn't like anything other than plain speaking. That's why Agrippina selected them both as Nero's advisors: so that neither one will gain an ascendancy above and beyond the other. Checks and balances, Majesties. Checks and balances."

After digesting the information, Boudica said, "We have to send an embassy to Rome to pay our respects to Nero. What else should we do, Abram?"

Abram smiled, and stood. "An embassy is a good idea, Your Majesty. Send gifts and supplications. Flattery is the coinage on which many Romans grow rich. But in the meanwhile, friends, it's late and I'm an old man. If Your Highnesses will excuse me, I have an early start and must leave your delightful home long before the sun rises if I am to catch the tide in the morning. Yes, I think that sending an embassy to Rome is a good idea. But might I suggest that before paying respects to the new Emperor, you pay obeisance to the real power behind the throne, Agrippina."

They watched him leave and sat for moments, thinking. Softly, Boudica said, "I think you should send Cassus. He will do very well for us in Rome. Yes, Cassus should be our ambassador."

Prasutagus looked at her in amazement. "But I thought you were furious with Cassus because of the way he's treated you."

Boudica shrugged. "It's time for him to leave the land of the Iceni and make his way in the world. A few months away, traveling to Rome and seeing the wide world, will do him a lot of good. And it'll give you and me a break from him, which will be good for us both."

Prasutagus smiled, and gripped her hand. "You have a good and forgiving nature," he said. "This embassy is important. And as for Cassus, he will either sink, or swim."

He didn't understand why Boudica burst out laughing.

It took only a week before all of Britain was aware of, and excited by, the news of a change of emperor. Few had the advantages of Abram's knowledge and insights, but all kings and queens realized the necessity of sending representatives to Rome to show their respect as clients of the new ruler of their world. Many believed that with the death of the old conqueror of Britain, the new, young and hopefully open-minded ruler might portray a different and more progressive attitude toward the provinces than his stepfather. Hope surged through the land at the prospect of some alleviation from the crippling taxes and tributes and theft of men, women and children as slaves.

On the day they farewelled Cassus, Prasutagus and Boudica were surprised by the sudden appearance of three Druid priests in their villa. Druids were very scarce these days in Britain; almost all those who still lived had fled to Wales and the island of Anglesea, and were issuing dire threats and warnings, condemnations and cajolings to the kings and queens of Britain who had made their peace with the Romans and turned their backs on the traditional ways.

Prasutagus felt nothing but contempt for the Druids. Never a man who believed in the power of their spells or potions or the presence of spirits in their sacred places, he had turned instead to the Roman gods, and found greater comfort in being able to see a statue representing what a god might look like, than trust in the invisible spirits of the Druids. Ever since he was a boy and was told that the Druid gods were in the trees or the air or the water, he'd always looked carefully but had never found any. When the Romans came to Britain, they had adopted the Druid spirits along with their own gods, which seemed eminently fair to Prasutagus. But the Druids had adamantly refused to acknowledge the presence of any gods or spirits other than their own, and rejected Rome's deities, which Prasutagus considered the height of arrogance.

Boudica, on the other hand, found great joy and comfort in the Druid gods. She believed with all her heart that the British gods did, indeed, reside in the lakes and trees of her land, and often, despite Prasutagus' open ridicule, she would take time while walking or riding somewhere to offer prayers or make a small sacrifice when she passed a sacred place. She, like her husband, had adopted the Roman gods as her own, and prayed fervently with the Roman priests when she visited one of their temples, but secretly, privately, silently she acknowledged the greater potency and ascendancy of her ancient gods over the new ones.

She was pleased, though surprised, to see the Druids appear at the door of her villa. Prasutagus was far from happy, although he greeted them with the respect which was their due.

When they were fed and rested, the three newcomers sought an immediate audience with the king and queen of the Iceni. As the chief Druid entered the atrium where Prasutagus and Boudica received their embassies and visitors, the priests looked around at the murals and frescoes and the disgust was evident on their faces. They had specially donned their Druid robes of white, embroidered with elm twigs, oak leaves and mistletoe; on their heads, they wore braided cloth, their hair piled high and stiffened with lime. Even with their additional height, they neither intimidated nor overwhelmed Prasutagus.

"Where are the Britons?" asked the chief Druid.

Immediately understanding the insult, Prasutagus said, "You speak with the king and queen of Britain's most important kingdom. Why have you come, Druid?"

"To seek out true Britons. To see where lies Britain's heart, and not its brain. To find the spirits of Britain, or to find whether they have all fled to the west where the true guardians of this land are living. Oh Prasutagus! Oh Boudica! How can you have fallen so deeply into the enemy's pocket?"

Boudica knew that at any moment her husband would rise from his seat and strike the Druid, so she said quickly, "Perhaps it is you, priest, who need to look deep into your heart to find what lies there. Neither my husband nor I like being the subjects of another country, but we have the choice of looking back into a past which will lead to the deaths of thousands of our people, or looking forward to a future in which our people will live in prosperity and security. We are no different from the peoples of other nations who have accepted the rule of Rome as an unfortunate but necessary reality."

"Have they, Boudica? Have the people of Germania, or Judea, or Gaul, accepted the rule of Rome? Or are these gallant peoples, like gallant Britons, fighting against the oppressors to free themselves of the shame of being an enslaved people?"

"Like Caratacus' shame? How many Britons died in the mud of Wales, living in caves like animals, just because he refused to accommodate Roman rule?" shouted Prasutagus.

Furious, the Druid hissed, "Had he not fled for sanctuary to the evil Queen Cartimandua of the Brigantes who betrayed him and handed him over to the enemy, the noble Caratacus would not have been captured and humiliated before all of Rome. He would still be leading our troops today."

"Fool! Caratacus was enslaved by the Romans, but the moment the Emperor Claudius listened to the dignity of his address and his bearing as a king of Britain, the emperor accorded him great respect, and allowed him and his family to live free in Rome. This, priest, is the enemy you want to fight. Live in peace with the Romans, and we'll all prosper. Fight them, and we'll all die," said Prasutagus.

"Better to die a Briton than live as a slave of Rome," the Druid responded.

The priests looked at the king and queen of the Iceni in contempt. Boudica was worried that those courtiers who were listening might think that the priests were gaining the upper hand.

"For what reason have you come here?" she asked. "Is it to pay tribute to us?"

The chief Druid sneered. "We came, Boudica, to see whether there was any Briton left in the east of the country, or whether they had all become Romans. I see from your dress and the house in which you live, that your eyes now turn toward Rome and no longer do you see Britain. I have come here with my brothers at a time of propitiation, a time when great things are happening. At the moment of the death of the accursed Claudius, three burning stars were seen in the skies, two of them lasting for no more than moments before they fell to earth; one fell in an instant where the sun falls into the sea. This signifies the end of the emperor.

"Another fell for a longer time, but even this one died quickly in the place where the sun rises. What does this signify? We say that it signifies the beginning of a new and vigorous empire, one which will burn brightly but will surely fade as it grows corrupt and evil . . . this is the empire of Nero."

The Druid looked at Prasutagus and Boudica with fire in his eyes. "But it is the third star which carries the greatest promise. For this star, Boudica, this third

star, has the greatest meaning of them all. This falling star rose in the heavens and
fell to earth, and its brightness lasted for the entire night. For that bright star fell
where the North Star shines over Britain. This, for us, is a clear prophecy, and
means that it is time for Britain to rise up against the new emperor; even before
Nero has a chance to grow a beard, even before his accursed mother Agrippina
weans him off her breast, now is the time for Britain to rise up again, and to strike
at the very heart of the Romans who dare to despoil our sacred places with their
iron shoes."

Prasutagus sneered. "And who, priest, will lead this revolt? The Britons are
still fighting the Romans in the west and are reduced to living like wild beasts.
Their weapons come from whoever they can kill. In Wales, the tribes are surrounded by Romans and have yet to gain a significant victory. Yet you believe
that we of the Iceni and the Regni and the Brigantes, we who prosper as never
before, should join you in this folly?" he said.

The priest suddenly stood, and pointed his stick at Prasutagus. A guard un-
sheathed his sword, but Prasutagus waved him down. The priest said, "The stars
which light the dark sky of Britain have foretold a great victory, obstinate king.
And not only the stars, but the lakes of our land are turning red with the blood
of Rome. Our trees have retained their summer colors long after they should
have faded. Sheep and goats are giving birth to healthy offspring long after their
season. Do you not see, blind one, that the gods are foretelling a great victory
for us?"

Coldly, Boudica said, "My husband the king asked you who would lead this
revolt. You haven't answered. And I have a question for you, priest. Why is it that
rivers and lakes and animals are behaving in these ways in other parts, yet we of
the Iceni have seen no such evidence?"

"Because, Boudica, the gods do not smile on the Iceni. Because just as you
have turned your back on them, they have turned their backs on you. And as to
who will lead the Britons, that is something which the gods will decide. The time
to fight is now, Boudica. We are here because the true men and women of Britain
are bogged in the marshes of kingdoms of the Silures and the Ordovicii in
Wales. Only the Britons of the east today are able to walk free, but their freedom

is an illusion, as real as the morning mists. That is why we need you and your men and women to join with us at this great moment in the life of Britain. We need you to raise an army of true Britons to be the arms and legs, the head and shoulders of our land in this final fight against the might of our nation's enemy. Because if not now, Prasutagus, then tomorrow, we will again be lost in the black night of Rome."

CHAPTER SEVEN

55 AD—The Emperor Nero's Rome

Septima Plantia had been waiting for so long that she was on the verge of walking back to her family home and telling them that once again, he had failed to appear. But she'd done that for the past three nights, and knew that if she did it again, her father would give her another beating. So despite the lecherous glances she was getting from the old sots who were staggering home from the tavern and the looks of disgust from the elderly matrons who were being carried on their litters from their evening's entertainment and who assumed that she was a low-money street prostitute rejected by the brothels, she remained where she was, standing beneath the glow of the guttering lamps which cast dull pools of illumination on the street.

In the three nights she'd been waiting for the emperor, she had been accosted and fondled by a handful of drunken equestrians and two lecherous senators and more citizens than she could count. Each time, she'd screamed and threatened and they'd hurried away, but Septima knew that it was only a matter of time before she was beaten unconscious, raped and left for dead in some alley, or thrown, like all the other dead and dying Romans, into the Tiber.

Her father's instructions had been quite clear. Whatever happened, she must remain standing in her spot for the emperor, and no matter how much she was offered by some other rich Roman, she must wait and continue to wait. But for the past three nights she waited until the cockcrow of the early morning and had only returned home when the bakers opened their shops and began to sell their bread. She'd been told later in the day that the emperor had, indeed, appeared on the streets, but in another part of the city, where he had entertained himself with girls and boys, or men and women. Rumor even had it that during one of his evening tours of the dens of the city, he had satisfied himself on a tethered goat in a garden, but that was probably nothing more than speculation.

Fortunately for Septima, it was a warm night, and she had bread and cheese and a flagon of white wine from Gaul to keep her company. And so she waited and waited. When her mind was dulled from the wine and her legs were aching from standing on the stones for half the night, she suddenly heard a commotion from the upper end of the street. Unlike previous strollers, who came individually or with silent and menacing guards, this was a party of young revelers, whose shouting and joking egged one on against the remarks of the other. And even though it might have been the wine or her imagination, she thought she heard the loud, girlish and squeaking voice which her father had told her was the voice of the emperor. Heart pounding, she prepared her theater in the event that it was Nero and his friends.

His German guards surveyed the street before allowing the emperor and his party to enter. It looked empty, and except for some figure at the bottom, a drunk weaving on the spot, it looked safe enough. The German unit of his Praetorian Guard accompanied the emperor at night every time he left the palace, ever since he'd knocked some stranger in the head, and the stranger had turned, failed to recognize the emperor, and had laid into him. The man had been crucified, but since that moment, Seneca had ordered that the emperor must be accompanied by a bodyguard at all times, even to be stationed outside of the door of a brothel and to allow nobody else inside, regardless of their rank or stature.

But this street looked safe enough to the Guard, and the emperor had been saying to his friends that he was desperate to find company. So they entered the road, followed by the seven young men and women from the palace. Behind them came another flanking contingent of guards ensuring the emperor's safety.

As they walked down the street, they noticed that the figure underneath the lamp was not weaving around drunk as they first thought, but was in fact crumpled up and appeared to be sobbing, praying imprecations to the gods. Hearing her, Nero suddenly ordered the laughter and ribald comments of his friends to come to an immediate end.

He listened, and said, "Do you think that this person needs the help of the most powerful man in the world?"

Drusilla, the emperor's friend, said, "Only the most powerful and the most perceptive man in the world, a god come to earth, would know such a thing, Nero. How do you expect mere mortals such as we to know what you understand? Your wisdom and knowledge are beyond human comprehension."

Nero walked over to the crouching sobbing figure, and stood over her. All he could see was a woman in a crumpled tunic, her cloak torn, her face hidden as though in shame.

"Why are you crying, woman?" he asked, knowing that his advisor, Seneca, would have approved mightily. The Stoic philosopher had taught him so much about the brotherhood of mankind, and he was always pleased to be able to put it into practice. Removing the cloak from her head, Nero saw that she was a young woman, a very attractive woman with dark hair and eyes the color of jet and a white skin which he found very appealing. "Tell me why you're crying. Have you been hurt?"

Septima immediately recognized Nero from the portraits of him in the forum and even from his face on coins. She had been tutored in what to say by her father, but suddenly, being this close to him, she was at a loss for words, and all of her practicing had come to nothing. And he was so much grosser than his portraits. Even in the dull light of the night lamp, his skin was ugly and mottled, spotted and pocked; as he stood closer to her, as though examining one of his prize beasts, she could smell that his breath stank of rotten flesh; and he was potbellied and appeared to be somehow shrunken as though he was an old man, yet he was barely seventeen.

So repellent did she find him, that as she looked closely at his face, the emperor's power seemed to diminish and the dominance she felt over customers when she worked in brothels revitalized her spirits. Suddenly the words came flooding back into her mind. "Leave me, sir, for I have been abused by my master, and I am a fallen woman. I must go now to the Tiber and put this evil world behind me."

Appalled by the thought of one so young and beautiful ending her life, Nero said, "You mustn't even think about committing suicide. You've so much to live for."

"Master," said Septima, "I have nothing to live for. I have been abducted from my home in the north, been enslaved to a cruel merchant from Gaul, and when he tried to force himself upon me tonight in one of his drunken fits, I pushed him away and ran. His guards caught me and beat me, and now he has gone from the city. I have no food or clothes or money, and I can't return home. There's nothing for me but the peace of death."

Turning to his friends, Nero said, "Do you hear that? Isn't this what my tutor has been teaching me? Isn't this the very cruelty of man against man which we must fight against if we are to leave this world a better place than we found it?"

He bent down to stroke her cheek, and whispered consolation in her ear. Septima Plantia stopped sobbing. Addressing his friends again, he said, "My teacher, Seneca, tells me that the path to personal happiness and inner peace is through the extinguishing of all desire to have or to affect things beyond one's control, and through living for the present without hope for or fear of the future beyond the power of opinion. I have no desire for this girl, other than the desire to make this moment, this present time for her, better. Seneca further teaches that we Stoics believe in the sequential reabsorption and re-creation of the universe by the Central Fire, the Conflagration, and if this child kills herself tonight, then a small part of the Conflagration will be extinguished before its time, which will damage the prospect of re-creation of the universe into a better place. That's why I need to help her."

His friends looked at him in incomprehension. They had come for a good time, not a philosophy lesson, especially from Seneca who was impossible to understand.

The Emperor Nero held out his hand in friendship to Septima, and told her, "Come, girl, come with me and I will ensure that your life improves from this moment onwards, so that you will continue to be a light within the Universal Flame."

But Septima didn't hold out her hand. Instead, she shrank back into her cloak, and whispered, "Sir, I don't know who you are, or why you're showing this kindness to me, and I don't understand the words you're using, but I am a fallen woman. I am disgraced. No decent man can ever look upon me again, without feeling disgust and contempt. I have only one course of action and that is to end my life."

"Because someone tried to force himself upon you?"

She remained silent.

"What if someone was able to absolve you of all guilt? What if the most powerful man on earth was to make a pronouncement that you have lived a guilt-free and blameless life—a Stoic life like the life that the philosopher Seneca lives? That your life until now has been null and void, and that from this moment on, you are a woman of decency and morality, as upstanding as Caesar's Calpurnia or as moral as any vestal virgin?"

Septima looked at him, and smiled. "Only one man is capable of that, and he is like a god to me. The blessed Nero would . . . but how could a person such as I . . ."

Nero burst out laughing. All his friends burst out laughing. Only the Germans in the Praetorian Guard failed to laugh, because as experts at it, they knew extortion when they saw it. But it was the emperor's money, and so long as he returned safe and secure to the palace by the morning, they had done their job. And as soon as the girl was out of the emperor's sight, one of them would follow her, relieve her of the emperor's money, and oblige her by throwing her into the Tiber. And they'd have a good laugh and a drink with the money they'd managed to rescue.

❋ ❋ ❋

"Proud? Yes, I suppose that I'm proud of the way in which you have considered the needs of another. But pride can be a stone block upon which a man will stumble as he ascends the path which leads to his place in a better world. Pride, Nero, is a sharp and hard-edged sword which hangs by a delicate thread around the neck of all but the most humble, ready to skewer those who would unbind themselves of the knot. Pride is a blinding light which prevents us from seeing the world as it is so that we see it in our own image alone. And only hubris makes us believe that the image we see of ourselves is also the image seen by others, who might perceive more about us and place us in a very different light. Who is more humble than a blind man; yet who hears better, or is more conscious of his surroundings? Who is more full of thoughts than the man who cannot speak, the man who says not a word, yet who listens to the words of others?"

The emperor wanted to interject, but Seneca continued. "But provided that your motives for helping this girl were selfless, then your deeds will be a shining example of the way in which all Rome must behave if it is to be saved from itself."

Beaming at the praise, Nero said enthusiastically, "When she accepted my help, and stood, I wanted to give her money, but she smiled at me in a most gracious way, and thanked me for listening. She walked away and refused any reward. So I had to insist that she take a purse of gold coins to ensure that she has enough to buy back her respectability."

Seneca put his hand on the young man's arm, and whispered, "The gods see our actions and see into the very essence of our thoughts. We might dress in finery for the eyes of mortals, but the gods see us naked and know the true language of our bodies. But I'm sure that great Jove himself is proud of you tonight."

Nero said good night to his advisor, and left his apartments. He walked down the labyrinthine corridors which made up the highways of his palace, a place he had visited many times when he became Claudius' adopted son, and then heir, and knew the secret ways and shortcuts. One of those which he knew best was the way to his mother's apartments.

He shuddered whenever he thought of his mother. He and Agrippina were no longer as close as they once were. He was becoming increasingly furious at her, and sometimes he had to admit that he hated her. And she, too, hated him, for she had let it be known that she was increasingly spurning him, and had recently made the great mistake of publicly favoring Claudius' natural son Britannicus, who was rapidly reaching adulthood, and who would, no doubt with her guidance, make a claim to the throne. But both Agrippina and Britannicus had badly underestimated him, and they would soon both pay a heavy price.

But in the meantime, there were things which he needed to say to Agrippina, and as he was emperor, and she was merely his mother, he would say them, no matter what the cost to her.

At last he reached her apartments, built at the western wing of the palace, looking out on the ground where Nero intended to build the biggest building in the world, an eternal monument to his emperorship, a great amphitheater with thousands of columns where great spectacles would be staged. He had it all planned in his mind. He would even call it the Neronium, although for the time being he had agreed with his architect that its true name should be kept secret and known only to the two of them, and that the building should be called the Colosseum so that when he officially opened and dedicated it, he would delight and surprise the world with its true and wonderful name. And he was also thinking of building a huge palace made of gold, his palace rather than that of Claudius, if only he could clear the squalid buildings between the Palatine and the Esquiline hills. But these were plans which could wait until later in his reign. Right now, he had words to say to his mother.

The doors to Agrippina's apartments were closed, and without knocking, as was the emperor's right, he walked in. Agrippina's servants and maids were sitting around the antechamber eating and drinking. The emperor's mother was nowhere to be seen. They all suddenly stood and abased themselves when he entered, the slaves dropping to the floor, the freedwomen bowing deeply.

"Where is the emperor's mother?" he asked.

The senior freedwoman, still bowing, said, "The Lady Agrippina went to bed early, Caesar, complaining of tiredness of the mind, and fatigue of the body."

Nero walked across the room and opened the door of Agrippina's bedroom. The shades were lowered, but he could make out the figure of Agrippina lying in the bed. He stood on the threshold of the room, and closed the door. All the anger which he felt toward his mother seemed to evaporate like water on a hot summer's day. He smiled when he saw her slender form in the bed. They had shared so much together: the exile, the return, her marriage to Claudius despite her detestation of him; and forcing him to make Nero the emperor designate over his own natural son Britannicus had been a stroke of genius. If only she hadn't tried to control him and become as powerful as the emperor when Nero rose to the purple; if only she had contented herself with being the most powerful woman in the empire, instead of trying to be the most powerful man.

But she looked so young and innocent as she lay breathing softly under the covers. He walked across the floor, and coughed gently. Agrippina stirred, and opened her eyes.

"Nero?"

She adjusted her eyes, and realized that her son had entered her room. He had hardly spoken to her in two months, and then only in a harsh and officious way. Now, just like old times, he had come into her room.

"Nero? What is it that you want?" she asked.

He had come to demand that she leave Rome because of her conniving with Britannicus, but instead, he suddenly yearned for her approval. "You would have been so proud of me tonight, Mother," he told her, his voice taking on the high-pitched squeak which he always seemed to affect when he was with her. "I went into the city with my friends, and I found this girl who had been robbed and beaten by her employer, and I helped her and gave her a purse. And she thanked me. Seneca said that I did a very good thing, and that the gods will smile on me. It was a good thing, wasn't it, Mother?"

Propping herself on her elbow, Agrippina said, "Oh, my lovely boy. It was a good and kind and generous thing. The sort of thing that your uncle Caligula would have done before the gods took his mind away. Yes, Nero, it was a fine and noble thing, and I'm very proud of you."

"Do I get a reward, Mother? For doing such a good thing? I didn't get a reward from the girl, although I'm sure she would have been willing. It just didn't seem like a Stoic thing to do. But I need a reward tonight, Mother. My body needs a reward."

She smiled, and threw open her bedsheets. She lay naked, her body warm and pink with the heat of the blankets. She held out her hands and said, "Come to me, my son, my husband and lover. Come to your Agrippina and make her ascend to the heights of joy which only a son and a mother can ever truly know. Come, my man, my son, my husband!"

55 AD—The Court of Prasutagus and Boudica

"Child," Boudica said to her youngest daughter Tasca, "you're too young."

Tasca shook her head insistently. "I'm not. I'm six. When you were six, you told me that you went on visits to holy shrines with your parents. Why can't I go with you?"

Boudica tried to restrain herself from smiling, knowing that only by acting the part of a stern mother would she quieten such a wild and rebellious spirit. "I have spoken!" said Boudica.

"And I am speaking," Tasca shouted, stamping her foot on the marble floor. "I will go with you and Camorra. I won't be left here!"

"Tasca," shouted her father. "Don't dare speak to your mother in that voice."

"Why? Because she's a queen? She won't take me, Father, and that's wrong. If I can't go with Mother and Camorra, then I'll never speak with any of you again. I'll go and live with the goats and sheep in the fields, and you'll never see me ever again. I'll leave home, and I'll run away, and you'll never see me again. I'll die in the fields and you'll be sorry. Forever!"

Boudica shook her head in amazement. While Camorra, a year older than her sister, was much like her father, quiet and determined, Tasca was a tiny version of Boudica, full of desire and life and excitement and hope and purpose. *Ah*, she thought, *may the gods help any man who takes Tasca to be his wife.*

"Tasca, my child. You must listen to me. I will take you next year, and the year after. But today you must accept my decision that you just aren't old enough to join me on my journey. Your sister Camorra is barely old enough, but I must take her. As she is the future queen of the Iceni, it is only right and proper that the people of Britain should see her. And she will be a companion for me on my journey. Anyway, if you both leave this villa, then who will look after your father? Who will ensure that he eats his food regularly, and that he doesn't overwork? You have important duties in your home, Tasca, from which you cannot be spared."

Tasca looked at her mother, and fought back the tears of disappointment. Her mother and sister would be gone for months . . . they wouldn't be back until at least the middle of the summer, and with whom would Tasca play? Who would comfort her when she was hurt or stung by a bee, or feed her when she was hungry, or console her by stroking her forehead when she was too excited or tired to sleep?

Tasca turned to Prasutagus, who shrugged his shoulders. He was just as mystified and alarmed about his wife's decision to go on a progress around Britain as was his younger daughter. Yet despite the fact that he'd forbidden her, ordered her, instructed her, advised her, pleaded with her and finally begged her not to risk her life by going, Boudica, always strong-willed and determined, said that she simply had to.

And more so now than at any time in their past together: with a new emperor and new hope, with Britons more divided than ever before, with the western half of the land in open rebellion against the empire, and the eastern and northern as its allies, now more than ever Boudica had to make alliances, and benefit from the new political landscape of Britain; to try to determine whether there was a better way of dealing with Rome, and of Rome dealing with her newest colony.

But privately, without confiding in Prasutagus, what Boudica really wanted to do was to meet with the great Queen Cartimandua whose realm in the most northern part of Britain was shrouded in mists and fogs, yet who was the closest of any monarch in Britain to the distant emperor in Rome. All of her life, Cartimandua had been like a specter in the north, a dark and malevolent force over

Boudica's life. From the time she had refused to fight the Romans when they invaded, to the time she had betrayed Caratacus, to the way in which the Roman army had fought on her behalf when her tribe rebelled against her, to her growing closeness to Rome, Cartimandua was a woman who seemed to have great influence, and a woman whom Boudica desperately wanted to meet.

Prasutagus knew, of course, that the decision Boudica had made to go on her progress had all been the fault of those damn priests. When the Druids had visited and told Boudica of what was happening in other parts of Britain, it seemed to awaken a long-dormant need in her to be associated with her upbringing. There had always been some hidden part of Boudica which Prasutagus couldn't reach, and the more he grew close to Rome, the more that hidden part of her grew inaccessible to him.

Since the arrival of the Druids at his home, and despite her treatment of them when they had insulted him, their very presence seemed to have opened up a desire in her to know more about what was happening in her nation. Only a few days after they left, Boudica announced that she would visit the whole of Britain for herself in order to meet her fellow kings and queens. Her reason, at least the reason she had told Prasutagus, was to try to convince those who still did not understand of the importance of living in peace and harmony with the Romans, rather than risk any more British lives in fighting them. But knowing Boudica as well as he did, he knew that there was an underlying reason, and he would only learn what it was when she returned from her visit and confronted him.

The only concession she had made to Prasutagus' concerns for her safety was that she would only travel to the west as far as the land of the Dobunni, and as far north as the land of the Brigantes. On no account would she travel into the lands of the Ordovices, where vicious fighting was taking place, and the Romans would kill her before asking who she was. The other concession she made was that she wouldn't only take her personal servants and cooks, but would also allow a troop of soldiers and bodyguards to accompany her, both to ensure her and Camorra's safety, and to provide her with the prestige which was her due as a queen of the Iceni. While it would slow her journey, she also recognized it as a sensible thing to do.

On the day before they were due to leave, unknown to Boudica, Prasutagus' son Cassus rode out of the village on the road to the Roman city of Camulodunum. Telling Prasutagus that he was visiting friends in another village, the young man used a series of minor paths and rode south through the Vitteline forest before ensuring that he wasn't being followed. He sat immobile on his horse for some time, looking cautiously back along the road before he was satisfied that he was completely alone. Then he turned north, meeting the road from Londinium to Camulodunum, and by the end of the afternoon, he arrived at the fortress.

Since the Roman conquest, a solid wooden wall had been built around the city. The gate was closed and guarded, and a centurion shouted to him, "What's your business, Briton?"

"I wish to see the governor of the city," he shouted up.

"And who are you?"

"Who I am, soldier, is none of your business. I have urgent information to give to the governor. Let me in, or is the Roman army too frightened of a lone man on a horse?"

The gate opened, and Cassus rode through the archway and into the road outside the guardhouse. Soldiers off duty came out to look at the stranger, and when the captain of the guard decided that he wasn't dangerous, he ordered an escort to take him to the center of the city. Riding slowly behind his escort down alleyways and straight roads, Cassus was surprised at the way the Romans had changed Camulodunum from the Celtic village which was large and spacious, boasting few buildings and no roads, into a planned city in which streets ran parallel and at right angles to each other, and buildings of all shapes and sizes prevented the eye from seeing the size of the city. But because the major roads led off the main intersection, it was easy to understand where a visitor was in the city.

And the houses were the colors of the rainbow; some were painted the blue of the sky, others yellow and red, and still others in the shades of the earth. In the village where he lived, all the houses were thatched or made of wattle and daub and were the color of mud or straw. Camulodunum was a feast for his eyes, and he couldn't believe the inventiveness of the Romans. And many of the houses weren't houses at all, but were crowded with people buying and selling things. He knew from listening to his father that these were shops, and different roads in the city had been dedicated to different crafts and activities, such as streets devoted only to metalworking, or butchering, or leatherwork and tanning. Large wooden signs were hung over the entry to the road to indicate which trade or activity the shops were devoted to.

The previous year, at the insistence of his father, Cassus had traveled out of Britain to Rome, where he had paid compliments to the new Caesar, Nero. Of course, he hadn't managed to see Nero; instead, a minor functionary of the court had come out to the steps of the palace to receive his felicitations, but he was assured that his greetings and respects would be passed on to the emperor, along with the thousands of other greetings from all over the world which had flooded in to pay compliments to the new ruler of the world.

Try as he might, Cassus couldn't remember too much about Rome. He'd spent much of his time drunk in taverns or ensconced in the numerous brothels along the banks of the Tiber; but the steward he had traveled with managed to extricate him, and the journey home had seemed to drag on forever.

Reentering a Roman city in Britain brought back his memories of Rome. In silence, in awe, Cassus and his escort continued into the heart of the city, where he saw that a huge stone building was being constructed. It looked like a temple, and he asked his escort what was its purpose.

"It's dedicated to the god Claudius," said the soldier. "The Emperor Nero made the old bastard into a god, so now we've got to worship him."

Cassus shook his head in amazement. "Claudius? The emperor who came here on an elephant?"

The guard laughed, and told Cassus that it was Claudius' way of amusing the local people.

Still mystified, Cassus asked, "But how can a man become a god?" Before the guard could answer, Cassus continued. "Surely a god has to be a god, and not a man." The guard shrugged, and told him tersely, "For me, he's a god. I've been given free land, so I couldn't care whether Claudius is a god or a donkey; I'll worship anybody who makes my life easier."

They passed by the new temple, and entered the large space in the middle of the town which Cassus recognized as the forum. It was surrounded by tall and impressive buildings, many of them made of stone, with large fluted columns holding up porticos and porches, archways and grand entrances. He hadn't been in a city as magnificent as this in Britain, and few outside of Rome. This, he realized, was where he wanted to live. Maybe here, or maybe he'd leave Britain if ever Boudica ruled, and live in Rome.

The escort told Cassus to dismount and walked into one of the buildings, ordering him to remain outside. After a while, a more important soldier with insignia on his uniform showing that he was a unit leader, maybe even a legate, came out and looked him up and down as though he were a beggar. The officer asked Cassus, "What is your name, Briton? What business do you have with the governor of Camulodunum?"

"I am Cassus, son of Prasutagus, king of the Iceni. I am here because I have information to give the governor."

The legate looked at the young man, and nodded. "Follow me."

They entered the building, and Cassus was immediately impressed by the grandeur. And again, as he always felt when he entered a Roman house, he was amazed by the warmth. It was as though the gods of winter had been expelled, and the gods of summer were resident. He looked around for a fire, but couldn't see one. His father's house had such heating which came from beneath the floors, and although he'd been told, he still found it hard to believe where the warmth of the room had come from. The Romans built fires outside the building, and somehow the heat traveled along pipes under the floor, but it was all too difficult for him to comprehend. When he was in Rome it had been summer, and everywhere was warm or hot. But in Britain, it was winter everywhere, except inside Roman villas.

And that wasn't all that impressed him. Statues of prominent Roman men and women were resting on plinths in every room; niches in the walls held smaller statues of gods and goddesses; some of the walls were painted with scenes of these same gods and goddesses at rest or at play, and the lintels were decorated with delicate yet lovely patterns of yellow and red and blue. It made his own house seem squalid and ordinary; even his father's villa wasn't as magnificent as this.

They walked along corridors and through antechambers, until the legate knocked on a door and opened it without being asked. Two guards stood to attention on the inside of the door, their lances fixed. At his desk was the governor of Britain.

"Excellency," said the legate, "the son of Prasutagus, king of the Iceni, wishes to speak with you."

The governor, Aulus Didius Gallus, looked up from his work and studied the young man. Without greeting him, he asked tersely, "How is your father?"

"My father does well. He is not the reason why I've come."

Surprised by the curt answer, the lack of respect, and the surly appearance of the youth, the governor beckoned him over. Accompanied by the legate, Cassus approached the desk and sat down.

"I have information to give you, but I will only tell you when we're alone."

Aulus Didius Gallus' spies in Prasutagus' court had often given him reports of his son, and the difficult nature of the young man. It was the first time they'd met, and he took an immediate dislike to him.

"I will decide who listens to your information. If you're unhappy with the legate being present, then you're free to go. I suggest instead of trying to dictate terms and conditions to me, you tell me why you've come, or return to your lands."

Stung by the rebuke, Cassus mumbled, "Do I have your assurance that my name and this visit will not be linked to me?"

"Young man, if you have information for me, then give it. If not, then leave."

"But my life will be in jeopardy if it gets out that I've told you."

"And why should your life have any meaning to me?" asked Didius.

"Look, I came here as a friend to give you secret information that could help you."

Relenting slightly, Didius said softly, "Very well, young man, if the information you wish to give me is so secret, then yes, I give you my word that your name won't be linked. Now what is it that you've come to me about?"

"My father's wife—"

"The Queen Boadicea?"

Cassus nodded. "She's going on a long trip around the country. She's going to Wales and to the north."

Didius remained silent, looking at the young man. His spies had already told him of this information, but he wanted to know why Cassus was relaying it to him. Embarrassed, Cassus continued, "I think you should arrest her and her daughter. Boudica is going to raise an army to fight the Romans. She's going to rebel against you. She's going to bring back soldiers, Britons, and she's going to fight you."

Still Didius looked at the young man. The silence became painful. "Aren't you going to do something? Why aren't you saying anything? I'm giving you valuable information, and you're just looking at me. Are you too stupid to understand what I'm saying . . . she's going to rebel against you! You have to arrest her."

Softly, Didius said, "If Boadicea raises an army against us, we will arrest her. I thank you for coming, Cassus, and now if you'd leave my office, I'm very busy."

The legate gripped Cassus' arm and began to lead him out of the governor's room. At the door, he turned, and said to Didius, "You obviously aren't intelligent enough to understand what this information could mean. Maybe I should go to see the procurator in Londinium, who speaks directly to the emperor, and tell him my information. He'll probably know the importance of what I'm telling you. I'm not a barbarian, you know. I've been to Rome."

Again, Didius simply looked at him, and then looked down and continued working on the papers on his table. In humiliation, Cassus walked silently out of the building and remounted his horse, riding away in fury and determined to seek an audience with the Roman procurator of Britain to report Didius' indifference. While Aulus might be the governor, the procurator had control of all taxes and finances, and spoke more directly to the emperor than did the governor.

The legate returned to the governor, and stood before his desk. Didius said, "So that was young Cassus. I've heard much about him. And what I've heard

seems to be true. I also had a report on his visit last year to Rome to see the emperor. He made a fool of himself, and was nearly arrested for fighting. Had it
not been for his steward telling the guards who he was, it could have been difficult. He's a youth who's not to be trusted. Actually, if he were my son, I'd have
him flogged and sent to the galleys. After a visit like that, I need a drink."

By the time Boudica was ready for her progress, her entourage had expanded to
fifty armed guards, seven cooks, four wagons carrying kitchen equipment, vast
amounts of smoked, dried and preserved food, arms, her treasury, tents, and
hangings to decorate her tents and any accommodation she would be given by
those whom she visited. Other wagons contained her and her daughter's clothes,
their personal cleansing items, gifts for the kings and queens she would be visiting, distractions and playthings for Camorra, and wood, leaves and flasks of water from the holy groves and springs to keep her personal gods happy as she
ventured far from her home.

In the cold of the early winter, the air already frosty after a long autumn of
rain and fogs, Prasutagus and Tasca came to bid them goodbye. "I can't believe
that I'm traveling with all this," she said to him, turning and pointing to the
small army of supporters. "When I was a girl and traveled to holy sites with my
parents, we took with us only what we could carry."

"Then you were a girl. Today you're a queen, and people must see the most
regal, most excellent queen in all of Britain."

She nodded. She loved her husband and would miss him greatly. He was
wise and clever and calm, compared with her impetuous and sometimes emo-
tional behavior. But she had to learn to be a queen, even though she'd ruled the
Iceni for many years. And she would miss her daughter Tasca very much. Just as
Prasutagus would miss Camorra, who had developed into the most beautiful of
girls, and whose voice was already mature and fluid. By the time she returned, no
doubt Tasca would have become the mistress of the house, and would be busily
instructing the slaves and servants in their duties. How would Boudica fit back
into a household with two mothers? But Prasutagus would know how to restrain

Tasca's natural urge to lead before her time, and would ensure that the absence of her mother didn't go to her head.

Boudica hesitated before spurring on her horse. She was dressed as a Roman matron. It was the way in which she'd dressed since she became queen, accepting her husband's decision to live in peace, and not to fight the empire. She dressed as a Roman in her own court, and others followed her style; however, traveling the roads of Britain, she now feared that she would be looked upon as a traitor to her people. But what truly frightened her was the prospect that the kings and queens whom she was visiting, and who hadn't accepted the Roman occupation of her land, might view her in a lesser light than if she were to look more like a British queen.

With an insight into what was disturbing her, Prasutagus smiled at his wife as she straddled her horse, very much the regal lady; he reached up and put his hand on her leg. Softly, gently, he gave her reassurance. "You are a magnificent woman, Boudica. You are a true queen of your people. You will leave the lesser monarchs dumbstruck in the path you take on your progress. You're an example which all others will inevitably follow." And with that, he said a silent prayer, kissed Camorra and lifted her onto her horse. He bade Boudica farewell, and slapped her mount on its flanks.

They remained standing, father and daughter, until the last wagon had trundled out of sight and silence descended upon the garden of their villa. Then, they turned and went back into their half-empty home.

The party attracted the attention of peasants in the fields, and of villagers wherever they went. Their first day was uneventful, traveling through land with which Boudica was familiar. The first stop after twenty-five miles was at the foot of the hill on which the Romans had built a wooden fort at Canteluvellum. It took them until the falling of night to erect their tents, get the fires lit and the food in the pots cooking. In the meantime, Boudica and Camorra rode up the hill to visit the Roman commander.

They were met at the palisade by three sentries, rough-looking Romans gripping their spears, looking down at the two women in suspicion. Because mother and daughter were dressed as Roman women, the sentries called down, "Greetings, ladies. What do you want?"

"Boudica, queen of the Iceni and friend of Rome, with her daughter Camorra, visits the commander of the fort of Canteluvellum, and wishes to pay her respects."

"You're Boadicea?" one of the men asked.

"Queen of the Iceni. Tell your commander immediately that I wish to pay my respects."

All the men disappeared from their parapet on the ramparts. From within the fort, Boudica and Camorra heard shouts and scrambling and movement. Their visit had caused a stir. Good! This was how a queen should behave, and should be treated, she whispered to her daughter.

Within moments, the heavy wooden door was opened, and a small delegation of soldiers, one of them wearing the epaulet and insignia of a commander of a Roman *centuria*, walked forward. He was a head shorter than Boudica, but stocky and powerful.

"My name is Maximillius Veronicus Africanus, centurion of the army of Rome. I greet Boadicea, queen of the Iceni, and her daughter. Will you honor me and my men by dining with us, Lady?"

Boudica smiled, and shook her head. She knew all too well what Roman army food tasted like. "I thank you, Centurion, but my cooks are preparing my meal. I have come to pay my respects as I am traveling through your lands, and I wanted you to be confident of my good intentions."

He smiled. "Lady, I have known about your progress since the middle of the day. My riders gave me the intelligence."

"Would you and your officers like to dine with me, Maximillius Veronicus? I'm sure that your meal will be delicious, but my cooks are preparing venison from a deer we killed this afternoon, accompanied by fresh field mushrooms, roots and tubers cooked in newly churned and salted butter, as well as a fresh pike which we're cooking in Roman olive oil, and all of this to be followed by summer fruits from our orchard which have been preserved in wine."

She could see the sudden look of desire in his eyes, and refrained from smiling. "Majesty," he said, "I and two of my officers would be honored to join you. My men will remain here and protect the area."

Later that evening, after the first decent meal the Roman had enjoyed since being sent into the middle of the country, he and Boudica sat under the canopy of stars, gazing over the blackness of the landscape. Only the occasional pinprick of light from a distant house shone in the blackness of the forest and the fields.

The Roman soldier had been drinking long and heavily all night. He was slurring his words badly, but it was what Boudica had planned.

"Nero?" he said softly. "I know only that I wouldn't trust my daughter to be in the same city as him." He giggled. "I've had far too much to drink. I shouldn't be say— But I'll tell you something, Your Majesty. Worse, a million times worse, than Nero is his mother. You know that she was the wife of the cursed Emperor Caligula, don't you?"

"You mean his sister," said Boudica.

"I mean his wife. What went on in that imperial family would disgust you, Majesty. Caligula slept with anything that moved. He slept with the pantomime actor Mnester, with his own sisters Agrippina and Drusilla, and with the family dog, cat and horse as far as I know." He burst into laughter, and quaffed another drink. "Rumor has it that he once made his horse, Incitatus, into a priest and a consul, and he gave the beast a stable of ivory and a golden goblet for him to drink wine. What he and the horse did at night, the gods only know."

Even Boudica burst out laughing, and it impelled the Roman on. "Unfortunately, it's not all funny. That murderous swine Caligula did hideous things. Did you know, Majesty, that when his sister Drusilla became pregnant by him, the bastard couldn't wait for the birth of the child he thought would be a god, and he disemboweled her in order to pluck the fetus out of her body and he ate it. When she died, Caligula had Drusilla deified. Now what kind of a monster is that?"

Sickened, Boudica listened in horror to the story. "And Nero?" she asked, trying to get the Roman to focus.

"By all accounts, Lady, he's starting off his rule quite well. His love interests are rampant and there are reports that he's worse than Caligula when it comes to having sex with men and women, boys and girls, but what counts as far as we're concerned is how he performs as emperor. Will he be a good emperor like Claudius started off? Who can say? Maybe he'll be excellent, but there again, as I remember, so were Caligula and Claudius after him at certain times of their rule." He sighed. "But they all go crazy in the end, these emperors. Remember Tiberius who was mad as a hare and let General Sejanus kill half of Rome on his behalf?" He stopped talking, drank another cup of wine, and said, "Majesty, I'm only a humble soldier. I've said too much. I could be crucified for what I've said tonight. It was the wine. Don't report this to my commanders, will you, or I'll be dead by morning."

"Don't worry, Centurion. My interest in Rome only lasts as long as Rome's interest in Britain."

He looked at her, but in his drunken state, all he could see was a tall, slender, magnificent-looking woman with long red hair. Before he fell asleep the last thought which went through his mind was that if Boudica were the wife of a Roman emperor, the empire wouldn't be in the dreadful state it was in.

CHAPTER EIGHT

55 AD—Approaching the Court of Queen Cartimandua

Boudica arrived with Camorra in the land of the Brigantes in the middle of the spring. The days were still cold, demanding that she keep wearing the woolen shawl she used in the winter, but the early fruit blossoms were beginning to grow on the apple, pear and plum trees and the winter flowers had disappeared to be replaced by spring buds.

She cursed her own stupidity for traveling in the winter, but she'd reasoned that Prasutagus would need her beside him in the summer during the harvest time, when so much was happening. Still, the days were beginning to warm up slightly, and she was nearing the end of her journey.

Boudica and Camorra removed themselves from their entourage, giving instruction for them to make camp, and went behind a hill to where they could be private. Boudica took out her favorite idol and set it down on a small hillock of grass which faced a river. Then, carefully pulling each third flower she saw— three being the birth number she had been given by the Druid priest—she wove them into a garland which she placed on the head of her beloved child. Standing, closing her eyes, Boudica chanted:

> *Great gods of sky and earth, gods of spring and brook and sea, gods of trees and flowers, of house and fields, look down upon us, your worshippers and friends. I see through my closed eyes my husband Prasutagus and my daughter Tasca, and I ask that you keep them safe and well until our return. Grant us the strength to deal with Cartimandua and to show her the power and mystery of your ways. Gods of woods and groves, protect us, feed us, nurture us, guide us, and love us.*

She and Camorra hugged, and removed their garlands. As they returned to the entourage, Camorra asked, "Why do we pray alone? Why don't we pray with the others when they pray?"

Boudica sighed. "The Romans want to take our gods and spirits and make them their own. They want to build temples and have our gods and their gods sit side by side. Your father and I have decided that for the peace of our land, we must learn to live with the Romans. But I will never allow them to take over our gods. So to save trouble for your father, I don't want anybody to know that I follow the old ways, and pray to our gods to the exclusion of the Roman gods. Your father doesn't like the Druids, and says that we're better now that they've all gone over to the west. I don't agree, but it's better that I pray silently and alone rather than upset him, or the Romans."

Camorra smiled and hugged her mother. She walked ahead, and as she rounded the hillock, Boudica couldn't restrain a smile at the way in which her beautiful child moved with such grace. Boudica was delighted every day in the way Camorra was maturing; always the more sensitive and grown-up of her two daughters, Camorra seemed to have developed rapidly in the time that they had been away. They had visited the homes of three kings and queens in the middle of Britain and the west before obeying her husband's injunction and turning north before they approached the border with the kings and queens of the Welsh tribes.

The reception she enjoyed in those kingdoms she visited was initially suspicious, but soon transformed into welcome and ease. She had stayed in the middle lands, in the city of Carvellus by the banks of the River Soar for two weeks, and enjoyed riding and hunting and fishing in the pristine streams. Wherever she went, she first paid tribute to the king and queen; then she visited the Roman fort or district governorship in order to inform the local Roman ruler of her presence in his territory, and to find out if he had any additional intelligence from Rome. And then, in privacy, she paid obeisance to those gods who protected the local people.

But more than any of the other kingdoms she traveled to, Boudica was particularly excited about visiting the far northern land of the Brigantes, and especially meeting with Queen Cartimandua, the woman who was the greatest friend that Rome had in Britain. Infamous among the rebels, Cartimandua had chained the defeated and fleeing Caratacus who sought refuge from the Romans in her kingdom. She had handed him and his family over to the emperor.

Hated by half of Britain, treated with suspicion and jealousy by the other half, Cartimandua was reputed to be a strong-willed ruler growing fabulously wealthy at the expense of others. Indeed, Prasutagus had told Boudica to be extremely wary of the Queen of the North, because she was so close to Rome that she might, for some perverse reason, believe that she could benefit by enslaving Boudica. Astounded, Prasutagus had told his wife before she left that Cartimandua was rumored to have enlisted the support of the Romans in a plot to overthrow her very own husband so that she could assume sole rights as heir to the Brigantian throne.

Now that they had arrived at the outskirts of Cartimandua's lands, Boudica suddenly felt alone, and realized how very much she missed the wisdom and counsel of Prasutagus. But this was a journey she had decided to undertake so that she could know more about her own country, and it was a journey she would have to finish.

Boudica returned with Camorra to their camp and settled down for the night. She preferred to make camp early rather than continue on for an additional few miles and have to set up her camp in the dark. She had chosen a flat plain which ran down to a river. To her left was a thick forest, where nobody could maneuver to conduct a surprise assault; to her right was an escarpment of rock, too high and steep for an ambush. Looking up, she saw a dozen or so men and women, who looked down at her party in bemusement but continued with their work as the afternoon drew toward night. They were laborers in the fields, working at the top of the ridge, and they were as interested in her arrival as she was in what they were doing. If they were a secret army preparing to attack, they weren't particularly skilled. She set guards and lookouts at the rear and in the front, the only places where she and her entourage were vulnerable.

Sore from riding, and having had her fill of hunting in the south, Boudica instructed her soldiers to search the forests and fields for game to kill, so that they could eat well that night. The cooks were already preparing the vegetables, leaves which they'd gathered the previous day, as well as cutting strips of smoked meat and dried fish. Her steward quickly prepared a large fire so that he could make for the queen and her daughter the mulled wine they enjoyed so much after a hard day's traveling.

Boudica and Camorra sat in front of the fire and warmed their bodies. Feeling better that they had prayed to their gods, they sipped their wine, and Boudica stole another glimpse at her beautiful and noble daughter. There was so much to say to her, so much to tell her of the world; yet whatever Boudica told her would be as nothing compared to the joys she would experience of learning everything for herself. Boudica had been born into a noble family, had worked hard to learn the different languages of the different tribes and of their conqueror, had quickly gleaned the differences in culture between the Romans and the Britons and had understood the need to adopt the customs which made her life easier and more prosperous than the lives of those Britons who resisted the change.

But what would life hold in store for Camorra and for Tasca? she wondered. Would the Romans still be in Britain when they were grown women, and they were leaders of their Iceni tribe? The centurion whom she had entertained on the first day of her progress had been sufficiently drunk to tell her of gossip which was beginning to emanate from Rome: that the constant assaults from the people in the west and in Wales were forcing the Romans to increase the numbers of troops they were sending to Britain. He told her of rumors that legions now in

Germany and Gaul, and possibly one in Syria under Vespasian, were going to be sent to Britain to put down the rebellion once and for all time.

But the centurion also said that there was talk in the corridors of the Senate of Rome that the costs of establishing such a huge force of men, and at such a distance from the capital, was simply not worth it. It would be different, the talk said, if Britain were connected by land to the rest of the world; but it was still seen as a barbarian outpost across the sea, disconnected from the rest of the world and unworthy of troops and governors and all the effort.

If the Romans did evacuate Britain, what would that mean for the Iceni, the Brigantes and all the other kingdoms which had sided with Rome and become clients of the empire? The visit which Cassus had made to Rome the previous year had been a complete waste of time and money. He should have presented Prasutagus' and Boudica's compliments directly to the emperor, but he hadn't been allowed near the palace. Instead, according to Cassus' steward, they had been treated like peasants, kept waiting on the steps of the palace, never getting close to the center of power. That, Boudica realized, was the contempt for Britain which the Romans felt. Yet she and Prasutagus had made their future dependent on Roman goodwill.

But if it suddenly came to an end, would the people who had spent so much time and suffered so greatly in fighting Rome ever forgive Boudica and Prasutagus and Cartimandua and all the others for dining with the enemy? Would the Druids encircle the lands of those kingdoms which had been Rome's clients and place a curse on them, damn them to the dark regions, prohibit trade between kingdom and kingdom? Would they rouse the victorious Britons and encourage them to overthrow the monarchies which had slept with Rome?

Boudica's fears were drowned out by the sudden and excited shouting of Camorra. Lost in her thoughts, Boudica didn't realize that it had grown dark, and Camorra was turning and pointing to the top of the escarpment. "Look," she shouted in excitement. "Look, Mother, up there. It's Beltane!" Boudica looked at the scene on the top of the escarpment, and suddenly realized just how she had misjudged the time. She was swept with guilt. How could she have allowed such an event to slip from her mind?

Boudica saw that the few peasants had been joined by hundreds of others. They had erected a maypole, a freshly felled tall young tree, stripped of its lower branches and bark, at the top of which were tied bunches of flowers and long strands of brightly colored cloth. The villagers had lit a huge bonfire at the top of the cliff. Now musical instruments like drums and pipes and harps were playing, and men and women, boys and girls, were starting to dance around the maypole, holding on to the ribbons and entwining them around the trunk of the tree, laughing and clapping and shouting as they wove in and out.

"I shall go up there, Mother, and join them," Camorra announced. "Why don't you come as well? You'll enjoy yourself."

Smiling, Boudica said, "No, my sweet child. You go. I shall stay here and rest."

But Camorra wouldn't have it. "Don't just sit around. You've had no fun since we left Father and Tasca. You know you love dancing. Come on," she said, pulling her mother's arm.

But Boudica resisted. "I don't want to go. Not without your father being here. You know what happens in the Beltane. I can't put myself into that position."

Camorra shrugged, and then she nodded. "I shall be back in the morning," she said, and ran to the foot of the cliff. Through the enveloping gloom of the evening, Boudica watched her as she ascended the track which led up to the plateau. She couldn't help herself but smiled yet again at her daughter's lovely graceful body. When she had been Camorra's age, she too had been like a deer, prancing around the fields with her long tireless legs, jumping into rivers, climbing trees . . . it had been a time of freedom and inspiration, of a constant search for knowledge and understanding, and a desire to know everything.

Boudica remembered the festivals of Beltane when she was only a girl: the heat from the fire, the celebration of the end of the dark half of the year and the beginning of the light and the sun; she remembered the delicate air when it was full of the new scent of blossoms which seemed to come out shortly after the lighting of the huge bonfires throughout the country as Britons said goodbye to winter and welcome to the spring.

Most especially, Boudica remembered her amazement and joy at seeing the tiny fruits begin to grow, and as the sun warmed them, how they'd increase in size until they were sweet and juicy and luscious—and the way in which the fields were stark and green one day, and suddenly brilliantly blazing with flowers the next. The young animals being born gave her the greatest thrills of all.

How she missed the Druids! They would have known the precise moment when Beltane would arrive. They wouldn't have been surprised by a bonfire on a cliff top. But how would she know, now that the Druids were being driven by the Romans into the west? Druids had always appeared on the day of the Beltane, as well as on the complementary festival of Samhain, a time when the entire village doused its hearth fires, and came to the home of the chieftain or the king and queen in order to light wooden brands from their fires. Then they took the fires to relight their own in order to give themselves the light and warmth of the king's protection to help them and see them safely through the winter. But who would guide the Britons now that the Druids were gone?

Boudica stood, and walked from her campfire toward the cliff in the gathering dusk. She looked up and saw that the dancing of the men and women was increasingly frantic, faster, more carefree. This was a time, at the end of a long and hard winter, when the men and women and the older boys and girls of all the villages of Britain came out into the field to dance around the maypole, the tree of the world.

She looked carefully, and saw that two rows of dancers were dancing around it, spiraling and weaving in and out, each holding a ribbon tied to the top of the pole. The weaving of the ribbons meant the turning of the seasons, the turning of the world, the turning of the stars. She heard music played and saw the happiness on peoples' faces.

And men and women, boys and girls, would pair off, and go and lie in the straw under the stars, with the heat of the fire warming their naked bodies, and they would join together and fulfill the demands of the gods and the priests and rise in ecstasy to the very zenith of joy.

Boudica sighed. More than at any time since she'd begun her journey, she missed Prasutagus as husband. Suddenly, she felt lonely and ached to be back in her home with the people she loved most in the world. She ached for his body, his strength, his gentleness; she yearned for him to touch her on her breasts, to kiss them and move his hands gently down toward her thighs. They had been married for years, had rarely enjoyed other partners, reveling in the closeness of each other; but although they considered themselves settled, they still made love many times a week, sometimes at night and often when she first stirred in the morning. She'd open her eyes and find Prasutagus lying with his head on the pillow, looking at her and smiling. She would smile back; he would move across and kiss her, and they'd hug and join as one.

Soon she would be back in her husband's arms. But she hadn't regretted coming on the journey. It was important for her, as one of the most important queens of a major tribe in Britain, to meet other monarchs and encourage trade and a closer relationship.

Her progress to date had been worthwhile. She had made good trading treaties with friendly kings and queens, had met most of the important Roman commanders and introduced herself and her daughter to the land of her birth. And tomorrow she would meet a queen who was, by all accounts, the most feared woman in Britain.

"Majesty," said the older woman, stepping down from her throne on the dais, "reports of your youth and beauty have lied and I shall behead the next person who tells me that you're lovely. For you are the most ravishing and divine of women. Beauty, not Boudica, is your name. You are a goddess, Queen of the Iceni, a goddess come to earth. Even your very name is that of our ancient goddess of victory in battle. Come here, Sovereign of the South, and kiss your sister."

Surprised by the overwhelming warmth and generosity of the welcome, Boudica and Camorra walked over the mosaic floor of Queen Cartimandua's vast and opulent palace, a floor of delicate river colors, depicting scenes of Cartimandua ruling her people as supreme queen of the Brigantes. Boudica and Camorra bowed long and low until released from their abasement.

"Stand, queen and daughter of the Iceni, and embrace Cartimandua, sister queen and friend of Rome," she said, walking over to the newcomers and enveloping them in the voluminous folds of her gown. Slightly shorter than Boudica, Queen Cartimandua was older and more buxom; her hair, once blond, was now streaked with gray, and her face no longer wore the smooth suppleness of youth. Yet despite her more mature appearance, Cartimandua was a handsome woman who must have looked fearsome to all who came before her.

Wondering why the queen was being so open and friendly, especially in front of all her councilors and advisors, instead of being the stern and uncompromising woman she had been warned to expect, Boudica kissed Cartimandua on both cheeks and whispered a prayer to Lugh, the god of light, in honor of her visit. The two women grasped each other in a sisterly hug, but a sudden scream from a distant part of the room made Camorra grasp her mother in fear. Terrified, the creature screamed again. It was a woman . . . no, a child . . . in danger, or being hurt. Camorra was distressed and hugged her mother. Even Boudica was horrified by the pain which was carried in the scream, especially when Cartimandua simply smiled, and snapped her fingers.

The press of courtiers parted, and at the end of the aisle they created, Boudica and Camorra saw the most extraordinary sight they had ever seen. Again, it—for they had no idea what it was—screamed, and started to walk forward on its scrawny legs. But when the bird—Boudica realized that it was a bird, though she had never seen a bird of such luminosity or brilliance—was halfway toward her, it suddenly stopped, bowed its crowned head to the two queens, and its tail feathers stood erect; then they splayed out into the most fantastic fan of the colors of the rainbow, with a thousand eyes within the tail which seemed to be looking in all directions.

Stunned, Boudica turned to Cartimandua, and didn't have to ask the obvious question. "It's called a peacock. It is a male bird . . . the female is very dull, unlike us, Boudica. It comes from the most northerly and eastern part of the Roman Empire, from a place called by those who live there after their god, Indus. It was given to me as a gift by the Emperor Claudius. He was my friend. A pity Agrippina gave him those mushrooms to eat, which didn't agree with him."

Ignoring the bird's display, Cartimandua gripped Boudica's and Camorra's hands and led them through the throng of courtiers to her dais. Neither Boudica nor Camorra could take their eyes off the bird, which walked imperiously through the aisle and followed them to the dais.

"Come, Queen of the Iceni, and tell me why you're traveling around Britain. I've heard everything you've been doing. My intelligence is the very best there is, you know. I know where you've been and who you've seen, but the one thing which nobody seems to understand is why. But where are my manners. You've had a hard journey, and I haven't offered you any refreshment."

Again, she snapped her fingers, and two black African slaves came forward bearing trays on which were placed three cups, steaming from their contents.

"Hot red wine, spiced and sweetened with honey. It's what you and Camorra prefer, as I understand it."

Boudica felt childlike and deflated. Wherever she'd been, she had been greeted as an equal, and had shared and gleaned information. But Queen Cartimandua seemed to know everything about her, and yet she knew little about the queen other than her fearsome and hostile reputation. Sipping the wine, Boudica proposed health and thanks to the queen of the Brigantes, and silently prayed to herself that she could learn enough during the evening so that by the morning, she would feel more of an equal than a subservient provincial.

Cartimandua took pleasure in showing her young visitors round the huge villa which had been built as a gift of the Romans. It was larger in every respect than the villa built for Boudica in the land of the Iceni, sprawling over a vast area and stretching to a seemingly impossible size. And there were atriums which seemed to bring the outside within the compass of the house, amazing interior gardens with trees and shrubs which seemed to grow high above the level of the ground, and two rooms where there were sunken baths.

Separate kitchens also had rooms where food could be stored on slabs and shelves, as well as places where, Cartimandua told her, piss from slaves was collected and stored and, when mixed with water, was used to eliminate grease when washing clothes. Throughout the huge villa, except for the closed washing room which reeked of the stench of urine, was the aroma of perfume which delighted the nose and excited the emotions. Boudica asked Cartimandua what the smell was, but the queen of the Brigantes shrugged her shoulders, and said, "Whenever I'm visited by a Roman nobleman, he always brings me gifts of spices and perfumes. I have a separate room where I collect and store these things, and the smells seem to insinuate themselves throughout the palace."

Boudica was beginning to understand the difference in the relationship which Cartimandua enjoyed with Rome, and that which she and Prasutagus had agreed to by force of circumstance. Cartimandua was a Roman queen by desire and actively courted her relationship, pursuing it at every opportunity, whereas she and Prasutagus were client rulers by force, rather than by choice.

Yet for all Cartimandua's fearsome reputation, as they toured the palace, Boudica looked on her more as a servant than as a friend of Rome, and determined to understand why such a great queen could have allowed herself to be so used.

Ending her tour of the palace, Cartimandua sat, surrounded by just a handful of advisors and courtiers, sending Camorra off to visit with her own children, and asked Boudica, "So, Queen of the Iceni, why are you visiting the north of Britain? Why have you and your beautiful daughter left King Prasutagus and your other daughter Tasca all alone? I hear that you have been securing trading relationships with the Dobunni, the Cornovii and the Coritani. Is it now the turn of the Brigantes to trade with the Iceni? Or is there another reason for your visit?"

Sipping another cup of wine, Boudica thought of how she should answer the queen. The other monarchs with whom she'd negotiated had been willing to listen to her, wanting to benefit from the visit of the monarch of such an important tribe as the Iceni; yet Cartimandua seemed to have been testing her since the moment she'd arrived.

"Because of the death of the Emperor Claudius, opportunities have arisen for the people of Britain to review their relationship with Rome. It seems a propitious time now, Cartimandua, for us to reassess why we are clients of Rome, and on what basis we continue to send them tributes. Every year, my husband and I pay half of our entire income to Rome. In return, they provide us with expertise which we otherwise don't have. They teach our children their language in schools, they've built roads and baths and have shown us ways of building houses, and much more. But in return, they strip our countryside of forests, they take young men and women as slaves, and they never seem satisfied with the amount of silver and lead we give them from our mines—"

"Give?"

"Sell. Yes, we've done very well from our trading with the Romans, Great Queen. And we will continue to do well. But Prasutagus and I feel that we are buying peace at a very high price, and wonder if now isn't the time to demand from a new emperor a new relationship, such as a reduction on the tributes and taxes we're forced to pay."

Queen Cartimandua looked at the younger woman, and asked, "Is that the only reason? I thought it was because the land of the Iceni is bordered by the might of the Catuvellauni tribe who, like me, have a warm and solid relationship with Rome. If you want to travel outside of your tribal area to trade goods, you have to cross their land, and so you and Prasutagus are indirectly controlled by the Catuvellauni and directly by the Romans."

Boudica was about to object, but Cartimandua continued. "But that's not the only reason why you should grow closer to Rome. You people of the Iceni sell the Romans a fortune's worth of silver and copper jewelry. Your craftsmen and women work day and night to supply the merchants with what they want."

"True," said Boudica, "but much of our income goes to repay the loan we were forced to take from the Emperor Claudius when he conquered our lands, a loan that was necessary to pay for grain from other parts of the world because the Roman soldiers took all of our food; and we had to borrow to pay tributes and taxes as well. My people were forced to borrow forty million sesterces. It's the interest we have to pay each year, as well as the continuing huge amount in tribute to Rome, which has caused my people such hardship, and which is causing such resentment.

"My journey around Britain is for many reasons: to determine whether other clients of Rome as treated as iniquitously as are we, and to talk to other rulers about a way out of our situation."

"We all have to pay tribute, Boudica. In return for this tribute, we enjoy the benefits of Rome's protection against our enemies, as well as the genius of Rome's finest talent, its builders and road makers and teachers. But you and Prasutagus are richer than you've ever been. Everything comes at a cost. Surely you now know this from your travels."

"Before the conquest, I only ever saw the lands of the Catuvellauni, and that of the Belgae," Boudica replied. "I went on prayer walks to our holy shrines and did what any young girl does. But now that I am queen, I felt it my duty to visit more of Britain, to see the land of my birth, and to meet with other monarchs— to discuss these things with them. But I have been met with great reluctance. They are willing to talk about trade and exchanging our crafts and much more; but the moment I raise the subject of their relations with Rome, they become silent. I find it strange. We're all Britons. We're all suffering."

"Some are perhaps suffering more than others. Was this the only reason you have been journeying?"

"That was what initially impelled me to leave my home and see the rest of my country. But in truth, Cartimandua, I wanted to see if those of us who do not fight against Rome might form some kind of coalition in order to meet with the new emperor, and convince him somehow to change the way in which he sees our land; to create a new relationship with him; to somehow convince him that Britain is more than just a place where he can acquire silver for his coins, wood for his ships and slaves for his peoples' service."

"But what more can Britain offer to Rome?" Cartimandua asked.

Smiling, Boudica said, "What a wife offers to a husband. A partnership of equals."

Cartimandua thought for a while. Boudica wondered if she was silent because something she had said had angered the queen. But sipping her wine, Cartimandua said softly, "And why do you think that the new emperor will suddenly and unexpectedly review his relationship with Britain? What about his mother Agrippina, who still whispers in his ear? What about Seneca and Burrus, who really are the powers behind young Nero's throne? Surely you can't think that an embassy to the emperor can have such an effect without the agreement of these others? Rome is a snake pit in which you tread at risk of your life. Young as you are, Boudica, surely your years on the throne have taught you that."

"I know about the dangers of sending an embassy to Rome. When Nero first became emperor, I sent Prasutagus' son, Cassus, to Rome to pay our respects. He was treated with contempt and failed to get close to the emperor. All he managed to see was a minor functionary. Cassus now hates the Romans, which has caused Prasutagus and me yet more problems."

Cartimandua looked at Boudica in surprise. "Hates them?"

Boudica nodded.

"Then you haven't heard of the meetings which Cassus has been having with the procurator, Decianus?"

Boudica looked at Cartimandua in shock.

"Oh yes, dear sister. Prasutagus' son has had three meetings with Procurator Decianus in Londinium. They've become quite friendly. Maybe if you were to send Cassus back to Rome, he would be treated in a very different manner," said Cartimandua.

Boudica fought to recover her composure. For the past year or two, Cassus had become warmer and friendlier toward Prasutagus and Boudica. She thought he was growing up; now she realized that he was far more devious than she had realized.

"Cassus leads his own life, Cartimandua. It is not my responsibility to spy on him. And no, he will not be returning to Rome. If anybody goes, it will be my husband, or me. Indeed, the intelligence which I've gathered tells me that Rome might be a different snake pit than it once was, with less dangerous snakes. Much seems to have changed since the ending of the reign of Claudius. Seneca, for instance, has advised Nero that gladiatorial fights to the death must be banned—that contests in which animals tear slaves and criminals to pieces in the arena must no longer be permitted. The traders who visit us tell us that Rome is a gentler and more tolerant place than it was under Claudius. This emperor seems to be different.

"My intelligence goes on to inform me that people are again laughing and feeling free in the streets of Rome. Compare that, Cartimandua, to the last years of the reign of Claudius, when so many great men were killed at his whim. And in order to show that things have changed in Rome, Nero has delighted everybody by reducing taxation for citizens. The influence of the advisor Seneca seems to have had a very real effect on the young emperor, who listens carefully when things are said to him."

"And Agrippina?" asked Cartimandua. "What of the empress behind the emperor? Does she still have a role in Rome, according to your intelligence? I ask, Boudica, because my intelligence comes from within the palace, and not from the streets."

Carefully, knowing how well informed Cartimandua was, Boudica said, "I am informed that Nero gets greater pleasure from music and art and theater and entertainment than from running the empire. I am informed that Agrippina's power is waning; that he no longer seeks her advice or comfort; that he pays more attention to the pursuit of pleasure and the advice of his friends than the comforts which were once offered by his mother.

"But most especially, Cartimandua, I am reliably informed by my intelligencers that Britain is a great burden on the purse of Rome; that stationing so many soldiers here is costing Rome a fortune, and that many in the Senate are questioning why Rome's empire needs to extend north, beyond Gaul. If we are cut adrift by Rome, Cartimandua, and if the empire withdraws its legions, then how will life be for those of us who have befriended Rome?"

Queen Cartimandua listened carefully to the younger woman. She continued to ponder while sipping her wine. And softly, she said, "Once you have slept and rested, Boudica, I think it would be wise for you to sit with me in council, and meet with my advisors. There is much for us to talk about. Especially some disturbing reports I'm hearing about the new emperor."

But reports about Nero weren't pressing on Boudica's mind as painfully as the information that Cassus was in league with the Roman procurator in Londinium. What was he up to? she wondered. What devious plans was he initiating? What dangers could he pose for Prasutagus . . . and more certainly, for her?

The Palace of the Emperor Nero

"Britannicus," shouted the Emperor Nero in delight. "Britannicus, dearest brother, and son of the god Claudius. Let us celebrate Saturnalia with a song. I want you to come into the middle of the room and sing us a song. Let us see your radiant lips, hear your sweet voice."

The banqueting hall came to a sudden and not unexpected silence. Always positioned on the couches at the bottom of the room, a place normally reserved for secondary guests, artists and junior senators and knights, Britannicus had long accepted his position in Nero's hierarchy. Always ignored, often ridiculed in public, Britannicus, stepbrother of Nero and natural son of the late Emperor Claudius, was a boy of slight appearance, delicate temperament and quiet disposition. Those who knew him realized that his withdrawn personality, like his father's, was merely the way in which he could escape the emperor's deadly gaze.

"Come, Britannicus," the emperor shouted, "into the center of the room where all can see you. You're honored, after all. I've made your father a god, and now it appears that you're my mother's favorite. For reasons which only the gods could possibly understand, she favors you above me. Let us see the reason why she has eschewed her natural-born son with all his gifts and talents, for . . . for you."

The guests looked in horror at what they knew must surely come to pass. The hatred between Nero and Britannicus had always been understood, but it had never before been public. Now it was naked and frightening.

Falteringly, Britannicus said, "Caesar, you know that I don't have a good singing voice. I'm sure we'd all rather listen to one of your delightful odes. Sing us a song, Nero, and let all your friends and admirers share in a voice which was taken from the gods themselves."

"No, dear brother. This time, you will sing for us. You will sing! Come along now, and stand up. Let us hear your song."

The thirteen-year-old Britannicus stood on his thin legs, shaking with sudden and overwhelming fear. He almost fell as he skirted the couches and stood in the center of the room, all eyes upon him. His jaw shaking, he asked, "What shall I sing, Nero?"

The emperor turned to his guests, and burst out laughing. "He asks me what he should sing? Do you hear that? The boy wants me to tell him. Does anybody tell me what to sing? No, for the gods put music into my mouth, and I sing the songs of the air and the sea and the mountaintops. My fingers are harps which soothe the frenzied spirits, my lips are the trumpets which call the gods to attention, and my mouth is the cornucopia in which the Muses live and from which all greatness derives. Yet this callow boy asks me what he should sing."

He expected laughter from his friends, but there was silence in the room, as all eyes were on Britannicus, all onlookers feeling the misery he was experiencing.

"I don't know, boy!" shouted Nero. "Sing what you want."

And in a thin and timorous voice, Britannicus began to sing the song he'd composed just a few days earlier in the silence of his distant room in the basement of the palace.

> I am a boy of tender years,
> An orphan boy who cries no tears.
> My father and my mother dead,
> No lap on which to rest my head.
> My noble family has now gone
> To sit among the godly throng
> And now, if Fates be as I fear
> My end as well will soon be here.
> For I . . .

"Enough!" shouted Nero. "Enough! What a dirge. What a hideous song." He looked around, and waited for people to nod in agreement and shout at the boy in anger. But the entire banqueting hall was silent. Indeed, some of the faces were averted so that Nero couldn't see their distress. In fury, Nero ordered Britannicus to sit down, and remained silent and incensed for the rest of the dinner.

Nero retired early to bed, and as the guests left, an elderly senator, who had lived precariously through the reigns of Tiberius and Caligula and Claudius, whispered into Britannicus' ear, "Take great care from this moment on. Your song could be your very own threnody. My advice, son of Claudius, is to leave this palace tonight and never return."

It would be a fine dinner. Everything had been carefully selected to be just right, just so. Nero himself had ensured that the entertainment was very ordinary so that he would be called upon by all his friends to rescue the evening from the mediocrities. Oh, it would be a glorious evening, and it would be a fitting way to pay Britannicus back for the dishonor he had done him all those weeks ago, when he'd embarrassed him in front of his friends.

And best of all would be the beginning of the demise of the dreadful remnant of the body of the awful Claudius, a brother and sister who posed a threat to Nero's throne. Britannicus would at last perish after causing him so much grief and consternation. And the hideous boy would soon be followed to the land of the Shades by Nero's own wife Octavia, the other festering relic of the diseased, crippled and dead emperor.

And then at long last he could turn his attention to the real problem of his reign. She was, all his friends argued, the most dangerous of all. Oh, the joy of killing Agrippina. How many great men could claim that they had been able to kill a woman who was at once their own mother and wife?

Yes, she would go. It would be difficult, for she was immensely powerful and was still considered by some to be the power behind his throne. But despite Nero having banished her from the palace, she was still a danger to him. Hadn't she made wild comments at a banquet in her home on the Bay of Neapolis about how her very own son was a usurper and didn't deserve to be emperor . . . of how Britannicus was the true and rightful emperor as Claudius' own natural son? The more Nero tried to remove his mother from the center of power, the more she supported Britannicus against him. Oh, he thought, a faithless mother would soon meet a faithless and painful end!

And tonight, the world would kneel and pay homage to the only true emperor; not the usurper as Agrippina so hurtfully put it, but emperor in his own right. A young man who listened carefully to the lessons taught by his tutor and adviser Seneca, a wise and stoic man; who learned well the advice given to him by the fearless and upright general Burrus; who was the joy and delight of Rome and who had earned the love and respect of all the people when he reduced their taxes, when he took blood sports out of the arena and made it into a place for the family, and especially when he staged the biggest and most fantastic performances that Rome had ever seen.

The Emperor Nero lay down on one of the banqueting couches, and took a moment to think about the contributions he had already made to the empire. His mind played over the map of his empire, from the hot and mysterious east to the cold and inhospitable north. He was told by Seneca that he should begin to develop an interest in the lands under his command; but he was only interested in theater and singing and music and enjoying himself. Why should he bother with details? Wasn't that the job of his advisors? Why were they there, if not to worry about the empire and Rome? His job as emperor was to be loved by the people, and he was working hard to fulfill his god-given role.

He looked at the banqueting table, starting to be laden with the pleasures which he and his guests would be enjoying. They would enjoy the food, but only he would know of the true and enduring pleasures which the night would bring. The awful Britannicus, loved by the Romans as the nephew of the great Germanicus and the son of the crippled and stuttering fool Claudius, the delight of the Senate who considered him a fine speaker and an excellent young man, soon would be writhing and wriggling on the floor; soon he would gasp for air and beg for water. And while he was in the throes of death, unloved and unnoticed by Nero's other guests, he would be ignored by everybody, because as Britannicus was dying, all eyes would be on Nero, their emperor; all ears would be listening to his godlike music and his divine voice, reveling in the brilliance of his words, thrilling to the harp and the lyre as he picked them up, one after the other, and trilled on notes which only the gods could hear. Oh! It would be a glorious night. And the delicious irony was so simple, yet so theatrical. For the last sound which Britannicus would hear upon this earth before the Shades took him and Charon the ferryman carried him over the Styx, would be the divine voice of Nero, his brother, his friend, his murderer!

The poisoner used by Agrippina to kill Claudius had given Nero a fine concoction. He'd tried on a couple of occasions to end the life of Britannicus, but the boy was too well guarded, and all his efforts had come to nothing; now he would have to resort to poison. But because Britannicus was so wary of his half-brother, special care had to be taken in administering the deadly drops. Again, Nero reviewed the evening in his mind, and felt a shudder of pleasure surge through his body as he rehearsed the carefully planned events which would terrify his mother and leave him without rivals to the empire.

His mother! Why did she always have to come into his dreams and spoil them? They had once been so close. When he became emperor, hadn't she taken him into her bed and made him her husband? Hadn't she insisted that he use her very own bed to entertain his men and women friends? Hadn't she supplied him with girls and boys to play with until all of his desires were completely satisfied?

But he had also been a good son. He had been just as considerate of her as she was of him in those early days of his rule. Hadn't he allowed her to listen to his speeches in the Senate, creating a special curtain for her to hide behind in a place where women were forbidden? Hadn't he allowed her to sit beside him when he received embassies from other countries? Hadn't he allowed the special minting of coins with their faces looking at each other to show the world that Rome was ruled by mother, as well as son? Didn't she often stay in his council chamber when Seneca and Burrus and his other advisors were discussing things? But that wasn't enough for her. No! She had to go and destroy everything because of her desire for equal power with the emperor. She wanted to make decisions and to command and control. She had forgotten that she was the mother and wife of the empire, and not the empire itself.

And what a fuss she'd made when Nero, advised by Seneca, had told her that she could no longer sit in on council meetings or go to the Senate, even in secret. It was then that he was able to see his mother properly for the first time, to see the woman she really was—a woman with little love for her son, just a love of the power that came with being the mother of the emperor.

As they drifted apart, Agrippina became vindictive and furtive and infinitely hurtful. She had even . . . Nero could hardly bear to think about what she'd said without a tear appearing on his cheek . . . it was the worst of all things, the most damaging and frightening and treasonous; for she had begun to support Britannicus in a claim for the purple, against her own son. How could any mother sacrifice her very own son for the son by another woman, a boy produced by a crippled and stuttering moron of a husband?

The slaves, standing around the walls of the banqueting hall in attendance on their emperor and master, suddenly heard him burst out laughing. It was a silly, high-pitched laugh. And they all knew enough about the emperor's moods to know that they mustn't respond, but must remain quiet and attentive.

They watched him as he stood from his couch, and again approached the banqueting table, which would soon groan under the weight of food and drink. And when the revelers eventually fell asleep or left to go to their beds, there would be plenty of food left over for the slaves and servants to enjoy their own feast.

On an upper level, watching the emperor from behind a screen, and wondering what his devious and perverted mind was planning, was Agrippina. She had been forced to leave the protection of her villa on the Bay of Neapolis, invited to this banquet by the emperor. There was no way she could refuse the invitation, not if she valued her life. She'd hoped that living so far away, she would be lost to Nero's mind.

But she knew enough about her son to know that nothing about her activities was lost to him. Even her support for Britannicus, supposedly a closely guarded secret known to only a few trusted senators, had somehow got back to him. She shuddered when she saw him, and wondered what the Fates had in store for her.

As evening fell, the guests for the banquet began to arrive. Agrippina had dressed very carefully. She had selected a red toga with gold trimming, cut very low to favor her breasts. In her hair were jewels given to her by Claudius, as well as a bronze comb brought back by him when he conquered Britain.

Agrippina was accorded the respect of the company as the mother of the emperor, and sat three seats away from him on the second divan couch. Farther round the banqueting table sat his friends and flunkies, his advisors Seneca and Burrus, Greek physicians and Egyptian astrologers, a couple of generals whose legions were camped on the hills outside Rome, as well as the usual number of senators, their wives and children, all looking particularly uncomfortable. At the bottom of the hall, facing Nero, was Britannicus, his sister Octavia, and his friend Titus, son of the great General Vespasian.

Nero was in a particularly good mood, telling and retelling stories of his exploits in the marketplace and the forum. But his laughter didn't manage to drown out the hideous music of musicians from some local tavern, who were singing bawdy songs simply not suitable for the emperor's home. It wasn't only Agrippina, but many other guests whose faces showed their disapproval of the vulgar words and the cacophonous strains.

When he returned from the vomitorium, Nero stood in the center of the room, and said in a loud voice, "Is anybody enjoying this music?"

Almost as one, the guests shouted that they thought it was awful. Stunned, the musicians and singers looked at the guests, and Nero said loudly, "Pack your things away, and leave this palace. Never return. You are to the god of music what shit is to a sandal. Now go."

Terrified, they grabbed whatever they could, and ran. One of the guests, a friend of Nero, said, "What a shame that there aren't any other musicians here tonight, Caesar. If only we could listen to the dulcet tones of the lyre, the beauty of the harp, the poetry of a well-turned phrase."

Another said loudly, "I wonder, Great Caesar, would you deign to play for us? Would you permit us mere mortals to hear your music?"

"No," said Nero, "no, after such a terrible performance, it wouldn't be right for me to perform. No, friends, we will dine in silence and appreciate the beauty of the song of the night birds and the evening music of the wind in the trees."

His friends shouted their sorrow and begged him to play, much to the mortification of the senators who knew what they were in for. Eventually, re-luctantly, Nero agreed to perform, and called for his harp and lyre which were stationed behind a nearby pillar.

As he stood in the center of the room, he said, "In order for me to play, you all must be relaxed. Wine for my guests," he shouted to the slaves. "Hot wine for the evening."

Ewers of hot wine were brought, and poured into cups. As he picked up his lyre, Nero looked carefully in Britannicus' direction. The boy's food taster picked up the cup, and sipped the wine. He nodded to Britannicus, who took it, and sipped it. Nero knew that Britannicus didn't like very hot drinks, and so the lad called for cold water to be poured into the cup. Trying not to shout for joy, Nero watched carefully as the poisoned water was poured. The emperor began to strum on his harp, and to sing a song he'd composed that morning about two shepherds in the hills who find a woman asleep in the fields, and how they trick her into thinking that they're gods and have their evil way with her.

He saw Britannicus sipping the cooler diluted wine, and then draining the entire cup. Nero sang louder as Britannicus put his cup down, and turned to Titus to discuss something with him. By the time Nero had come to the end of the eighth verse of his song, Britannicus was already mopping his brow and ex-cusing himself to Titus for feeling so unwell. The boy began to stand, but his legs were too weak, paralyzed, and incapable of moving him away from the table. He was now gasping audibly, interrupting Nero's song. Nero glanced at Agrip-pina who was looking in consternation at the sudden illness of her protégé.

Oh, the joy which surged through Nero's body as his rival tried to open his mouth wider in order to breathe, but his throat was constricting, just as the poi-soner Locusta said it would. He collapsed noisily onto the floor, again inter-rupting Nero in his singing. People stood to go to Britannicus' aid. At last, realizing that he was no longer the center of the room's attention, Nero stopped playing. Sullenly, angry that nobody was listening to his carefully composed words, he shouted, "Oh, he's just having a fit. He'll regain his voice and his body by the morning. Carry him to his room, and put him to bed. There are many more songs I have to sing for you on this most wonderful of nights."

And as the slaves carried out the dying body of Claudius' son and the guests reluctantly returned to their couches, Nero looked into the eyes of the one woman who hadn't moved; the one woman who knew precisely what had just happened.

The fear in Agrippina's eyes nearly made Nero weep for joy. And to his profound amusement, he felt the start of an erection growing beneath his toga.

CHAPTER NINE

58 AD—Londinium, the Temporary Quarters
of Decianus Catus

Vast as it was, the stench from the River Thames was hideous; he was told by
one of the Britons who lived close by that before the Romans came, the
mighty river had been a lovely, clean and joyous length of water, full of fish and
eels. But in the few years since the arrival of the Romans, it had turned into a
river like the Tiber, large, languid, dirty and as unappetizing as an imperial bath
after a feast. From time to time, bodies floated past, some of them animal, some
human. It was all he could do not to turn up his nose and leave the city. But it
had been decreed that this would be his residence, and so be it.

Decianus Catus, procurator of Britain, had put a strict time limit on his stay
in this distant outpost of the nurturing civilization he so loved. Other procurators,
especially those in provinces such as Lusitania and Syria, had made enough money
so that they would never need to work again. Of course, as a still relatively minor
knight of Rome, he enjoyed limited power to determine his own future, and the

post of procurator of Britain, purchased by him for an obscenely large payment to the emperor's advisor, Seneca, was still somewhat tenuous, but if he worked hard, and extracted sufficient taxes, he was assured of a more prestigious post, closer to Rome, on his next appointment. Gaul, maybe, or even an eastern province.

Londinium was a squalid, fetid little place. He'd wanted to make his home in the more established capital, Camulodunum, but the new governor, Quintus Veranius, had taken an instant dislike to him, and insisted that they should work in separate cities. So Decianus established his home on a hill overlooking the river, and had his servants and guards demolish the surrounding dirty little huts in which the Britons lived.

Sitting at his table covered in scrolls and demands for taxation, he viewed the young man standing opposite him. Still suspicious, and somewhat offended by the man's presumption in arriving without an escort, he decided to listen to him just in case he had something important to say.

He invited the young man to sit. Decianus had first met Cassus, son of Prasutagus, some years previously, when he'd come bleating to him about not being accorded respect by Aulus Didius Gallus. But Didius and Decianus were friends, and so he'd done nothing, other than turn the young man away. But like a family dog, Cassus had returned several months later with information he'd heard about the Trinovantes hiding stocks of grain which were due to the emperor, and which he'd managed to retrieve, even at the cost of ten of his soldiers. Next time he'd come, the boy had been arrogant, and made demands of Decianus, and so again, he'd been shown the door. Now the lad was here for a third time, and the real reason he'd come, the procurator knew from long experience with traitors, would slowly emerge as he grew comfortable in the Roman surroundings.

"Tell me again what Quintus Veranius said to you when you went to see him in Camulodunum," he asked gently.

The young man had begged for food when he arrived, saying he hadn't eaten properly since he'd begun his journey; so in deciding to feed him, Decianus was forced to watch him eat and listen to him at the same time. Finishing a bowl of chicken stew, and mopping up the juices with a crust of bread, Cassus said, "I informed the new governor what I told the previous governor three years ago.

I said that Boudica intended to raise an army against the Romans and that she's in league with the rebels." He stuffed more bread into his mouth, a globule of chicken stew dropping onto his tunic, which the boy didn't seem to notice. Decianus tried not to sneer, and waited until the young man continued. "But like Didius, this new governor just ignored me. Who does he think he is? I'm the son of the most important king of Britain, and he just ignores me. You must write to the emperor, and—"

"Please don't tell me what to do, Briton. Just tell me what Governor Quintus Veranius said to you."

"He thanked me for the information, and told me that he would consider it, but I knew from the look on his face that he wasn't interested. I hadn't even left the room, when he continued with his work. Why does Quintus Veranius treat me like a peasant? Doesn't he realize who I am? He had no right to ignore me and treat me with contempt."

Cassus took a drink of wine from a beaker, and complimented Decianus on his good table. Acknowledging the compliment, the procurator asked, "And your mother, the Lady Boadicea?"

"She's not my mother," Cassus shouted. "She married my father and she's a whore and a traitor."

Decianus eyed Cassus suspiciously. "A traitor? To whom?"

Cassus said swiftly, "To Rome. My father is a loyal servant of Rome. He loves the emperor and wants to work with Rome to make the emperor rich. But his wife is secretly working to stab him in the back. My father Prasutagus knows nothing of this. I heard her plans when she was speaking to one of her friends in a corridor of the house. She said that she was going to murder Prasutagus, and take control of the kingdom; then she was going to lead her army against you. She plans to murder every single Roman in Britain. It's against our Druid religion to have foreign feet on our soil, and that's why she went on her travels. She's receiving secret embassies from other kings and queens and she's plotting. All the while, she's plotting. You have to arrest her, and both of her daughters."

The young man was starting to bring the procurator useful information. If he could be managed, then perhaps Cassus was an ally that Decianus could use to find out where the rest of the Britons were hiding their caches of weaponry, where their food was hidden, and most importantly, where their gold, silver and tin was stored. So much wealth was hidden from the eyes of Rome; if only he could uncover it, he would become a hero, he would be wealthy, and he would become the most obvious candidate for a senatorial appointment.

Decianus stood from his desk, and walked around it. He put his arm around the young man's shoulders, and said softly, "It must have taken great courage for you to come and see me, especially after your information had been rejected by your father and by the governor of Britain—"

"I haven't told my father. He knows nothing, and he mustn't know anything."

Surprised, Decianus said, "But why haven't you informed your father? Surely he must be told in order to take action against this traitor of a wife."

"No!" shouted Cassus. "He mustn't be told. He mustn't know that I've told you anything. Do what I say, and take your troops, ride to the land of the Iceni, and kill her. Why can't you do something so simple?"

Decianus said softly, "I can, Cassus, and I will. But if I am to do you this favor, then in return, I will need something done for me. Unlike governors, procurators have a much more subtle form of power. We don't control huge armies, but we're the real power behind the imperial throne. And while ever we are responsible for the finances of an imperial province, it's we procurators who make the important decisions. Oh, certainly the governor appears to those who don't understand these things to hold the reins of office, but men like you and me know who is really in charge."

"And you speak directly to the emperor?" asked Cassus.

"Of course; and more importantly, I speak directly to the emperor's advisor, Seneca, who is a dear and valued friend. You might say, Cassus, that the emperor is the most important man in the world, Seneca is the next most important, and I am the third in line. So even though I might appear to defer to the governor in terms of the ruling of Britain, all defer to me in terms of my importance in the empire of Rome. Which is why, Cassus, I want you to work for me. Because a man of your intelligence needs the world as a stage, and not a small nation on its northern borders. If you work hard and intelligently for me, Cassus, I will take you to the very top of the Roman Empire. Why, who knows, in time, you could be dining with the emperor himself. Now, does that excite you?"

Decianus fought a smile as he saw a leer spread over the young man's lips.

"I can help you, Procurator. I'm not like most Britons. I've been to Rome," said Cassus, "where I was treated like a visiting king. They said to me that I might return whenever I want, and that I might be given an audience with the emperor himself."

Cassus looked at Decianus to see the procurator's reaction. The older man nodded and smiled. "All good things happen for a reason, Cassus. And it is a good thing that you've come to see me."

58 AD—The Palace of the Emperor Nero

Why had he been sent for? And why had he been sent to the balcony overlooking the banqueting hall? What on earth could Seneca want with him? His mind was reeling with questions. And if there was one thing which General of the Armies of Africa Gaius Suetonius Paulinus hated more than anything else, it was questions to which he didn't know the answers.

Standing tall and martial in his soldier's uniform, the prematurely gray-haired general, skin taut and leathery from a lifetime of fighting in hot lands, had been resting in his villa in the Tuscan hills when an order came from Seneca to travel immediately to Rome in order to discuss certain military matters.

He'd arrived the previous day and had been put into a small but comfortable room on the northern wing of the palace. He'd waited during the whole of that day, and the following morning, but no word had come either from Seneca or Nero that they even knew he was in the palace. If he wasn't granted an interview by the afternoon, he'd pack his bag and ride north back to his home. Hating Rome and its politics at the best of times, stories he'd heard about what was happening in the capital told him that this wasn't a moment to be in the center of things. The growing evil and debauchery of Rome were beginning to infest the whole of the empire, and he wanted nothing to do with it.

Happiest when he was on campaign with his army, or at home in Tuscany on his estates with his wife and children, Suetonius resented this intrusion into his private time. He had been four years on campaign without seeing his son or daughters. They had grown so much, and he desperately wanted to be with them. He had been in the middle of a conversation with his oldest daughter concerning a young man of lower rank who wanted to marry her when the call from Rome came. In the middle of his precious time with his family, a detachment of armed men suddenly arrived, protecting an imperial courier who proffered a note to Suetonius, and within the hour, he was riding south to Rome surrounded by mean-looking and somewhat menacing German Praetorian Guards, his petrified wife and children looking on as he descended the hill riding toward the Via Cassia.

Knowing as much about Rome as he did, Suetonius realized that the sudden arrival of an armed guard meant that for some reason, for something he'd done or not done, at the erratic will of the emperor, his life was to be ended. That he could live with, so to speak, but what really infuriated him was that he hadn't been given the opportunity to bid farewell to his family, or seek solace from his gods. What kind of an empire was it which failed to allow a man about to go to his death to make peace with the world he was about to leave?

But Suetonius was wrong, and he entered the city he most detested being treated with respect by the guards on the northern gate, and hailed by people in the streets whom he had never seen before. By the time he reached Nero's palace, Suetonius had no idea why he had been summoned. The letter itself was enigmatic, asking him to come to Rome for consultations. Well, he would soon find out whether he would hear the emperor's voice, or feel his sword.

Whenever he was in Rome—as rarely as possible—he liked to enjoy the buildings and the theater, but beneath the magnificent edifices with their beautiful façades and their graceful columns and the ornate rooms with their mosaics and frescoes lay a rotten heart. The Senate was putrid and corrupt with wealthy timeservers having no love of the empire or the people, but only concerned with increasing their power and influence; the marketplace was riddled with thieves and scoundrels robbing citizens blind; the inns and taverns and brothels were hotbeds of vice and evil; and sexual perversions seemed to infest everywhere.

From everything he'd heard, the licentiousness was led by the emperor himself, and even the temples to the gods had become amoral places, with the priests and priestesses ignoring the demands of their deities, and bowing instead to the wishes of the rich and powerful.

But the sacrilege was compounded when he realized, in the face of holiness, decency and morality, that even the awful Claudius, probably the most effete of all emperors, had now been made into a god and was to be worshipped along with other mortals raised up into the divine pantheon.

Suetonius always followed the maxim that a rotting fish began to stink from its head. When he'd taken control of his legions in the north of Africa, he'd found that the military leadership had become soft and lazy; women infested the thoughts of the commanders; prostitutes were regular visitors to the camp; North African tradesmen were buying swords and spears from soldiers, who then lied and reported them lost to their quartermasters.

Suetonius soon cleared out the rottenness and immorality he'd found on his return to his legions. First, he'd sent half of the commanders back to Rome in disgrace, ordering the forfeiture of their year's salary. Then he'd elevated clever and brave young men who had been prevented from gaining their deserved status. And finally, to drive home the need for honesty and morality within the army, he'd crucified a few local miscreants, and then made an example to every rank by publicly executing a particularly corrupt Syrian centurion. As the man slowly and publicly died on the cross, fear had surged throughout the entire army, and within days, he had not only regained control, but within a month had trained his exhausted men well enough to be the first Roman legion to climb the fearsome Atlas Mountains.

Now he was in Rome, the very heart of the evil which was undermining the empire, and he was standing around, gazing on a sexually immoral and corrupt palace, wondering what in the name of the gods he was doing here.

"My dear General," said a voice behind him from a man who had entered the balcony quietly. "My sincerest apologies for keeping you waiting. I am Seneca, the advisor to the emperor. I pay you respects and greetings."

"Respects? I'll accept your greetings, sir, but not your respects. You treat me with no respect when you demand my attendance and then keep me waiting for nearly two days before acknowledging my presence."

Taken aback, not having been spoken to in that manner since he'd returned to Rome, Seneca said, "Perhaps the General will come with me and we can eat and drink before we discuss the business for which I've asked you to travel to Rome. And as for not attending on you since your arrival, General, it's simply because of the pressures of the work I do. I have the entire weight of the empire on my shoulders, and there are many matters to which I have to give my person. My lack of courtesy was not intended, and I do apologize."

Silently, General Suetonius followed Seneca out of the balcony room overlooking the banqueting hall, and eventually reached the advisor's apartments. Compared to those which he'd been allotted, these were sumptuous: vast rooms with huge ceilings, delicate gauze curtains wafting in breezes from the nearby Tiber, ornate carvings from many different parts of the empire, colorful wall hangings decorating every room, and intricate mosaics on the floor.

Noticing the soldier looking at the décor, Seneca said, "It isn't my choice. I am a devotee and follower of the philosophies of Zeno the Stoic. We practice the values of modesty rather than excess. We don't appreciate the expenditure of vast sums of money for the glorification of mankind, but rather on improving the behavior of one man toward another. These apartments once belonged to the Empress Julia, wife of Tiberius, daughter of Julius Caesar; in respect for Julius, I have sought not to redecorate them."

The dour soldier shrugged. "So, Seneca, why have you brought me here? I have duties to my wife and family."

"Straight to the point, General! I have been told that you don't waste time in unnecessary talk. Tell me, what do you know of Britain?"

"A land of snow and mists and evil weather, with an even more evil people who live there. Why?"

"What do you know of our current disposition of forces?" asked Seneca.

"Why don't you just tell me why you want to see me, instead of questioning my knowledge? What I know or don't know about Britain is not the reason you've brought me here. You want something from me. Whether I know about the workings of Britain has nothing to do with my ability to perform the task you want."

Seneca could barely restrain himself from smiling. Why couldn't all conversations in Rome be like this one? Direct and without the pretence and dangers of hidden meanings. "Rome has good relationships with many of the kings and queens of Britain, but there are still many problems with a continuous and seemingly never-ending revolt in the west and north. We also have terrible problems with the Druid priests . . . but most especially, we are being crippled by the cost of keeping so many of our legions there. We must reduce the expenditure of maintaining such huge forces in a land which is valuable, but difficult to control. When he was alive, the Emperor Claudius lent forty million sesterces to the Iceni, one of the kingdoms of Britain, to assist them in paying their tributes. I have decided that, for reasons of which I will inform you in great secrecy, I am going to issue instructions for the return of that money. You see, General, the Emperor Nero is considering withdrawing from Britain and reducing the size of our empire, because—"

"What! Who would be so stupid as to advise the emperor to make that decision? No, more than stupid . . . if that's your advice, Seneca, then it must rank as treasonous. Your forty million sesterces can go to Hades. If we reduce the size of the empire at its margins, the word will spread like a summer fire to every province and region in the entire world. There'll be uprisings in Africa, in Judea, in Syria and everywhere else. The emperor holds these lands in trust for the Roman people. Surely he wouldn't be so naïve as to follow that course of action. He must realize that doing so would make him a traitor to the memory of Germanicus and Augustus and all those who lived and died to bring civilization to the barbarians."

Horrified, Seneca looked around to ensure that no slave or servant was in the room. "Please, General, have a care for whom you criticize. Nobody speaks of the emperor in that manner."

Suetonius shrugged. "I say things as I see them. If Rome can no longer bear honesty from a man who has devoted his life to her security and splendor, then perhaps Rome is not the place for me."

"General," said Seneca, "there's little wrong with you, and a lot wrong with Rome. My colleague, your good friend General Burrus, and I are trying to return to the glory of the time when Augustus ruled. But in the meantime, we must clean out the Augean stable which this city has become. Perhaps with your help—"

Suetonius shook his head. "No! I'll give you no help in your work. I'll leave that to philosophers and men of words. Me? I'm just a soldier. And as a soldier, I say that to abandon Britain is a very bad decision."

Seneca continued in a lower tone of voice. "Whether we abandon it or not, we currently have General Quintus Veranius as our governor in Britain, and he's—"

"An excellent man. He deserves the rapid promotion he's been given. His campaigns on the eastern front in Lycia and Pamphylia were brilliant. If any man can defeat the Britons, it's Veranius."

"Unfortunately, the governor has been taken ill, and it seems his condition is serious. The word is that he will not live out the month."

"That's a shame. Rome can't afford to lose men of his caliber."

"Which brings me to what I need to discuss with you," said Seneca.

"You want me to replace him," said Suetonius.

Seneca was getting used to the man's directness. But he decided to teach him a bit of diplomacy, despite his protestations. "You are one of a number of choices the emperor and I are considering, General. We are fortunate to have many good soldiers in our empire."

Again, Suetonius shrugged. "When you've made your choice, let me know. In the meantime, I will return to my villa and continue to run my estates."

The general stood, but an exasperated Seneca begged him to remain. "The emperor has expressed a desire to meet with you. He commands you to join him at the banquet tonight. He says that he has composed a special song in honor of your victories in Africa."

Suetonius smiled for the first time since entering the room. "If my commander desires my presence, I shall be there. And I shall dine with the emperor. But that's all I will be doing. If the emperor wants anything more from me other than my professionalism, he'll be disappointed. So be aware, philosopher, that I shall not be part of the revels; nor shall my name become a plaything which is abused in the inns and taverns of this city," he said, bowing and leaving the room.

Seneca watched him retreat. With his abilities in mountain warfare, proven in the Atlas Mountains of Mauretania, Suetonius should have no problems in eliminating the rebels in Wales and the hills of the northwest of that cold and inhospitable land. Once they were quashed, then all of Britain would at last be at peace. Instead of active legions being stationed there costing a fortune, more and more garrisons of retired legionaries would be established. There was already one at Camulodunum where the veterans were building some simple shrine to the god Claudius; and there was another at Londinium on the banks of the Thames which was rapidly growing as a trading port because it was a river with two tides a day and therefore excellent for carrying materials to and fro.

Seneca intended to establish others. The veterans of the army and their families would be given free land to farm in return for forfeiting the money they would otherwise have been given for their pensions. That would enable the emperor to withdraw most of the army, populate Britain with tough old Roman veterans to defend the emperor's possessions, and reduce the vast sums which were paid to the former soldiers. It was a clever, simple and elegant formula for the future. And most urgent of all was to reclaim the huge sums of money which had been loaned to the Britons when Claudius had conquered the land. Rome desperately needed these moneys. Seneca smiled to himself as he thought of the principal returning to his personal coffers to add to the interest he had been receiving for many years. Since his return from exile, he had lent money out to nations on the periphery of the empire at embarrassingly high interest rates, and had earned a fortune. Rumor had it that he was the richest man in Rome.

Traditional Roman law didn't permit a citizen to lend money to another citizen at a rate of interest, but Seneca was the first to decide that the law said nothing about lending to the barbarians to enable them to pay their tributes and taxes, or to buy the foodstuffs they needed, or to trade with Rome. Nobody knew that the money Claudius lent to the Britons had come from Seneca's personal coffers. And when the forty million sesterces would be returned, with ten million interest, then he would rank not only as one of richest, but also one of the most powerful men in the empire.

But everything depended on quelling the uprising, and if anybody could do it, it was this tough-talking soldier who wanted nothing to do with Rome. Yes, he thought, Suetonius was an excellent choice to rule Britain . . . and the gods help any Briton who rose against him.

58 AD—The Lands of the Iceni in Britain

Gray with worry, unsure how to tell his wife, King Prasutagus wandered alone in his orchard, gazing at the bounty of nature, pondering what to do next. He walked from apple tree to apple tree, admiring the rosy hues of the maturing fruit, clustered in bunches, ripe with expectation, full with juice and flavor. It was the Romans who had taught him how to cluster trees together into an orchard. Before they came, the Britons had gathered fruit from wherever the trees had grown; but the economy of bringing them all together, so that at harvest time the slaves didn't have to walk so far, was eminently sensible. The Romans' expertise at growing food and wine was extraordinary, and the skills which they'd taught him and his servants would ensure that more food grew from the same amount of land than in any previous year. The Romans had even planted vines in fields from ancient grape stock which were now starting to grow and would soon make wine.

The Romans had so much to teach the people of Britain. Their roads were long and straight, and made traveling not just much easier, but far safer; their schools were introducing a curriculum for boys and girls to learn Latin and grammar and mathematics and philosophy, things which neither Prasutagus nor Boudica could understand, yet which Camorra and Tasca seemed to comprehend easily. Britons could learn so much from Rome!

But Rome could also learn much from the ancient wisdoms of the Britons.

British craftsmen and women made far finer and better jewelry and weaponry than Romans, and the new port at Londinium on the banks of the Thames was crowded with Roman merchants eager to purchase as much as Britain could manufacture. Britons could also teach their knowledge of the stars and the times of the year, knowledge of the seasons and when heavenly events were taking place. If only the Romans weren't trying to kill all the Druid priests, they could learn a lot more.

There was so much that each nation could contribute to the other. He sighed. Looking down, he noticed an apple which had recently fallen onto the orchard ground, and stooped to pick it up. It was still full and moist from the tree, yet there was a greenness in its skin, telling Prasutagus that the spirits of the tree hadn't yet decided to allow the ripe apple to fall, knowing that it needed a few more days to ripen in the sunshine. Some malign spirit must have entered the apple. He examined it and saw the cause of its demise; a tiny hole had been burrowed in the skin. A wasp or some other insect had landed on the ripening fruit, laid its eggs inside the apple, and flown away. Now the inside of the apple was being eaten by worms. Rapidly, the rich and lustrous fruit, moist with potential, was becoming rotten and putrid with dankness and decay from within.

It was the story of Britain. A rich and rosy land, fresh and open and honest, peopled with strong and hale men and women, had been invaded by Rome, and now corruption and rottenness were everywhere. Instead of sharing, there was avarice and greed.

Yes, Prasutagus and Boudica had grown wealthy from their trade, but the Romans were building towns on British land, worshipping Roman gods, violating British women and girls, destroying Britain's priesthood and the right of Britons to worship Druid gods, forcing her soldiers into an ever-shrinking area in Wales and now Anglesea where only the gods could save them. And for years, Prasutagus had closed his eyes to the reality of what was happening, happy to sup with the Romans, dress like a Roman, speak and even think like a Roman.

Even his adopted son, Cassus, was turning against him. But what could he do? Prasutagus had no concern for any danger Cassus might pose to him or his daughters while he was alive, but when Cassus learned of the contents of the will that Prasutagus was intent on making, the erratic and ominous young man had the potential to turn very nasty. Why had Cassus grown from such a loving and gentle boy into such a surly and ungrateful young man? Prasutagus would never understand the ways of youth.

But for now, Cassus was the least of his troubles. He looked around the orchard for somewhere to sit, and decided upon the shade of a tree. He looked at the scroll in his hands, and shuddered in disgust as he tried to come to terms with the way in which his trust in Rome had been so badly abused. He unrolled the vellum scroll, and reread the demand made in the name of the Emperor Nero for the return of forty million sesterces, with ten million sesterces of interest, money to be repaid immediately and without thought to the consequences; money which he'd been forced to borrow from Claudius because the Roman army had stolen so much food; money which had to be paid in vast tributes to the glory of an emperor he was forced to call his own. The taxes he was charged had denuded his coffers and he wasn't able to support his people with their needs for grain and oats and other foodstuffs to keep them alive through the winter without borrowing such a vast sum from the emperor; and now the emperor wanted his money back.

How was he going to pay? From where was he going to find such a fortune when every year half of the money he and Boudica earned was lost on tributes and taxes to Rome? He could refuse, and then the new governor Suetonius would send a massive army and lay waste to his land. He could go to Rome and beg for understanding, but last night, he was told by Abram the Jew that Nero's reign, despite its early promise, was going the same way as that of Tiberius and Caligula and Claudius. He could pay a tenth, and tell the Romans that more would follow shortly, in the hope that Rome might look elsewhere or might even forget!

But he knew better than most that none of these were options. Boudica would have to be told, and then all hell would break loose. There were times when he'd rather face a Roman army alone and defenseless, than face the wrath of his wife when he was being an apologist for the ways of the Romans.

When they had first been married, she had grudgingly accepted her role as queen of a client nation of Rome. The money they earned, the status they had been given, the education which Rome had provided for Camorra and Tasca, the houses they had been provided, all pleased her greatly. She appeared to revel in the standing she enjoyed in the eyes of the Roman veterans and their ladies from nearby Camulodunum.

But things changed three years ago when she returned from her progress around Britain. She had been away for the better part of half a year, and when she regaled Prasutagus with her adventures, it became very obvious to him that her regard for Rome seemed to have diminished to a point nearing contempt.

She reveled when she told Prasutagus of all the wondrous sights she'd seen, the sacred places she'd visited, the agreements and treaties she'd arranged with other kings and queens, and especially her relationship with Queen Cartimandua of the Brigantes. But her joy evaporated when she told him of the rapacity of the Romans. The Iceni were in a better position than all of Britain except for the Brigantes. Rome, for some reason, seemed to pay greater regard to these two kingdoms than to all of the others, even those who were willing clients. For in other kingdoms, the Romans were little more than an evil occupying force, and reports of rape and violence by the soldiers against innocent Britons were widespread.

Since Boudica had returned, her relations with the local Romans had cooled considerably, and often during his conversations with her in bed at night, she would tell him that she intended to diminish her relationship even further, and perhaps to write to the emperor and complain about the treatment her people were receiving. Always cautious of the effects such action might have on a power such as Rome, Prasutagus managed to persuade her to remain quiet until the time was more apposite.

Grasping the scroll tightly, he wondered whether now was the appropriate time to stand up to Rome and— A sharp and vicious pain in his chest caused Prasutagus to shout out aloud in shock. It felt as if a horse were sitting on his body. Barely able to breathe, he fell to the ground, legs kicking in spasms, clutching his chest. It was the grip again. His mind reeled at the suddenness and intensity of it this time. His shortness of breath, the unbearable pain, the ache beneath his arm, all terrified him. What was happening to his body, once so fit and strong? He lay stretched out on the orchard floor, thankful that nobody could see their great king in such distress, and allowed the pain to go, as it always did.

When he had the pain under control and could again breathe without gasping, he slowly walked back to his villa. He had seen many older men in this pain, and knew that soon the gods would take him and he would be no more. But before he died, he had to do one thing to ensure that his beautiful and wonderful wife and his beauteous daughters were safe from Rome. As he slowly and painfully walked back to his villa, he felt increasingly confident that his action would protect them from the emperor—but would it protect them from Cassus?

Abram the Jew looked at the king in consternation. Trained as a physician in Alexandria, but preferring the life of a traveling merchant, Abram knew that the man's gray skin and blue tinge around the mouth presaged his imminent death. And the king knew it, too, because of his question.

"Will you?"

"Of course, Majesty. I still don't understand why."

"Because if the will is kept here, then Boudica will find it after my death and destroy it. That will be disastrous to her and my daughters. Abram, my friend, you know Boudica. You know how she'll react when she learns of my desires."

The old Jew smiled and nodded. "Very well, Prasutagus, I'll take the will to Camulodunum. But I still fail to understand why you're following this course of action."

"Then you fail to understand Boudica."

He smiled again, and after a moment, asked, "When are you going to tell Boudica about the forty million sesterces?"

Rubbing his chest and underneath his arms, which still ached, Prasutagus said softly, "I will take her into a distant field, tie her arms and legs to stakes buried in the ground, retreat to another field, and then shout the news at her from a distance."

Abram laughed. "I fear, Majesty, that a thousand fields won't be far enough to guarantee your safety."

Draining his cup of wine, which seemed to ease the pain he was feeling, Prasutagus signed his will with a flourish, and handed the duck feather over to Abram, who signed as witness. Then he melted wax into a bowl, sealed the scroll with his ring, and rolled it up in the way of the Romans, sealing it again over the join. Handing it to Abram, Prasutagus said softly, "This is the way it must be."

Abram nodded, and accepted the scroll. "I will leave for Camulodunum in the morning. What instructions do you want me to give to the garrison commander?"

"That when he learns of my death, he is to ride here and take half of everything to give to Nero, regardless of Boudica's protestations. Tell him to bring with him a force of men."

Abram shook his head. "You know that's not what I mean."

Prasutagus sighed. "That's something which Boudica will have to come to terms with. I shall write a letter to Camorra, explaining things. Maybe she'll have the power to tell Boudica."

"But why can't you tell the queen yourself, Prasutagus? Why leave it to a Roman to inform her? Or a daughter? Surely any husband—"

"It's not the husband, old friend. It's the wife. Can you imagine if I told Boudica what is contained in my will? She'd skewer me from head to tail. Nobody, regardless of how brave they are, would have the courage to tell her."

59 AD—En Route to the Island of Anglesea (Mona)

General Suetonius knew of the complaints, and he wasn't interested. If the men couldn't march twenty-five miles a day, they were of no use to him. His African legions marched that far through the loose sands of the deserts, much more difficult terrain than this. Here the men were marching on green fields and solid roads. If anything, they should be marching farther!

Suetonius had heard stories, though he didn't know whether or not they were true, of black men in the south of Africa, beyond the impenetrable jungles, who spent their lives naked, and who were the fiercest warriors on the face of the earth. It was said that these men formed armies of tens of thousands of warriors which could run—run, mind you—fifty miles in a day, and then immediately fight a battle.

Yet his so-called battle-hardened troops were sprawled out on hillsides and underneath the leather of their tents at the end of the day looking as though they'd drowned in the sea, too exhausted to eat and drink. It had taken him a month to toughen up his African army. It would take him longer to toughen up these troops, fresh from the vineyards and villages of Gaul.

And these were dangerous lands, even more dangerous than in Africa. There, in the hot and dusty deserts, he could post a patrol and they would warn him of an enemy long before it was close enough for battle; but Britain was a land of mists and forests and hills and caves where the enemy hid and conducted raids as swift as lightning. They had marched westward and then north into the land of the Silures, where they had already engaged in a number of pitched battles with insurgents; quelling these rebels, they marched in close file north and west into the deadly land of the Ordovicii, where the former rebel leader Caratacus had caused terrible trouble for the army. Here they were suffering terribly from pinpricks. Every night, a few guards or soldiers who were drunk, or those who wandered into the dark away from the fires, were found dead in the morning with their throats cut. Some had their heads cut from their bodies, which he was told was the way of the Druids. The men were utterly demoralized, as downcast as the army of Caligula on the shores of Gaul, which had refused to cross the sea to Britain because of the fearsome reputation of the Druids.

What made matters so much worse wasn't the numbers of men he was losing, but the fact that when he sent out punitive parties to round the devils up or even to find them, they appeared to have disappeared into the air. The hills and cliffs surrounding them were riddled with caves, and it would have taken years to search every cave to find the killers. So he issued orders that every man was to take responsibility for a fellow soldier, and never let the man out of his sight; all men who went to the latrines at the edge of the encampment must go with three others and each must have lighted brands; no man was to leave the protection or light of a fire without permission from a senior officer; all men were to sleep under leather, and each tent was to be guarded throughout the night, the soldiers taking three-hour shifts. Further, ditches filled with wood and dry straw were to be dug around every campsite and the wood lit so that the perimeter of the camp was aflame. All his instructions were carried out to the letter; yet still headless men were found the following morning.

How wrong he'd been when he'd first arrived. Then, he thought the situation would be easy to administer and control. Veranius had begun to do an excellent job in continuing the task of clearing up the resistance to Roman rule, but had been taken ill and died; the last words on his soldier's lips were that if he had another two years, he could have delivered all Britain to the emperor—which was precisely what Suetonius intended to do.

Show the Britons that the might of Rome was unstoppable, and they'd go to water. Bring sufficient force to bear, show utter mercilessness in gaining victory, and resistance would be crushed. Show clemency and leniency in the Roman victory to all but the leaders of the rebellion, and he would win the love and affection of the British peoples.

But first he had to crush the strengthening resistance in Wales and eliminate the Druids who had gathered in huge numbers on the distant island of Mona, called by the Druids Anglesea, sending messages of encouragement and blessings to the rebel commanders in their caves and hideouts. In Londinium and Camulodunum, talking to his generals and senior commanders, it had all sounded as if the war would be over within the year. The rebels were being concentrated into an increasingly small area; more and more British people in the east and north were accepting Rome as the ruler of their lands, and were actually making weapons and armaments for them; the Druids were nowhere to be seen in the conquered parts of the land, and so their influence was waning. And Suetonius had even written to the emperor that his predecessor Veranius had done a commendable job in the short time that the greatly mourned soldier had been governor of Britain.

But all of that was discussed in the safety and ease of his forts and camps in

the east. Now that he was leading a dispirited army through the wilds of an un-
tamed land, full of thick forests and towering cliffs, the practice of defeating the
British was looking very different to the theory. And surveying the thousands of
exhausted men under his command, he wondered whether or not he'd have the
power to do the job Nero had commissioned him to do. Failure would not only
end his career, but with Nero's current erratic disposition, it could very well end
his life.

Drinking his cup of apple juice, recommended to him by an equestrian, he
pondered how he was going to get the men to march harder and faster without
inviting a revolt. Punishment would only make them resentful, and they'd drag
their feet even more. Appealing to their patriotism would be ridiculed, as they
were overdue for leave anyway and instead of being sent home from Gaul had
been sent north across the sea. But worse was that Britain was considered, along
with Germania, a dreadful posting. Word of the human sacrifices of the Druids
was on everybody's lips. And now that headless Roman soldiers were being discovered every morning, morale was the lowest Suetonius had ever experienced in
a Roman army.

So he decided to resort to incentive. He'd once tried offering an incentive in
North Africa, and the results had been excellent; however, those troops weren't
demoralized. These were! And an incentive offered which didn't work would
make matters worse. But it was a risk he decided to take.

Calling for his amanuensis, he dictated a letter to be read out by every centurion. Those who couldn't read would be offered assistance by their commanding officer. The incentive was simple and dramatic. General Suetonius
would ride ahead of the army, and select a campsite for the night. One hundred
sesterces would be paid to every soldier in the *centuria* which was first to arrive
at the designated campsite. And this reward would be offered every day. The
general smiled to himself, because if he knew anything about Roman soldiers,
and he thought he knew a lot, it would add five or more miles a day to their
progress.

He prayed to his personal god, Mars, that the incentive would work. For if
it did, then he would surprise the Druids on the island of Mona by arriving

days before they anticipated his appearance, and kill them all along with their families. Once their priests were gone, the rebel Britons would be so demoralized that all fight would leave them.

He finished off his apple juice, and ordered a cup of wine to be poured. He'd brought the wine from Rome; it had been a farewell present from the emperor. Suetonius shuddered when he thought of his one and only meeting with Nero. He shook his head, and wondered why the emperor's mother hadn't drowned the ugly, smelly youth at birth.

59 AD—Baiae, the Bay of Neapolis

Anicetus, commander of the imperial fleet in the Bay of Neapolis, and onetime tutor to Nero, had anticipated the emperor's visit with almost unbridled enthusiasm. He knew he was a good commander, liked by his men, but until he'd proven himself in a great sea battle, he would be forgotten by the Senate and the emperor, and his glorious career, so promising at the start, would come to an untimely and unworthy end. There was no chance of his being remembered by being at sea, because virtually all battles these days were fought on land. The fleet seemed to be used only to fight pirates, or to transport men and equipment, or occasionally to protect the emperor when he went sailing along the coast. Not like in the great days of the Roman fleet, during the Punic Wars, when great naval battles had determined the fate of empires. He knew this when he accepted the sinecure, having been sidestepped and marginalized by Seneca.

So to remind the emperor of the existence of his former tutor and friend, Anicetus had read the signs, anticipated the emperor's desire to rid himself of Agrippina, and written a secret communication, delivered to Nero's private apartments by a woman whom both the commander and the emperor shared.

It was so simple, so elegant, so sophisticated. Agrippina would be put to sea in a boat which would collapse when she was far offshore. She would drown, and the whole of Rome would mourn and nobody would blame Nero. And in gratitude, Anicetus would be invited back into the palace and his life would return to its once-glorious position in the center of power, rather than telling ignorant sailors to scrape the barnacles off the bottoms of boats.

The date which Anicetus had suggested to the emperor was the festival of the goddess Minerva, which the fleet would celebrate off Misenum in the Bay of Neapolis. The emperor and all of his friends would spend the night at the noisy resort of Baiae, close to the fleet. Agrippina had been informed that the emperor would first dine with her in her villa overlooking the bay, and then she had been ordered to join her son at the festivities to the goddess. Gazing across the narrow stretch of water which separated his command ship from the mainland, Anicetus wondered what the emperor and Agrippina were discussing. He saw them in his mind, dining in private at her villa in Bauli very close by, talking about their former relationship, and where it had gone wrong. Oh, he'd give a thousand sesterces just to be a fly on the wall, listening to Nero explain why his mother had to travel to Baiae by ship, while he must go there by land.

Agrippina was nearly beside herself with relief. Nero, estranged for more than three years, had finally decided to become her son once more. Their dinner at her villa in Bauli had been sumptuous; her cooks had worked especially hard to ensure that the emperor ate everything which he most enjoyed. And they had relaxed afterward on couches set up on the balcony. The view was spectacular, looking over the water at the far distant cities of Pompeii and Herculaneum, the tendrils of their light illuminating the blackness of the sea as a radiance which seemed to dance in long filaments in the water. It was a clear, warm and still night, the very best which Rome's resorts, clustered around the Bay of Neapolis, had to offer.

Now that Nero had expressed his remorse and apologies for the way in which Agrippina had been excluded from power for these years, she determined that she would create an entire suite of rooms for him and his friends in her villa, to use whenever they wanted. It would be so much more private, so much more erotic, than the very public and gossip-ridden corridors of the palace in nearby Rome, or the brothels which he frequented.

Agrippina stepped gingerly onto the ship, helped down by her maid Acerronia, and she lay on a bunk while the captain set sail for the town of Baiae, ordering his rowers to pull the ship into the depths of the bay. She looked carefully onto the land, but it was too dark to see whether Nero's litter had left her home yet. She looked forward to seeing him later in the evening at Baiae, where they would pray together and then celebrate Minerva's festival. Maybe, just maybe, she would offer him her body, just like in the old days. Or if he had his own amusements, there were plenty of young men and women who would satisfy her sexual needs.

Deep out in the bay, Agrippina sat beneath the canopy of the ship, and lazily watched the lights of the shore gently glide past. Soon, she thought, they should be turning course and sailing back to land and into the harbor of Baiae. But a sudden light from shore, weaving back and forth, back and forth, like some warning sign about bad weather, caught her attention. And that was when she heard a splash, then a crack, and suddenly the roof of the boat shuddered. Acerronia looked up and screamed, diving across the room to protect her mistress from the ceiling which was falling onto them. In horror, Agrippina sank down into her couch as the roof of the boat collapsed, falling to within a hairsbreadth of her face. But by a miracle, the collapsing roof was supported by the arms of her couch.

"Murder, mistress!" screamed Acerronia. "Murder! They're trying to murder us!"

But Agrippina didn't properly understand what was happening. She struggled from under the collapsed roof, and saw the amazed look on the face of the oarsmen. At that moment she realized that somebody was trying to crush her to death. When the astonished rowers realized that she wasn't dead, they fell on one side of the ship in order to overbalance her so that she fell into the water.

Terrified, Agrippina launched herself into the water and struck out for the shore. It was a long swim, and she turned around, only to see the oarsmen pummeling Acerronia with hammers and mallets and poles. Agrippina, thanking the gods that she'd escaped, saw the sailors toss the dead body of her servant into the sea.

As she swam silently, so as to be lost in the night and invisible to the murderers on the ship, Agrippina's mind cleared. And then she realized with a sickening feeling that she had seen this event before. Nero himself had used the precise trick years earlier in the aquatic games, when he'd organize for gladiators to be surprised and attacked by animals who escaped from a collapsing ship. And now he was playing the same trick on his mother. Furious at the way she had been so easily deceived by his friendship and desire for reconciliation, she determined to swim to shore, and petition the Senate for his removal and imprisonment.

It took her an age, but Agrippina reached some rowing boats, and begged them to take her to shore. Eventually she found her way home, and when she was composed, she sent word to Nero that by divine intervention, she had been saved, begging him not to visit her because she was resting.

Immediately after she had sent the letter, she wrote a series of letters to senators, begging them to convene a meeting of the Senate so that they could address the question of Nero's fitness to reign. Yes, the Praetorian Guard would be a problem, but there were enough loyal soldiers near to Rome to deal with the Germans. Agrippina was beside herself with fury. Now, she thought, she would finally be avenged for the curse of giving birth to such an ungrateful boy.

When he received his mother's letter, Nero panicked at the news, and immediately sent for Anicetus. The naval commander was astonished to see his former pupil hiding underneath blankets in his bed, shaking with fear. The stench of urine suffused the room. It was like being in the nursery of a spoiled child.

Before Anicetus could say a word, Nero blubbered, "Friend, tutor, revered sailor," he began. "Your plan didn't work. My mother has escaped. Now I'm frightened . . . Anicetus, I've never been more terrified in all my life. Was it the gods who intervened? Will I be punished?"

"Great Caesar, nobody can harm your godlike person. The other gods, even great Jove and warlike Mars, drop to their knees when you enter a room. No, I always thought that the gods would play a trick on your mother by making her think that she's escaped death, only to be disappointed when certain death comes later. Nero, great emperor of the world, let me take a couple of sailors, rough and reliable men, and we'll go to your mother's villa, and there we'll ensure that this is the very last night your mother spends on this earth."

"Yes," Nero cried. "Yes, do that, friend, and I'll reward you with anything you want. But there must be no body found. Agrippina must be destroyed. She must be burned, cremated, with not a bone nor a hair left of her body. Nobody in Rome must ever be able to say that Nero, who loved his mother, had anything to do with her death. And I shall mourn her passing over the River Styx for a full year."

Anicetus smiled and bowed low. His troubles were now at an end. As he was leaving, Nero said softly, "You know, Anicetus, a year seems like an awfully long time to mourn."

Chapter Ten

60 AD—The Lands of the Iceni in Britain

All eyes were upon the queen—all eyes, except those of her daughters Camorra and Tasca, who were in their rooms, quietly weeping to themselves, being consoled by their friends and servants. Also noticeably absent was Cassus, who, the moment he was told of his stepfather's death, immediately removed himself to Londinium. But all others, from his slaves to his servants to his villagers to the leaders of his tribe, had come to pay tribute to Prasutagus. And everyone was looking at Boudica.

The moment she was informed of her husband's death, Boudica immediately removed all of her clothes, and walked naked from the house to wash in the sacred river to remove the stains of her previous life as the wife of a dead man.

On her return, shivering and wet, the hetman of the village laid oak leaves in her path and she was invited to pass beneath a canopy of preserved mistletoe leaves intertwined within branches of the poplar tree, a sign to all of the passing of a life and the continuation of those left behind. As Boudica emerged from the canopy of leaves and branches, the hetman asked all the men and women of the nearby village to join him in chanting paeans to the gods to grant her freedom and peace in her new life as a widow.

Her slaves rubbed her down with towels and then dressed her in a shroud of white cloth, the color of purity, of mortification, of death, which she would wear for seven days and seven nights. She would wear neither jewelry nor ornaments, and every morning and every night she would walk naked to the sacred river and immerse herself fully to wash away her own and her husband's sins.

The ritual was comforting, but all she really wanted to do was to weep, to howl at the light of the sun, to curse at the coldness of the moon and to grieve for the man who had made a woman from the girl; the man who had stood beside her when she wore a green wedding dress all those years ago and who had loved her from that day to the moment of his death.

Boudica wanted to shout to the world that Prasutagus was the best of men, a man who was gentle and loving as husband and father, but valiant and courageous as king and leader of the largest tribe in Britain, but custom and religion demanded of her that she remain silent about her love of Prasutagus. Instead she must abase herself in the cleansing waters of the river until all Prasutagus' and Boudica's sins had been washed away, and life could be renewed.

But the time for her personal grieving would come and go; the time for recollection of past years and past joys would present themselves when her official duties as widow and queen of her people had been satisfied. For now, though, she had to tell the assembly of her thoughts and give them her blessing. It was a huge crowd, all of them her subjects, her neighbors and her friends; also in the crowd were some slaves, some servants and many workers who had come from other tribes to share in the bounty of the people of the Iceni.

Standing in the warmth of the sun, Boudica thought for a moment of what she would say. Words came easily to her, but she had never been a widow, or a sole ruler, and she said a short prayer to the goddess Lagalla that her words would enter the minds of her people, and allow them that same assurance they had felt when they met and spoke with Prasutagus.

She looked into the eyes of her tribe as she stood on a stool, and spoke.

"My people, my friends. As you know, the great Prasutagus is dead. He died this morning. But in death, there is life. Life and hope. Were death the end of things, then what of our children and our grandchildren, who carry with them our spirit, as well as our hopes and dreams. Yes, Prasutagus is dead and as his body becomes dust, his soul will fly off to the land of the ancestors and he will be re-united with those whom we revere.

"Your king turned the catastrophe of the invasion of Rome seventeen years ago into prosperity for us all. What could have been a land at war became, under the wise rule of Prasutagus, a land in which you all live in peace. Prasutagus knew that fighting Rome would lead to our enslavement; learning to live with Rome would lead to wealth and safety. Many disagreed with him. I disagreed with him. But time is a great teacher, and in his understanding, we must now all see how wise were his ideas, and how far was his vision.

"Friends, I stand before you as queen of the Iceni. You all know me. I am not a queen for today, but for tomorrow and tomorrow. I will continue with Prasutagus' work. I will ensure that you remain safe in your homes; that your old and sick will be comforted; that your children will learn with the benefit of the Romans; that the fruits of your labor will be sold and you will profit. But most especially, friends, I will ensure that you will always be proud to call yourselves People of the Iceni, and in that, you will have dignity and respect. None of us here is a servant of Rome. All of us are friends of Rome. Now go to your homes and say prayers for Prasutagus. He is dead, but he lives on forever."

The last of her words drifted over the heads of the crowd, who listened dolefully to everything she had said. She stood on her stool, wondering whether her words had had the desired effect. And then some began to smile, then a few nodded and said words which showed they approved of her as their queen. And suddenly, without any prompting, two, then five, then all of the assembly of her people began to sing the traditional burial dirge of her tribe, a song which spoke of the journey from earth into the stars, of a full life ahead and the way in which Prasutagus would join with his ancestors and would look down upon them and ensure their welfare forevermore. Pleased, and without waiting for the song to end, Boudica stepped down and entered her villa, alone.

Prasutagus' death hadn't been unexpected. A few days earlier, Abram the Jew had visited them to sell a consignment of tin for their bronzeworkers which he had bought in the west of the country, and he had had a private word to Boudica about Prasutagus' illness. She, herself, had noticed for some time that her husband's movements had become slower, his breath more labored and his color grayer. The previous day, she had found him bent double, clutching the corner of a table to prevent himself from falling onto the floor. And this morning, when the slave brought him a hot cup of mint water, and had screamed in fear and panic to Boudica, who was downstairs eating the morning meal, she knew immediately what had happened, even before she ran up the steps.

Sending the distressed girl out of the room, Boudica stood over her dead husband's body for what seemed like an age in order to settle the raging emotions which threatened to overwhelm her. How was she going to manage without him? How would Camorra and Tasca, who loved him so dearly, fare without him? What problems would she encounter with Cassus now that the restraining hand of his father was gone?

But she had duties to perform, and so she closed his dead eyes, straightened his clothing, cleaned up the vomit drying on the side of his face, and said a silent prayer to the goddess Ankala to protect him on his journey to the stars where good men and women gather to watch the antics of those they leave behind.

As the morning gathered heat, people heard the news and began to arrive to pay their respects and to receive her blessing as their sole ruler. Some came with rye bread to enable Prasutagus to eat on his journey to the stars, some came with bottles of ale for him to drink, children came with dolls so that he would have companions on his voyage, and the elderly came with wreaths of flowers for Boudica to wear in her hair to tell the world that she was now a widow. All that night, and all the following morning, men and women, boys and girls, gathered at her door and pressed gifts into her hand for Prasutagus' journey to the heavens, as well as for herself and her daughters.

It was not until late in the night that she was at last alone, and went to her bed. The servant had cleaned up the room from Prasutagus' illness, but she wasn't used to sleeping alone. She tossed and turned all night, occasionally waking up realizing that she was crying. Twice, Camorra and Tasca came into her bed to be comforted; twice, she'd carried the two sleeping children back, and tried to return to sleep.

In the morning, exhausted from such a dreadful night, she rose, ate, and realized with a shock that this was her first meal alone since she had been a girl about to marry. Every morning, she'd broken the night's fast by eating with Prasutagus. And when she and Camorra had traveled throughout Britain, she had broken the fast with her daughter.

But this wasn't just her first day of eating alone. It was also the first true day of her reign as queen of the Iceni, her first day of ruling alone. The enormity of what had happened made her gasp. She would have to decide things alone, make life and death judgments alone, defend and advance her people alone, order and instruct everyone alone, and run the entire tribe alone and unhelped. To whom could she turn? Camorra and Tasca were still little more than girls; Cassus was her enemy. And her helpmate for half her life, Prasutagus, was no longer beside her.

She was suddenly overcome by panic. Whenever she had needed to make a decision, she always sought Prasutagus' opinion. Now he was gone, and these decisions would begin and end with her. But what of areas of their lives in which she'd played no part? What of paying a good price when a merchant brought timber or tin or copper for sale? What about trading with the Romans when they tried to tell her that the silver or lead she was extracting was of poor quality, and they demanded that she reduce the price? How would she manage without Prasutagus by her side?

Deep in thought, listlessly spooning oats into her mouth, she was disturbed by the sound of horses. She listened, and realized that it wasn't just one or a couple of riders, but that a lot of riders had suddenly galloped into the area. She went outside, and saw that a detachment of Romans, dusty from a hard ride, had descended on her home. She recognized the man at the head of the column; it was Marcus Vitellus Publicus, commander of the fort of veterans at Camulodunum. She and Prasutagus had visited him on a number of occasions. He was honest and decent, and treated them as friends, despite the fact that he was a retired commander, and they were the king and queen of Britain's largest tribe. No doubt he had come to pay his respects, but all she wanted was to be left alone.

"Marcus Vitellus Publicus bids greetings to Boadicea, and on behalf of the emperor wishes you to know the depth of sorrow he feels for the loss of such a fine man as Prasutagus."

She bowed slightly, and responded, "Boudica, queen of the Iceni, thanks Marcus Vitellus, and his emperor. Would you and your men like refreshment after your ride?"

He shook his head, and dismounted from his horse. "Thank you, Boadicea, but no. I am here on official business."

Taking a vellum scroll out of the saddlebag, he handed it to Boudica. "Boadicea, this is your husband's will. He deposited it with me a few days ago. His instruction was to bring it to you when I received news of his death. This is a sad day for me, and it will be even sadder for you, my friend. Lady, take your husband's wishes."

She frowned and accepted the scroll. Why in the name of all the gods had Prasutagus given his will to the Romans? She hadn't even thought of his will since she'd discovered his body the previous day. It was a mystery.

"I thank you, Roman, for bringing this to me. Now I must ask you to leave, because I am in mourning, and I would like to read this will alone."

He sighed. "Boadicea, I've known you for some time, and have come to respect you. As a mark of that respect, I beg of you to read this will now, in front of me. I know in general terms what are its contents, and you will need the support of a friend, even a Roman friend, when you see what Prasutagus has determined."

"But this will is sealed. How can you—"

"I know. The man who brought it to me told me of what it contains. Please, Boadicea, read the will."

Mystified, Boudica broke the wax seal and unrolled the vellum. It was written in Prasutagus' beautiful hand, the writing careful and precise. She read the document to herself.

To the gods of this world and to the gods of the next, to the god Lugh and the god Atta who have been my companions, guides and teachers since my childhood, greetings from your friend and servant Prasutagus, King and Omnipotent Ruler of the Iceni.

To my ancestors from whom I derive my strength and wisdom, greetings. To the Druids who are the knowers of the unknowable and the unknown, the keepers of the secrets of our nation and the healers and teachers of my people, greetings.

To my wife Boudica and my children Camorra and Tasca, Prasutagus, your husband and father, proffers his greetings and his eternal devotion. To my son Cassus who came to me as a baby from my first wife Issult, greetings.

Greetings from Prasutagus, King of the People of the Iceni in the nation of Britain, owner and possessor of all that is contained and encompassed within the lands therein, friend of the people of Rome, friend of the Senate and the Governors of Rome, friend of the soldiers and justices of Rome, friend of Nero, Emperor of Rome, may the gods bless and preserve him now and forever.

Let it be known that I, Prasutagus, am soon to pass into the next world, and I bid greetings and farewell to all who read this, my last demands while I am a part of this earth and before my spirit flies hence into the very heavens themselves.

To my friend and master, Nero, Emperor of Rome, I bequeath my daughters Camorra and Tasca to be his godchildren; I ask my friend Nero, Emperor, to take pains over their welfare, to protect them from the dark and those who might wish them ill.

In furtherance of this task, I bequeath half of all my monies, lands and possessions to the Emperor Nero and the people of Rome. Furthermore, I beg of Nero, Emperor of Rome, to crown Camorra my eldest daughter, and Tasca, my youngest daughter, to be joint Queens of the People of the Iceni from now until the time of their deaths, when their kingdom will pass to any eldest child the gods grant them able to bear. And in furtherance of this bequest, on the moment of my death, I appoint the Emperor of Rome, Nero, to be joint ruler of the lands of the Iceni, co-regent with my daughters, to rule my people in kindness and wisdom and to share in the glories, wealth and majesty which I beg you to accept. Treat my people well, Nero, and they will be a blessing unto you.

To my excellent, noble and loving wife Boudica, I bequeath one quarter of all

*those monies which remain when the tributes and taxes to be paid to the Emperor of
Rome have been distributed. To my son Cassus, I bequeath ten thousand sesterces for
his benefit without condition or preferment.*

*And this is the final demand of Prasutagus, King of Iceni. Cursed be he who
fails to carry out these demands. May the gods bless and preserve all others within
this Land of Britain, our nation.*

Boudica read the scroll, and blinked twice to ensure that her eyes weren't de-
ceiving her. She looked up at Marcus Vitellus and shook her head in disbelief.

"Lady, this is the will of your husband. Was he right in his head when he
wrote it? It seems to me a very strange will. I am told that he makes your daughters and the emperor co-regents and rulers of your land over and above you.
I am shocked that Prasutagus would have written such a will, yet it is my duty,
painful but necessary, to deliver this to you, and having delivered it, I am then
commanded to withdraw."

Boudica's mind was reeling, trying to grasp the implications of what she'd
just read. Prasutagus, her beloved and loving husband, had ceded the kingdom to
her daughters and to Nero! To Nero! And what of her? What of Boudica, by
rights and by inheritance, queen of the Iceni? Hadn't a thousand people, just yesterday, gathered at her door and paid her homage and tribute as their queen?
Hadn't she addressed them as their ruler, told them how life would be?

Yet in her hands, she held an instrument of destruction which Prasutagus
had just wielded from the grave, a sword which cut off her legs, which felled her
to the ground, so that she was now not just a grieving widow, but a groveling
woman without power, without influence, and without position. She began to
sway and the very air was so thick that she found she could barely breathe.

"Lady, are you unwell? You look faint. Shall I call your daughters that they
may look after you?"

A voice, distant and weak, said, "No, thank you. I need to sit."

The Roman helped Boudica back inside the villa and put her hot drink into
her hand. He looked at her in concern. "Boadicea, knowing the love which you and
Prasutagus had for each other, I asked the old Judean who put this will into my

hands why your husband had done such a terrible thing as to depose you as queen. I asked whether your marriage was at an end or whether this was his way of repaying you for some evil deed which you had committed. The messenger said that I was completely wrong; that you and Prasutagus were then and always had been lovers and your marriage was the most joyous he had ever witnessed. He said that only Camorra, your daughter, had the true answer, but he wouldn't tell me anything other than that.

"Lady, I must return to Camulodunum, for I soon have to ride to Londinium where it will be my duty to inform the procurator of Britain, Decianus Catus, of the death of your husband. I'm sure you know of the strictures of Roman law when it comes to inheritance. I pray that the will your husband has written will prevent the awful things happening to you which have happened to other widows. But I must bid you greetings, Lady, and wish your future well."

He saluted, and left the villa. She vaguely heard his troop of men remount and ride swiftly away. She had no idea of how long she sat at the table, reading and rereading the death sentences of Prasutagus' will. She couldn't destroy it, because a copy would have been kept in Camulodunum. She couldn't ignore it, because her husband's wishes on his deathbed had to be obeyed or furious gods and their rampant spirits would make her life a misery from that moment onward. She couldn't contest the will, because its contents were clear and unambiguous.

But the overwhelming question in Boudica's mind was why? Why had Prasutagus destroyed her future by taking the kingdom away from her? Why had he made their daughters rulers of the land? And most disastrous of all, why had he made Nero the children's godfather, and then made the Roman emperor coregent on the lands of the Iceni? She heard a woman scream out. The name "Prasutagus" rebounded off the walls of the room. Shocked, she realized that she was screaming his name in rage.

Camorra and Tasca, beautiful and innocent, looked at their mother in terror. Never, ever, had they seen her in such a mood of fury. Her eyes were wild with an injustice they couldn't understand, her words were spat out in sentences which they couldn't comprehend. The two girls, who had been in each other's arms crying over the death of their father, were suddenly commanded to appear before their mother, and then assailed by a tirade cursing their father's actions.

"So you aren't the queen?" whispered Camorra.

"No, child! You and your sister rule this land in conjunction with the Emperor Nero. Your father in his wisdom has ensured that every member of the tribe will now suffer because of a brain fever which must have come over him before he died. And he didn't have the courage to speak out and tell me what he was doing. For years, children, I loved a man whom I didn't know. For years, your father was planning the sale of his people into the slavery of the emperor of Rome, and all of this was behind my back. Now, I must bow down to you, my children, and call you queen."

The two girls remained silent, too petrified to say anything. Boudica was walking around the room like a caged beast, picking up things and putting them down, scratching her head as though she had lice, standing and then sitting. It was a mother they had never met, and Tasca began to cry.

Breathing deeply, Boudica suddenly realized that she was terrifying her child, and went over to comfort her. But Camorra stepped forward.

"Father gave me a letter four days ago. He told me not to open it until the Romans had been and gone. He said that it must only be opened after you had read the will. I'll get it. He made me promise." She began to weep. "I'm sorry, Mother."

In tears, the girl ran up the steps to her room, and ran downstairs quickly, thrusting the letter into her mother's hands. Boudica tore open the seal, and saw again the familiar handwriting of her husband, writing which now brought such foreboding.

Beloved family,

I, Prasutagus, your husband and father, am writing this letter to you while I am still walking the earth. But you will read this letter when my body is cold and my spirits soar upward to the stars to rest with the gods.

By the time you read this letter, you will also know the contents and desires of my will, which I have deposited with the Romans at Camulodunum.

Boudica, if I know the woman to whom I have been married for many years, whom I have loved and revered as wife and mother, then I know that you will be cursing the name Prasutagus and wishing to the gods that I suffer eternal torments, returning to this earth as a frog or a worm. But Boudica, I beg of you to know and believe that everything I have done this day has been undertaken for your protection and the protection of my beloved children. I love you, Boudica, more than I have ever loved anything or anyone, except, of course, for my beautiful girls, who are flesh of my flesh, life of my life.

And you, Boudica, are my other hand, my life and my hopes and my spirit. Never in all of time has a man loved a woman as I love and have loved you.

So you may wonder, wife, why I have taken from you that which, by rights, is yours and given it both to our children, and to a crazed Emperor across the seas.

I did it, Boudica, because if I had not done so, the Procurator of Britain would have taken everything from us in the name of the Emperor and would have left you and our children bereft, prey to the beasts of the forest and the birds of the air.

By making Nero co-regent of the lands of the Iceni, I have, I pray and hope, prevented you from losing everything on the day of my death. I know too well what other Roman procurators have done in other parts of the Roman Empire—in Gaul and Lusitania and Judea—and I had to prevent this from happening in Britain. Know this, wife . . . that had I not made the Emperor co-regent, had I not willingly given him half of our possessions, he would have taken everything, and left you and the girls without means.

My actions will have caused you grief and fury, Boudica. But my inaction would have brought you abandonment and destitution. I beg you to forgive your loving husband and to understand this, his last will.

In the name of the spirits who guard us and the gods who love us, we will meet again in the heavens . . .

Prasutagus

Numb, Boudica shook her head in disbelief. She looked at the girls whose eyes gazed expectantly on hers. And they were stunned when their mother sat heavily on a stool, and wept bitterly and loudly for the first time since their father had died.

* * *

Decianus Catus, the emperor's procurator in Britain, sneered with contempt at the villa. He'd been told by Marcus Vitellus Publicus, some old veteran of the legions now living in Camulodunum who had visited him in Londinium, a man all puffed up with self-importance, that Boadicea and her dead husband lived in a palace. But from the hilltop where he sat and rested with his fifty collectors and hundred guards, he looked down on the house and town which surrounded it and saw a hovel without substantial walls or any serious fortification. In Rome, it would be the house of some functionary, an impoverished nobleman. Decianus realized that it was nothing more than the biggest house in a country village in an insignificant part of the Roman Empire. But it contained money, and that was why he was here.

As he spurred his horse down the hill, he was reminded of his own villa in Rome, a magnificent edifice with Grecian columns lining the road which led to the doors, and rooms for eating, resting, bathing, playing, sleeping and much more. Not that Decianus' house in Londinium was anything to be proud of. It was comfortable, and certainly far larger and more imposing than anything else in the town, especially now that he'd demolished the hovels which once surrounded it; but compared to his domicile in Rome, his Londinium residence was little more than a hovel.

What was important, though, was Decianus' position in the hierarchy which ruled Britain, not where he lived. He was making a fortune as the emperor's procurator. For every million sesterces of tribute he extracted from the people and sent to the emperor, he took one hundred thousand for himself. For every million sesterces in taxes, he kept nearly two hundred thousand, though much of this was shared among his tax collectors; every time some Briton of importance died, he would raid the house and take all the furniture, acquire the land and property, take the food and any livestock or foodstuffs, and in the name of the emperor, ship it to Rome, except for that which he kept for himself. One of his frustrations with the Britons was that the moment one of their own died, they'd scurry around like squirrels, hiding their valuables. By the time he or his men arrived, it was often impossible to find the more valuable of the property, and in the desolate landscape, his collectors sometimes disappeared and were never seen again, until their headless bodies floated down to the sea.

But this time, it would be different. The moment Prasutagus had died, his stepson, Cassus, had ridden hard to Londinium and told him of all the places where Boadicea would think of hiding the family valuables. Soon, all of the late king's wonderful and expensive property would become that of the emperor. As he had ridden from Londinium, he was barely able to stop salivating about the riches which would be contained in the house. Gold and silver dishes, bronze statues and ornaments which would bring a fortune when sold to the wealthy of Rome, mines for taking, cattle and sheep for collection . . . his mind reeled with how much he would soon make for the emperor, and how much would stay in his pocket. And he knew in which barn, and where, the real valuables such as bags of gold and silver were kept.

But as he looked down upon the town, he wondered whether such a dismal peasant place could possibly hide a fortune. It was squalid, ordinary and in every way unexceptional. The only thing of any significance was the villa in the center, built in the Roman style, affecting the values of the empire, yet which was too small to be considered even a wing in the mansion of some great man. Where was the forum surrounded by its columns and colonnades? Where were the public buildings?

Spurring his horse to a gallop and ordering his tax collectors and guards to hurry, Decianus Catus rode down and saw that he had been wrong when he believed that the town was largely undefended. In fact, as he drew nearer, he saw that there was indeed a large earthen bank and a deep ditch; on top of the bank he saw a wooden palisade which had been erected, but as it seemed to blend in to the colors of the ground, it was really only visible as one rode toward the gates of the road.

Being daytime, the gates were open, and Decianus rode through, heading straight for the villa. There, he was met by a tall, red-haired woman who looked fierce and uncompromising. To prevent the prospect of trouble in advance, his arrival hadn't been announced, and so this woman, whom he assumed was the former queen, Boadicea, came out alone.

"I am Decianus Catus, procurator of Britain. I am here in the name of the Senate and the people of Rome. I am commanded by the most excellent ruler of the world, Nero, Emperor, to assess your home and lands for the benefit of Rome. As the widow of the once-king of the Iceni, you are liable to give to the emperor everything which is in your possession. That includes this house, your lands and servants and slaves, your furniture and property, as well as all that which is above and all that which is below these, which once were your lands. Further, you are to give up all of your animals and your foodstuffs.

"In return, the emperor will generously grant you and your family one half of one tenth of all he takes into his possession, so that you might live your lives in fullness and luxury. Long live the emperor of Rome."

He looked at Boadicea, who stared back.

Quietly, so that he had to strain to hear her, she said, "My husband Prasutagus has left a will with the Romans at Camulodunum in which he leaves—"

Decianus sneered from on top of his horse. "What your husband wrote in his will is of no interest to me or the emperor. As a servant of the empire, woman, you obey my orders and are subject to my conditions. Now, step aside and allow the emperor's procurator of all Britain to enter."

She stood motionless. Decianus Catus had done this many times, and most widows reacted by weeping or screaming or shouting or fainting. But none had merely stood there as though she were deaf and dumb.

"Did you hear what I said, woman? I commanded you to step aside in the name of the emperor," he commanded, raising his voice.

Softly, Boudica said, "I heard."

"Get out of the way, so that my men can enter your house. The carts are on their way to assemble your possessions and remove them. Move aside, I say, or I will have my men remove you."

He turned to his tax collectors. "Over there, in that barn, you'll find bags of gold and silver in a compartment at the back of the fifth stall, hidden beneath bales of straw. Go and fetch it!"

They dismounted, and Boudica watched in horror as five of the men strode toward the barn.

"Cassus!" she hissed, spitting the word at Decianus.

"You will move, woman, or I'll have you trussed up and thrown into a river. I am the emperor's procurator."

Still, she stood there. Furious at his commands not being obeyed immediately, Decianus Catus dismounted. He stood a head shorter than Boudica, but he wasn't afraid of her, as he had fifty strong tax collectors and a hundred armed soldiers behind him.

"Stand aside, woman," he ordered.

But still she blocked his path.

He shouted, "In the name of the emperor of Rome, I, Decianus Catus, command you to stand aside—"

Boudica let out a deep-throated cry of hatred, reached behind her flowing tunic and pulled a huge sword out of a hidden scabbard strapped to her back. The weapon glinted in the sunlight as it flashed upward and in a movement too quick for the eye, Boudica cleaved the air as she brought it to a sudden stop directly above Decianus' head, her arms raised to the heavens. Decianus shouted in surprise, his eyes widened in fear as Boudica brandished the bronze sword above her head, poised to be brought crashing down on his skull and splitting his body from head to foot. He screamed. His men reached for their swords, but each knew instinctively that Decianus' head would be cut from his body before they could unsheathe them.

The sword remained erect, unmoving, threatening to end the procurator's life in a bloody instant. There was murder in Boudica's eyes as she stared down at him, her face a mask of fury and loathing. Nothing except her will separated Decianus from instant death. Too petrified to speak, his mouth gaping in terror, he looked up at her as she spat the words.

"Now you listen carefully to me, little man! I, Boudica, queen of the Iceni, tell you this. Let no man think that he can take from her with impunity that which is hers. Today you come as a thief with an army. Tomorrow Boudica will ride with an army to take back that which you steal. Today Rome rules; tomorrow, Rome will bleed for the harm it does to me and my family. Roman men, women and children will wail in the forum for the sin which you commit in the name of the emperor against those whom Rome has enslaved to her avarice. Understand me well, Romans. Each man here, each thief and robber who enters this house, stealing its contents and defiling its spirit, each man will pay a mortal price. Each and every one of you will be killed by this, my sword. Each man among you will die a lonely and painful death, his blood leaching into British soil, his dying breath carrying the name Boudica. Each one of you will leave behind a widow and grieving children for the insult you do to Boudica this day. And first among you to die will be Cassus. I have spoken!"

With that, Boudica lowered the sword, turned, and walked into the villa to collect her children and to leave the place where she lived. Decianus Catus' legs went to water and he collapsed in a dead faint.

60 AD—The Island of Anglesea (Mona)

By the time the army arrived at the stretch of sea which separated the mainland from the island of Mona, he had already surveyed the situation and decided on the best plan of military assault.

Suetonius allowed his army to rest for the entire day. After all, they had done well, and were looking fitter and stronger than when he'd first taken command of them. On their way across Britain to Mona, they had fought battle after battle with the rebels; but then the rebels had changed their tack. As they neared Wales, his army never fought anything more than skirmishes; each battle had caused delays and frustration, for when they inevitably saw the rebels attack, and then swiftly withdraw, Suetonius sent his men to follow them but accepted that they would return empty-handed, having lost them to the ravines and hills and valleys and caves.

He had no idea of how many rebels he had killed, and how many of his own men he would continue to lose. His troops were still being killed and decapitated in the most gruesome way. Suetonius had even taken to mimicking the actions of the rebels. Whenever he managed to capture one of them, he'd stick the Briton's head on a pole on some hilltop to show the rest of the rebels that he had no fear of them. But in the end, Suetonius knew that for every one he killed, it was one fewer who would resist Roman rule, and so the deaths of his own men were not wasted.

His army erected their leather tents on the grassy hillocks above the sea overlooking the island. They were tired but in high spirits, now that their journey had come to an end. The rumor was that they wouldn't have to walk back, but a fleet of boats would be built and would carry them south and then along the coast to safer lands where the tribes respected and lived in peace with the Roman Empire.

They had arrived a month earlier than he had anticipated. Since Suetonius had introduced his financial incentives, many had earned an additional three months' pay, just by reaching the campsite faster. It was money which they would either send back to their families, or spend in the towns on whores and drink.

Astride his horse, General Suetonius could see the island of Mona in the distance. The strait which divided the island from the mainland was, at that point, only a quarter of a mile in distance, and from the color and disposition of the water which lay between them, he realized that it was so shallow that at low tide, a man could possibly wade the distance with the water rising no higher than his neck.

He could see hundreds of men and women on the opposite shore. Some of them were very tall, with their hair combed into tall spikes. They, no doubt, were the Druids who often stood on the tops of hills as his army was passing by in the valleys, and who screamed curses and imprecations down on them. The other people could have been farmers or cattlemen. Many of the men and women were naked and had painted their bodies with woad, expecting to frighten the Romans. But with instructions he would issue, he was sure that a blue-painted man didn't necessarily have to be frightening.

Suetonius allowed his men several days of rest to sharpen their swords and spears, repair their armor and equipment, and relax before the crossing and the fight. Just in case the water was deeper than he believed it to be, he had ordered his constructors to build a hundred flat-bottomed boats with wood taken from the forests which lined the coast. Simple and crude, they would enable those who were not equestrians to cross the strait without getting their armor and bodies wet. Suetonius knew from bitter experience of fighting in other parts of the Roman world how difficult it was for men to cross a river or a lake and then go into a fight when their leather was wet and heavy. If he, like Julius Caesar, was going to cross his Rubicon, then his men would be dry by the time they got to the other side. And from the looks of preparation on the opposite shore, the Britons and Druids were preparing to resist the Roman advance at all costs.

It was morning by the time the last boat had been made ready. The constructors had worked day and night in preparation, and the hundred flat-bottomed boats now lined the shore. In some consternation, the chief constructor told the general that flat-bottomed boats were not as stable as proper boats with a solid keel, but Suetonius assured him that if one capsized, the men would be in more danger of catching a cold than drowning.

His legionaries arranged the huge army into ranks, then into *centuriae*, and sent those on horseback ahead into the water, as they would be slower getting across. When all the horses and their riders were safely into the waves and swimming across the slow-moving narrows, Suetonius gave the command for his men and the battle equipment to be put into the boats and to strike out for the opposite shore. The sea was as calm as a mountain lake, the sun pleasantly warm as it rose over the mountains behind them, and the air was full of screaming birds ascending from the tussocks of grass in the hillocks lining the beach.

When the last boat had pushed off from the mainland shore, and the entire army of General Suetonius was halfway across the strait, a loud and insistent drumbeat rent the air. The horses, panicked by the noise and less than happy being ridden through the water, started to whinny and became unstable for their riders.

"What's that, for the sake of the gods?" asked a soldier in Suetonius' boat.

"That's the sound of the Druids," said another, who had been in Britain longer than anyone else. "I know that noise. I've heard it before, when the Druids cut out the heart of a living man or woman. It's the sound they make to tell the gods when they're about to perform a human sacrifice."

Suetonius could feel the sudden fear in his men. He looked across at the opposite beach, and suddenly, as if out of nowhere, thousands of Britons appeared in a huge line. They were ten deep on the beach, some carrying swords and spears, but most unarmed. Many were standing there naked and unashamed, both men and women. All were painted blue. It was an awesome sight, a host of Shades from the very depths of Hades. In between the soldiers, Suetonius could see hundreds of Druid priests. *Gods,* he thought, *the whole of the nation's priesthood is here!*

All conversation in the boat, and in other nearby boats, ebbed away as the Roman soldiers looked in horror at the vast army who had appeared from nowhere on the shore. But most fearsome were the Druids, and their drums beating a death volley.

The Druids all stepped forward to the margin of the water, and at a signal from their leader, began a fearsome chant, waving their fists and kicking their legs, and moaning in a horrible manner, presaging the deaths of the Roman soldiers. The priests raised their arms collectively to the sky, invoking their gods to come down and smite the Romans.

Suetonius' men were close to panic. They could cope with rebel soldiers; they could cope with some of their number being decapitated; they could cope with a fearsome army, even when they were outnumbered three to one; but the one thing they couldn't cope with was their fear of the Druids, these fiends from the lowest regions of the demonic abyss. All rowing now had stopped. The boats were beginning to drift in the gentle current as his men sat transfixed by the horrific sight which met them. They weren't even halfway, yet they were as good as defeated.

Suddenly Druid priests parted to allow Harpies to walk beyond them into the shallows of the sea. These were no ordinary women. They were not even Furies. They were demons of an altogether more terrifying dimension. Their nightmarish faces were blue-painted and lined with brown so that their eyes appeared to stare like the dead; their hair, coated in white clay, stood up in spikes to give them an extra head. Screaming and baring their blue- and red-painted breasts, they taunted the Romans to go back or die on the beach.

The air, once so morning-still and pleasing, rang with the moaning and curses of the Druids, the high-pitched screeching of the inhuman women-beasts, and the insistent beat of drums. Suetonius looked from boat to boat, and realized that his looming battle was as good as lost. These men, even assuming that they could land, would be too terrified to fight. Yes, they were able enough against an army, against a soldier, but not against these devils from a nether world.

Desperate now to regain the initiative, Suetonius stood in his boat, and at the top of his voice began to sing a lewd Roman drinking song.

As though released from a bad dream, his men looked at him in amazement. Normally dour and unwavering, General Suetonius was not only smiling, but was almost laughing as he sang the bawdy song about a woman who pretends to be a man so that she can join her lover in the ranks.

Slowly one, then another, and then the whole boat joined their general. At first, their singing was relatively soft, tentative; but then they gained courage one from the other, and their voices rose in pitch and enthusiasm. Then the next boat, and then the next joined in, until within a short space of time, the entire Roman army sailing across the strait was singing this song with gusto.

By the time they landed, the noise of the moaning Druids and the screeching women was almost drowned out by the song of the woman, wailing in pleasure with her lover as the two of them made love in front of the entire legion.

It was Suetonius who struck the first blow. It was a deliberate blow. Risking his own life, he ordered the surrounding boats to hold back so that his was the first to strike land. Then leading his men, he jumped onto the shore. He held his sword aloft, and shouted, "For the Senate and the people of Rome. For the emperor and all we live for. Strength, honor and glory to the army."

His men crowded around him as they walked up the beach. They faced a line of hysterical Druids who shook white bones at them, and spat at their faces. The women taunted them with their bare breasts, and pointed toward the Romans' legs, making obscene gestures.

But Suetonius knew that he had to prove that these were no warriors, or all of his men's resolve would disappear. He strode to the tallest and most impressive Druid he could find, a man whose eyes shone with hatred of him, and swung his sword through the air, cleaving the man's head off in one massive blow. The head hit the sand noiselessly; the Druid's body crumpled to the beach, his hands seeming to reach out toward his head which rolled into the sea.

The Harpies hissed and attacked him, but Suetonius swung his sword again and again, felling three with one blow, slashing the women across their naked breasts, and slicing off an arm of two of them. His men let out a Roman war cry, and heaved at the Druids with their swords, slicing and thrusting and slashing at anything which stood before them. Suetonius also slashed and thrust. He, as his men, was stunned that they were meeting no resistance.

He was so overwhelmed by the hissing and screeching from the women that he almost didn't hear the roar of fury and war cries from the rest of the boatloads of Romans who landed, running forward with their swords and daggers swinging, and thrusting them into whatever body they met.

Suddenly the rigidity of the Druid line appeared to collapse. They turned and began to run back up the beach, but the Romans were too fast, and they chased them up the hill, stabbing them in the back and killing them as they tried to escape. Flinging lances and spears into the retreating line, the soldiers felled dozens as they ran.

Surveying the carnage, Suetonius couldn't understand why the rebel Britons, the remnant of the army he'd been fighting all the way across Britain and into Wales, were just standing there, as though they were refusing to fight. Why were only the Druids and the Harpies in the forefront of this battle? Why weren't the warriors charging down to the beach to defend their island against the Romans? As the Druids and the women fled up the beach to avoid the daggers and swords of the now merciless and no longer fearful Romans, there was a sudden roar of hatred from the Celtic men and women who stood on the grassy crest of the beach. Those with weapons drew them; those without waved their bare hands in the air; all ran headlong toward the advancing Roman army.

Seeing the charge, Suetonius shouted an order. "Stand, army, and fix weapons. Swords at the ready. Stand fast to repel an advance."

There was no need for further instructions, or for deciding upon particular military maneuvers. And neither was there need for a Turtle or other deployment or stratagem which he would have ordered were they fighting against a professional infantry or cavalry. These were merely peasants, barbarians, brutes and cannibals, some armed with wooden staves, others with swords and spears, most without weapons of any kind, a disorganized rabble hurling themselves onto the deadly and unyielding line of a Roman legion.

Shaking his head in disgust at the inevitability of the coming slaughter, Suetonius gave another order: "Romans, advance in file; weapons prone; first rank spears, second rank swords; equestrians, form up in the flanks and ride to surround the enemy from the rear."

Following orders with precision, the Romans now presented a formidable two-tier line of attack. The first assault was impaled on spears. Not a single Roman was hurt. Those barbarians who escaped the spears were slaughtered by the swords of the back row. The mountain of Celtic bodies quickly grew so high that it made it difficult for the Romans to advance.

But it was the horsemen who did the most damage. The Britons' advance had come to a halt against the impenetrable line of Roman foot soldiers. The cavalry had ridden along the beach to the north and south to outflank the Britons, and then galloped up the hill behind the rabble of British. And as they cantered into the fray, they slashed at British necks and backs and legs, felling men and women fighters as if they were cutting stalks of wheat.

It took almost no time at all to reduce the thousands of British warriors to heaps of dead and dying men and women, legs and arms dismembered, heads hacked off, noses and eyes and lips pulped and bloody. The sand, soaked from the blood, could absorb no more, and the gore which oozed from the dead and dying ran in rivulets to the sea until the waves were incarnadine.

The Roman army had left their camp on the opposite shore when the sun was low in the east in the still, warm morning. By the time the last Briton—Celt or Druid or Harpy—had ceased fighting, the sun was barely in the middle of the sky.

Suetonius surveyed the scene. Were these the same fearless warriors they had encountered as they passed through the lands of the Dobunni or the Ordovicii: men who braved his sentries and who abducted and killed experienced soldiers; men who led fearless raids and then faded into the night; men for whom Suetonius had held some elemental form of respect? How could these be of the same breed? These thousands and thousands of dead and dying had barely fought, had sent Druids into the front row, had allowed Harpy women to protect them. Yet it had been! These warriors must be the same as the Celts they had fought on the mainland, for they dressed and smelled and seemed the same.

His second in command and personal aide, Fabius Tertius, came up to him and saluted. "A great victory, General."

Suetonius smiled grimly, "Do you think so, Fabius?"

"No. It was a massacre. But what else can I say?"

The following day, leaving the dead on the beach for the birds and crabs to demolish, the Romans marched inland. Knowing that there must still be Britons on the island, Suetonius ordered his men to kill everybody, men, women and children, regardless of whether or not they tried to surrender or to defend themselves.

By the end of the day, not one single Celtic man, woman or child was alive on the isle of Mona. The general's intelligence told him that every Druid priest had fled to Mona for the final battle with the Romans. Now the Druids, once the bane of every Roman soldier in Britain, were finally expunged. Now Roman soldiers had no further need to fear the Druids and their murderous rituals.

"These Druids," Suetonius shouted to his army during their victory celebrations, "worship oak and other trees, sacred springs and groves. Our job here is to salt the waters to make them undrinkable, to dig up the groves and trample them into the ground so that they are forever despoiled, and then, when the land is barren, to set fire to the trees so that nothing, not even a blade of grass, will ever grow on this accursed island again. That is my order. See to it."

He mounted his horse in order to ride to the coast. He would ride to the south of the island, as the very last thing he wanted to see, or smell, was thousands of British bodies still rotting on the shore. He had ordered a boat—a proper seagoing boat—to be sent to collect him, so that he could sail back to the land of the Cantiaci, where he would rest before riding to Camulodunum, supervise the building of the temple to the god Claudius, and then continue with his duties as Governor of Britain.

CHAPTER ELEVEN

60 AD—The Roman City of Camulodunum

She dismounted from her chariot, instructing her two daughters to remain aboard. Dressed in the clothes she had worn when she got out of bed in the morning, unable to change because she had been expelled from her home, Boudica surveyed the barricade which surrounded the city before she proceeded toward the guard's tower. Suddenly she felt naked and exposed, like a British warrior on a battlefield.

In her past, whenever she and Prasutagus had ridden up to this tower, the guard had recognized them, and the gate had swung open in welcome. Now it was closed and prevented her entry. She walked up to the gate and shouted to the guard in the watchtower, "You know me. I am Boudica, queen of the Iceni. I command you to open your gates and allow me and my daughters inside your city."

The guard looked down at the tall, robust figure who had just ridden along the road as if followed by the Furies. He had been told by the watch commander in the early morning of the arrival in their area of the procurator of Britain, and had been ordered to be both alert and efficient—not to allow strangers into the city. Concerned to follow orders, the guard was in no mood to accept any insolence from anybody, especially a woman's disrespect.

"I'm a bit deaf. Who did you say you are?" he shouted down.

"Boudica, queen of the Iceni. Open your gates immediately, Roman."

"Never heard of you! Now piss off and take your chariot and your daughters with you."

He and his fellow guards burst out laughing. But his laughter stopped when Boudica not only refused to move away from the gate, but shouted up, "My daughters rule my land with the emperor of Rome. I shall write to Nero and inform him of your rudeness. What is your name, guard? I shall make special note to tell the emperor of you."

Without saying another word, the guard told his colleague to go down and open the wooden gate to allow the chariot inside. Boudica and her daughters were no strangers to the city, so he wasn't being derelict in his duty. Anyway, the best course with a woman like her was to let the problem rest with the city leaders. The women looked at the guards in contempt as they rode past.

Boudica had been in Camulodunum many times since it was first taken in conquest by the Catuvellauni from the Trinovantes. In those days it was called Camulos, named to celebrate the Celtic god of war. She had seen it grow from a few wattle-and-daub houses before the Romans arrived, to its present state of tall and impressive buildings, wood and stone houses, and large public squares. And in the center, to celebrate the conquest of Britain by the Emperor Claudius, a huge temple was being built to contain a massive marble bust of the dead emperor made god by his adopted son, the Emperor Nero. And the greatest insult was that the Britons were being taxed into poverty by the Romans to help them build this sacrilege to a foreign man-god.

Aware of its rectangular order of streets and buildings and public spaces, she surveyed the many hundreds of men and women going about their business making purchases from the shops, or carrying things here and there. The Romans, she knew, loved cities and considered them the zenith of culture and sophistication, whereas Britons were people of the land and enjoyed nothing more than the forests and the freedom of the hills. Wherever the Romans went, they built forts which became towns which grew into cities. She hated towns at the best of times, feeling uncomfortable and trapped inside a walled city; she hated the noise and the crowding and the smells. But she knew that her only salvation from the disaster that had occurred to her because of her husband's death lay not in the countryside, but within the bosom of the cities of Rome.

Boudica strapped her horses, and steered them to the home of Marcus Vitellus Publicus, the man who had been given charge of Prasutagus' will. He was the most high-ranking veteran in the city, and effectively the city's commander, even though the governor of the whole of Britain had made his home here. She knew that he, more than any other, would listen to her.

As the chariot drew up to his door, he came outside, but the look on his face made her realize that her troubles were not at an end.

"Boadicea, I beg you to leave this place and not to return. This is not a good place for you. The procurator of Britain, Decianus Catus, is on his way to your villa. The gods only know what he will say to you. Go back to your home, Boadicea, and when you greet him, behave in a restrained way. You can't fight the will of Rome without bringing destruction upon yourselves. Live for tomorrow and accept the injustice of today."

"He has already been, Marcus Vitellus. I and my daughters are bereft. We are paupers, peasants. He has been told of our hidden cache of gold and silver by Prasutagus' son Cassus, may the gods cause him a painful death. Knowing what he knew, the procurator has taken everything for Rome and the emperor. We are denuded of our lands, our property, and our jewelry. We have no money and no food. We have been left with nothing."

Marcus Vitellus' body sagged in distress. "It's worse than I feared. As you know, the emperor takes half and usually allows the dependents to keep the rest. When Prasutagus wrote his will, he did so with the intention of persuading the emperor not to allow what the procurator has just done. I'm afraid that your husband created his will in vain. I didn't know what his cursed son Cassus had done, but now that you've told me, many things begin to make sense. For some time, the procurator has been more than usually busy in this area. Cassus was obviously giving him information. Unfortunately, the procurator has the right to take as much as he wants in the name of the emperor. This is the course of action he has chosen. What did you say to him? I pray you didn't insult him. He's a nasty and vindictive little man. When I delivered the will to you, I should have warned you to be compliant—"

"You know me, Marcus Vitellus. You know I couldn't stand by and allow myself to be so badly used. Cassus might have told the procurator in Londinium about our wealth, but the emperor couldn't possibly have known about Prasutagus' death. There hasn't been sufficient time for a copy of the will you sent to him to reach Rome. This abuse against me and my daughters is not the doing of Nero, but of Cassus, and for this act of treachery, he will die on my sword.

"Understand this, Marcus Vitellus: The procurator has acted against the interests of Rome and the emperor. I am here, friend, to write a letter to Nero himself, to explain to him that if he reinstates me and my daughters, we will be far more valuable to him than if he steals all of our property. If I enter your home and write this letter, can you ensure that it gets to Rome as quickly as possible, so that the abuses of this procurator can be stopped?"

Marcus Vitellus looked at Boudica for a long moment. By rights, he, as a veteran and a man who owed a lifetime of allegiance to the emperor, should refuse her request and dismiss her from his sight. But what she was saying was sensible; and the procurator had taken an excessive liberty with a queen of Britain and against the expressed will of a king of one of the most important client tribes. Marcus Vitellus nodded, and invited Boudica into his home.

It took her the entire day and long into the night to write the epistle. In it, Boudica outlined the way in which, since his elevation to the kingship, Prasutagus had worked tirelessly to be a good friend and supporter of the Roman emperor. Yet suddenly a charge of forty million sesterces, plus ten million in interest, had been demanded for repayment by Seneca, which could not possibly be met immediately. The shock of this alone, Boudica claimed, had been sufficient to kill her husband. And yet the conditions of his will had been mercilessly ignored by the procurator, even though the terms were immensely favorable to Rome and the emperor himself.

She was just finishing the letter and was about to seal it, when she heard a commotion in the streets outside Marcus Vitellus' home. She looked outside the window, and her heart dropped when she saw the procurator, riding with fifty or so men, straight to Marcus' house. Cassus rode with him, a leer spreading on his face. Fury rose in her throat, but she was mindful of her daughters, and fought to remain calm.

The procurator's voice rebounded off the walls of the street, and entered every room in the house. "Boadicea! Hideous crone. Woman who dares to raise a sword against the person of the procurator of Britain. Come out into the street, and face your accuser."

She didn't move, and saw Marcus Vitellus step outside the house, and salute the procurator.

"You are the senior veteran?"

Marcus nodded.

"You give aid and sustenance to a woman who defied the majesty of Rome, a woman who nearly murdered your procurator?"

"No, sir. I give no comfort. I had no knowledge of what Boadicea did to you. She came here to write a letter to the emperor."

Boudica joined Marcus on the portico. The look she gave to Cassus made him stop smiling. But Decianus Catus merely sneered in contempt when he saw her emerge, and before he could say anything, Boudica said to him, "Marcus Vitellus is innocent. He is a loyal Roman. I didn't inform him of the way in which you and your thieves came to rob me and my children. Neither did I tell him that Prasutagus' son was a coward and a traitor and a dog.

"But what Marcus Vitellus said is correct. I am writing to the Emperor Nero, named by my late husband as co-regent of the land of the Iceni. I have informed him of what you have done, and demanded of him that you be recalled to Rome and examined by the justices for your treatment of the friends of the empire."

Decianus Catus burst out laughing. He turned to a tax collector who had ridden next to him, and said, "Enter the house and find the letter. Burn it." Then he ordered the forward contingent, "Dismount and arrest this woman and her daughters. This excellent young man, Cassus," he said to Boudica, "has told me much about you which is of interest. It is you, woman, who are the traitor to Rome. It is not I who will be reported to the emperor, but you. You've been raising an army against our interests, with the intention of starting an insurrection. I shall put an end to your plans, and teach you to learn respect for Rome. Chain them and take them to the forum," he told his men.

Boudica screamed, "No!"

She turned and ran inside the house to gather her daughters and the letter. But the tax collectors, brutish ex-soldiers who hated the British, ran after her. They pushed her to the floor and restrained her while Decianus' second in command searched Marcus' home for the letter Boudica had spent so long writing. Without even reading it, he threw it into the fire which burned in the hearth. The vellum curled, turned brown, and then burst into flame.

Boudica was screaming to warn her children to escape, but it was too late. By the time she had been roped like an animal and she and her daughters dragged outside, a large crowd of citizens had gathered to watch the extraordinary events. Marcus Vitellus averted his gaze. He knew only too well what was going to happen and wanted no part of it.

Tethered and chained, the mother and her two terrified screaming daughters were marched from Marcus' house down the narrow streets toward the forum in the center of the city. Cassus followed on his horse.

Boudica turned and looked up at him. She sneered and hissed at him, "Soon, boy, you will meet your father in death, and he will do to you what he should have done all those years ago. You aren't fit to tread the same land as other Britons."

"Oh, dearest Mother," he taunted. "You think I'm scared of you. I know what they're going to do to you, and it's me who'll be laughing. Not you."

Boudica fell to the ground, but she was pulled up roughly by her hair. She screamed at the pain, and she heard Tasca burst into tears. Camorra called out her name, but one of the soldiers hit Boudica over the ears. They began to ring, which blotted out any other noise.

The party arrived at the forum. On one side was the building which housed the city governance; on the other side of the forum was the huge new edifice of burning white marble embedded with mosaics of scenes of heaven—a half-built temple dedicated to the god Claudius—and nearby were the barracks of those veteran soldiers who had no wives or children.

To the crowd which had assembled in the forum, Decianus Catus called out, "This woman is called Boadicea. She is a woman of no status. She is a Briton. She was once a queen, but the imperial majesty of the Emperor Nero has decided that he and he alone will rule Britain. You all know me. I am Decianus Catus, the procurator of Britain. This woman Boadicea raised her sword and tried to strike me dead. Only by my courage and daring did I escape her blade. In punishment, I order the said Boadicea to be stripped of her clothes, and be whipped naked before all the populace."

Boudica was grabbed roughly and the bonds holding her arms and legs were severed. Her dress was cut from her body, and it fell to the ground. She stood there, naked, tall and regal, unashamed and defiant. The crowd gasped at her nakedness, and even the men were shamed by her scorn.

Cassus pushed forward through the press of men and women, and his eyes widened in a shudder of excitement as he saw her naked. Other men and women in the audience looked at her body in admiration. Her long red hair fell to her waist and her breasts were erect, almost as a sign of indifference to their stares. Not only Cassus, but many Roman men were stirred by the sight of her regal beauty.

Decianus Catus turned to his subordinate and said, "Take the two children into the barracks, and tell the men to have their way with them." Turning to the young man, he said, "Cassus, would you like to enjoy your stepsisters?"

To her horror, Boudica saw Cassus' eyes widen in pleasure. At that moment, she vowed that no matter what happened to her now, Cassus would die on the blade of her knife.

"No, thank you," said Cassus. "I'll reserve my pleasures for girls who are older."

Decianus shrugged, and turned to one of his soldiers. "Take the children now. Let them be playthings for our veterans. Let the children of Britain get to know the nature of Roman manhood."

Wide-eyed in horror, Boudica screamed, "No! Do to me what you want, but leave my children alone. Don't hurt them. I beg of you, Decianus, don't take them away. I have to protect them."

She turned to Cassus, and shouted, "For the sake of your father, Cassus, I beg you not to allow them to hurt my daughters." Tears began to well up in her eyes, but Cassus merely smiled, and looked at the two struggling girls as the guards approached them.

"I said you shouldn't have married my father," he sneered. "I always knew that one day, you'd be naked and helpless before me." He turned away and walked toward the barracks.

Decianus Catus nodded to his men, and Camorra and Tasca were viciously gripped by the strong hands of the soldiers and force-marched, screaming and struggling, from their mother. They screamed for her, but she was held fast and couldn't free herself. She watched in despair as her two little daughters were dragged away from her. In utter despair, Boudica cried out their names.

Tasca and Camorra continued to wail in fear. Boudica struggled, helpless, calling her daughters, shouting to them not to be frightened. The crowd closed in and Boudica lost sight of the girls being dragged to their fate, thrashing against the iron grip of the guards.

Another nod from Decianus Catus, and the whip man cracked his leather thong in the air. The crowd, momentarily distracted by the abduction of the children, now turned back to Boudica and saw the first blow of the whip brought down against the skin of her back; the leather thong whistled in the air and cracked as it hit her flesh. Men and women winced at the strike. Boudica screamed in pain as a vicious red wheal erupted where the strap sliced against her skin. Before the whip man could draw back his arm for the second blow, blood began to ooze out of the wound. Boudica began to cry out, "Camorra, Tasca," but barely had the words left her mouth when the second blow struck her back.

This time the pain was so severe that her legs couldn't support her body, and she crumpled to the ground. She screamed again with the pain, a high-pitched animal cry, like a sparrow suddenly crushed by the sharp talons of an eagle.

Looking at her crumpled on the ground, blood now flowing freely from her wounds, the whip man stepped forward to get a better aim and to ensure that when the whip hit the skin, it did so at its maximum velocity.

Now that she was lying in the dirt, twitching, the whip man was able to swing the thongs vertically, causing more pain and allowing him greater accuracy. It was good, because he preferred a grounded target to one that was standing. But by the fourth swing, Boudica was no longer aware of what was happening.

From a vast gulf which spanned a deep and troubled ocean, Boudica vaguely heard the sound of birds chirping in the trees. Throbbing consciousness was beginning to return, and with its dawning came the pain. A terrible pain. A pain so all-encompassing that she thought she might be dead, and if she wasn't dead, then she wished she were. But in her ears, there was a throbbing. She tried to reason what the noise was, but the pain was too great for reason. All she could hear was the sound of crying in the distance—the crying of a child.

She tried to open her eyes, but they, too, were painful and seemed to be matted together. She moved her fingers and felt dirt. And then she felt cold and began to shiver uncontrollably. If only she could open her eyes, she would be able to see what was happening to her.

A rough hand gently grasped her beneath her arms, and tried to lift her. She felt the sudden sting of liquid. It cascaded over her forehead and down her cheeks, some of it finding its way into her mouth. As she sipped the water, she realized how thirsty she was. But the feeling which overwhelmed her was the pain—a sharp cutting pain in her back, her buttocks, and her legs, a pain which overlaid a deep throbbing and twitching in her muscles. She cried out at the pain. Why was she in such pain?

"Boadicea?"

A man's voice.

"Queen Boadicea, can you hear me?"

A familiar voice, one she'd heard recently. Not her husband Prasutagus, but a familiar voice.

"Drink this wine. It will make you feel better. Boadicea?"

She felt the spout of a wine bladder being pushed into her mouth, but it was too painful for her to open it. The voice? Was it a Roman's voice? The language? It was Latin. Marcus Vitellus' voice?

She struggled to open her eyes. The light was unbearable and she squinted. She tried to form his name, but no sound came from her dry lips.

"Don't speak, Lady. Just try to drink this wine. It will refresh your spirits."

And then the memory came flooding back, opening the gates to the horror she and her daughters had suffered. Her daughters! Despite the pain, she opened her eyes in panic, and gasped, "Camorra? Tasca?"

"They are here. They are safe. Tasca is asleep, Camorra between sleeping and waking. I have made them warm and comfortable. And safe."

"What happened?" she rasped, her voice hoarse and manlike.

"Time to tell you later. For the moment, Lady, rest, and I'll . . ."

"What happened to them!" she demanded.

His protracted silence told her everything she needed to know.

"How badly are they damaged?"

He shook his head.

"You're badly hurt. Time to tell of these things when . . ."

"What happened!"

"Many men pleasured themselves on your daughters. I have stopped the girls' bleeding with balm, but they were in a great deal of pain and shock when I brought them from the barracks. Their bodies were not . . . they were too small to . . . but they are young and strong and they will recover. As will you, Boadicea. Your back is badly cut, but I've put salt in the wound to dry the bleeding and wood balm to heal the cuts. It will be painful but the remedy is what we use in the army to heal wounds after a battle, and it's effective. I've also mixed the balm with a salve of crushed wheat and oil and laid it over your wounds on a bandage. In time, you will all recover. This is a nightmare from which you will gain strength. And when you are strong enough, you can return to your home. I have brought a wagon for you all. When you feel able, I and my horse will ensure that the journey back to your village is as comfortable as possible."

Boudica struggled to sit up, but the movement opened the wounds in her back, and she winced in pain. But the pain of her mind was greater than all other bodily hurts.

"How long have I been like this? When was I . . . where am I?" she asked.

"After your whipping, you were carried unconscious to the city gates and thrown outside. Shortly afterward, your daughters were ejected as well. When the crowd had dispersed, I came looking for you. I covered your and your daughters' nakedness with clothes from my wife and children, and carried you into the woods so that you would be out of sight of the city. You have been here for a long time, Boadicea, and it will soon be dark. That's why I want to leave you for a short while, and get the wagon so that I can take you home. Once it's dark and the city gates are locked, I will not be allowed to leave the city in order to help you and you will spend the night in the open. With so many wolves, it's too dangerous to be in the woods. I cannot allow that to happen."

"Go, Marcus. We need no help from Rome. We will care for ourselves. I thank you for your kindness, but we must be left alone to tend our wounds."

"No, Boadicea. Now is not the time for you to reject a friend. The gods know that I played no part in the hideous things which were done to you, but with the smell of blood on you and being alone in the woods at night, defenseless and without weapons, wolves will prey on you. If not wolves, then forest bears. I will return shortly and bring transport and lighted brands to scare off the animals. Queen Boadicea, I beg you to let me do this, not as a Roman but as a friend."

Silently, wordlessly, knowing that without his protection, she and her children would be dead by morning, she nodded.

She knew that her daughters would never recover. Ever. Since their birth, she had relished the thought of her daughters enjoying the love and comfort of men, lying with them, accept them into their bodies, and knowing the pleasures which would be theirs by right of being women. But how could they look upon men now without feelings of hatred and revenge?

Despite her entreaties, her daughters would not talk about what had happened to them in the barracks. In the beginning, resting in the home of one of her former servants, Boudica had gently questioned the girls, but every time she asked, tears welled up in their eyes, and they became mute, shaking their heads as if to throw off the hideousness of the memory. So Boudica determined to allow the demons in their heads to leave of their own accord, and to wait for her daughters to talk about the nightmare of their own volition.

Every night the girls, who seemed to be constantly exhausted and listless during the day, would wake up in tears or screaming; and despite her own pain from the whipping she had received and other ravages against her person, Boudica would lie with the girls and comfort them, singing them their favorite songs or telling them of the wonders of the gods and the stories of how the world was first created: of how the birds and the rivers and the mountains first came to the earth, and of how the gods of the Celts looked on at everything which was happening, and remembered all the evil things which men did. The girls seemed comforted when Boudica said the gods would ensure that they avenged evil.

During the day, when the girls were safe and dressed, Boudica would wander over to her villa and enter through the now unhinged door. The house was bare, stripped of its once beautiful possessions, its rugs and carpets and hangings; all the jewelry she had once taken such pride in wearing had been stolen from her; all the cups and plates and knives were gone. The tax collectors had pissed on the walls and floor of every room to show their disgust at being within a Briton's home, and the house now reeked.

Boudica enjoyed going back into her home, because it gave her the strength she often lost when she held her children in her arms, and wanted to sink into the bed and disappear from this life. But the destruction of everything she once held dear needed to be avenged. And once her back was healed, once she was able to ride without pain and speak without bursting into tears of fury, then vengeance would be hers for the taking. She would be avenged on Decianus Catus, on the Romans who had done these things to her family, but most especially on her stepson, Cassus. The pleasure she would enjoy in slicing his throat was unimaginable.

While she was recovering, men and women came from far-flung parts of her land to see their former queen, to pay their respects, and to show their sympathy and disgust at her treatment. Embassies were sent from neighboring kingdoms. Leaders of other tribes came to see her and tell her of their horror when they learned what had been done by the Romans to Boudica and her daughters.

And from these Iceni travelers, Boudica learned how the Roman tax collectors, under instructions from Nero's advisor Seneca, had stripped her country bare of almost everything as a way of recouping the forty million sesterces plus interest which had been demanded. Never had her people been so oppressed and exploited; never had the whip of the tax man been applied so harshly, or stung so viciously. Life under the Romans, even for British friends of Rome, had become bare and bitter.

It took a full month for Boudica's wounds to heal sufficiently so that she could mount a horse without wincing in pain. It took a further month for her to feel comfortable riding. During those two months, she spent all day with her daughters, walking with them through the fields, sitting beside the river and fishing, watching the ducks swimming in nearby lakes, cuddling and protecting her girls, drying their tears when they cried, stroking their hair as they stared at the heavens.

But Boudica had a mission to fulfill, and when she was confident of being able to leave her children without their panicking at her absence, she borrowed a horse from a neighbor, promising to return it within the week. She bade her two children a fond goodbye, promising them that if they woke in a nightmare, their friend and former servant would comfort them.

Her clothes having been rescued by her former servant, Boudica dressed in a long flowing red robe, covered with a green cloak gathered together at her neck by a bronze clasp. By her outward appearance, she was a queen; but she would never allow anybody to know the pain of the woman within. She gave her children a final farewell kiss, reassuring them that she would soon return, and then she rode south, to the land of her people's ancient enemies, the Trinovantes.

Mandubracus, king of the Trinovantes, deliberately remained seated as Boudica entered the longhouse which was in the center of the town. As a meeting hall, it was traditionally Celtic, with statues of ancient gods set in wall niches, swords and shields hanging from the walls, and branches of oak and mistletoe suspended from the roof beams for good fortune. The longhouse supported none of the Roman features which she and Prasutagus had constructed as friends of the emperor. It was a normal courtesy for a monarch to rise in the presence of another monarch; but the Iceni and the Trinovantes had been enemies for longer than anybody could remember, and there was no love between Mandubracus and Boudica.

"I greet Mandubracus in friendship and sisterly love," she said at the entrance to the great house. Watched by a multitude of his people and advisors, she walked down the length of the building, smelling the earthy smells of a Celtic village; it was so much richer, so much more like her childhood than the smell of stone and marble in what once was her own home.

As she walked to the midway point of the longhouse, she called out, "I, Boudica, queen of the Iceni, beg permission from Mandubracus, king of the Trinovantes, to enter his kingdom."

She waited for his permission. He remained silent. The entire room, once abuzz with her appearance at the entryway, fell into silence. All eyes were on the king, trying to deduce his response. To deny her entry would be a sign of a future war; to force her to stand in the midsection would be an insult.

"Why should Mandubracus grant entry to a Roman?" he asked.

"Once a Roman, I am a Roman no longer, great king and ruler of the Trinovantes! I stand before you, a Briton and a queen, deposed by Rome. I am naked in my fury and vengeful in my desires."

He nodded. "I have heard what the Romans did to you at Camulodunum, our former capital, stolen from us by the Catuvellauni and then from them by the Romans. I have also heard what they did to your daughters. I cry for your distress and for the insult to your womanhood, and the crime against your children is something which cannot be forgiven.

"But I ask again, Boudica, why should Mandubracus grant entry to one who was joined to Rome like an infant joined to its mother's breast? For years, you and your husband sneered at those of us who were robbed and pillaged and forced into servitude by Rome, while you and he suckled on the Roman teat, growing rich and fat and soft trading with the enemy."

"I have come, Great King, to do homage, to pay penance, and to apologize for the disdain which we wrongly felt toward you. Mandubracus, we of the Iceni erred when we joined with the Romans. I and my husband Prasutagus were wrong. I see that now, and I come to kneel and beg you to understand and forgive."

There were gasps from the entire community. The great and noble Boudica was groveling at the foot of their king. She, who was proud and unbending!

"Hear me well, Mandubracus. I and my daughters have paid the heaviest of prices for our errors. Now it is time for Rome to pay. Not just a few deaths like the rebels in the west, but a mass of bodies as high as a forest. Not just the defeat of an army, but the elimination of every legion which dares to set foot on Britain's sacred ground."

Mandubracus shook his head, and said to her, "Many have tried to defeat Rome, and all have failed. Many widows are grieving for their husbands who died defending their homes from the invaders. You and Prasutagus welcomed the Romans as guests. But you are here because you seek vengeance against Rome.

"Boudica! Let me tell you this. There are those who rightly demand vengeance. The spirit of Caratacus of the Catuvellauni demands vengeance for the defeats he suffered. The spirits of all the Druids murdered on the isle of Mona demand righteous vengeance. But if you are here to beg for the help of my people in gaining vengeance against Rome for what they did to your family, then my answer is no. When the time is propitious, then I and my people will fight our battles, not yours."

All eyes of the Trinovante people were on her. Slowly, regally, she walked the remaining length of the room, and stood before the king.

She nodded. "Mandubracus is right when he says that there are others more deserving of vengeance. While Britons were living like animals in caves and bravely fighting the legions, my husband and I were lying on couches eating grapes and drinking goblets of wine. But I have learned a painful lesson from my mistakes. I have learned that the bite of the Roman snake is deep and dangerous. I understand why Mandubracus feels anger against me and the Iceni for our errors of the past. But to avenge the wrongs done to me and my children, I am going to teach the empire such a lesson that Roman widows will wail in the streets while their dead menfolk's blood spills into British soil; I am going to hurt the emperor so badly that he will curse the name Britain for all time. When Boudica is finished, songs will be sung by all people about the time when the Britons turned the relentless Roman tide and forced it to flood back on itself, drowning its evil ways.

"I, Boudica, am raising an army from among the people of the Iceni. Thousands will flock to my sword. They will be armed and fearless, dedicating their lives to avenging the crimes done to the tribe of Prasutagus and to the people of the Iceni. But even these thousands will not be enough to fight the might of Rome. I need men and women who will bear arms and stand shoulder to shoulder with other tribes. I am here, Mandubracus, to beg you and the people of the Trinovantes to join the men and women of the Iceni in the greatest battle we will ever fight."

The king burst out laughing. "You want us to join you? Is this why you have come, Boudica? I can taste your fury and understand the cause upon which you wish to embark, but why would I risk the lives of my people in doing what men like Caratacus have been unable to do?"

"Because, O King, unlike Caratacus and the Druids and all the others who died on the Roman sword, I know the Roman ways. I know their thoughts. I have studied their battle plans and dispositions. I know their strengths and weaknesses. Caratacus was defeated because he led a rabble. He was brave, but ignorant of what the Romans would do when he attacked them. And many men and women died because he refused to learn the lessons of the new world which the Romans forced upon us. Had Caratacus fought the Romans like a Roman, today there would be no civic capital at Camulodunum, no Romans in Britain.

"I came here, Mandubracus, to beg your understanding and your brotherly cooperation. But this is the last time ever that you will hear Boudica beg. Join me in my fight against Rome and we will be unbeatable, and then we will be free of servitude forever. Believe this, Mandubracus, I will join together all the tribes of Britain into the greatest and most powerful army we have ever seen. I will create an army out of the tribes from the north and south, from the east and west of Britain. In this army, Great King, there will be no Icenii or Regnii or Trinovantii. There will only be Britons."

"And who will lead this great army of yours?" he asked.

"Each king and queen will lead. Every tribe of Britain will be led by its rulers. And the rulers will sit together and together we will determine our battle plans. Together we will be the greatest army the world has ever seen. The very earth itself will shake when we march; the Roman army will quake in fear when they hear our footsteps. The Senate and the people of Rome will weep and rend their clothes when they listen to our battle cry. Mothers and fathers, sons and daughters, will howl at the moon for the gore of their loved ones spilled upon our soil. And our sacred trees will be nourished by Roman blood. Will you and your people join me?" she shouted, drawing her sword and brandishing it above her head.

Before he could answer, a hundred voices in the room shouted out as one, "Yes!"

Men took out their swords and held them above their heads, a forest of gleaming silver pointing at the roof.

Smiling, Boudica said, "Your people have spoken, Mandubracus."

60 AD—The Palace of the Emperor Nero

General Burrus, friend and advisor to the emperor, read and reread the scroll. He handed it back to Seneca, and said, "You're a fool, Spaniard. A fool and a scoundrel and a greedy usurer. Your actions will bring about great resentment and then Roman soldiers will have to pay with their lives for your avarice."

"And you, soldier, are an ill-mannered, ill-tempered, ignorant buffoon who would ruin the emperor's treasury just so you could take up with a whore from a portside tavern."

"Imbecile!" said Burrus.

"Deceiver!" responded Seneca.

The two men looked at each other. "Drink?" asked Burrus.

"My usual, and not too much spice this time. I was coughing all yesterday afternoon. I thought you must have been trying to poison me."

"Now there's an idea, Spaniard. Is poisoning a philosopher a crime? I would have thought I'd be rewarded by the Senate."

He handed him a cup of hot wine, and sat beside him on the couch. Their vantage point gave them a panoramic view of the city. "Seriously, Seneca, demanding back the forty million will surely cause problems for our men over there. Won't it?"

"We have enough men to deal with any resentment. The emperor needs the money—"

"But it was your money. You lent it to Claudius, and now you're demanding it back in Nero's name. Once it's repatriated to Rome, the emperor won't see any of it, so how will the emperor benefit?"

Seneca turned in surprise. "How did you know that? I've told nobody. The loan documents are in my possession."

Burrus shrugged. "You're not the only one with good intelligencers."

Indignantly, Seneca said, "You have a man in my service?"

"Two. Just like you have three in mine . . . my dresser, my armorer and my treasurer. Really, Seneca, didn't you think I'd find out? You're only paying them half what I pay them to tell you lies about me." The older man burst out laughing.

Seneca sighed. "Alright, the money will go back to me—"

"Plus the ten million in interest. So I ask again, apart from your avarice as the richest man in the empire, why are you putting such pressure on the Britons by demanding the return of your loan? I've seen this sort of thing before, old friend, and it's always led to uprisings and riots. We Romans are wonderful at conquering, but the money we extract from our provinces causes such bitterness toward us that you have to wonder about our tactics when all we do is drain the empire just for the benefit of Rome."

"But you know as well as I that things have to be paid for. Roads and bridges and the army and food for the people, and—"

"—and games in the arena which are ruining our treasury. But this money you're repatriating won't even go to the emperor, but will go to you. The emperor and Rome aren't going to benefit, and you're causing an uprising. You don't need the money."

"By the gods, Burrus, you sound like a philosopher rather than a soldier. The truth is, friend, that the Senate itself is beginning to wonder why it is that we're spending all this money on maintaining such vast armies and legions, when in return all we're really getting are goods and services and slaves which we could purchase without conquering the country. Yes, Rome has to control the world, but it has to be at a reasonable cost.

"People are beginning to ask themselves whether it would be better to reduce the size of the army, reduce the costs of maintaining such a huge empire, consolidate back to the borders before Augustus, and live a less complex life. You more than anybody would know that we have terrible problems in Armenia, in Judea, in northern Gaul, in Germania and now, it seems, in Britain—"

"I told you Britain would be a problem. When Suetonius wrote and told us of his successes in destroying those damnable Druids in the west of the country, I expressed my fears about the effect that would have on the rest of the people. Look at the Jews in Judea if you want to know what can happen when we undermine the worship of their gods and try to force them to worship ours. At least in Judea, we haven't slaughtered their priests . . . yet," Burrus said.

"My fear, Burrus, is that if we do withdraw from Britain, all the money I've lent will be lost. The decision could be made within the next year, if Suetonius has managed to put an end to the main rebellion. He's on his way back now to Londinium on the banks of the River Thames. I'm waiting for a report from him giving an assessment of the conditions of Britain now that the rebellion has finally been put down. If he says that we no longer have troubles, then I will recommend to the emperor that we withdraw, leaving only a few forts and trading outlets. Gaul and Germania are where our interests should lie, not the lands beyond the sea."

"And Judea? Parthia? Africa? Are we to pull away from all of these lands on which our blood has been spilled? When I became a soldier, Seneca, it was to fight for my emperor and my people. In the army, I learned to value the civilization we brought to savages and barbarians. We would fight a battle, subdue the people and on their mud huts or desert tents, we'd build stone and marble buildings which would last for all time. We introduced learning to them—mathematics and skills of reading and writing and philosophy and rhetoric—and in return we benefited from the things they produced, the slaves they sent and the taxes they paid.

"But since the time of Caligula, we've been bleeding the empire dry. It's becoming like a rotting carcass hanging on a butcher's hook. All the vital organs have been extracted, all the blood drained out of it, until it's just a gray and festering mass of resentment. And why do we suck the vitality and money out of the empire? To pay for the emperor's games, his banquets, his amusements, his plays and performances, his obscenities . . . ."

Looking round in shock, Seneca hissed, "For the sake of the gods, Burrus, keep silent."

"There are no servants around. I dismissed them all and I checked just moments ago. What I'm saying is for your ears, and your ears only. But it's only what's being whispered in the halls of the Senate every morning. You must have overheard such talk."

"Of course, but why do you think it's whispered and not discussed aloud in the halls of the chamber? Haven't you been seeing the wives of important men being forced to perform in lewd plays written by the emperor? Haven't you been party to the orgies in which the most elegant Roman matrons, some of them even grandmothers, are forced to cavort naked and pretend to be Grecian nymphs? The reason that Nero is allowed to do these things is precisely because any opposition to him leads to the disappearance of the man who opposes, and the forfeiture of all his money and property. And the same will happen to you, Burrus, if you continue to talk in this way. I'm trying to make the emperor realize the values of the Stoic way of life, but his hedonism is beating down my philosophy. Frankly, friend, I'm at a loss as to what to do."

Burrus shrugged. This time he moved closer to Seneca, and whispered, "Perhaps he'll go the same way as Caligula and Claudius. Perhaps you could use some of your money to persuade certain Germans in the Praetorian Guard."

Seneca looked at his friend in shock. He was smiling, but there was something in his eyes which told the philosopher that the soldier was only partially joking.

CHAPTER TWELVE

60 AD—The Roman City of Camulodunum

Only a month previously, she had ridden in distress along this very road, along the path which led to the gates of Camulodunum, she and her daughters having been robbed of their wealth. Tears had filled her eyes, knowing that the procurator was ransacking her home with its precious contents, and stealing her jewelry and possessions.

And only a month previously, she had been carried in a filthy cart like some butchered beast, along this very road, away from Camulodunum, having been scourged by a whip and humiliated in front of the entire town. And worse, a million times worse, had been the treatment meted out to her daughters who were robbed of their youth. Tears no longer filled her eyes as she returned to Camulodunum. The pain was too great even for tears. Instead, her eyes were full of fury and hatred. And today, she was again riding in her chariot with her daughters toward the locked gates of the city, but her intentions this time were altogether different. Today, she would extract the eternal revenge.

As the walls of the city loomed closer, Boudica wished that she had known a month earlier what was in store for her and her daughters. For had she even begun to comprehend the depth of Roman cruelty, she would never have traveled this road. She would, like other widows of Britons, have accepted her lot, and thrown herself on the mercy of her people. But when Boudica thought of her two girls, she felt afresh a surge of self-righteousness and hatred at the merciless Roman veterans in the barracks. She had a special treat reserved for them, just as she had rehearsed in her mind the punishment she would mete out to the procurator of Britain, the execrable Decianus Catus, living safely in Londinium. And to Cassus, who would soon meet Prasutagus in a slow and agonizing dance of death!

Boudica reined in her horses as she neared the gate. Behind her, hiding in the woods, armed and gorged on her fury, thousands of men and women of the Iceni and Trinovantes, now calling themselves Britons, had silently amassed overnight, waiting in anticipation of striking their first blow.

By common consent, all had agreed to wait until Boudica had made the first move before they would assault the walls. By rights and custom, Boudica and her daughters were the wronged, the victims of Roman criminals; by rights and custom, Boudica and her daughters should be the first to see their assailants kneel and beg for mercy.

They had journeyed throughout the night from all over the outlying districts to hide in the woods, a vast host of Britons who looked on Boudica as their leader and first warrior. None, not one in the British army, held any doubts about their mission. All knew of Caratacus' failure years earlier; all now believed the victory would be theirs under the leadership of their kings and queens, and in the wake of the fury of Boudica and her daughters.

The queen of the Iceni, for she now assumed the title, had explained to them carefully the previous day what would be the battle plan. They were still half a day's march from Camulodunum and knew they would be preparing for the battle which would be fought at first light. Without sleep, silently creeping like wolves through the dark forests, without lanterns and relying only on the weak light of the moon, they had arrived at the surrounds of Camulodunum.

And now they waited, watching from the distant woods as Boudica and her daughters rode slowly along the road toward the eastern gate of the city. Swords and spears in their hands, they crouched in anticipation.

The Roman guard, a veteran of the army in Parthia and Syria, first saw the dust when he turned to the east to look at the rising sun and try to estimate how much longer before he was relieved and could get some sleep. Wondering whether the dust was caused by an animal or a vehicle on the road that early in the morning, the guard blinked to clear the tiredness from his eyes, and stared at the distance. It wasn't long before the chariot approaching the gates came into view. Odd that somebody would be arriving at the city before the curfew was ended and the gates could be opened.

He waited until the chariot was close before he called out, "Who wants entry before the curfew is lifted?" He looked down, and saw it was a woman and her two children. The woman was dressed in bronze armor covered by a cloak. Her long red hair spilled out of the horned bronze helmet. The guard looked closely at her . . . and then with a shock realized that it was the same woman who had come to Camulodunum some time ago and had been whipped. And she was riding with her daughters, the girls who had been raped. He himself had enjoyed some time on top of the body of the younger one.

He turned and called down to the guardhouse. "Commander. You'd better come up here. Now!"

"I am Boudica, queen of the Iceni. I command you to open your gates," she called out in a strong and confident voice.

The guard looked down at her. "I told you when you came here last time, piss off. Go away. Turn around and leave, or do you want the same welcome as last time?" But there was no confidence in his voice.

"Open the gates, guard, or you will regret the day you were born," she shouted, enfolding Camorra and Tasca in her cloak. The horses whinnied. This tall, red-haired woman with blue eyes—the eyes of a Siren or Medusa—wearing a brilliant red cloak over her armor, showed neither fear nor concern.

The guard commander joined his colleague on the parapet. "What's going on here? Who is this woman? Turn around, woman, and go back the way you came, or I'll unleash my men on you."

Staring up in naked hatred, Boudica said nothing. Slowly she pulled her bow out of its harness and took an arrow from the quiver on her back.

"Shoot that arrow, woman, and you and your children will die. Guards . . . arm yourselves. Listen to me carefully, woman. Turn around immediately, or you will die in your next breath," said the commander.

But ignoring him, she turned slowly and deliberately in her chariot, and instead of shooting the arrow at the guards, Boudica instead shot it away from the city and upward in the direction of the wood. The guard commander, mystified, held up his hands to prevent the archers on the parapet from unleashing their arrows. He wanted to know what game she was playing. And the Romans watched in surprise as first a few men and women slowly emerged from the woods and stood on the road; then more and more emerged from the trees, until the road was full of thousands of heavily armed Britons. His eyes widened in shock. Some of the men and women were naked, some dressed in armor and battle gear. All had their faces painted in the blue woad of a Celtic warrior, their bodies wearing painted symbols of circles and arrowheads and waves.

The guard commander cried out, "By the gods . . ."

He turned to run, but before he could take a pace, Boudica let fly an arrow which hit him in the neck. He screamed and gasped, and fell off the parapet onto the ground below. Camorra quickly picked up her bow and let fly an arrow. The other guard opened his mouth to cry a warning, but the girl's arrow caught him also in his throat. He crumpled to his knees, trying to pull the arrow out before darkness descended. Immediately, the few archers on the parapet unleashed their arrows at the Britons, and Boudica pulled her children down onto their knees in the protection of the chariot's metal front shield.

Crouching, Boudica whispered to her children, "The first blow. One to the mother, and one to the daughter. Oh, by the gods, it feels good. Soon, Tasca, you'll have the chance to kill a Roman. And both of you will avenge the wrongs done to you. Soon, you'll see the men who terrified you become terrified of you. Soon, you'll know the joy of revenge, the feeling of power."

When Boudica heard the sound of her army screaming battle cries as they ran toward the walls, she stood and began to fire arrows over the fence and into the city. Hearing the commotion and seeing arrows flying through the air, other Roman guards ran up to the parapet. Agape with surprise at seeing a huge army suddenly appearing out of nowhere at their door, they turned and shouted the alarm to the town below. One of the guards rang the warning bell.

Taking a dozen arrows out of her quiver, Boudica loosed them one after the other at the guards and citizens who had climbed the parapet and were running along the walkway to see what was happening. Guards began to throw spears down at Boudica's chariot, but they landed short. However, fearing for the continued safety of her children, she tugged on the reins and turned her horses around to ride out of the fray.

By now, the front ranks of her army were at the gates, and were lighting arrowheads with rags soaked in tar to set the city on fire. At her command, they shot the flame arrows into the air and over the walls. She gave orders for the battering ram to be carried to the gate. Ten men hefted the newly cut tree into the middle of the road and, protected by a barrage of arrows fired at the guards, forcing the Romans to cower below the level of the fence, they ran at the gate, shouting imprecations and war cries to their gods.

The gate was stouter than first it seemed, and the ram rebounded off it, tripping up four of the men and causing the others to collapse. They fell to the ground, pinned under the huge tree.

"Stand, fools, and do it again," Boudica screamed.

The men struggled from under the tree, picked it up and again ran at the gate, this time with a vengeance. As the ram hit the wood of the gate, they heard the satisfying sound of tearing struts and beams coming from the other side of the door.

"Again!" Boudica commanded. For the third time, and then a final fourth, the men ran the battering ram at the wall. All the time, she commanded her archers to fire at the parapet to engage the Romans, and ensure that her batterers would not be fired upon from above.

Many citizens, alarmed out of their beds by the ringing of the warning bell, gathered in the streets. And many were killed by the flights of burning arrows which fell like Jove's thunderbolts from the sky. A wail of screaming and crying grew in the city. Hysterical men and women ran for cover into their homes. Guards who had been sleeping were rudely awakened and commanded to take up arms and repel the invaders. They ran to the walls, and saw that the eastern gate was about to give way, its crossbeams splintered and fractured. The flame arrows had set fire to bales of straw and wooden buildings, as well as to the leaves on terra-cotta roofs. The fires spread beneath the roof tiles into the cavities and set fire to the wood of the ceiling.

When the building was well alight, the flames spread from one house to the next. And fires in the streets from burning wagons and hay were making the eastern access to the city into an inferno.

The news of the impending breach of the city walls was quickly transmitted to the commander of the west gate, who looked in horror at the vast army which had suddenly materialized out of nowhere. There weren't enough guards or soldiers to protect the city, and so he immediately wrote orders and gave them to a rider who raced out of the western gate of the city with instructions to ride to the fort twelve miles away and instruct the garrison commander to send reinforcements immediately.

Boudica saw the horseman ride off into the distance, and cursed herself for failing to secure the other two gates of the city before attacking from the east. But it was too late to worry about that now. She had to breach the eastern gate quickly to keep up the momentum.

The centurion of the forces ordered his men to gather into a Tortoise so that when the gates were breached and opened by the enemy, the Romans would march out, shields protecting them, and fight in open ground.

With the final assault by the battering ram, the eastern gate burst open with a loud crack, and a cheer rose from the Britons. Boudica knew the likely next move of the Romans, and had warned her army the previous night of what to expect. Instead of rushing into the open maw to their certain deaths, all of her men and women drew back, her archers still firing shots up onto the parapet to prevent the Romans from shooting arrows and throwing lances downward at her exposed soldiers.

Unsure of what to do at the standoff, and anticipating the rabble would come flooding through the gates where they could be dealt with one by one, the watch commander ordered his men to move forward through the gate in the disposition of the Tortoise. Shields closed one on the other to protect themselves, the hundred Romans walked slowly forward through the gate, staring through the joins in their shields to glimpse the nature of the enemy.

Knowing that a Tortoise was a solid defense, and knowing that the protruding spears made it too deadly to approach, Boudica gave the order for her army to pull back, while the archers were still firing volley after volley at the parapet to force the Roman archers and guards to keep their heads down.

Then she nodded to the leader of the men who held the battering ram. They withdrew from the wall, and ran back along the road. As the Tortoise slowly edged its way through the gate and into the open ground to prepare for combat, Boudica gave the order for the batterers to turn and run forward as fast as possible. The ramming party ran full tilt into the Roman Tortoise, something which Boudica doubted had ever happened before in the history of Roman warfare. Those in the front were knocked over, and fell back heavily into the Tortoise at the feet of those behind, causing them to fall, arms and legs akimbo.

Smiling at the simplicity of her device, Boudica saw with enormous satisfaction that the mighty and invincible Roman Tortoise was collapsing like reeds in a wind, the men flailing on the ground, shields now useless to defend them. Soon, the famed Tortoise was lying on its back, hundreds of legs and arms weaving in despair, the men trying urgently to stand.

"Attack," Boudica screamed, and a hundred archers and spearmen and women ran forward and shot volley upon volley of deadly arrows into the struggling mass of Roman soldiers. They screamed and clawed the air in pain, but were defenseless against the fury of the Britons.

"Kill them," shouted Camorra.

"Kill them all," screamed Tasca.

"No, not all," shouted Boudica over the noise of the Britons. "Bring two of them to me in ropes."

Stabbing them with lances, hacking off arms and heads with swords, it took only a short time for the Britons to kill the hundred Roman defenders. Two, however, were dragged to their feet, terrified, and force-marched toward Boudica's chariot.

Surveying the battle, it was now obvious that with the gate open, the eastern sector of the city surrounded by her army and the remnants of the Roman forces on the parapet pinned down beneath the fence by continuous arrow fire, Camulodunum was hers for the taking. But before she and her daughters rode in, there was something she had to do.

Boudica and her two daughters stepped down from their chariot, and looked at the Roman soldiers who were bowed before them on their knees. Their uniforms were dusty and tattered, and their helmets were on the ground in front of them. One was bleeding from a wound to his arm.

"Look, girls. Look at the might of Rome. Look at Roman manhood. This is what hurt you so badly. And this is when you shall have your revenge."

She gave Camorra and Tasca each a dagger, and nodded to them. Tasca walked the two paces to the Roman, her face a snarl of hatred, and plunged the dagger into his neck. The man screamed in pain, gasped and then pitched forward onto the ground. His fellow soldier, seeing what had just happened, cried and began to beg. Undaunted, Tasca plunged the dagger again and again into the dead man's back, her mouth rigid with hatred.

"Tasca!" shouted her sister.

"No. Be silent, Camorra. It is Tasca's right to do so. It is her way of ridding herself of the evil inside of her. You must do the same."

The soldier shouted in tears, "No! I beg of you to spare me. I'm a married man. I have children."

Hearing him, Camorra turned and frowned. "You have children?" the young girl asked quietly.

He looked up and nodded. "Three. I beg you, Lady, to spare me for the sake of my children." He started to cry.

Suddenly furious, Camorra shouted at him. "You have children, yet you did this to me? You raped me and my sister, even though you have children? You are a father, and you would let this happen to a girl like one of your daughters. Did you laugh, Roman, when those beasts were hurting and raping me and my sister? Did you watch? Did you! Or were you one of those who hurt me?" she screamed, her rage rising until she was unstoppable. Grasping the dagger tightly, Camorra paced over to the soldier and plunged it into his back. Blood spurted out of the wound and Camorra looked at his death in satisfaction.

Boudica smiled. Yes, it was a hard and cruel lesson for her girls, but they had been brutalized, and the healing would now begin.

Leaving the dagger in his back as he lay on the ground, Camorra stepped back into the chariot. "Come, Mother, we have a battle to win."

Pride welled up inside Boudica for her two wonderful girls. She and her daughters resumed their places on the chariot, and wheeled it around. She looked at her army. Twenty or thirty Britons lay dead on the ground, but the hundred Roman soldiers lay in what remained of the shape of the Tortoise, along with those who had emerged from the gate to engage in battle. How many were dead and dying on the parapet or in the now-burning eastern edge of the city, she had no idea. But she would shortly find out.

Whipping her horses, she shouted to her army, "Advance! Move into the city. Kill every Roman man and woman inside. Leave not one Roman alive, except for Marcus Vitellus Publicus. I will deal with him. Now march!" Her army cheered. As they entered the city, she gave instructions that this gate, and all the others which would enable the citizens to flee, were each to be guarded by fifty men and women. She hadn't realized how easy it would be to demolish this gate, the city's first line of defense, but she didn't want any of the gates to continue to be used for escape. She thought about the horseman who had ridden off as she was attacking the eastern gate, and assumed that his task was to bring reinforcements.

As the army entered the eastern edge of Camulodunum, they were faced with a scene from the very realm of Hades. Buildings were burning, and black and gray smoke was pouring out of roofs and doors and windows. Hundreds of men and women lay in the streets, some trying to crawl, others in the stillness of death. Some of the citizens were charred, their clothes and bodies having been burnt by the falling conflagration of pitch arrows bringing fire from the skies.

Others had arrows sticking out of their bodies, their blood pooling into the dust and mud of the roadways. But nowhere were there living and active citizens or soldiers or civic officials standing in a line to prevent their entry.

Boudica wondered what the city would do to defend itself, and her question was soon answered. The noise of an army running into a battle formation could be heard over the shouts and screams and crackling of fires. She looked through the smoke, and saw hundreds of Roman soldiers arranging themselves into a military line at the distant end of the street.

"Quickly," she commanded, "form up into the positions you practiced yesterday."

Her men and women hastily assembled into five rows, with spearmen and women in the front row protected by their shields; behind them were archers; behind them more lancers; and in the last row were more archers. She knew from Prasutagus that Romans prefer to fight in open country where they can perform their maneuvers. In open ground, they had wings and flanks, fighting lines and supporting lines, and hidden areas behind nearby hills or forests where they could keep their secondary fighting men in reserve. But in the close confines of a town, it would be hand-to-hand combat, where the rage and hatred of the Britons would give them an advantage. The Romans were fighting for a distant emperor; the Britons were fighting for the return of their country.

The Romans began to advance, and Boudica sent her troops at a slow forward pace. She had ordered them not to rush forward as was their inclination, but to remain calm, to consolidate their positions as they advanced upon the enemy.

She ordered her rear archers to shoot their first volley into the face of the enemy. Dozens of Romans were felled by the swarm of arrows which flew over the heads of her army, but despite the losses, they continued to pace forward slowly and menacingly.

Roman archers also sent volleys of arrows into the Britons, who fell screaming in large numbers. The Roman front line continued to advance up the street, stepping over the bodies of their dead and wounded comrades, and soon the two armies met. Boudica rode her chariot through the throng and toward the Romans. She screamed a battle cry and picked up one of the lances, which she flung at the centurion who led his troops. It flew through the air and struck him in the breast, piercing his thick leather tunic and metal armor. He screamed in pain as he fell, dead.

The two armies fought until the Romans, realizing that they were defeated by the vast numbers of Britons, and now leaderless with the deliberate targeting of their commanders, turned and ran back in the direction of the forum and their barracks. Boudica surveyed the ground. She had lost another hundred or more men and women, and at least the same number were moaning on the ground, badly wounded. She gave orders for the evacuation of the wounded, but for the dead to be left where they were, as there was no time for burial or sacred rites.

Now, where there had been screaming and mayhem, there was quiet. Only the sounds of men grunting and gasping, and of the fires crackling, disturbed the silence. And then the air became mysteriously still. Slowly, Boudica and her army marched forward and entered the town center, which looked as if all living humanity had evacuated, leaving only the dead to testify to its former glory. She spurred her chariot farther into the city she knew so well, and looked around.

Could this be victory? Could success be so easy?

Boudica ordered her men and women to march into the forum and assemble there, taking control of the remaining two gates in the city walls; she anticipated that they would meet little or no resistance, as the veterans were probably cowering in their barracks, and the citizens, all retired soldiers who had been given land stolen from the Britons, were too frightened to come out of their houses.

Leaving further defensive forces at the remaining gates of the city to ensure no more escapees, Boudica cut away from the main body of her army and steered her chariot out of the main street into the road which led to the baths. There, she saw the house of Marcus Vitellus Publicus, and reined in her horses. Telling the girls to remain in the chariot, and to ride away quickly if there was any trouble, Boudica drew her sword. She entered Marcus' home, and called out, "Boudica, queen of the Iceni, seeks Marcus Vitellus Publicus."

He walked slowly, unsteadily, out of the shadows, and stood in the center of the room. In his hands were a sword and a dagger, pointing at her. Boudica looked behind him, and saw his wife and children, cowering and terrified.

"I greet you as a friend, Marcus Vitellus Publicus. Some time ago, when my life was in peril and my daughters had been raped and left for dead, you were the only man in this city who came to our aid. You saved my life and restored me to my people. Boudica does not forget such kindness. But you must know, Marcus Vitellus, that I have raised a great army to right the wrongs which Rome has done to my people. Once we have destroyed Camulodunum and killed all its inhabitants, we will march on other Roman cities and towns and destroy them, too."

He remained impassive, but his wife gasped and put her hand to her mouth. The children began to whimper. Boudica continued. "Not one Roman will be left alive in all of Britain by the time that Boudica has finished. The soil of Britain will grow rich with Roman blood. But I don't wish this fate for you, Marcus Vitellus. You are a good man. You gave me friendship and tried to build a bridge over the turbulent sea which separates our people. You clothed me when I was naked, you rescued my babies, and I will reward this kindness by giving you a day to gather your family and a few possessions, and leave this land to return to where you belong.

"My men on the east gate have been given orders to allow you and your family to leave. Go now, Marcus Vitellus Publicus, while you are under the protection of Boudica. But delay until morning, and you will suffer the same fate which all of your people will suffer on my land. May the gods go with you and your family."

Boudica turned to leave the house.

"Wait!"

She turned in surprise and looked at Marcus Vitellus. "If you wish to beg for the lives of your friends—"

"I wish nothing of you, Boadicea. I am a former Roman soldier. I was commanded by General Vespasian; he was one of the noblest of all Romans. He would be merciless to an enemy nation in order to quell its resistance, but he would never have allowed his men to do to you what was done by Procurator Catus. You and your daughters were not dishonored by what was done to you, Boadicea. The whole of Rome and its empire was dishonored. Men such as Decianus are evil and line their own pockets at the expense of us all.

"I know that you're going to kill many here in Camulodunum, and I can't find it in my heart to blame you. But the man you should bring to justice is the one man who will find an excuse to escape back to Rome.

"Therefore I say this to you, Boadicea. For every Roman that you kill, Rome will ensure that a hundred Britons die. So make sure that the one Roman who shouldn't escape your vengeance is brought before you for justice. The moment Decianus hears of your uprising, he will probably sail for Gaul. Send a party of your warriors to the River Thames east of Londinium, for the moment he hears of your assault against Camulodunum, he'll set sail, and that's where you'll find him. And just before you kill him, tell him that Marcus Vitellus Publicus will curse his name forever."

Boudica breathed deeply, nodded, and left the house.

During the three days of skirmishing and fighting it took her to quell the last of the resistance to her invasion, Boudica and her army faced the biggest challenge they had yet contemplated. When she had first appeared at the eastern gate, a rider had been dispatched through the western gate to summon troops from the fort nearby. Yet when he'd described to the local commander how many Britons were attacking Camulodunum, he had been immediately dispatched to the north where a legion was encamped. When he arrived, without the authority of the military governor, Gaius Suetonius Paulinus, the commander of the fort, Petillius Cerialis, made an immediate decision to end the revolt right there and then. He ordered five thousand legionaries of the IX Legion Hispana to march immediately south toward Camulodunum. He gave orders that not one single rebel Briton was to be left alive.

But Boudica had already been warned of their arrival by lookouts posted on the distant hills, who had ridden in swiftly to tell her of the appearance of the Romans and informed her that they would be at Camulodunum by the end of the day. Having planned for the Romans sending reinforcements, Boudica ordered ten thousand of her men and women to leave the city by the west gate, and to gather sticks and branches in the woods north of the city through which the legion would have to march in order to reach Camulodunum.

Examining the preparations, Boudica checked that the branches and leaves and bushes retained the appearance of the forest. Then she ordered her army to pour oil at the base of the woodpiles. Satisfied, she ordered her army to hide in the undergrowth and behind trees which lined the approach road to the city.

Quietly, vigilantly, they lay in wait as the Romans headed for Camulodunum at full pace, assuming that these barbarians would be as disorganized as Caratacus and other rebels of the past.

When the legion was into the wood, blinded by the thickness of the undergrowth and the trees, Boudica screamed her war cry. Petillius Cerialis reined in his horse and watched in terror as thousands of Britons suddenly stood up from the undergrowth and let loose a continuous barrage of arrows. Hundreds of Romans fell in the first few moments, taken completely by surprise.

Petillius Cerialis, arrogant and impulsive, quickly but incorrectly summed up the situation, and ordered his men into crouching defensive positions behind their shields. He had to purchase time to make a more considered judgment of the situation, to determine the position and strength of the enemy and the countermeasures he could impose.

It was a deadly mistake. After the first torrent of arrows, the next salvo was flame arrows aimed at the base of the piles of branches and sticks, which suddenly burst into a roaring conflagration. More flame arrows pierced armor, ignited wagons, terrified horses into stampeding, and caused fear and havoc among the men. These flame arrows were immediately followed by lighted spears which ignited other oil-soaked bales of sticks and twigs and branches which had been stacked along the roadside.

A wall of smoke and flame on both sides of the road erupted like a volcano. The men cried in despair at the way they had walked into such a trap. Unable to breach the conflagration, unable to breathe in the oily smoke which filled their lungs, their only exit was via the front and rear, but hundreds of heavily armed Britons were gathered there to prevent escape.

The Roman army was now completely hemmed in by a flaming inferno which prevented them from breaking through and chasing the Britons. And while the troops were forced to defend themselves on the road, incapable of moving, the Britons loosed volley after volley of flame arrows until every single man of the IX Hispana was dead; every man, except for Petillius Cerialis, the son-in-law of the great General Vespasian, who whipped his horse through the flame and escaped into the dense scrub with a small personal guard while his men were being slaughtered.

Boudica prayed that the flames from the roadside wouldn't set fire to the forest. Her prayers were answered when the oil had burned away. The fire slowly died down, enabling Boudica to ensure that every single Roman had been killed. Those who were wounded or begging for a drink, or mercy, were swiftly dispatched to their gods by a dagger to the heart or throat.

She ordered many of their heads to be hacked off and stuck onto poles by the roadside as an offering to the Druid gods who protected the Britons.

Free now from outside interference, Boudica rode in triumph back into the city and toward the huge open forum. But as she entered, she sensed that something was not right. They had been fighting for three days only, yet the city seemed to have given in, as though surrender were preferable to fighting to the death. She couldn't understand how her victory had been that simple. Could she have taken the city in only a few days? A city as large as Camulodunum with its thousands of Roman inhabitants?

Surely not! Surely any citizens of any town would have turned out in greater numbers to fight in the streets against an invading army? Since the fighting within the walls had finished, most of the inhabitants had hidden in their homes instead of coming out to defend themselves. Was this the real strength of Rome? Cities of weak, bloated and cringing men and women hiding behind the tunics of a vast and merciless army?

One thing she knew with absolute conviction: After today, no Briton would ever again cower at the sound of Romans marching along the highways.

She lashed her horses and her chariot wheels clattered over the stones and mud as she rode toward the forum. There, she looked upon her army. Most of her men and women looked exhausted. Three days of hard fighting with minimal rations, three days of slaughtering Roman soldiers and seeing their friends and comrades being killed had weakened even the strongest. Some were still cautious, carrying their weapons close at hand, concerned about the element of a sudden attack, looking around and peering into streets and corners, into houses and doors and windows, to preempt a sudden counterattack by the veterans.

Others in her army, flushed by their victory at the cost of so few British lives compared to the thousands of Romans they'd slaughtered, were laughing and hugging the women; some were lying on the ground, others were drinking flagons of wine which they'd stolen in the search among the houses.

Boudica drew her chariot to a halt, and a roar of approval greeted her. Both her own Iceni and the Trinovantes greeted her as their supreme commander after three grueling days of battle in which she'd proved fearless, inexhaustible and unstoppable. In the beginning, they had followed her because they were ordered to. Now they would follow her because she was victorious.

But there was no smile on Boudica's face. Instead, her face was a mask of fury. She pushed through the outer ring of her guards into the middle of the forum, where the revelers had gathered.

One, leering and offensively friendly, thrust a flagon of wine at her, but with her sword, she knocked it out of his hand. Shocked, he drew back, and the laughter and cheering in the army came slowly to silence.

"This is how you will all die," she shouted. "Drunk and debauched and as a rabble. This is how Rome will defeat you. If you think we've won a great victory and that now it is your right to celebrate, then tomorrow you will surely die. This is how Caratacus and his army were defeated. This is how he caused the deaths of thousands of Britons and why he was dragged to Rome in chains instead of reigning as your king. You," she said, pointing to a seminaked woman of the Iceni people who had been lying on the floor, kissing several men in her ecstasy as victor over the Romans.

Wide-eyed in fear, the woman covered her breasts and stood. "You," repeated Boudica, "come here to your queen."

Gulping, the woman came forward and stood before Boudica. "You and all those who have put down their swords to cavort and revel are guilty of dereliction of your duty. You, who have drunk wine and clouded your judgment, are guilty of a crime against the Britons who have risked their lives to defeat the Romans. For the crimes of dereliction and treason, I sentence you to death."

A gasp was heard from the entire army. In their triumph was their downfall.

"Kneel," said Boudica, whose anger was boiling over.

The woman fell to her knees wailing, her body suddenly racked with sobs.

Boudica raised her sword high into the air, and called out, "This is the punishment which will be meted out to any British man or woman who fails to follow my orders."

The men and women of the Iceni and Trinovantes looked on in horror as Boudica swung her sword down toward the woman's naked back. But at the last fraction of a second, she twisted the blade, so that it cleft the air and landed just in front of the woman's head, striking the stone paving of the forum and sending up sparks.

Again, there was a gasp as the woman screamed and collapsed in a dead faint.

"Hear me, Britons. Two days ago, when we first entered this city, I saved the life of one good Roman. So it is right that today, now that the city is almost ours, I have decided to save the life of one stupid Briton. But be certain that this is the last time I will show leniency to any of you. Any infraction of my orders, by whomsoever, and it will lead to your immediate death; any cowardice before the enemy will be punishable by death; and most especially, any rebellious behavior by breaking ranks or failure to maintain your positions on the battlefield will result in your immediate deaths. I have spoken."

There was shuffling in the assembly. Men and women were looking at each other and wondering why she was being so harsh. Had they not just scored a great victory? Yet now they were being castigated in their moment of triumph. Was this why they had fought and risked their lives?

Sensing the mood, she shouted out, "Boudica's army will surely lose to Rome if you drink and dance and cavort like merrymakers at the Beltane, when instead you should be fighting Romans and using your eyes and ears to be alert and guard your own lives and those of your comrades. The only way we're going to defeat a Roman army is by discipline as rigid and unbending as a Roman's iron heel. From this moment onward, Britons, you will eat when I tell you, sleep when I tell you, smile and breathe when I tell you. Anyone who wishes to go his or her own way must leave my army now—but do so, and you will live like slaves for the rest of your lives. Those who wish to stay will swear by the mighty gods that they will obey me in everything; for I know Rome and its army; and only I, Boudica, your queen, will lead you to freedom and victory."

She stopped speaking, and waited breathlessly for a response. But her rhetoric was greeted by a heavy silence. Her heart sank. Had she won a minor skirmish and lost the war before it had even begun? Was this what her victory entailed? Did it end at the beginning? Her face stern, she silently prayed to the gods to come to her aid and make her fellow Britons understand that only rigid discipline would win over their enemy.

Still the silence continued; only the air crackled with the noise and stench of burning houses and flesh. She had lost! She was a queen with no followers, a debased and abused woman who could command nobody. Bereft, she was about to turn and join her daughters on the chariot to take her into hiding and oblivion, when suddenly, from a distance, one man from deep within the throng shouted out, "I swear by the gods that I will follow you, Boudica, and do as you command."

And then another; and then a hundred; and then the entire army shouted out their approval of her tactics and of Boudica as their leader. She bit her lip to prevent herself from crying.

Her first order of the new day was to send a party of twenty of her soldiers to travel south and to the east of the city of Londinium; there, they were to wait patiently, and to stop any boat which was sailing seaward. All Roman passengers were to be taken from the boats and their possessions examined. If one of them was the procurator of Britain, one Decianus Catus, he was to be brought in chains before Boudica.

Her second order of the day was for her men to search all the houses which were still standing in the southern quarter of the city, beginning at the outskirts of the forum, and working outward to the walls of the city. She and a troop of her soldiers would continue to search the public buildings, the roofs and cellars, looking for anyone who was still hiding. Her instructions were that when every house was searched, it was to be torched and burnt to the ground. She would take personal control of the destruction of the public buildings, especially the huge temple to Claudius, which had caused so much additional taxation to be levied against the British people. Boudica would take great pleasure in destroying that, as well as the statue of the goddess of victory which stood before it. The huge and ugly head of the so-called god, Claudius, came off the shoulders at a stroke of her axe. She ordered it to be carried to the outside of the city, and then thrown into the nearby river as an obeisance to the gods for enabling this great victory.

She also ensured that the great statue of the goddess of victory be pulled down off its pedestal, and that its back be turned away from the forum and the barracks, as a sign that Victory had turned her back on the Roman people.

And then, Boudica ordered that all living Romans captured were to be brought in chains to the forum for humiliation and execution. What she especially wanted to do was to search for the veterans of the Roman army who lived in the barracks. She had deliberately left the barracks until last, to ensure that the men waited days locked inside the house where her daughters had been raped, so that each and every man there knew with absolute certainty that all others in the city had been defeated by her, and now she was coming after them. The longer they waited in fear of the inevitable, the sweeter would be her revenge. She set out with a searching party of a hundred men and women, and stood outside the barracks on the southeast edge of the forum.

Boudica addressed her soldiers. "I have a special punishment in mind for the men in here. These animals raped my daughters. Kill as few as possible. I want to capture most of them alive."

Pushing open the wooden doors with her boot, she was confronted by the darkness of the interior and the stench of men living in close quarters. It had been closed up for days and the airless atmosphere stank of urine and fear. Sword held high in one hand, dagger held low in the other, Boudica walked forward into the gloom, anticipating a sudden assault.

It came when she and ten of her army were in the building. A impulsive shout of "Die, British whore," resounded through the building as twenty older men, dressed in full army gear and heavy armor, ran toward her, lances held horizontal, swords held aloft.

Boudica stood and faced the first line of assault, three men running shoulder to shoulder and filling the width of the corridor. As they raced toward her, anticipating a fight, she cried an order and she and her men suddenly sank to their knees. Without their target standing before them, the three leading veterans slowed their advance, not understanding what was happening.

By instruction, the men behind Boudica let loose a flight of arrows from their raised bows, striking the veterans in parts of their bodies which weren't protected. Armor saved one, but two others fell as the arrows pierced neck and groin and face. As they fell, Boudica stood and ordered her men to advance. The Romans behind their fallen colleagues were suddenly boxed in, finding the advance difficult over the bodies. They had lost their advantage of surprise and force, and now they saw that Boudica, tall and fearsome in her armor and horned helmet, swinging her sword, was advancing toward them.

One of the veterans ordered his men to stand and fight. They stood shoulder to shoulder as best they could in the confines of the barracks, but Boudica again surprised them by stopping her advance. Without warning, she and her men in the front fell to their knees as the archers at the back again let loose another volley. More Romans screamed in pain, and dropped down dead or injured to the floor.

"You are defeated. Do you surrender?" Boudica shouted at them.

The elderly men looked at their fallen comrades, and realized that it would be a slaughter if they continued. At least by surrendering, they stood some chance of leniency, or at best a few hours of extended life before their inevitable death. They nodded and threw their swords, daggers and spears to the ground. "Ensure that they are completely disarmed, and then bring them to the forum.

Search the building, and bring any others who might be hiding. As soon as you've ensured nobody is in the building, set it ablaze. I will continue to search the other buildings."

It was the beginning of the evening of the fourth day of the battle of Camulodunum before all the still-living residents of the city had been arrested, gathered into the forum, and restrained. Men and women, though only the occasional child, sat or lay like farm animals, trussed with ropes or chains, looking at the Britons in fear and contempt. How had it come to this? they wondered. Why were the Britons so vicious as to attack those who brought civilization to their midst?

There must have been four or five hundred in the forum, Boudica thought as she stood on the edge of the square, and surveyed the results of the first of many victories she would enjoy. Thousands had already died in the streets, as well as many of her British army.

Most of the buildings in the western and southern city were still ablaze and crackling with fire. The east of the city was a smoldering black ruin. The bodies of Romans who had died in the streets, shot with arrows as they tried to escape, or killed trying to defend their homes, were now stiffening, their fingers and arms making them look like statues, their faces drawn and grimacing in the throes of death. Those who hadn't died by arrows had been killed by sword or lance, their bodies livid with vicious scars and wounds. Some of the walls of the houses were daubed in blood where somebody, mortally wounded, had fallen against them. The ground, once shining with colorful mosaics, was now stained and slippery with the gore and innards of the dead.

Those who had chosen life over death now suffered the fear and indignity of being bound captives, nervously awaiting their fate. Most of the residents who had escaped death were dressed in togas or tunics; the veterans of the barracks had decided to put on military uniforms and armor for their last-ditch stand. It was a moment Boudica had dreamed of since the day she was abused and humiliated on this very spot, before these same people. Then, in her moment of agony, these men and women had been full of contempt, laughing and carefree, as the procurator of Britain had had her stripped naked and whipped. Where, Boudica wondered, were the smiles now? And when news reached Decianus, and his dog Cassus, how would they react? She ached to see the look on their faces when they were brought news of Boudica, and the revenge she had begun to exact for what they had done to her.

"Romans," she called out above the noise of the fires and the occasional explosion from a perfume bottle or a flagon of wine. "You are all guilty of crimes against the people of Britain. You are all guilty of being party to my humiliation and the rape of my daughters. I, Boudica, queen of the Iceni, was dragged before you a month ago, and was mercilessly abused by a thief and robber and tax collector you call procurator of Britain; yet not one of you raised a hand to stay the sting of the whip or to help my children when their precious and innocent young bodies were brutalized by the beasts from your barracks."

Women prisoners began to cry as they remembered where they had seen this tall, furious red-haired woman. They now knew with certainty what their fate would be.

"You are further guilty of the theft of British land, of the enslavement of British people, and of sacrilege against British gods. For all these crimes, and more, you are sentenced to death. All of the men here who were not responsible for the rape of my daughters, yet who were witnesses to my whipping, will be beheaded. All the women who witnessed my shame and nakedness, and who have suckled the might of Roman manhood on their breasts, will be hanged, and then they will have their teats cut from their bodies and sewn into their mouths as a sign of my contempt for your weakness.

"And finally, those veteran soldiers from the barracks who raped my two lovely and innocent girls will have their penises cut from their bodies while they are alive, their eyelids will be sliced off so they will not be able to close their eyes to their guilt, and they will be crucified. They will depart this world slowly and in the most excruciating pain. It is the most merciless death of which I know—I learned it from Rome—and as you expire, look on the destruction I have wreaked, and think on what you did to my daughters. Then, Romans, ponder how your moment of enjoyment begins to equal the hours of agony you will suffer nailed to the cross. That is my order. Boudica has spoken."

She turned and left the forum, gathering her children in the chariot as she listened with satisfaction to the wailing and pleading and screaming which came from the mouths of her enemies. This, she now realized, was the real and ultimate joy of victory.

CHAPTER THIRTEEN

60 AD—On the Southern Coast of Britain

It first appeared in the daylight sky, catching him and the other sailors by surprise. It caught the lookout's attention, and he followed its arc from the high cliff top, up into the heavens, until it descended, falling like a thunderbolt into the sea far in front of the ship. At first, for some peculiar reason, the sailor thought that it might have been a bird—not an albatross, which was white and far bigger, but a bird of prey like an eagle or an osprey or even a falcon. As it flew from land over the sea in a heavenly parabola, the sailor fancied that it could be a sea eagle, searching for some shiny fish. But the trail of smoke told him that it was a warning arrow.

"General," he shouted over the noise of the wind in the sail slapping against the mast, and the splash and crack of the oars propelling the ship eastward along the narrow sea which separated Gaul from Britain. General Suetonius, governor of Britain, continued to stare out of the seaward side of the boat, toward the far distant land of Gaul, where many of his army compatriots commanded legions.

Returning from a major victory on the island of Mona, his mind was elsewhere, and he was unaware either of the arrow, or of the sailor's cry.

"General, sir," the lookout shouted. One of the general's entourage heard and turned. The sailor pointed, but by this time, the arrow had landed in the sea and been extinguished, and there was nothing to show the governor. Anxiously, the sailor pointed toward the land, and thankfully, the distant archer fired another arrow, which left another smoky trail as it followed its predecessor into the water.

Suetonius immediately walked from the stern toward the bow. "Up there, General. An archer," said the sailor, his voice urgent.

And the distant archer loosed a third arrow. This time, the general ordered that an arrow dipped in tar be flamed and loosed at the land to show the archer that he had been noticed. "Tell the steersman to put in at the nearest beach where there are no cliffs," the general ordered the sailor. As the ship's arrow traveled toward land, the archer mounted his horse, and began to slowly follow along with the ship, each looking for a place where the messenger could descend from the high cliff tops to the sea and the ship could safely put into shallows.

When eventually they met, the messenger saluted the general and said, "I am commanded to bring greetings to the governor from the procurator of Britain, Decianus Catus. His Excellency sends his felicitations, and begs you to read this urgent message."

Suddenly furious that his passage from the island of Mona should have been curtailed by the fat, pompous, greedy, arrogant numbskull of a procurator, the general took the scroll and tore open the seal. He read the letter, and snorted in disgust.

To:
The most noble and honorable Governor Gaius Suetonius Paulinus
From:
The Procurator of Britain, Decianus Catus
In the name of the most excellent Nero, Emperor of Rome, Greetings.

I, Decianus Catus, do humbly beg to inform the Governor of a disturbance in our realm. Be it known that a Harpy whose name is Boadicea, known in her tongue as

Boudica and audaciously calling herself Queen of Britannia, has raised a vast army of hundreds of thousands of peasant Britons and loosed it upon our sacred veterans in violation of the order of the Emperor Nero.

This impudent lady, dressed as a man in armor and with sword and daggers, has laid waste our land, and slaughtered the entire population of our capital of Camulodunum in a most gruesome and hideous manner, worthy only of a barbarian. And Excellency, she has also slaughtered five thousand of the very finest Roman soldiers in the IX Legion Hispana. Only their commander, Petillius Cerialis, and his personal guard have managed to survive.

It is said, Governor, that this insolent wretch is even now marching upon the helpless and unprotected men and women of Londinium. I therefore beg you, Excellency, to make all haste and to take control of this worsening situation, in the name of the Emperor.

I regret, Sir, that I must leave Britain immediately for Gaul on the most urgent business of the Emperor, despite the dangers to my person in that barbaric nation, or I would willingly and most assuredly have taken up arms and fought beside our gallant citizens to repulse this woman. I would have done so, Governor, despite being a mere civilian administrator and servant of Rome with no experience of the military mind.

I beg you to understand, General, that you must, as a matter of the greatest priority, recall the army from the west, and stand to defend the people of Londinium against this most evil and treasonous of women, who should be flayed alive and her flesh eaten by carrion crows.

In the name of the Emperor, General, I bid you speed and success.

Signed by the Office and Hand of the Procurator of Britain this XX of the Month of Iunius in the VI Year of the Glorious Reign of our Emperor Nero by me,

Decianus Catus

Suetonius gave the scroll to his second in command, Fabius Tertius, to read. He thought about the IX Legion Hispana, and shuddered at the enormity of the loss. It was comparable to losses which the army had suffered recently in

Germania. It was terrible. How could Petillius Cerialis have allowed such a catastrophe? And why did he still live when all of his men had been slaughtered? He would instigate an inquiry at the appropriate time.

But now wasn't the time to show his feelings of distress at the deaths of so many Romans. Now was the time for leadership . . . if anything this buffoon of a man said could be believed.

Fabius shook his head in amazement. "Five thousand of the Hispana? Five thousand? Is that possible?"

Suetonius shrugged his shoulders.

Fabius continued to sneer at the contents of the letter. "It might just be that he's telling the truth, General. After all, why would the coward run away if not?" said Fabius.

"I would have expected nothing more of a pig who feeds at the trough of the emperor. Do you know of this Boadicea? A woman leading an army? Can he be right?"

Fabius said, "Queen Cartimandua has led an army!"

Suetonius laughed. "Yes, with the full might of Roman backing, she led her army against her own people who revolted against her in support of her husband. But this sounds different, Fabius. This sounds like a woman who is the equivalent of a man. She must have led a large force in battle against those veterans in Camulodunum, because some of them fought with me in North Africa, and they're a tough grizzled bunch of old swine. What Decianus says might be true, because the city was understrength militarily, with half of the army from Camulodunum with us in Wales. But to slaughter five thousand of the Ninth! By the gods, that would take a military strategist of the highest order. We have a very real problem, if, that is, what the oaf writes can be believed."

"There's truth here, General. Think about it, sir. The procurator is making so much money in Britain, that he would hardly run off to Gaul of all places, unless he had good reason to be very afraid."

Suetonius nodded. "True. Very true."

"Shall I send to Wales to withdraw our troops and prepare to fight this Boadicea?"

"Not yet. First, I want to examine the details of what happened at Camulo-dunum. Decianus Catus writes that Boadicea's army numbers hundreds of thou-sands. If his numbers are anything like the sums of taxation he documents for the emperor, then you can guarantee they're wildly inaccurate and hugely exag-gerated. But I fail to understand why once-peaceful tribes have risen up against us. They know we'll destroy them, like we destroyed the rebels in the west. Some-thing must have caused them such fury as to raise their weapons against Rome."

Fabius nodded. "Perhaps, sir, if I can speak plainly . . ."

"I wouldn't have appointed you unless you did, Fabius."

"Sir, when we arrived in Britain, I asked a lot of people about conditions for the population. They spoke quite plainly about what was really infuriating them. It was the increases in taxation, and especially the demand by the emperor for the return of the sums Claudius had lent from the imperial treasury. It's a huge amount, and is causing terrible hardship and even starvation among the Britons. You've always taught me, sir, to be merciless in battle and merciful in peace. With respect, General, I see little mercy in the peace we've brought to this land."

"And there's little I can do about it. I am duty bound to carry out the com-mands of the emperor and the Senate. However, if it is the emperor's demands for more and more money which has caused this rebellion, and has cost so many Roman lives, then as soon as I've assessed the situation, I'll write to Seneca, the emperor's chief advisor, and inform him of what I see."

Shaking his head, Fabius asked, "Why inform him, General? Why not write directly to the emperor himself, or to the Senate? Your post is created by them, not by some advisor."

Suetonius laughed. "How little you know about Rome, Fabius. That's why you're by my side—precisely because you're a stranger in that city."

60 AD—On the Road to Londinium

The numbers were increasing every day. By tens, by fifties and by hundreds, men and women walked down the roads, over fields and through woods to join the army. All came with daggers, some with shields, and some even with swords. Almost none came with lances and spears.

Boudica had sent to the many surrounding villages for blacksmiths and toolmakers, ironworkers and armorers, wagoners and wheelwrights and horsemen, breadmakers and cooks and anybody else who could equip her army with what they needed when they eventually met a real force of Romans. They had taken what food they needed from nearby fields and woods—taken livestock from farms and grain from fields. These actions had infuriated some of the Britons, but Boudica knew that once Britain was under her control, she would reward those who had, even unwillingly and unwittingly, assisted her.

After the battle to destroy Camulodunum, her army was jubilant, exultant. They had taken on the might of Rome, and they had scored a stunning and miraculous victory. Now that they could afford to relax for a day or two, Boudica had allowed them the joy of being victors. But when the celebrations came to an end, as they trudged the weary miles from Camulodunum to Londinium, it was time for Boudica to talk sense and make her army see reality.

Rather than gather everybody around her and make another speech, she preferred to visit their encampments, group by group. It took her two full nights to visit every single fire, spread now over a huge area because so many fighters had come to join her. At each camp, she told them that while the Romans would soon be reeling from news of the destruction of Camulodunum, they mustn't underestimate the power of Rome's response. It would be swift and utterly merciless. And she explained that while many would die, those who were left would live in freedom forevermore.

She cautiously told everyone that they had beaten a modest city of retired and underprotected legionaries and civilians; that when they met a true and proper Roman army in a field, it would be an altogether different matter, and that was when militaristic discipline would be essential. She assured them that she knew the Roman battle plans, she understood Roman tactics, and she had strategies which she'd put into effect that would make her army of Britons the equivalent of anything Rome could put into the field.

As she explained these things and saw the looks of relief and approval on their faces, silently, privately, she prayed to all of her gods that the stories she was telling everybody about her understanding of war and battles would come true. She thanked the gods that none of her people knew that she enjoyed no special knowledge of Roman tactics, only those which had been told to her by Prasutagus. It was he who had told her of the strength and purpose of the Roman Tortoise, of the Wedge which was used to divide enemy lines, of the Skirmish used against horsemen and of the Orb, in which the Roman soldiers formed a tight circle and defended their standard. As she talked to those who followed her, Boudica realized the depth of regard she felt for Prasutagus, and just how much she had depended upon him. And now she realized how much she missed him.

Drinking their mead and wine, eating the fresh breads and roasted meats which the cooks had worked all day to prepare, the army sprawled over the fields in an exultant mood. Yes, they listened carefully to her, paid her the courtesy of showing their approval; but she knew that they were inexperienced and unprepared for the reality of what Rome would pit against them. And it terrified her.

But what she also noticed in her travels from campfire to campfire was a mood of joy and cooperation. Increasingly, men and women from different tribes, identifiable from their dress or the metal clasps on their cloaks, were sitting together and talking. It had started to happen after the victory in Camulodunum; marching there and hiding in the woods, they had formed up as two separate parts of her army, the Iceni and the Trinovantes. But as they marched away from the burning city, the two peoples mingled, slapped each other on the back, linked arms and rested and drank together. And the latest arrivals, noticing how the different tribes sat together, also began to mingle. It was strange. And delightful.

They were seven days' march out of Londinium when Boudica decided that the time was right for her to take a horse and make her first trip to the ruler of the kingdom through whose land they were passing on their way to destroy the new Roman city on the banks of the River Thames. It was the land of the Catuvellauni, mortal enemies of the Trinovantes. Caratacus and his brother Togodumnus had been rulers of the Catuvellauni people, and had been great warriors against the Roman invasion. Now she must ride to the capital, Magiovinium, and speak to its ruler, Cassivellaunus, a man who had taken the name of the king who had fought against Julius Caesar himself a hundred years earlier, when the emperor had landed in Britain.

She had only received fierce and uncompromising signs of aggression from him when she and Prasutagus ruled the Iceni. Now that she was joined with his enemies, the Trinovantes, she had no idea how he would react. And since she had destroyed Camulodunum, a city on his land, she was even more dubious. Still, Cassivellaunus had thousands of men under his command, and he had to be persuaded to join their rebellion if it was to have any greater and more permanent victories than the destruction of a veteran's city.

Requesting King Mandubracus of the Trinovantes to take charge of her own people until her return, she rode northwest. She knew that King Cassivellaunus would be difficult to deal with, because it was well known that he wanted to expand his kingdom outward to reach the sea. He was making good money from traders crossing his land, but he realized that he would increase his wealth considerably if he were able to provide port facilities.

With these things in her mind, accompanied by a retinue, Boudica rode off thinking about ways of entering the dangerous field of embassy. If convincing Mandubracus to join her had been difficult, requiring tact and diplomacy, then getting the same reaction from Cassivellaunus would likely be impossible. His dislike of the Iceni was far more naked and aggressive. Still, it had to be done, because without him, every other British ruler would see her army as a local uprising, and would hesitate to associate with her. But if the Iceni, the Trinovantes and the Catuvellauni became a single army, then the whole of Britain would realize what was happening, and would rise up.

When she and her escort arrived at Magiovinium, the guards immediately opened the gate without questioning who she was, as though they had been expecting her. She rode through the wooden archway and nodded her appreciation. They smiled at her, and mouthed the words, "Gods be with you, woman of the Iceni."

She rode slowly deeper into the city, through the convolution of streets and workplaces, smelling the familiar smell of old Britain: smoke and red-hot metals and baking bread and roasting meats. No stone buildings or marble pillars here, no painted walls or mosaic floors; here was earth and wood and reeds and wattle.

Boudica looked into the huts and saw women and children who came to the doors to view the tall red-haired lady on the big horse. Some of the people whom she passed cheered as she rode by them; others looked at her in curiosity; yet others seemed sullen and unyielding. But all, it seemed, knew her.

She rode deeper and deeper into Magiovinium. In the days of Prasutagus, she would have felt uncomfortable with people staring at her, but here she felt no fear. By the looks on their faces, they knew her not as Boudica, but as the woman who had conquered a Roman city, a woman who had accomplished what no Briton had done before. And being armed with sword, shield and breastplate, a queen riding a large and imposing horse, she felt surprisingly confident and assured.

Boudica saw the great house in the center of the city. She rode slowly toward it, giving time for Cassivellaunus to prepare for her arrival. Unlike her previous encounter with the king of the Trinovantes, this was of a different order of priorities; then, she had been a supplicant, almost a beggar. Now, she was a warrior queen, proven in battle, demanding fealty from another of equal rank.

Dismounting from her horse, she tethered it to a post and walked into the great house. Unlike that of the Trinovantes, this great house was larger, more ornately decorated with large statues, niches in the walls with idols for prayer to the different gods who guarded the residents, a huge circular table surrounded by chairs, and on the walls, shields and banners displaying the rank and arrogance of those who owed loyalty to the king.

Cassivellaunus was sitting at the table, surrounded by men and women who, by their dress, held title in his kingdom. He stood as Boudica walked into the room. But she stopped and stood still just beyond the doorway, surveying the scene. The room was heavy with people, though not as full as had been the great hall of the king of the Trinovantes.

Boudica bowed her head slightly as she acknowledged Cassivellaunus. And one by one, those who sat with him, men and women, wives and daughters, sons and sons-in-law, stood as Boudica walked through the great house toward the meeting table.

"Boudica, queen of the Iceni, bids greetings to the great King Cassivellaunus, ruler of the Catuvellauni."

"Boudica? Is this the woman of the Iceni who destroyed a village of old Romans?"

He was a tall and rugged-looking man in his early forties, his hair already turning white from the cares of his rule. She had never met him, but had been told of his fearsome reputation. He was no friend of the Romans, although since the defeat of Caratacus, she knew that he had lived in an uncomfortable acceptance of their strength as conquerors.

"This is the Boudica who slaughtered trespassers on our sacred land. This, King Cassivellaunus, is the queen of the Iceni who destroyed an entire Roman legion in a holy forest."

They looked at each other, neither flinching, until one of the women seated beside the king stood and nodded her head. "I am Vella, queen of the Catuvellauni. I welcome Boudica, queen of the Iceni, and invite her to sit at our table."

Cassivellaunus looked in anger at his wife, but Boudica stepped forward and took her place at the end of the table.

The king introduced Boudica to the other women at the table, his children and his advisors. The reception she was receiving was vastly different than she had anticipated. She had expected hostility, rejection, aggression. Instead, except for the coldness of the king, Boudica was being treated as an honored visitor.

Drinking his ale, Cassivellaunus said, "I'm told that Mandubracus follows you. Is that why you're here? For Cassivellaunus of the Catuvellauni to follow you?"

"Mandubracus doesn't follow me, Great King. He walks beside me. He sees that together we are stronger than we would be separately. He acknowledges my understanding of Roman ways, my knowledge of their tactics, and the need to join together as Britons, rather than as separate tribes. Separately, we will always be prey to the Roman army; together, we will be invincible."

Cassivellaunus laughed. "And who will lead this invincible army? You?"

"We will lead it. You will lead your people, Mandubracus will lead the Trinovantes, and I will lead the Iceni. At a council table, we leaders will plan strategy, plan battles, plan dispositions. Then we each will instruct and lead our people. With a common cause, there need be no dissent."

Cassivellaunus nodded. The others around the table showed by their faces that they believed in the approach. But a cloud hung over the king. "And after the Romans are defeated, when they have been driven from our shores? Who will lead our people then, Boudica?"

"As a nation of tribes, we will be attacked again and again by those who seek our land, our fields, our metals, our people to be slaves. As a united nation, as Britain, we will never be conquered. Germania is in peril because it is still, like us, a nation of tribes."

"You haven't answered my question," he said.

"We will form a council of kings and queens. The council will elect a ruler over all Britain."

Cassivellaunus laughed. "And will you seek to be queen?"

"Will you seek to be king?"

His wife laughed, and lifted her goblet in a toast to Boudica. "You speak plainly but well, Queen of the Iceni."

But Cassivellaunus hadn't finished. "Why should the Catuvellauni join with you? Yes, the Iceni are a great people, but for many years, they have been bed partners with Rome. Your people, more than any other Britons, have become more Roman than the Romans. I am informed that you and your dead husband wore Roman clothes, ate Roman food, and lived in a villa built as though it was sited on one of the hills of Rome. Yet now you ask British kings and queens who have fought and lost friends and relations to forgo their responsibilities to their peoples, and to join with you in seeking vengeance against the Romans for what they did to you and your daughters. Why should we do it? Remember that my cousins Caratacus and Togodumnus died fighting Rome."

"It's precisely for that reason that you must join me, Cassivellaunus. If you don't fight, the taxes imposed will become even more harsh; more of your people will become slaves. But if you do fight, then you will only succeed if you are joined with a host of others, from other tribes. You and your family are seen as great warriors who fought but were defeated by the might of Rome. The Iceni have never fought Rome. So for us to rise up and strike at the heart of the invaders will carry a weight and significance which will resound throughout all of Britain. Word will quickly spread about the havoc I have wreaked upon them for their crimes.

"I am determined on revenge. Every Briton, man or woman, will understand the hatred I feel, and that hatred will spread to every house, every village and every British city."

Her words rose to the roof and engulfed everybody within the room. Her visceral fury was naked and held a potency which threatened to overwhelm good judgment.

Cassivellaunus nodded, but said softly, "These are the words of a woman who nurses hatred as though it were her infant. But how good is that woman on the battlefield? General Suetonius is the most renowned and feared of all Roman generals. He feels no hatred, just a strong sense of duty; he is a skilled tactician and he doesn't throw himself wildly into a battle. He uses mind and skill and strategy to defeat us."

"I won a great victory at Camulodunum—" she began.

She was interrupted by Cassivellaunus' laughter. "An undefended city, populated by Romans too old and drunk to pick up a sword. Half of the city was in the west, fighting against the rebels. That, Boudica, is not a victory."

"You forget that I slaughtered five thousand Roman troops who came as reinforcements," she said haughtily.

He looked at her, and nodded. "Yes, I've heard what you did, and you're right. I was being dismissive and belittling what you accomplished. But even so, you had the element of surprise and luck on your side. Now that the Romans know what you're capable of doing, they'll pitch everything at you in order to stop you."

She nodded. He was right. She had come here to win him over, and she realized that she was losing this, her most crucial battle. "My destruction of Londinium in a week's time will show them that Camulodunum wasn't just a stroke of luck—"

"Again, Boudica, Londinium cannot be defended. It has no walls, no fortifications. It has administrators and merchants and sailors; it is peopled by money changers and whorehouse-keepers and taverners and their wives and children. Their army is small compared to the forces fighting in Wales. I'm not talking about leading a huge number of tribespeople in the massacre of Roman citizens. I'm talking about what's going to happen when you find yourself fighting the greatest army in the world. How will Boudica fare when she faces a hundred thousand Romans in a field of battle, when she has to fight the combined strength of battle-hardened Roman legions?"

She nodded. These thoughts had been flowing through her mind for a month. "Boudica will not face Roman armies. Nor will the Iceni or the Trinovantes or the Catuvellauni. But what will face the Romans is an army of Britons. What you are saying, Cassivellaunus, is the truth, known well to me. But I ask you to remember the Roman symbol of supreme power, the fasces. Simple though its reasoning, as an emblem it resounds throughout the world. A single stick can easily be broken; five sticks can be broken; but bundle many sticks together and bind them, and they become unbreakable, even by the most powerful force. Inside the fasces, as the center of the bundle, the Romans place an axe to show their potency and to warn any enemy of the dangers of fighting their army.

"There are twenty-three separate kingdoms in our land, Cassivellaunus. The Romans are making treaties and assailing us one by one. If we had been united when Claudius landed, we would have repelled his armies and we would never have been beaten. We must think as one people, not as many. We live in one land, not in many. Only by being one can we be free.

"It is my life now, Cassivellaunus, to bring together all of the kingdoms, tribes and peoples of Britain into a single force, a fasces, with the fury of Britons as the axe in the middle, ready to cleave the body of any Roman who dares to stand against us."

Cassivellaunus again nodded, and drank his ale. "There is truth in what you say, Boudica. If I were to rise up against the Romans, no other tribe would join me because they would see Cassivellaunus of the Catuvellauni, and the rivalries and ancient hatreds would get in the way of the common cause.

"That's why I know that I can never lead such a force. But you have been shamed and abused, and in your shame, all Britain is shamed. You're brave and robust, but if I am to commit my men and women to join you against the Romans, I have to know that you have the skills to join with me in such an army. How can you prove to me that you're able?"

Dare she challenge him? It was the only way to break the deadlock. "How can Cassivellaunus prove to me that he is a sufficiently brave warrior to join me?"

Suddenly furious, he said, "No warrior is braver or more worthy in the whole of Britain than me!"

"Has Cassivellaunus won a battle?" she said softly. "Does Cassivellaunus have any knowledge of Roman tactics? Do you understand the Roman mind? I do. So prove to me, Cassivellaunus, that you are capable of action as well as words. If not, I shall leave and find another king who is more worthy."

They stared at each other, Boudica forcing herself to remain calm and composed, Cassivellaunus enraged and red-faced for having been so insulted in front of his family and advisors. Boudica prayed that her challenge wouldn't see her skewered on his sword.

Suddenly, Vella burst out laughing. Cassivellaunus looked at her in surprise. And then others at the table also started to laugh. Over the laughter, the queen of the Catuvellauni said, "Queen Boudica. You argue well. My husband has no answer, and neither does anybody else. What you say is right. Only on the battlefield can any one of us prove our value and worth, and since the time of Caratacus, none of us has fought the Romans."

She looked around at her family and the kingdom's advisors, and said, "I say that the people of the Catuvellauni join you and your army in a rebellion against the Romans. I say that we march with you, shoulder to shoulder, and that we fight as Britons."

Her sister, sitting beside her, said, "I agree. We join and fight. As Britons."

Others at the table raised their hands, and shouted their assent. Only King Cassivellaunus remained silent, still fuming at the insult. Boudica looked at him in concern. His vote would sway all others.

"Well, Great King? Will you join me?" she asked.

Softly, slowly and deliberately, Cassivellaunus said, "I will join and fight with you, Boudica. I shall stand beside you and not behind you. The men and women of the Catuvellauni will be subservient to no other Britons."

"Good," she said, "because each Briton is as worthy as the one he stands beside, no matter where he was born and to which tribe he belongs."

It was the best she could hope for. She stood and walked around the table. She kissed each of the women and called each one sister. When she reached the seat of King Cassivellaunus, she embraced him.

"Never have I felt greater pride or confidence in who we are, and what we are doing. I embrace you, Cassivellaunus, both as a king and as my brother. I salute you and your people. May the gods be with us."

60 AD—Approaching Londinium on the Banks of the River Thames

They rode through much of the night, until riding on the pitted roads became too dangerous for their horses' legs. But barely resting, rising from their blankets even as the sun was just beginning to illuminate the eastern sky, they ate soldier's rations and rode hard again the following day. Unerringly, they found what they were looking for on the second day of their travels, when they had covered a total of over a hundred and twenty-five miles.

The XX Legion Valeria was camped in a valley seventy miles to the west of Londinium. General Suetonius and his most senior legate and second in command, Fabius Tertius, stopped on the hill, and rested themselves and their horses.

He thanked the gods that he'd found the legion so quickly. With all the intelligence coming in from around the south and east about the growing numbers of

Britons joining this sudden uprising, the words of Decianus Catus had proven to be correct. Instead of traveling to Camulodunum to see the devastation for himself, Suetonius had relied upon the reports he was receiving, and ordered an immediate ride to Londinium for himself and his escort; he intended to pick up the XX Legion Valeria, as well as hopefully the XIV Legion Gemina, and bring this revolt to an immediate and harsh end.

Riding down the hill as swiftly as he could, Suetonius saw that the prefect commanding the legion had posted double guards on the periphery. Good! He had taken stock of the changed circumstances and reacted accordingly.

Suetonius rode toward the ten guards minding the southern flank.

"Halt, riders," shouted the guard, pointing his lance in their direction. "Identify yourselves."

"Gaius Suetonius Paulinus, governor of Britain and general of all the armies, escorted by *Legatus Legionis* Fabius Tertius and my personal escort."

Realizing he'd questioned the most important man in Britain, the soldier saluted, and said, "I'm sorry, General. I didn't recognize you. Or the legate."

"You have no need to apologize, soldier. You have the right and duty to question everyone who wishes to enter a Roman army camp, no matter who they are."

"Sir!" he shouted, and allowed the governor and his escort to ride through.

Suetonius and his escort thundered through the camp, looking for the command tent. Soldiers came out of their tents to see what the sudden noise was. Those who recognized him saluted; others asked who he was.

Entering the command tent, the surprised *Praefectus Legionis* turned from his map table and looked with anger at the men had suddenly walked in without requesting permission. When he saw who it was, he snapped to attention, and saluted.

"Prefect Callistus Marcus Antinios at your service, General."

Suetonius entered the tent, and took a cup of wine from the buffet. He came straight to the point. "How soon can your men march, Prefect?" he asked.

"Three days, General."

"They will begin to march eastward toward Londinium in the morning. And how far can your men march in a day, Prefect?"

"Twenty miles, General."

Suetonius glanced at Fabius, and turned to the map table to remind himself of the disposition of the British tribes.

"They will march twenty-five, or we will order the crucifixion of ten of them a day," Fabius said sternly.

Callistus stared at the legate, his jaw dropping. Fabius could barely restrain himself from laughing.

"Your men will march twenty-five miles in a day, just as my Ninth Legion Hispana learned to march when I first took charge of them," Suetonius said.

He turned, and looked at the prefect. The man's eyes were staring in disbelief. "Don't look so shocked, Prefect. I'm sure Legate Fabius doesn't really intend to crucify anybody. I'll reward them with extra rations and more salary for every additional mile they give me each day. Now tell me what intelligence you've had on the uprising of this Boadicea."

"The news gets worse every day, General. Since her destruction of Camulodunum, and especially since she defeated a Roman army of reinforcements, this woman has Britons flocking to her. My intelligence is that she now has over one hundred thousand fighters; she has somehow managed to join together the kingdoms of the Trinovantes, the Iceni and the Catuvellauni, and just today, I heard that the kings of the Coritani, the Dobunni and the Atrebates have all sent word to her that they will join in the revolt."

Suetonius shook his head in confusion; Fabius went to the map table, and pointed out the locations of the kingdoms to the general.

"By the gods, if this is true, then the whole of Britain will go up in flames. What's the current disposition of her army?" he asked.

"She is camped thirty miles to the northeast of Londinium. I've had deputations from the administrators, begging me to move my legion there to protect the city."

"And why haven't you, Prefect?" asked the general.

"I have no orders to do so, General. I didn't know whether you'd want me to defend the city, or join with you in attacking her advance. I'm sorry, sir, but I've had riders out for three days looking for you to get orders. Each carries a letter from me, saying that in the absence of your orders, I request permission to decamp and march immediately for Londinium. I had no idea whether you wanted me to join you in Wales and wait for her to come to us, or whether you wanted me to return to Londinium and defend our people. I'm sorry, General, but until I have orders . . ."

Suetonius nodded, realizing that he'd been hard on the man. "You did right in waiting, Prefect. But we must march first thing in the morning. Make the arrangements immediately."

"But General," said Callistus, "we won't be ready to march for three days—two at the very earliest. We have equipment to repair, food to cook for the march, the sick and injured to consider—"

"We march tomorrow morning at first light. Battle-order rations. Any soldier not ready will be left behind, and he'll have to do his best to catch us up. This isn't a moment to consider our weakest links, Prefect, but to capitalize on our greatest strengths. If she's half the woman she appears to be, then Boadicea knows that we're a full week's distance from Londinium. If we arrive before she does, the surprise will be the equivalent of a dozen *centuriae*. Now, Prefect, I suggest that you leave your planning, and ready your men for the fastest march they've ever made."

They were exhausted and in a state of clutter and disorganized mess: uniforms in disarray, weaponry haphazardly carried and jumbled, and provision wagons lagging miles and miles behind. But they had reached the outskirts of Londinium in a mere two and a half days, and the prefect was exultant. Not so Suetonius and Fabius, who viewed the geography of the river, the hills surrounding it, and the haphazard expansion of the city of Londinium with great concern.

Regardless of army precision and organization, the exhausted men threw themselves onto the ground, and lay looking up at the setting afternoon sun, trying to regain their breath and composure. Never, they vowed, in the history of the Roman Empire, had so many men marched so far, so fast as the XX Legion Valeria in the past two days. Not marching, exactly, but running, then walking, then running, then marching, then running, then resting for a few moments.

And then repeating the same thing again and again. When they'd finally rounded a bend in the road, and first caught sight of the vast silver band of the River Thames, and when the first house on the outskirts had come into view, a huge cheer had gone up from the front ranks. Instinctively, a roar of approbation had risen from the entire army.

But there was no approbation from either General Suetonius or Legate Fabius. For they had been sitting on their horses for the better part of an hour, surveying the sprawling layout of Londinium as it sat on the northern, and to a lesser extent on the southern, bank of the huge river. Between them a wooden bridge had been constructed by Roman engineers to span the river, and it was obvious to a practiced military mind like Suetonius that this was the focal point of the city, where the road system would be at its most vulnerable to Boadicea.

It was the first time that either Fabius or Suetonius had seen Londinium since they had first landed in Britain, so busy had they been in putting down the rebellion in the west.

"Who in the name of the great gods put a city there without sufficient means of defense?" asked Fabius. "There must be fifty or seventy thousand inhabitants there. And from the river, from the north and south, the east and west, they're exposed to attack. It's madness. Sheer negligence. Madness!"

Joining them, Prefect Callistus said softly, "Nobody put it there, sir. It just grew. It began as a few houses on the bend yonder which belonged to fishermen. Then tanners came because of the fresh water; then our engineers realized that even though we're far inland, the flow of the river is still tidal at this point because it's so deep. With two tides a day, they reasoned that it would be a good place for their shipping, and the merchants soon followed. From there, General, it just grew and grew and spread out farther and farther, until it's as you see it."

"Fabius is right. It's hopeless," said Suetonius. "Indefensible. There are far too few defensive walls, almost no fortifications, absolutely no way of stopping an insurgent army—"

"We could remove the bridge, sir, and try to defend just the north bank. The south bank should be safe while we fight off Boadicea," said Fabius.

Suetonius nodded. "But the north bank is the worst place of all to try to defend. Look at it," he said, pointing from the distance. "We'd need ten legions just to give sufficient depth to our defenses. How can I possibly protect this city against the hordes of Boadicea? We could be fighting for our lives in the west, while she's destroying the east, and there's no way we could get to her."

Fabius was about to suggest building boats to transport the army quickly from one location to another, but as the assault was due within the next two days, there wouldn't be time.

"Then what does the General order?" asked the Prefect.

"Fabius?" said Suetonius, instead of answering himself.

"Evacuate as many Roman citizens from Londinium as possible in the time we have, and find a suitable spot to our benefit in which to marshal our forces. Get her to come to us. Force her to fight us on our terms."

Suetonius nodded. "Precisely."

Calling himself, somewhat arrogantly, the Father of the City, the short, stout and rumpled man who stood before General Suetonius and his second in command in the forefront of his delegation, hands on hips and jaw jutting, said, "I'm not a fool, Governor, but kindly explain to me again precisely why we have to evacuate Londinium when you have a full Roman legion camped on the hill over there. Is the Roman army now running away from a woman? Does the Roman army now retreat at the first sign of a battle?"

Fabius was concerned that the governor was going to lose his temper and cause even more problems with the civic administration. So far, the governor had found it difficult to convey to the city the immense dangers from the rapidly approaching army of Britons. Because he had arrived with the XX Legion Valeria he had been greeted with wild cheers and flowers strewn in his path by the grateful inhabitants of the city. He had immediately called a meeting in the crude wooden amphitheater, where thousands of inhabitants had quickly gathered. There he had explained to the crowd that because the city was impossible to defend, and because his legion would be heavily outnumbered by Boadicea's forces in places where it would be impossible to conduct military tactics, he had decided not to remain to defend the city, but to take the legion north to the middle lands of the country, and there to engage her in battle in a place of his choosing, rather than hers.

The cries of horror and distress had initially concerned him. Parties of men and women had come out to his camp and offered him bribes and gifts to stay with them to fight. Some had fallen and mumbled prayers at his feet. But he was resolute in demanding that anybody who could march must do so immediately. And in his resolution, most of the population quickly realized that without the army to support them, they must flee immediately, and continue to enjoy whatever protection the army could provide while they marched quickly away on the road north. Some refused and said that they would remain, but most began packing a minimum of possessions for the rapid flight.

Word spread quickly throughout the rest of the city that it was to be evacuated in the face of Boadicea's imminent arrival, but Suetonius knew that only so many residents would actually leave. The very young, the sick, the injured, the bedridden, and the disbelievers would all stay behind, and would be slaughtered—which was why the elders of the city had sent a delegation under this man calling himself the Father of the City, Lucius Marcus Columbanus.

"What use, then, is our army, if it is so ineffectual that it can't defend a Roman city?" he demanded.

Before Suetonius lost his temper at the man's impertinence, Fabius interrupted quickly. "Sir, the army didn't build this city. Had it done so, it would have ensured an adequate defense. However, the people who built Londinium obviously believed that the city was in peaceful territory, and had no eye for any prospect of a future assault, and so the city has become indefensible. The Roman army will not allow itself to be subject to a massacre if there are good grounds for a tactical withdrawal so that we can fight to our full advantage sometime in the future—which is precisely what we're doing."

A young and weak-looking man, affecting the clothes of a Celt and not a Roman, stepped from beyond the crowd and addressed General Suetonius directly.

"Sir, my name is Cassus. I am in Londinium as a friend and advisor to the procurator, Decianus Catus. I am also the stepson of Boudica, the woman you call Boadicea. It is she who is leading this rebellion. I know more about her and her ways than anybody. I can be of assistance to you in conquering her and ensuring that this rebellion is put down."

Astonished, Suetonius looked at the young man, and asked, "And why would a Celt want to do that, Cassus? Why would a son stab his mother in the back?"

"Because she and her daughters robbed me of my inheritance. They were made queens by my dead father, whose mind had been twisted by this woman. It is I who should have been made king of the Iceni. I would have been the greatest friend Rome ever had. What happened to me was unjust, a breach of the natural order. I should have been king."

Feeling an immediate dislike of the young man, and comparing him to his own sons and daughters, Suetonius turned to Fabius and said softly, "So this is the honor of the British?"

He turned back to address Cassus, and asked, "Why didn't you travel to Gaul with Decianus Catus? Why stay here and endanger your life?"

"The procurator had to leave in a hurry," the youth said softly.

Suetonius nodded. He understood perfectly what had happened. Still, to have the son of Boadicea with him would be an advantage. He would get to know his enemy, if he could separate Cassus' bile from truth. Suetonius said to Cassus, "You may travel with us. I might call upon you for your information. Now, Lucius Marcus, are you going to abandon this city?"

Lucius Marcus Columbanus drew himself up fully to his middle height, and said, "General, while naturally I respect your authority as governor, Londinium isn't a fort or a *colonia*, but a peaceful city where trade is conducted. Before I can authorize the evacuation of the city, I must first consult with my fellow councilors. Then, and only then, will I—"

Utterly losing patience, Suetonius snapped, "Yes, I think that's a good idea, Lucius Marcus. You consult with whomsoever you want to consult with. Spend the next month consulting if you want. In the meantime, I order the evacuation of as many men, women and children as are able to walk or ride north with the army. And when Boadicea and her tens of thousands arrive here to an almost empty city, then why not consult with her."

Suetonius and Fabius swung on their heels and left the astonished man alone. Cassus scurried after them.

CHAPTER FOURTEEN

60 AD—Londinium

She smelled fear in the air. She heard silence. Sitting on her horse, she felt the
fear of a terrified city, its houses, streets and spaces petrified into stillness.
Smoke from dead hearth fires, the odor of rotting animal flesh in tanners' yards
and the stink of horse droppings told her everything she needed to know as a
warrior, but it was the silence which shouted loud in her ears that this was her
next victory. Silence and the stench of fear gave her inestimable pleasure.

But the closer she rode, the more the dead city seemed to come alive. With
every pace her horse took, Boudica could hear the muffled wailing of women and
children crying in distant cellars. Closer, and she perceived the tremor in voices
of men praying to their gods. Closer still, and she thought she could hear the
susurration of men and women begging the deities of Rome to intervene and
give them another day's life. It was as though the spirits of dead Romans were
already walking the streets, urgently mumbling imprecations to her to set them
free. This fear, this collective murmur of urgently whispered entreaties, wasn't

of this world, but of the next, as though the spirit world were all around her.

Boudica had come here to fight; to destroy; to gain the satisfaction which only horror in the eyes of an enemy, and the desolation around him, can bring. Her joy came when death clouded the eyes of her enemies and the last thing they saw was her face. Here was another portion of the revenge which she and her children so richly deserved; the reward she would extract for the beatings, the humiliation, the impoverishment, the dishonor to her husband, the avarice of Rome . . . but most of all, to the destruction of her children's innocence.

But where were the people whose eyes would stare questioningly at her in their last moments as the darkness of death drew their lives to an end? Where were the citizens of Londinium? She surveyed the empty streets, but could see that no citizens were falling to their knees, no boats plied the river, no horses or dogs or cats roamed the alleyways looking for food. This was a city where the people were hiding in basements; a city where she could feel the fear!

Boudica sat astride her gray horse, looking down on the city of Londinium from a hill to the northeast. She had been sitting there, still and full of thought, for some time. Could it be a trap, a typical Roman tactic to lure her onto some innocent-looking ground, only to see her hopes devastated by a legion suddenly appearing and squeezing the lifeblood out of her? Could they, perhaps, have laid some shattering device which could destroy her men and women as they entered the city, just as she had laid the fire trap for the Roman legion on the road to Camulodunum? Were there trenches or redoubts or defenses that she couldn't see from this distance which hid thousands of Romans who would bear down on her from all sides and make her dreams crumble into dust? Were there ballistae and catapults and cauldrons of boiling oil ready to make her people die in agony? And if not, where was the army, and where had all the people gone?

She had been sitting here for long enough. She had allocated herself time to make a considered decision; any longer and she would seem indecisive. Now she had to ride back down the hill to where her army had camped overnight and face a dozen stern-faced men and women, leaders of their people, who expected her to know all the answers. Yes, they would follow her and do as she commanded, but Boudica knew that one mistake, one foot placed falsely in quicksand, and they'd turn against her and flee. Boudica as war leader was as successful as her last battle, and she had enjoyed only one successful battle. Now she was facing her second fight, this against a city which looked as quiet as a barrow, as still as a dawn forest, yet which could house a viper in its bosom whose fangs would surely kill her. And with her death would swiftly follow the death of Britain.

But she had to tell her council something, and from viewing the disposition of the city, some thoughts had occurred to her. She kicked her horse's flanks and wheeled around, riding back quickly to the tent where the other kings and their queens had gathered.

As she rode she saw the huge numbers of men and women sprawled out on the ground, or emerging from their tents, cooking their breakfasts or cleaning and sharpening their weapons. The smoke from a thousand campfires wafted into the cool morning air, flattening out into a dull brown cloud which hung over the hillside where they had all gathered in preparation for the final day's march to battle. Londinium was only three hours' march away; then they would finally meet their enemy. But where were the people?

Dismounting, Boudica entered the command tent and confronted the leaders of the Britons. They looked at her eagerly. Mandubracus of the Trinovantes and Cassivellaunus of the Catuvellauni were at opposite sides of the tent, patently uncomfortable being in the same place, as were their wives and families, who sat or stood in clusters. Other kings and their queens of lesser tribes who had joined her more recently were huddling together, speaking quietly. All conversation in the tent came to an end as Boudica entered and crossed to the table to take a cup of wine.

"I ask you all to sit down," she said, acknowledging each king and queen in the room. Leaders of six tribes had journeyed to join her in her fight to conquer the Romans. She had met some of them on her progress, but never before had she addressed them together.

"My friends, my fellow rulers of the tribes of Britain. We are here by agreement that we will contribute to the destruction of Rome in Britain. Is this not correct?"

They looked at each other, and nodded in agreement with her. Boudica continued. "We are seven voices, all equal, all representing the most important tribes in the land. As a council, we must acknowledge the importance of agreeing on any decisions we make. If we are not united, we will fail. Are we all agreed on that?"

Again, there was agreement.

"Then are we all agreed that we march this morning? We divide up into three wedges, each entering the north of the city from three different points, one to the east, one in the center and one to the west. The Romans will expect us to enter along the roadway which leads to the bridge across the Thames in order to assault the north and south banks of the river. We won't. We'll avoid the road completely, and enter over the fields. It'll be slower, but safer, and the ground is quite firm, but we must stay close to each other like an army marching. By assaulting the city through the east and west flanks of the northern bank, we'll have the element of surprise on our side. Our spies tell us that their leader hasn't had time to gather all of his legions. There aren't enough of their soldiers to fight us on open ground. By going over the fields, we'll outflank the Romans.

"And they'll almost certainly have marshaled their defenses on the opposite side of the bridge, hidden in the warehouses and buildings at the edge of the water, knowing that we have to cross the river by the bridge in order to attack the southern bank. They'll hope to concentrate us in order to make it easier for them to destroy us. They know we won't be able to fight in such a narrow confine. But instead of crossing to the south by the bridge, we'll take all the boats which are moored along the north bank and cross at a hundred different points. We'll assemble on the south bank to the left and right of the bridge, and then attack the Roman army from their rear."

Cassivellaunus looked darkly at Boudica. "I thought this was supposed to be a council of kings and queens—a council of equals. Yet you seem to have determined a battle strategy without having consulted any of us."

Boudica nodded. "I have, King Cassivellaunus. I have spoken to our spies; I've been to Londinium and examined the city. But I am reporting my conclusions to the council, and asking for your support. This is the moment when you are free to disagree with me, and suggest another battle plan."

She had been careful not to challenge him in front of the other rulers, for to do so would have alienated them all. She had tried to be deferential in her tone, while firm in her resolve.

King Cassivellaunus nodded, and said, "Your battle plan is good, Boudica. It makes sense. But my people will follow me, and nobody else."

"And only you and Queen Vella will lead them."

Mandubracus interrupted, and said, "Regardless of who leads our army, surely the Romans will see us crossing the river by boat, and redeploy. As we land, they'll slaughter our men and women."

"We won't just kill all those inhabitants in the north. We'll round up hundreds of Roman citizens and force them to cross the bridge instead of us. As they flee across, the Roman army in hiding won't know what to do. They'll be confused, thinking it might be a trick, or that we Britons are secreted within the fleeing Romans. They'll be paralyzed. And as to being seen, Mandubracus, the river twists and turns on either side of the bridge. As we cross, we'll be like invisible spirits to the army waiting on the south bank."

"You're assuming that the army will be concentrated on the south bank, Boudica," said Cassivellaunus. "Why? Why shouldn't we meet the entire army as we bear down from the north? After all, they know where we're coming from, and so surely they'll be there to greet us before we enter the city. That's what I'd do," he said.

"That's what any great British king would do to protect his people, Cassivellaunus," she said gently, paying him great deference and courtesy. "But it's not what the Romans will do. They have grown into the largest empire in the world because of their military tactics. General Suetonius must surely realize that this city is incapable of defense. He realizes that with the size of our forces, we can have him in too many different places, and overwhelm his forces if he concentrates them into a fixed position for battle.

"The Roman army detests thinly spread-out forces. They like it best when they're concentrated into a wedge or a close cavalry line. And so he will retreat into the city. He has few walls behind which he can hide his men. He can't defend it as though it were a fort, and so he will try to lure us into a confined area, and try to destroy us that way. And there is no better place to confine us than as we cross the river over the bridge. So rather than going to him where he has stationed his men, we will disappoint him and come at him from many different directions."

She stopped talking, and waited for any further discussion. But there was none. Boudica broke the silence.

"Friends. Since my kingdom was taken from me, since my humiliation at the hands of the Romans, I have thought long and hard about who I am, and what my future will be. I have decided to change my name. From now on, I will no longer be Boudica, queen of the Iceni. From this moment, to Rome and to the people of this land, I will be called Britannia."

Her words were greeted by silence, the meaning not clearly registering in their minds, until slowly, purposefully, Queen Vella of the Catuvellauni raised her goblet of wine, and said, "Hail Britannia."

"Britons," said Boudica, "we march."

Cassivellaunus grabbed his sword and shield, and began to leave the tent with his wife and family. So did the other kings and queens. When nobody was left except for Boudica and Mandubracus, he softly asked her, "How do you know so much about Roman tactics?"

She smiled, and said softly, "When you sleep with the enemy, you know how his mind works and what his body looks like without armor. My husband Prasutagus and I lived like Romans for years—wrongly, I now see to my eternal shame. We had many Romans come to our house, and they treated us like friends. They explained to us the way their armies had won great battles, about how their forces were deployed, and much more. I tell you, Mandubracus, I know more about Rome and Romans than I do about Britain and the British. And it fills me with shame and grief."

He nodded and as he left the tent to face the morning, he said softly, "Soon, Boudica, you will no longer feel shame, but the sweet taste of revenge on your lips."

✳   ✳   ✳

The occasional scream of a child or cry of a woman told her that the city was still inhabited, though barely. It was obvious that most of its residents had left. She had never been in such a place as this: empty houses, empty taverns, and workshops with fires still smoking weakly, dead from lack of attention. In the houses, washing still hung over balconies, food was left on plates and drinks still in cups on tables. It looked as though the inhabitants had suddenly been sucked up into the heavens by the mischievous god Lugh. Indeed, some of her soldiers looked heavenward just to ensure that no legs were hanging from clouds in the sky.

Mandubracus rode up to her, and shook his head. "They've evacuated the city," he said. "There's almost nobody left!"

She nodded. "It's empty. They must have fled a day or two ago when they heard of our arrival. But where could they have gone? There must be fifty thousand people in this city, and they've just disappeared."

"Not all," said Mandubracus. "My men have rounded up hundreds of inhabitants who were hiding in their houses. But they're old men and women, sick and injured people, and mothers of babies and young children still being carried. Where are the soldiers, the fighters, the battle-ready men and women we came to fight?"

"Perhaps," she said, "they've all moved across to the southern bank of the Thames."

But Mandubracus shook his head. "My men have been standing on the banks, and they report no movement over there, except for the occasional man or woman whom they see on a rooftop, looking over at us. It's a mystery, Boudica. Where have all the inhabitants gone?"

Her instincts of the early morning had been confirmed. The fear she had smelled was the fear which caused people to flee in panic. The people of Londinium, those who could walk or march, had left their homes and business places and fled in the face of her arrival. There was satisfaction in that, though the satisfaction of slaughtering tens of thousands of inhabitants would have been greater.

She turned to Mandubracus, and ordered, "Set fire to the buildings on the northern bank. Flame everything. Not a single building is to be left standing. It is to be a fire whose flames will light up the night sky and will be seen in Rome."

The flames still leapt toward the sky three days after she had first ordered the buildings to be torched. And the people who were hiding inside them, those who weren't burnt to death, had fled into the streets and cried for mercy. But like the citizens of Camulodunum, they were rounded up, and brought to the banks of the river, trussed up like animals, and ordered to remain quiet on pain of death.

As the flames roared from house to house, Boudica and her men sailed and rowed across the river, and were met by the same empty city. The south bank housed far fewer buildings, and was easier and quicker to search. They found only a few hundred souls who, like their northern colleagues, begged Boudica and her army to spare their lives. These were marched over the bridge to the north of the River Thames, and tied up with rope. They watched in horror as Boudica and her army set fire to the buildings on the southern bank. By the end of the third day, the whole of Londinium looked like a tortured beast, growling with the roar of the fire, glowing yellow and red in the conflagration.

Keen to leave and attack another Roman city, Boudica addressed her captives by the bank of the river, downstream from the burning city. It was a scene from the very depths of Hades itself: the sky was black with smoke, the acrid air thick and unbreathable, and the entire landscape lit in nightmare colors as the flames digested the wood and thatch of every single house.

"Listen to me, Romans," she shouted over the distant roar. "Your army has deserted you to your fate. You have no right to place your feet on our precious soil; you have no place on our River Thames; you have no purpose in being here.

"For the crimes which you and Rome have committed against the British people, you are sentenced to death. The men will be beheaded by the sword, and their bodies will be left here for the birds to gorge themselves on. Their heads will be thrown into the Thames to appease our gods. The women will be hanged and their bodies will be impaled on spikes—this is Britain's way of making love to Rome—then their breasts will be cut off and sewn into their mouths for daring to suckle upon the pure milk of a land which does not belong to them. Britannia has spoken."

She spurred her horse away, and for the second time since the rebellion began, Boudica heard the screams and wails of the hundreds of Roman men and women whose lives she had now determined. *Yes!* she thought. This was a joyous sound, a din so loud that it blocked out the voices screaming in her head which commanded her to avenge the harm done to her and her children.

So it was! So it would be!

Looting was rampant. British men and women, knowing that the city was undefended, ran screaming and laughing into houses and ransacked every room, looking for things to take, before they set them alight. Jewelry, pottery, plates and knives, dresses and cloth, household and trade implements, were all carried out into the streets and dumped into sacks, which were carried away by stronger men along the streets and out into the northern fields. The carts were weighed down with booty. Additional carts had to be pressed into service.

Warehouses beside the river were ransacked. Shops and tradesmen's workrooms were raided. Houses which still held food inside were a prime target. The food was gobbled on the spot, or carried away for later consumption. Women walked away from open houses in thin voile the color of rainbows draped over their crude woolen cloaks and tunics; men struggled under the weight of plates and cups and knives, and jugs full of wine. Every house which was cleared was put to the torch.

The looting was more widespread in Londinium than it had been in Camulodunum, as was the wild drinking, the debauchery, and the inevitable contests of strength between the drunkards in the fields beyond the city.

But great pleasure was gained in the torturing of Roman men and women before they were killed. Their deaths by beheading and crucifixion had been prescribed by Boudica; to slake their bloodlust, the Britons began impaling the women on long spikes and emasculating the men even before they were dead. They died screaming in agony. It was not what Boudica had ordered, but it was good.

And the Britons took even greater pleasure in the slow and agonizing death of many Romans when they threw them onto the blazing fires. Wagers were taken as to which of the hundreds of victims would die immediately, and which would flail in the murderous heat of the flames, and whether fat men would burn faster than thin men.

Boudica allowed them to do whatever they wanted to do, because she had made a pact with her goddess Andasta the Unconquerable that the Romans would suffer tenfold for every crime they had committed against the Britons since the conquest seventeen years earlier. It was Boudica's way of appeasing her own spirits.

When her children Camorra and Tasca became distressed at so many women suffering so badly, Boudica realized that it was time to leave Londinium and travel to the next Roman city they would destroy. Her plan was to take the northern Roman road which ran through the military zone, and to lay assault to any fort which was on the way. The reason for this was that it would bring on the inevitable battle with General Suetonius even more rapidly. Her fight with him, her ultimate victory, would end Roman hopes for the continued occupation of her land. Once he was defeated, it would then be an easy job to destroy every Roman fort and encampment. Even if the emperor sent ten new legions, they would be defeated by the host of Britons, and she would be forever queen.

Boudica met with Mandubracus of the Trinovantes and Cassivellaunus of the Catuvellauni in her tent, pitched on the hills on the north, outside of the still-burning city. She told them of her plans, and they agreed. The Romans had to be led to them, and the Romans would come to where she was assaulting their forts and *coloniae*. By that method, Boudica would be able to choose the ground upon which the final battle would be fought.

They looked at a map, looted from one of the few large official stone buildings in the city, and studied their route. It was a good plan, and when light dawned in the morning, she would order her men and women to end their plunder and to begin their march north along what the Romans called Watling Street, a name they had copied from the Britons' own tongue, Waechlinga Straet.

Cassivellaunus looked carefully at the map, and shook his head, frowning.

"Do you have a problem, my friend?" Boudica asked.

He stabbed a position on the road with the point of his dagger. "Here," he said.

Mandubracus and Boudica looked carefully. It was the *colonia* of Verulamium, on the land of the Catuvellauni, directly north of Londinium. Boudica didn't understand what his problem was.

"This is a town which was originally inhabited by men and women of my own tribe, the Catuvellauni. But no longer."

"I know this city," said Mandubracus. "It has no Roman citizens or soldiers in it. It's a British city."

"No, you're wrong. Since the conquest, men and women from Gaul have crossed the sea in increasing numbers, and have driven out my people. These Gauls are more Roman than the Romans. They live under Rome's protection. They're arrogant and have even levied taxes upon the farms nearby; they pay only a fraction of the real price of produce and when there's a complaint, they go to the local fort. The commander enslaves the British farmer and his family. My people are starving as a result of the avarice of these Verulamians."

"And you want this city destroyed?" asked Boudica.

Cassivellaunus nodded. "And every Gaul killed. I shall be avenged."

"Even though this city is on the land of the Catuvellauni, and not a Roman city?"

Again, he nodded.

"So it shall be," she said. "In four days' time, Verulamium will be no more."

Her daughters entered the tent and bowed to the kings who were now their mother's closest friends and advisors. She could see the look of concern on their faces.

"May we talk to you, Mother?" asked Camorra.

Boudica looked at her colleagues; her expression asked them to leave the tent and allow her time with her family. When they had gone, Camorra continued, "Tasca and I want to go home. We're frightened. We don't want to kill anybody else. And we don't want you to kill any more and we don't want more people to die. All the killing and burning and the screaming. It's . . ." Both girls started to whimper; Tasca burst into tears, hiding her face in disgrace in her cloak.

Boudica walked the two paces to where her children were standing at the doorway of the tent, and enfolded them in her arms. She led them over to chairs, and they sat, still whimpering. It was, Boudica realized in shame, the first time that she had paid attention to her children since Camulodunum. Every moment of her day, and of her night, she had been engaged in the battle of reclaiming Britain from the Romans. Now she realized that in her quest, she had ignored the very reason for which she was fighting.

"Children, believe your mother when I tell you that nothing I am doing is more important to me than the two of you. And yes, it is right that you should be at home, running through the fields and swimming with the spirits in the river, and enjoying your youth. When I was your age, summers were always warm, the sun was always golden and my life was an adventure from one day to the next. But my youth came to an end when the Romans attacked our land, and I am fighting them so that you two, and the other children of Britain, can continue to have your freedom, your youth.

"Understand this, my lovely children. Because of the Romans, you have no home. They have destroyed our heritage, and hurt us all so badly that in order for us to be loved and respected by our gods, we have to drive them from here. Because of the Romans, we can never return to that villa in which you grew up. It no longer belongs to me. It belongs to Nero.

"We, your father and I, wanted to be friendly with Nero, but he has decided to take from us our home, our land, our money, our possessions, and to leave us with nothing. Your father decided that he wanted you to rule our people with Nero, but the emperor said, 'No, I want to rule the Iceni myself.' Yet, girls, he has never been to Britain; he has never met one of the Iceni; he has no idea about us.

"I am fighting to restore those things which you love so much. I fight against the Romans so that you can again swim in a river which belongs to Britain, and grow food which is British food."

The girls listened respectfully to everything Boudica told them. Then Camorra said quietly, "But we aren't killing Roman soldiers; we're killing men and women and children like us. And their screaming is giving us nightmares and keeping Tasca and me awake at night. And we don't like the fires and the smells of flesh burning in the air. And we don't like the people here, in this camp; they're always drunk and shouting and fighting."

Boudica sighed. A military camp was no place for girls. As she marched along Waechlinga Straet, she would find a safe British town and leave them there with a guard of a dozen men and women, and when she had won her final victory, she would retrieve them and begin the process of building a home. Once she was no longer queen of the Iceni, she would have to find a safe and permanent home for herself and her family. She would like to return to the Iceni, but for the time being, while the Romans were still in command, this was impossible. Perhaps she could live along the southern coast, near to where there were many sacred groves—near to where she had once traveled, all those years ago, when she had been free as a bird, and the burdens of who she had become were a faraway dream.

She was woken from her sleep by the sound of somebody entering her tent. Instinctively, Boudica reached for a dagger beneath her pillow, but by the light of the beacon outside her tent, she could see that it was a Briton who entered.

"Boudica?"

"Yes."

"We have found him," said the man.

"Him?"

"The man you sent us to find. The procurator. He was sailing and we had to ram his boat with our own, but we dragged him ashore and he commanded us in the name of Rome, and told us who he was, so we chained him like you told us, and we—"

"What!" she shouted, suddenly wide awake. "Decianus Catus? Here?"

"Yes," said her soldier.

She leapt out of her bed, and felt like kissing him, but restrained herself. Almost naked despite the cold, Boudica threw on a fur wrap and followed her soldier to the middle of her encampment, where a roaring fire gave light to a fat pathetic figure crumpled up on the filthy ground, his once glorious toga now ragged and stained.

Decianus Catus struggled to his feet, but the weight of the chains and a kick from one of the guards held him down. Boudica walked over, feeling bile rise in her throat.

"So," she said, spitting the words as she strode toward him. "So, Decianus Catus. You are humbled at my feet. You are where I was all those days ago."

When he saw Boudica, the Roman procurator's eyes widened in sudden fear. He stammered, but only noise came out. Then something within him strengthened, and he said in a voice hoarse with restrained terror, "I am the procurator of Britain. I order you, Boadicea, to unchain me and let me go. Failure to do so will go heavily against you. But if you free me now, I will intercede with the emperor himself, and I will ensure that you and your men are—"

"Silence, fool," she spat. "Your only assurance is that you are about to die. Just as you whipped me, so will you be whipped. Just as you arranged for my daughters to be raped, so will you be raped. Some of my men enjoy themselves with other men, some with animals of the field. So they will enjoy themselves with you. Hundreds of them. And when your body is torn and bloody, then I will hack it limb from limb and each limb will be fed to the dogs."

Boudica's men looked at her in astonishment. The procurator of Britain opened his mouth to speak, but the only sound which emerged was a muffled scream. He fainted.

She looked at his fat, ungainly and pampered body, and turned to one of her soldiers. In disgust, she said, "Crucify him. High on a hill overlooking his city. Let the fire warm his last moments on earth, and the flames light his way into never-ending torment."

The Encampment of Suetonius, Seventy Miles North of Londinium

Gaius Suetonius Paulinus sat nursing a cup of wine. Beside him in his tent were his second in command, *Legatus Legionis* Fabius Tertius, and Prefect Callistus Marcus Antinios, in temporary command of the XX Legion Valeria while its commander was engaged with the rest of the legion marching back from the borders of Wales to join in the fight against Boadicea.

Also seated was Cassus, Boadicea's stepson, a fund of useful information about her. Thanks to him, Suetonius believed that he understood the woman he was fighting—and more importantly, why. Once Cassus had stopped defending himself and being aggressive in his demands, once he settled down as merely somebody of use to Rome, rather than the aggrieved party, Suetonius had been able to extract important information. Now he knew about Seneca's demand for the return of his money; now he knew about the testament Prasutagus had written in the vain hope of persuading Rome not to appropriate all of his possessions when he died; and most importantly, he now knew about Boadicea's and her daughters' disgraceful treatment before the public of Camulodunum. No wonder the woman had raised an army to avenge herself. He would have expected no less from a warrior queen.

Suetonius had developed a severe headache during the day. Rarely did he suffer the torments which made other men's lives a living nightmare, especially—or so it was reputed—the Emperor Caligula. But when he had eaten quickly and badly, and ridden hard for the entire day with barely a break, and when he was worried about an uncertain future, then sometimes the demons of the head assaulted him, and only wine seemed able to quell their ravages.

And the arrival of the messenger from Londinium hadn't helped his head. He knew that it would be bad news, and had deliberately kept the man waiting outside his tent while he, Fabius and Callistus continued to talk about their progress in the march to the north and west. But he had delayed long enough, and it was time to receive the intelligence from the beleaguered city. He just prayed that those who hadn't or couldn't have escaped with him and his legions had managed to take his advice and flee to the east of the city, where they might find some boats and a rapid tide which could carry them toward the sea and away from the certainty of death at Boadicea's hands. But in his heart, he knew that many would have been slaughtered by her, and that he, as governor, would be held responsible by the emperor for the destruction of the city.

Suetonius nodded to the tent guard, who opened the leather flap and ordered the messenger inside. He stood at the entrance, saluted, and marched to the middle of the semicircle of military commanders. He stared at the Briton, Cassus, unsure of whether to speak.

"What news of Londinium, Centurion?" asked Suetonius.

"The entire city is destroyed, General. Flames have consumed every building, every warehouse, every shop and tavern. The gutted stone buildings of the municipal capital were then demolished by the barbarians."

Suetonius sighed. "Buildings can be rebuilt. What of the citizens?"

The centurion shook his head.

Softly, Suetonius said, "Tell me . . ."

"A massacre, General. Men, women and children. Crucified, burned, beheaded, throttled. Every one . . ."

"Everyone? All? Not one was allowed to live to be sold as a slave?"

Again, the messenger shook his head. "Not one. All of the women were hanged, and many had their breasts cut from their bodies and sewn into their mouths. It was ghastly, General. I've never seen anything like it, and I've fought the wild men in Germania and the desert dwellers in Syria. I rode into Londinium after the last of the rebels had left. General, the expressions on the faces of the dead children . . . I've never seen children look so completely . . ." He dissolved into silence.

"Continue with your report, Centurion," said Fabius sternly.

Drawing on reserves of strength, the messenger said, "But that wasn't the worst, General. Before they were killed, while they were hanging by their arms, some of the women had spikes and stakes thrust through their bodies. Through the whole length of their bodies. General, it was . . . and the men . . . their heads were cut from their bodies. I saw some floating in the river. They'd just been thrown there, sir. Remember what the Egyptians did to the head of General Pompey a century ago? We've never forgotten that, have we, sir? And nor will we ever forget what these barbarians did to our people. General, it was . . ."

"You're dismissed, Centurion," said Fabius.

He stood there, looking from one commander to the other, waiting for the strength to walk away. Suetonius nodded to the man and thanked him for his report. The centurion saluted, turned on his heel, and left the tent. Silence brooded over the three commanders for many moments. It was broken by Callistus, who said, "It must have been their priests, the Druids, who did this. It's they who pray to gods who demand such evil."

Suetonius shook his head. "I'm assured that we have killed all of the Druid priests. There are none left. No, this was the work of Boadicea and her army. They, and they alone."

"I told you," Cassus said loudly. "I told you what she was like. She's the very worst of women. She's the spirit devil walking the earth. We have to destroy her, because if she lives she'll come after me, and—"

Ignoring him, Suetonius said, "Yes, she's evil, but we must remember that this was an undefended city."

"But this is a horror on a scale which we have never encountered, General," said Callistus, reeling in shock from what the messenger had said.

"Yes, Prefect! This is the very basest of barbarism. But is it any more barbaric than what we Romans do in the arena, getting animals to tear men to pieces . . . more evil than pitting to the death man against man in the name of entertainment?" asked Suetonius.

"Yes, General," interrupted Fabius. "Far more so! The deaths in the arena are of criminals or slaves or men who make a good living as professional gladiators, knowing the deadly risks they face. But this . . . ," he said, pointing in the direction of Londinium. "This is the torture of innocents. Roman men, women and children! This is torture for enjoyment. Worse than anything I've ever known. To impale women on spikes . . . to cut off—"

"Enough, Fabius! I've heard what the messenger had to say. Yes, it's sickening and inhuman and the very opposite of the civilization we Romans bring to the far-flung world. Evil, though, is relative. Today, Roman men, except for the most depraved, wouldn't dream of having sex with a little boy. Yet the Greeks thought it the very height of sophistication and morality to teach a catamite the joys of the body. In Rome, it is a crime today to criticize the emperor, yet in the days of the divine Augustus, it was commonplace . . . indeed, Augustus encouraged criticism as a way of sharpening the wits of his commanders and himself.

"Things change in different times and in different places. What we consider hideous and inhuman in the behavior of these barbarians might have been quite normal in the time of Tarquinius Superbus. And look at the behavior of our gods: They eat children and rape women and create contests between mortals and divines for their own amusements and do all sorts of hideous things, which we willingly teach to our children as part of their lessons."

"You're surely not excusing this Fury Boadicea for her behavior, are you, General?" asked Callistus.

"Excuse her? No, I will never excuse her for slaughtering so many Roman citizens. And I certainly wouldn't behave in the way that she did; neither would any of you. But wasn't it Crassus who crucified six thousand of the followers of the rebel Thracian gladiator Spartacus on the Appian Way? Now imagine, gentlemen, if one of these barbarians had been visiting Rome a hundred and thirty years ago, and happened to be wandering down the Appian Way. What would he have seen? He would have been witness to thousands of men on crosses screaming in agony, gasping for water or an end to their suffering by the mercy of being pierced by a lance. Might not that barbarian have very well reacted in precisely the same way as did we when the messenger was giving his report of what occurred in Londinium? We are all soldiers, paid to kill Rome's enemies. And while we would never contemplate torture as have these barbarians, we live in barbaric times. Now, if you'll excuse me, my headache has become much worse, and I must take myself to my bed. We continue our march north at sunrise."

The sun was already lighting the landscape by the time Suetonius led his army along Watling Street. He knew from his maps that five miles north, a road branched off to the west where it ran all the way to the southwesternmost corner of the land; it was where the II Legion Augusta was based. Suetonius planned to march off in that direction, and to send to the commander of the legion, Poenius Postumus, for reinforcements. Once he was joined by the XIV Legion Gemina, then with the two legions and cohorts from the Augusta, he should have enough strength, placed strategically, to deal with Boadicea's army, even if it numbered one hundred thousand. But most essential would be choosing the right ground on which to do battle.

What he knew with absolute certainty was that Boadicea had attacked indefensible cities, where it was impossible for the Roman soldiers to fight the invaders in the manner and style they had been trained to do.

Roman armies were trained to defend forts behind barricades, to fight army against army in open ground, and to attack cities with their catapults and ballistae and other terrifying war machines. But fighting a vast mob of ruffians in the crowded streets of a city wasn't the Roman style, and so Boadicea had won significant victories in Camulodunum and Londinium. But she had won victories against buildings . . . not Rome's military might!

Now, according to Cassus, she would be confident that she could take on a Roman legion and win. And that, Suetonius knew, was how he would destroy her. He spurred on his horse. He had sent orders to the commanders of other legions that he wanted them to force-march and meet him in four days. He would assemble his troops. Then, somehow, he would have to force Boadicea to come to him. He smiled for the first time in days. Her confidence was her fatal weakness.

Toward Verulamium

Was Suetonius so weak that he was avoiding fighting her? Boudica sat on her horse, high on a hill, watching the vast numbers of men and women, horses and wagons, trudge up the Waechlinga Straet toward Verulamium. Spread out before her like a gigantic snake, the end so distant that she could barely make it out, were a hundred thousand or more British men and women: a colossal army to meet and defeat any challenge.

But where were the Romans? Where was Suetonius? Every day since destroying Camulodunum, she had anticipated the clarion call of Roman trumpets and drums signaling the arrival of the combined legions led by a standard bearer dressed in the skin of a crouching lion. She anticipated that they would ride her down and assault her. Every single day she prepared herself for the decisive battle in which her military might would be pitted against Suetonius' famed military genius. And every night, she had retired to her bed in a state of consternation and anxiety, wondering whether the next day, or the next, the Romans would surprise her and come screaming over the hill like a swarm of furious wasps.

But fears of Rome subsided as she viewed from on high the astounding numbers of men and women under her command. She was continually told by those around her that thanks to them, what she had accomplished so far was more than any British man or woman had previously accomplished: more than Caratacus and more than Cogidubnus in past days, and certainly much more than Queen Cartimandua who lived under Roman protection today. No Briton had achieved so much by conquest, had driven a dagger so deep into the hearts of their enemy, nor caused Rome to be so utterly terrified, they told her. They were now composing songs to her, and many were including her name in their prayers to their gods. Most of the praise she ignored or viewed as the lapping water which washed her feet when she stood at the edge of the sea. But she was beginning to believe that in the future, when people spoke of these happenings, her name would resound, and she would be called Victory.

Every day, as word spread of her successes in demolishing Roman cities, more and more men and women flocked from all over to join her. And her people were being rewarded by the loot which they took from the Romans. Even the gods were appeased, having received in conquest the bodies of thousands of victims. And next would be the traitorous city of Verulamium: not a Roman city, but its defeat would send a message to every city and town and village in Britain that there was no compromise, no cooperation with the Romans.

And she was enjoying her relationship with the kings and queens who had come to join her in her rebellion. Initially skeptical and unconvinced, Mandubracus of the Trinovantes and Cassivellaunus of the Catuvellauni had become admirers. Indeed, they seemed to agree with all her decisions. They had begun to speak to each other, asking counsel and giving well-received advice. But best of all, each and every one called her Britannia. The Roman emperor might well have refused to acknowledge her right to be monarch of the Iceni, but far more important than some creature thousands of miles to the south, British monarchs who ruled over other tribes recognized, respected and cherished her.

Despite the numbers which had gathered around her and despite the rank which she now held among her peers, Boudica knew with a terrifying certainty that she had not yet met her greatest test. Yes, she'd destroyed a couple of cities. But she had yet to meet a Roman army on the field, and that was where she was most vulnerable.

General Suetonius had a reputation as a great Roman fighter and tactician. She'd heard stories of what he had achieved in Mauretania in the north of Africa, where he had put down a serious revolt among the dwellers in their sand deserts. And she had recently learned of the devastation he had wreaked on the island of Mona when he murdered all the Druids and Britons who had sheltered there for protection.

But where was he? Why wasn't he riding toward her with his legions and taking battle against her? Why was he allowing her to roam so freely over Britain without raising a sword against her? None of it made any sense to her.

And when he eventually did meet her in the field, she knew that her greatest challenge was to keep her men and women fighters in order; to prevent them from an undisciplined charge into the jaws of the Roman war animal. She had devised battle plans for when her followers would fight Suetonius. She knew that thousands of men and women would die, but this was a price she and they were willing to pay for freedom. But she would only win the battle, conquer Suetonius and see him impaled on her sword, if her army kept its discipline and followed her battle plan. From what she'd seen in Londinium, she was concerned that the men and women under her command would open themselves up to disaster through greed, glory or plain stupidity. She hadn't tried to control their plunder in Londinium; but an army which sought only riches for itself would never win against the discipline of Rome.

It was not until the middle of the following day that Verulamium came into sight. And from her experience with looking at Londinium from a distance, she knew that the city had already emptied itself of inhabitants. Intelligence had obviously reached them early, and like many citizens of Londinium, they had escaped Boudica's wrath and were now somewhere in the protection of the Roman army.

The city gates were open; no guards were walking the walls; the streets were devoid of men or women, boys or girls. Not even a dog could be seen wandering the alleys, looking for scraps. Her bloodlust would have to wait and be slaked when eventually she took on the might of a Roman army. And what a day that would be!

Boudica sat on her horse and viewed the thousands of eager faces before her. How would they react when they realized that, yet again, there were so few inhabitants to slaughter? They had been sharpening their swords and daggers and spears since leaving Londinium, eager for their weapons to feel the bite of human flesh . . . Roman flesh. Their eyes wanted to feast again on the fear in Roman faces as proud Britons wielded an axe or a sword or a dagger. But once again they would be disappointed. Would they view her as a failure? A leader who promised, yet failed to satisfy?

She cleared her throat, and shouted to the multitude, "Fellow Britons . . ."

A huge cheer erupted from the crowd. She allowed it to die down before continuing. "Again, we have terrified the enemy. Again, like frightened rabbits, they have scurried from their burrows and disappeared into the woods. Again, my Britons, Rome has retreated before our might, and returned our Britain safely back to us.

"The city of Verulamium is empty. Empty of citizens. Empty of enemies. But they have left behind their valuables, their possessions, their food and jewelry and plates and much more for us to take. No, we aren't robbers and thieves stealing from those who have little. We are Britons, retrieving from robbers and thieves what was taken from us in the first place. These citizens of Verulamium have come to our country from Gaul, and have lived better than the Romans lived. They are not Britons; they have no love for this land, only what they can steal and take to their own bosoms. They have risen upon the backs of downtrodden Britons who toil from morning to night, just to support the rot and corruption which lives behind those walls," she said, pointing to Verulamium in the distance.

"In the name of your kings and queens, I command you now, Britons, to enter the city, enter every house and temple and warehouse and building. Take that which belongs to Britain and not to Rome. And then cleanse the stench of Rome out of British soil forever by setting a fire whose flames will burst over the rooftops and touch the very clouds themselves. Go now, Britons, and avenge your brothers and sisters. Go and light the cleansing flame of Britannia!" she screamed.

Her words were lost in the roar of anger and approbation which rose like an enormous thunderclap into the surrounding hills and valleys. Boudica watched as her locusts turned and prepared to swarm over the hapless empty land.

CHAPTER FIFTEEN

In the Middle Lands of Britain

It had come to him in the darkness of the night. He had awoken from a disturbed sleep, and suddenly it was so clear to him. And because it was so obvious, he became annoyed with his own simple mind for not having thought of it before.

Suetonius rose and relieved himself of night soil in a piss pot. He walked out of the tent, and his guards snapped to attention. Acknowledging them, he looked up at the still-dark sky and pulled his cloak around his shoulders to protect him from the cold. Suetonius walked to the edge of the camp. Almost everyone was still asleep. Though he could hear coughing and stirring in some of the tents, most of the noises came from men snoring.

As he was looking into the distant east to see if there was any trace of the rising sun, he heard a noise behind him.

"Can't the General sleep?" asked Fabius.

"By the gods, Fabius, do you shadow me at every moment of the day and night? Why aren't you sleeping, friend? You retired even later than I did."

"I sleep enough, General," he said. "I need less sleep when I'm on maneuvers. I followed you to see whether you needed something."

Suetonius smiled, and placed a fatherly hand on Fabius' shoulder. "You followed me because you didn't want me to be alone. You're a good and loyal deputy, Fabius. But soon you must leave my side and take up a command of your own. You've done well as a legate; now you need to rise to the very top. And you're well able, despite your youth. I just hope, Fabius, that you find a deputy as skilled, intelligent and generous as I have found in you."

Despite the dark, Suetonius could sense that Fabius was flushed at the unexpected and rare praise.

"Is the General thinking of retiring?" he asked.

Suetonius smiled. "The General has been thinking of retiring for a number of years. I yearn for my family and my farm in Tuscany. But I need one final battle, one victory which will be the subject of songs in Roman taverns . . ."

"And one victory parade. You deserve it, sir. When the Senate wouldn't award you a parade for your victory in Mauretania, it was an insult to the whole army."

"I don't clamor for parades, Fabius; I can leave those to the Neros and the Caligulas of this world. I fight for Rome and our people. But I do need a final victory for me to retire and tell my grandchildren how brave their grandfather was. And I feel that this victory will be coming to me very soon. In a week, two at the most."

"But we still don't know how to force her to come to us, General. She's clever and knows our ways. It's obvious that she's trying to force us to fight on terrain chosen by her."

Suetonius shook his head. "Yes, she's clever, and yes, she knows our ways. But at heart, she's a Briton, and that is her weakness. A Briton reveres his gods. They see them in every stream and tree and rock. They're in the very air they breathe. In Rome, our gods sit in their pantheon and direct the affairs of mankind. But the Britons walk and talk with their gods as though they were invisible but ever-present. And that, Fabius, is where we'll defeat her. Through her gods.

Through her streams and rocks and trees. That's how we'll get Boadicea to come to us. Wake the Briton, and bring him to my tent. I'd like to see what he thinks of my idea."

Suetonius laughed, and turned to face Fabius. He could barely make out the features of the young man in the darkness. But he could sense that he was frowning.

Grumbling at being woken before sunrise, Cassus listened in amazement to what General Suetonius was suggesting.

"It's monstrous," he said, wiping his eyes and drinking a cup of cold leftover mulled wine.

"I'm not interested in your opinion. Just in whether you think it will work."

"Oh, it'll work alright. I can just see her righteous indignation now. She'll come running," said Cassus, with a grin on his face.

When the centurions had received the general's dispatches and had their orders read to them, they first thought that it was a joke. Suetonius accepted the camp-wide laughter. It was good to unleash the tension in the men. But soon they would learn that there was a serious purpose to what he was ordering.

Burn trees; tip cooking waste into streams to make them undrinkable; urinate and defecate not in waste trenches and ditches dug specially outside of the camps, but in groves and hollows; set fire to woods and fields after they'd marched through them. It was like telling children to create mess and havoc in a room.

No explanation was given, no reasons presented. Just the bland order:

> Whenever a century, cohort or legion takes a scheduled rest break, soldiers shall not relieve themselves of their waste in the drains of one place, but shall void their waste widely throughout woods and fields and any places which the commander deems sacred to the barbarian gods. Further, the wet sponges used by soldiers to wipe their waste from the backsides of their bodies are, when the army moves on, to be left hanging on trees in full view of passersby, with the excrement still adhering to the sponge.

Suetonius insisted that the army slow its march to the north and west of the land, allowing copses and forests along his trail to be burnt. Now pristine streams and rivers were suddenly polluted with human excrement, with the detritus of cooking waste, and with the smelt left from the fires of the ironworkers who were creating or repairing weapons. Boudica would be angry.

The desecration was reported to Boudica by Britons who were in the wake of the Roman army. They pleaded with her to prevent the Romans from the further despoliation of their sacred groves and the defilement of their holy woods.

In tears, one elderly woman who had walked for four days just to see Boudica and tell her of what was happening, sobbed, "All my life, I have been guarded by the goddess Brigid. Since childhood, I have always had a fire lit for her, even in the warmth of summer. It's never gone out, Boudica. Not once in all my many years of life. And my parents before me kept Brigid's fires burning."

The old woman took out from her bodice a figure woven from reeds. It was the shape of a woman, and it possessed four arms which seemed to move as the old woman held it. To her, the goddess was more precious than a baby.

"I hang my goddess over the hearth in my home and before I make any food which needs a fire to heat it, I pray to Brigid for her love. She's helped me in giving birth to four children, and has taken into her breast six more whom I lost.

"And now, Boudica, these Romans have left her grove in filth. It's sacrilege what they've done, deliberately desecrated it so that no goddess would want to live there. They've thrown hot coals and lumps of iron onto the ground where my goddess sleeps. They've pissed and shat on her moss bed. They've . . ." She dissolved into tears.

Boudica walked two paces and put her arms around her to comfort her. Mandubracus looked on and wanted to say something, but declined, until Boudica had finished consoling the old woman and assured her that soon, with the help of Brigid and the other Druid gods, the Romans would be beaten back and pushed into the sea, never again to despoil the sacred realm of Britain.

Seeming pleased by her words, the woman left the tent. As Boudica turned to Mandubracus, he shook his head in fury, and hissed, "This is the very end! This will mean the death of every Roman in Britain. No slaves, no truce, no withdrawal. How dare these animals insult our gods, our land?"

When the old woman was no longer in earshot, his voice rose as his fury increased. "Desecrating holy groves and rivers and lakes. Is there no end to the infamy, the evil of Rome? This is the work of the most malignant forces. I'll strangle the sons of whores with my own hands, I swear before all of the gods. This vile and evil provocation by Suetonius is done to insult us. Worse than taking our men and women as slaves, worse than stealing from widows, this is defiling our sacred lands. First, they've killed our priests—every Druid hacked to pieces on Anglesea—then they've killed our bravest men and women, children and the elderly and sick. And now they've deliberately defiled our sacred places. Well, no more, I say, Boudica. We ride after them, and we slit their throats from ear to ear."

Boudica listened, and decided to remain silent until his fury had abated. He began to calm, and said, "First the Romans insult us as kings and queens, then as Britons; and now this general is insulting our gods. This man and those who follow him must be destroyed. We must unleash the full fury of the British tribes. We must crush and destroy him. We—"

"And that is precisely why he's doing it, my friend. To provoke us into righteous anger, to insult us and make us rise up to strike him," she said.

"And that's exactly what we'll do. We'll destroy his army and cut off ten thousand heads from their bodies, and hurl them into the seas from the southern cliffs. Their heads will ride on the crests of waves until they beat against the shores of Rome. Their blood will—"

"Wolves."

He looked at her in silence, wondering what she'd just said. She repeated it. "Wolves."

"What?" asked Mandubracus.

"Wolves. A dangerous animal, King Mandubracus. Think of a pack of wolves for a moment."

Mandubracus nodded his head. Boudica was restraining a smile.

"Wolves?" he repeated.

"Yes. And now think of a pack of dogs."

"Dogs?"

"Dogs!" she insisted.

"Queen Boudica, what are you talking about?"

"Alone in a wood, and armed with only a sword, would you rather be at-tacked by a pack of wolves, or a pack of dogs?"

Mandubracus knew the answer immediately. "Dogs, of course," he said emphatically.

"Why?"

"Because wolves are clever; they hunt together. They're cautious and you never know what they're thinking. They circle and tire out their prey; they take small snaps at his flesh until he's worn out. They'll wait for an entire day for the prey to falter and fall in exhaustion before they move in for the kill."

"And dogs?" she asked.

"Wild dogs? They're crazed. They throw themselves at you and you can kill one after the other, so long as you don't let them get their fangs into you. They're not clever. They—"

He stopped talking, and suddenly understood. "The Romans are trying to make us furious and mad so that we rush into an attack against them. And in our fury, they'll win." She nodded. "But if we behave like wolves," he continued, "and we're clever and cunning . . ."

She smiled.

"But how do we know that this is Suetonius' tactic? He might simply be des-ecrating our land because he is foul."

"Did he do that before? When he was in Wales and fighting the rebels, did anyone tell us that he was despoiling our land? The Romans don't want to defile our land, because they want to incorporate our gods into their heavens. And they want to live in this land and drink its pure water and use its tall trees for their ships and their houses. No, Mandubracus, General Suetonius is deliberately pro-voking me into a state of fury and wrath, hoping to make my British blood fume with rage; hoping to make me rush headlong into an attack. For in that way, I'll lose control of my army, and then we're lost. If that happens, then be sure that one of his disciplined soldiers will be worth ten of our rabble. And that's been my biggest fear since I destroyed Camulodunum."

Along the Watling Road

Even Fabius was becoming increasingly irritated by the way the delays were preventing the company from its forced march, and he idolized the general and had never found reason to question his judgment. The commanders of the legions were equally concerned about his procrastination. Yet nobody would, or could, tell General Suetonius that his constant forays were damaging the progress they would have to make.

Everyone guessed that he was looking for a position to station his troops and deciding how they would be deployed, but only he knew what he was looking for. And three or four times during every morning, and every afternoon, Suetonius would ride away from the main body of the army as it tramped north and west on Watling Street into the middle lands of England, approaching the Roman vexillation fortress of Manduessendum, known to the local Britons as Mancetter.

The army would march several miles, and the general, lost in thought, would suddenly and without any explanation kick his horse in the flanks and gallop halfway up a hill to the west or the east of the column, and stay there for some time surveying the surrounding land and its formations. Then, still lost in his thoughts, he would ride down again and continue to lead his thousands of soldiers. And the numbers who were walking with him had swelled substantially with exhausted citizens from the destroyed cities of Londinium and Verulamium.

When the general had returned from his fifth or sixth scouting mission of that day, Fabius whipped his horse and rode from the middle of the column to the head, drawing up alongside Suetonius.

Before he had even uttered a word, the general said, "These are decisions which I and I alone must make. The fate of the army, the fate of Britain, and even the ultimate fate of Rome depends upon my decision. If I choose wrongly,

Fabius, and if we lose, we're lost in Britain; and that will encourage all nations to think to themselves, 'If a barbarian woman can beat the best Roman legions in the world, then we can, too.' If that happens, the empire will collapse."

Fabius knew precisely why the general was speaking in this way, and allowed him to continue. "We're suffering rebel assaults and losses in Germania, in Judea, in Syria and now in Africa. If these losses continue, the opposition to Roman rule will be unstoppable. Tribes and malcontents everywhere will rise up and will strike at our heart. Our Senate is so utterly corrupt, and our emperor showing all the signs of going the way of Caligula and Claudius, that we can expect little leadership. So it is up to us generals and leaders of the army to protect our empire—which is why I am so long in deciding on the best position to meet Boadicea.

"When Aulus Plautius and Titus Vespasian invaded Britain and worked so hard and successfully to put down the resistance, it sent a shudder through the whole of the world. Rome, everybody thought, is invincible; Rome is the greatest power in all of history; we cannot fight Rome, and so we must live in peace under Roman rule.

"That was then, Fabius; but much has changed in these past two decades. There is a feeling of great discontent and mischief on all of our borders. Much of it, and I say this to you as a friend and confidant, is due to the hideous comedians and disgusting perverts we've enjoyed as our last three emperors.

"Which makes this coming fight imperative, Fabius. That's why we must deal with Boadicea in the harshest and most merciless manner imaginable. The world must again shudder at the might of Rome. If we weaken, if we resile, if we are beaten, if we even blink, then the whole world will ignite in an anti-Roman conflagration which will be the funeral pyre of our nation and our empire."

He looked at the young man, whose face was creased in concern. Smiling, he reached over and put his hand on his shoulder. "But these aren't your worries. It's the job of young men to fight the battles initiated by old men. I know you and the other commanders are concerned about the time I'm taking to find the right place to fight against Boadicea, Fabius. But understand me; I'm scouting the land carefully to ensure that the coming battle is more in our favor than the numbers would suggest. This woman seems to have raised half of Britain in revolt against us. The numbers of fighters flocking to her like birds are amazing.

"My caution in picking the spot to lure Boadicea to us is to minimize the loss of Roman life, and to ensure the maximum destruction of this Fury and her army. According to our intelligence, she has more than one hundred thousand men and women who are bearing arms, but if even one Briton walks away alive from this coming encounter, then I will count it in part as a defeat. She must be demolished. Her name must be expunged from history. Not one of her soldiers, man or woman, must remain alive after this engagement. This forthcoming battle, Fabius, will be like a clash of the very gods themselves. Mount Olympus will resound to the cries of orphans and widows by the time I'm finished with Queen Boadicea."

Fabius remained silent, and watched his general kick his horse, and suddenly ride off toward the west.

"When I have finished with General Suetonius and the rest of the Roman army," she screamed to make herself heard over the cawing of crows and the rustling of the leaves, "there will only be enough left of him and his soldiers to fill a corn sack."

A huge roar of laughter rose from the assembly; those at the back and on the sides, who couldn't hear, roared anyway in approval of what she might have said.

"His army has come from the west, from Mona, where they have slaughtered thousands of our holy Druid priests, where mothers and fathers, sons and daughters, grandparents and babies, have all been murdered to satisfy the bloodlust of a crazed emperor in Rome."

Another yell, but this was one of hatred and fury. It startled Boudica, because although she had been building her army up into a state of frenzy, she knew that she must retain control and not allow them to become a rabble.

"General Suetonius has gathered together the might and strength of the Roman army to the north and west of us. They are hoping to lure us into a trap. I know the way the minds of the Romans work. But no matter what the trap, no matter how fearsome are the Romans in battle, we will win."

The roar of approbation erupted and threatened to engulf Boudica's more important words. Yet because of the shouting and cheering, she had to wait until the vast sea of soldiers had calmed down and was prepared to listen. Many of them had been drinking since early morning, and their spirits were excitable. Yet what could she do? They would follow her as long as she led them to victory, and so far they had not enjoyed a victory. Yes, the first battle she had fought against Camulodunum had been a victory, but only half of the soldiers who now followed her had been involved; the rest had participated in a massacre at Londinium, and the destruction of the empty town of Verulamium. So only half of her soldiers had fought a battle.

"The Roman general has called for reinforcements from the Second Legion Augusta who are far to the west. If we attack him soon, they won't have time to reach him. That means that he'll be fighting us with the Fourteenth and the Twentieth Legions. Now these are fearsome men, valiant and resourceful. And most importantly, they're disciplined. Remember that one disciplined soldier is worth ten men in a rabble. Never has there been greater certainty of victory than the battle we'll be fighting tomorrow or the day following. Why? Because we are Britons, and they are not!"

Again there was a huge roar.

"Because we number ten times the forces that Suetonius can put up against us."

Again, a roar of approval. They were waiting on her every word. She saw the look of adoration in their eyes, and loved this moment more than any of her life until now. She glanced aside, and saw her two daughters hugging each other, sharing in their mother's moment.

"Because we live in this land and they will die in this land."

She waited for her army to stop whistling and clapping; she had reached her climax, and she wanted to send them into battle with this sound of courage ringing in their ears.

"And one final thing which will give us victory over the Romans: They are protected by their god of vengeance, Mars Ultor; but he lives in Rome on a sacred mountain. The Romans think that this god will protect them, and give them victory. But I have invoked the most awesome and powerful god in all the heavens and on the earth. I have invoked the power of Teutates to protect us and to fight by our side."

At the mention of the fearsome Druid god's name, the huge crowd became silent and uneasy. Each of them had his or her own personal god, whether in a niche in the wall beside the hearth, or carried as a good luck charm in a pocket. None, though, would ever consider associating with the awesome Teutates. His name was rarely, if ever, spoken aloud. Only the Druids were permitted to speak of him, and then only among themselves before a battle. Teutates demanded human sacrifice as his payment for coming to the aid of his people. They knew that he had been invoked by the Druids before the battle of the island of Mona, but for reasons which none understood, he had abandoned his people.

And now Boudica was invoking him to fly from Mona and to be present at the coming battle between Rome and themselves. The men and women looked at each other, shaking their heads in wonder.

Loudly, and with complete confidence in her voice, Boudica shouted, "Teutates came to me in a vision last night. He entered my tent and stood by the foot of my bed. I tried to look at his face, but it was a mask of utter horror and I averted my eyes. But I heard his voice, which was like a loud noise in my head, a clap of thunder. He said to me, 'Queen Britannia, I have allowed the Romans to kill all of my Druid priests on Mona because they were unworthy. I need a strong people to live in my land. The men and women under your command are strong and faithful to Britain, and I will support and defend them. Through my hand, they will slay all the Romans. And from the end of the battle, there will never be another Roman who sets foot on our sacred soil.'

"Then he disappeared in a cloud of smoke. So this is the promise which Teutates makes to me, Britannia, and to you Britons: When we engage with the enemy, our god will ensure that we fight in a strong, determined and disciplined manner. Our god demands that you listen to my orders. Then, and only then, will you be protected by a god who will fight against Mars Ultor of the Romans, and our god will prevail."

Any fears which might have surfaced when Boudica mentioned Teutates' name evaporated, and the army cried out in ecstasy. They cheered, and cried out in their joy, war cries splitting the air, arms raised to the heavens, swords and lances stabbing the clouds. Then they pulled flasks and bottles from their pockets, and drank and shared their drink with those around them.

As Boudica turned and walked toward her children, the clamor in the air was of people laughing. She smiled as she embraced her daughters.

"Soon, Tasca, soon, Camorra, you and I will finally be avenged. The memory of the pain you suffered at the hands of those beasts will be gone forever."

Along the Watling Road

After the general's final speech, the army had retired, confident of their coming victory. They had been exultant, giving him a series of cheers for his leadership. It had been a good and rousing speech, and the army's nerves at fighting the barbarians were calmed. The night had passed peacefully and the men would soon wake, rested and secure.

So Fabius was unsure how to present the report which the messenger had just given him: news so disastrous it spelled death to every man in the camp; news which meant not only calamity for the coming battle, but disaster for Rome and its empire; for as the general had so often pointed out, revolts which succeeded could spread like a forest fire throughout every province. Yet it was news which was undeniable, and the general had to be told.

The young man hesitated before walking across the camp compound, and wondered how to frame the words. He surveyed the campsite. Hundreds of leather tents grew like mushrooms over the fields and hillside. The perimeter which they had dug just the previous day was heavily guarded, the final guard having changed two hours earlier in preparation for morning muster. Men were now stirring in their tents, coughing and belching and farting. Soon they would emerge to void their night soil. Normally, they'd do it in the latrine trenches dug away from the camp, but since the general had given orders to befoul the countryside, they were now doing it in urns, bowls, and buckets which were collected by orderlies and dispatched under guard to streams and copses. And it seemed to be working. Their intelligencers reported that Boadicea's army was in a state of great agitation, and was moving rapidly toward where the Romans were camped.

But these things didn't concern Fabius that morning. Where once he had assumed a great victory, he was now profoundly disturbed. The army the Britons would meet was far smaller than the general had initially conceived. His planning had not materialized. And not only that, but when news of the coming battle with Queen Boadicea and the Britons had circulated around the camp, the civilians from Londinium and Verulamium had found reason to excuse themselves, and had scurried away into the countryside like rats in a state of panic.

When he had first come from Wales and Mona to confront the uprising, the general believed that he could rely on fielding fifty thousand soldiers. But the need to retain so many men in the west in order to clean up the continuing resistance had reduced his army to no more than twenty thousand. He also believed that he could count on an additional twenty thousand auxiliaries in the form of armed civilians from the towns which Boadicea had destroyed, but these cowards were now running away. So to have to tell him the latest news would compound the disaster and make him furious.

Preparing himself for the onslaught, Fabius crossed the campground, and nodded to the soldiers guarding the general's tent. They opened the flaps for him, and he saw Suetonius bent over a bowl, washing his face.

As he toweled himself, Suetonius saw a look of concern on Fabius' face. "Tell me," he said without preamble.

"Sir, the *Praefectus Castrorum* of the Second *Augusta*, Poenius Postumus, has sent a messenger saying that he cannot obey your command and that regretfully he is unable to send his legion to our aid."

Fabius braced himself.

"Why?" asked Suetonius softly.

"Because he says that he is under siege from the Durotriges tribe and that he must stay where he is in order to defend his fort. He says his men will have to march nearly two hundred miles through enemy territory, and his casualties will be terrible before he reaches you."

Fabius grew silent. Knowing him as well as he did, Suetonius asked gently, "There's more, isn't there?"

Fabius nodded. "He adds in his note that the general should be able to fight against a woman without needing to be rescued by the Augusta."

Suetonius sat heavily in his chair, and looked at the table. Fabius, holding his breath and not knowing whether to retreat from the tent, waited, standing there.

Breathing deeply, Suetonius calmed himself and stood, going over to his uniform and armor. He drew his sword and gave it to Fabius.

"Send the messenger back with my sword. Tell him to inform Prefect Poenius Postumus that he is to keep this sword by his side from now on. If he hears that Suetonius has lost the coming battle with Boadicea, he is to seek out her army, engage them, and then use this sword to strike her dead. However, if the prefect hears that General Suetonius has succeeded and has won the battle, he is to fall on this sword in front of his entire army. Tell him that this is the price for failing to obey an order, and the salary of a coward. Go!"

Toward Manduessendum, in the Middle Lands of Britain

Flushed with excitement, Mandubracus and Cassivellaunus returned from their tour around the encampment, where they had given last-minute instructions to their subjects and servants. Even their slaves had been sent to the armorers in order to be given swords and daggers, though not shields. The slaves were told by their owners that even though they were bound in servitude for the rest of their lives, they would not be freed, but killed by the Romans if Britain lost the looming battle, and so it was in their interests to fight for their masters and mistresses.

The two monarchs met Boudica who was returning from her visit to where the thousands of men and women from the Iceni tribe had encamped. But unlike them, her face was dark with concern. She had seen drunkenness and was worried about the lack of preparation.

"Did you see how many have arrived to join us?" shouted Cassivellaunus exultantly as they approached. "They've come from everywhere. Like grass in the fields, there are thousands of grandfathers and grandmothers, aunts and uncles, sons and daughters. All have traveled from far and near to be here at the final victory. Word has spread throughout Britain of this battle, and our freedom. By all the gods, Boudica, all of Britain has come here to stand by our sides. It's beyond my dreams. We've achieved what a thousand years of British history have failed to do. We've united a people and made Britain whole. Rivalries have been put aside. For the first time, we are one, like Gaul and Spain, and we will speak with one voice." He grew silent, uncertain how to phrase the next thoughts. "And they've come here because of you, Boudica. They really see you as Britannia." He shook his head. "I never would have believed it."

She looked at him in amazement. Her concerns about the preparedness of her British army were put to one side as her once mortal enemy spoke to her with praise on his lips.

Mandubracus smiled in agreement and said, "Cassivellaunus is right. All of Britain is traveling here to see the final victory. They've walked for many miles, or come by carts. They're the families of the men and women who will lay down their lives for you. They number as many as we have in our army. Cassivellaunus is correct when he says that the people of Britain have come to worship at your feet. Because when the last Roman head has been severed from his shoulders, the people of Britain will see you as the leader who has defeated the enemy."

"But will you?" she asked Cassivellaunus. "Will you?" she asked Mandubracus. "When I first came to your kingdoms, begging you to join me in ridding Britain of Romans, you were hesitant. Victory has made you certain. But your hesitancy wasn't just in supporting my demands; you insisted that all decisions had to be made in a council. Yet it is my tactics, my leadership, which has brought us victory. So when Rome is no longer in Britain, who will lead us? Or will we go back to being a nation of tribes, each fighting the other?"

The men looked at one another. Their silence spoke eloquently of the future for Britain once it was no longer part of the empire of Rome. These onetime mortal enemies, men who would have killed each other on sight, were now brothers in arms, prepared to die side by side against the forces of Suetonius.

But Boudica knew that each would use her coming victory to increase his own power and the land and wealth of his own people. She knew with certainty that Rome would only be her first enemy. The battle to regain not just her land and people, but the whole of Britain, would continue long after the last Roman had left British shores.

It was Camorra who first saw that her mother was in a state of distress. Boudica sat down heavily in a chair, weighed down by the worries which threatened to overwhelm her.

"Mother?" asked her daughter. "Are you worried about the battle?"

Boudica smiled, and hugged her child to her breast. "Victory, darling girl, is merely a prelude to the real battles which are looming. We will win against our enemies; but the day after we defeat the Romans, we will have to begin the long battle against our friends."

Camorra frowned and shook her head. Boudica kissed her young daughter on the forehead. "If a man smiles at you, is he your friend, or your enemy?"

"Your friend."

"And if, after the smile, you turn around and walk away, but he stabs you in the back, is he your friend or your enemy?"

"Your enemy."

"That is your first lesson, but I regret to say that there is much that you have to learn about life, dearest child. I pray to all the gods that you learn the lessons quickly and without too much pain."

As her mother held her close, Camorra could feel her begin to sob. Alarmed, she asked softly, "What's the matter? Is there anything I can do?"

"No," Boudica said, trying to control her weeping. "There are times at which your father's loss is so very great that I feel as if I just can't carry on without him."

Mystified, Camorra said, "But people are bowing down to you. They're calling you 'saviour.' They're saying that only you can lead them. You've won victories against the Romans. You've—"

"And all of this on my own. Understand me, child. When your father was alive, he and I ruled together. Any decision I made was discussed with him. And he always discussed everything with me."

Camorra thought about the will Prasutagus had made which he hadn't discussed with her mother, but knew that she had to remain silent.

"Now I am expected to be sole ruler not just of the Iceni, but of all of Britain; I'm expected to be a great general, better than a man whose whole life has been steeped in the ways of warfare; I'm expected to be a lawgiver, a judge of the disputes of people whom I have never met. So much is expected of me, Camorra. And I am alone in making those decisions."

She sighed, and dried her eyes.

Camorra said, "I'm here, Mother. I can help you make those decisions."

Boudica smiled for the first time since returning to her tent. "You? Dearest, you can't even tell the difference between a friend and an enemy."

Boudica hugged her young daughter, felt her soft and willing body, and said to herself, *But maybe neither can I.*

CHAPTER SIXTEEN

Manduessendum, Along Watling Street

Everything about it told him that it was right. He knew it the moment it came slowly into view along the straight road. Was it the tall cliff at the rear which allowed him to decide, or was it the wood to the left and rear which made his heart skip a beat? No, those he'd seen many times on the road. But what led him to select the place for the battle was the way in which the landscape led upward into a narrow gorge between two hills and became a bottleneck which then widened out into a large flat area on which he could position his army. It was the defile leading up to the cliff which made the place perfect. Any one of the peculiarities of the landscape—the sheer cliff, the woods on the right and left, or the narrowing defile—would have made for a strong defensive position, but all three together made it perfect. And tomorrow, or whenever the Britons arrived, he would need all the help which the terrain and his gods could give him.

He wheeled his horse around and galloped back to his army, riding furiously over a plain which soon would be swarming with the largest mob of

Britons ever to gather in one place. And from his intelligencers, he knew that they were near ... just a half day's march away. There were times when the wind was still and the air was cool, and he felt he could hear them; but that was fanciful, the mind playing tricks on a grizzled old commander.

Suetonius rode like a madman toward the front of the column. He saw his standards being born aloft and felt a surge of pride. Days of indecision, of trying to find a suitable location, of keeping a day or so ahead of Boadicea's army, had suddenly and unexpectedly come to an end. Every instinct in his soldier's body told him that the plain which narrowed into a defile which led to a hill which was supported by a steep and unclimbable cliff and defended on its flanks by thick woods, was worth at least an additional legion.

Fabius saw the general riding like the very wind itself across the grasslands. He broke rank and rode out to meet and greet him. Saluting, and watched by every exhausted man in the long snake of a column, Fabius said, "You've found it, haven't you, General."

Suetonius smiled and nodded. He turned in his saddle, and Fabius followed the direction of his gaze.

"Tell me, *Legatus,* why is that my preferred battlefield?" he said, pointing to the hill and the cliff behind it.

Fabius looked for a moment and summed up the terrain. "Our men will be stationed on top of the hill. The enemy will have to climb up to fight us. We have the advantage of height and dominance. Because of the woods on either side of the hill, we can't be surprised by an attack from the flanks or the rear. However, our cavalry can hide in the woods, and swoop down on the rear of the enemy army, forcing them to defend both sides of the pincer. The cliff at the rear protects us from a sudden attack by the barbarians as our men face the opposite way and are fighting the hordes who ascend the hill and come through the defile."

Suetonius nodded and said, "But we've seen similar terrains on the way here. Why is this the one I've chosen?"

Now Fabius was more circumspect. This was the question which would define the difference between a general and a legion commander. He had been promised advancement by Suetonius; now he had to earn it.

He delayed answering until he was certain, and then confidently, he said, "The geography of the terrain means that the Britons will approach the hill on a wide front. But as they cross the grass plain, the land will force them into an increasingly narrow defile. This will cause them to be concentrated to the point where there will be so many of them standing side by side, trying to get at us through the narrow point of the defile of the hills, that they won't have the space to swing swords and axes. Further, our troops will only be presented with a small number of attackers as the Britons advance through the defile toward us."

Suetonius was delighted, and encouraged his protégé. "Go on," he said.

"The concentration of enemy forces at their rear will immobilize those who are not in the front ranks; their progress will be halted, making them easier targets for our cavalry. Further, when we begin to slaughter them as they emerge through the defile, many will turn and try to retreat, but they'll find that impossible. They'll fall over those who are trying to get through. Their confusion will aid us greatly."

Looking at him to see whether he had determined the strategy correctly, Suetonius said softly, "And one further thing."

Fabius looked long and hard at the future battleground, but shook his head and shrugged.

Smiling, Suetonius said, "The archers?"

And then the final part of Suetonius' strategy fell into place. Grinning, Fabius said, "Of course. How stupid of me. As the Britons are halted in their determination to get through the defile, they'll be concentrated into a mass of people, and they'll be completely still, waiting to ascend. A huge body of men and women will make a simple target for our archers, stationed on the wings of the defile. They'll just pick them off, a hundred at a time. It'll be more butchery than warfare. It's brilliant, General. My congratulations."

Nodding, Suetonius said, "Now do you understand why I've taken so long to make the choice? We are ten thousand, compared to Boadicea's one hundred thousand and more. The terrain here will give us the equivalent of fifty thousand extra soldiers. And one Roman soldier is worth five of these Britons."

They turned their horses, and began to ride back to their troops. "You've done well, Fabius. When we have finished with this rebellious upstart Boadicea, I will recommend that you return to Rome, and that the Senate give you the rank of military tribune."

Fabius looked at him in amazement. "Tribune . . . but General . . . I don't know what to say . . . ."

"Of course, if we lose the battle tomorrow, your chances of survival, let alone advancement, are severely reduced. So I suggest that we now order the men to set up their camp and prepare themselves for the greatest clash this country will ever see. I want extra guards posted. The men will sharpen weapons and check their armor. Everything is to be inspected by centurions tonight or before dawn in the morning. Any weapon which isn't sharp or which is broken will cause the soldier to be flogged. Further, there will be only food served tonight. No wine. Just water and this apple juice which they've taken a fancy to. Any drinking of wine, any drunkenness tonight or in the early hours of the morning will earn the miscreant two months' cancellation of his salary and a double flogging. All men are to be roused an hour before sunrise and formed up into *centuriae*. They will march to their hill as though they're taking part in a triumphal procession through the streets of Rome; and they'll guard their hill as though they were guarding their family homes. Their very lives depend upon it. Discipline will be rigid, Fabius. There will be no exceptions."

Fabius saluted again, and rode off to brief his centurions on their roles and to post the orders. The restriction on wine wouldn't be welcomed, but it was a sensible precaution, especially if the British arrived in the early hours of the morning soon after sunrise.

The Roman camp was established beside the river so that it would not interfere with the path of the Britons. Suetonius continued to ride around the defile, which narrowed into a bottleneck as it ascended the hill where he would station his troops.

A nagging doubt began to surface. Was this spot good enough to accomplish his aims? If not, if he had made the wrong decision, then instead of his name being heaped with paeans of glory, instead of being welcomed by cheering masses in adoring Rome and accorded a triumph—maybe even an arch—instead of those glories which should conclude his fabulous military career, if he had made a mistake, then his flesh would be stripped from his body, his head severed from his neck, flies would begin to consume his body and those of his men, and the bones of Rome's glory would bleach in the sun.

But any doubts quickly vanished when he started to determine the military maneuvers needed to meet the coming of the hordes. At the bottleneck which led up through the defile caused by rock formations to left and right, he would place three lines of spearmen: One line in the front would hold short javelins to stab at the naked chests of the first men and women through the narrow entryway; immediately behind the front row he would station men with stabbing swords and longer spears; and the third line would just have long spears. Those would be his repulse troops to stop the forward movement of the Britons. The sudden halt to their charge up the hill would cause chaos for the tens of thousands behind as they continued their push up the hill to join their colleagues. Mayhem would ensue, and then he could go on the attack.

The formidable defensive barrier to slow down the British onslaught and create havoc with their advance would enable his equestrians to do their job. Once the casualties began to mount and the British fell at his soldiers' feet, he would order the drummers and trumpeters to sound the advance. The lines of spearmen would separate to allow swordsmen to step past them, over the bodies of the British, and hack away at anybody who stood there.

But was that the best military tactic, or should his archers first fire their volleys into the oncoming mob to slow them down as they advanced for the fight, or should he order them to fire into the retreating mob to create mayhem? And should he load up some ballistae with rocks to demoralize the onrushing barbarians or hurl the rocks at them as they ran away? With the drastic imbalance between his forces and Boadicea's, these decisions about tactics could spell the difference between the sweetest of victories or the greatest defeat in history. And if the gods ordained the second, then his name and family honor would be doomed forever.

Approaching Manduessendum, Along Watling Street

Their step wasn't as quick or light as it had been when they left Londinium. In the weeks since setting it, and Verulamium, on fire, they had been drinking, loving, eating, drinking and loving. It was as though the whole of Britain had suddenly stopped and was celebrating a long continuous festival of merriment. But the ale and wine and cider they had drunk was taking its toll, and today, their march was a slow trudge.

Everybody was walking slower, their bodies lacking enthusiasm, and all seemed to be complaining about the pace of their walk, and the shortage of resting stops. While many were still enthused about driving the Romans from their homes, and many more continued to be incensed about the sacrilege against their land, most seemed to be following for the sake of following.

Some in her army were even stopping by the wayside, assuring their friends that they'd catch up soon and rejoin the army, but Boudica knew that they'd disappear into the woods and grasslands and return to their homes, content to let her fight on their behalf. The massacre at Camulodunum, the rape of Londinium and the looting at Verulamium had slaked their thirst and satisfied their lust for vengeance. Now the holiday was over, and they wanted to go home.

But for every man and woman who apologetically wandered away, ten times ten additional Britons bounded over the fields, booming out cries of joy and welcome and bolstering her army until it was too big for her to count. Nor could she blame anybody for leaving. Had she the opportunity, she would take her daughters and slink away into the night to return to her home and her hearth and her friends and to close her door and shut out memories of the previous months forever. There were times when she believed that she was a plaything of the god Lugh, and that she would wake in the morning and find Prasutagus lying next to her, snoring and smiling in his sleep, and her two daughters safe in their beds.

But she wasn't in Lugh's hands; she was in the hands of the terrible god Teutates, and he was dictating her every move, her thoughts, her fears and her desire for Roman blood. Boudica was tired, and she knew that those who had been with her since the start were also tired. But unlike her, their exhaustion wasn't attributable to pressures of responsibility and leadership along Waechlinga Straet, but in drink and cavorting and wrestling and gaming.

She had ridden around the hillsides on which her army was camped. She was now a familiar sight on her horse; she cajoled her followers, demanded that they behave like an army, and ordered them to restrain their drinking. She had punished some of them severely, but the vast numbers weren't cowed by discipline. And they had cheered her onward, confident in their coming victory, secure in their vastly superior numbers and knowing that the Druid gods would ensure their ultimate success. The more she remonstrated with them, commanded their obedience, the more they promised that they would behave like Roman soldiers; and as she rode away, she knew that once she was no longer in sight, they would begin their drinking again.

In silence, Boudica rode at the head of her vast army. She turned and looked at the huge line that snaked into the distance and was lost in the clouds of dust which the hundreds of thousands of feet had created from the dry roadway. Up ahead lay the Roman army. The previous day, she had been told by her spies that they were in disarray, nervous, tense, shouting orders and in a state of panic.

Up ahead, General Suetonius was no doubt aware that she had caught up to him and his legions, and he was preparing for a fight to the death. Her spies told her that most of the civilians from the three cities she'd destroyed had already deserted him, had turned and run like panicked dogs. The men and women from Londinium and Verulamium, who had joined the army's advance for protection, were now disappearing into the countryside. They obviously realized that the Romans were doomed and that if they were caught with them, they would die.

So now the great General Suetonius was left with only a fraction of her numbers. Her spies estimated his army at two legions—about ten thousand men. Her army was like grass in a field. At least a hundred thousand Britons, who, when they shook off their drink-induced lethargy, would be clamoring to cleave a Roman's head from his shoulders. It would be a massacre, which gave her great cause for concern. Her victory, on numbers alone, was certain. Yet a fear gripped her body and her heart pounded. Was it a fear that she herself might not be the leader her people deserved? If so, why did great kings like Mandubracus and Cas-sivellaunus defer to her? They had far more experience of fighting battles than she. Yet there must be a reason why so many had flocked to join her. And it couldn't simply be their hatred of the Romans, for if it was, then Caratacus would have been supported by ten times the number who had actually fought with him.

No, the simple answer was that because she and her daughters had been hu-miliated, she had come to symbolize everything which was wrong in a Britain controlled by a mad emperor and his ferocious servants. That was why tens of thousands of Britons had suddenly become roused in their fury and tramped across the land to join her. If she could rekindle that ferocity, then in the morn-ing victory would be hers and Britain would be free forever.

But if it was such a certain victory, why was she so worried?

As she rode at the head of the column, she saw a runner at the far point of her vision. He was fording a stream, and running up the valley which led to the crest of the hill on which Waechlinga Straet had been built and improved by the Ro-mans. He was still a long way off, but Boudica knew the man and realized that his haste in running toward her meant that he was carrying important information.

She kicked her horse and rode across the land to where he stood, trying to regain his breath. When they met, he fell to ground in exhaustion and lay there panting. Boudica dismounted and gave him a drink from her flask, cradling his head in her lap.

Gasping, the runner told her, "Your Majesty, over there." He pointed to a distant hill.

"What?" she asked, already sensing his answer.

Recovering quickly from his exertions, he said, "Roman army. There, be-yond the hill. They're camped. We can catch them by surprise. They're a short march for us now. If we run, we can surprise them while they're setting up their camp."

He took another long draught of water, and continued. "They're camped in the valley beside the sacred river. If we swoop down on them like birds of prey, we can slaughter them. They're not ready, Boudica. They're sharpening their weapons and making repairs and doing things which men in the army do. They're unprepared for a battle now. If we go immediately, we can win. There are ten of us to every one of them. Don't you understand? We must move now!"

She shook her head. "We aren't ready ourselves. Our men and women are exhausted. Some are drunk. And the wagons aren't yet arrived with our weapons and our food. The Romans might be setting up their camp and unready for battle, but if we attack them now, we'll be fighting them with our bare hands. And," she said, looking up at the sky, "it will be dark soon. No. We'll camp here, and in the morning, when we've eaten and rested, when we're armed and ready, then and only then will we march around the hill and attack them."

Suddenly energized with a courage which had drained out of her body just moments earlier, an energy and confidence which she realized had slowly been seeping out of her since the looting at Verulamium, she gave the runner food from her pack and told him to jump onto the back of her horse, and to ride with her the rest of the way.

They arrived back at her British army, which was now sprawling all over the roadway and into the surrounding hills. Everybody had assumed that as night was beginning to fall, Boudica would order them to remain here for the rest of the night.

Her tent was always the first to be erected, as she had matters of war to discuss with her colleagues. As she rode into the camp, she smelled the burning of wood which were the fires to warm the spirits of her subjects, and which would shortly be heating their food. Hungry, having eaten nothing since the middle of the morning, Boudica began to think of roasted meats and vegetables, and her mouth began to water; but before she would allow herself the joy of eating and drinking, she had to determine the tactics for the morning.

According to her spy, it was a two-hour march for her army to reach the Romans' camp. Assuming that they didn't move off at the break of day, and if she could rouse her army by sunrise, then by the middle of the next morning, she and her British subjects should be in the midst of a battle to reclaim Britain for her people.

Suddenly, the enormity of what she was about to undertake made her gasp. The cities she'd destroyed had been nothing compared to what she was facing. The legion she had destroyed at Camulodunum was led by a fool. But tomorrow she would meet a true Roman. Then she would prove her worth against the best that the empire could produce.

She felt a pain in her back. It still hurt from the scars of the lash, and she knew with absolute certainty that even though Camorra and Tasca seemed to be well enough, and to have slaked their thirst for vengeance by their killing of Romans, they would always be scarred by their experiences with the beasts in the barracks. Boudica's wounds were on the surface of her skin; but her children's wounds were deep and incapable of healing. For them, for herself, for the thousands of Britons made slaves to the Roman empire, for the despoliation of her sacred lands by the filth of the army . . . for all of these reasons, tomorrow would be a day of reckoning. It would be a day when she would drink from the well of vengeance and satisfy her thirst for revenge on the blood and bones of the fiends who were assembling before her.

As she entered her tent, she saw Mandubracus and Cassivellaunus were already there; their faces betrayed their excitement.

"Is it true?" asked Mandubracus.

Boudica nodded. "They're just beyond the hill. They're in a state of panic and disarray, according to the spy. They're setting up camp right now. We will wait for our wagons; then we'll arm our men and women and I'll talk to them. We'll march from here before sunrise so that we catch the Romans preparing for the day. We'll be on the high road, and they're camped in the valley. We'll swoop down on them like an eagle swoops on its prey. We'll crush them in our talons and squeeze the life force from their bodies. This will be the most glorious day in the whole history of Britain."

Mandubracus and Cassivellaunus had never seen her like this. It was as though the clouds which had dulled her since leaving Londinium and Verulamium had lifted, and a new and young and energetic Boudica was among them again. She put on her breastplate and her helmet, which shone in the slanting rays of the late sun, and she seemed to illuminate the entire tent. "I will talk to my people," she said, walking out of the tent. "King Mandubracus, King Cassivellaunus, please assemble everybody after their evening meal, so that I can address them."

Some had been drinking. But for once, she forced herself not to be critical. When tomorrow came, the numbers on her side would eliminate any deficiencies her army might suffer; and the victory would give her time to raise a permanent army like the Romans, fund them from levies on the tribal leaders, equip them and train them properly to be soldiers.

Boudica knew that any failings in her men would be made good by the god Teutates. Most had quietly been sharpening their swords; many men and women had removed all of their clothes and anointed their bodies with oils and fragrances before painting them with blue woad and red ochre so that they looked fearsome and would strike terror into the hearts of their enemy.

Their mood seemed subdued; it was as though all had suddenly realized that for once they wouldn't be fighting retired elderly soldiers, or raping and looting civilians, but would be facing the real might of Rome. She needed to raise their spirits, to elevate them to a level where hatred coursed through their bodies and they felt the fury of earlier days. Tomorrow, they had to be exultant, to be ecstatic, for if they went into a fight against the Romans in a state of fear and consternation, they would be at a severe disadvantage.

All now assembled before her. She had ridden in her chariot, preferring it to the back of her horse; it spoke of her power, of her warrior status, of the destruction which she and her weapons, and the murderous swords on the wheels of the vehicle, would wreak on the Romans.

The noise of the hundred thousand Britons had been overwhelmingly loud; but she seemed to feel a nervous tension in the air. She whipped her horses and rode down the hill to where her army was assembled. Now she was ready to speak to them, not as a woman, but as a leader, a general. Now she would give them courage.

"Men and women of Britain's army, if ever an army was invincible, then this is the army."

She waited for the shouts, laughter and applause to quieten. "The Romans once were a fierce and noble army, but today, they are a dull shadow in a weak and fading sun. How many soldiers does Suetonius have with him?"

She didn't wait for an answer. Instead, she continued to shout. "He wanted double our number, but all but a handful have deserted him. He wanted two hundred thousand Romans to face us tomorrow, but our spies tell us that he has fewer than ten thousand. And we are ten times ten thousand. Victory tomorrow is assured. Listen to me, men and women of Britain. We are an ancient people, a proud people. Our leaders in the past have led us astray. They have allowed their people to eat at the same table as the hated Roman, sleep with Romans, and even to kiss the Roman arse. And what has the Roman done for Britain? He has raped us and beaten us and savaged us and destroyed our land. Our forests are being cut down to make masts for his ships and wood for his houses. Our mines are being exhausted for his coins. Our young men and women are being abducted to be his slaves. Enough, I say. Enough! Tomorrow, you will strike at the Roman heart. Tomorrow, every Roman standing upon our sacred hill will be dead, his blood enriching our earth, his flesh and bones rotting and becoming the dust of the air. Tonight, I command you to celebrate. Make love to each other, wrestle and play dice. Comb your hair and sharpen your swords. This is your last night of slavery, for tomorrow freedom will begin for all of Britain."

The cheer which erupted sounded as though it would wake the very gods themselves. She whipped her horses, wheeled her chariot around, and returned to her lodgings. Entering her tent, Boudica suddenly felt exhausted. And she felt her age. Perhaps it was the beating, or seeing her children brutalized. Perhaps it was the battles she'd fought, or the slaughters in which she'd participated. There were many reasons for her body to feel so tired.

Yet somehow she had the strength not just to recover from all she had been through during the traumas of the previous months, but she had also been able to rouse the entire nation of Britain behind her, to become the queen of all of her people, and to inflict three of the most awful defeats which Rome had suffered in a thousand years. She knew that her three defeats of the Romans were making the entire empire reel in shock. Not even the wild-eyed Germans had managed to inflict such damage on once-invincible Rome.

But with little sleep in a month, and with the weight of the whole country on her shoulders, Boudica needed her rest. Her body ached for respite; for sleep, for the dreams she once enjoyed so much as a child.

She stepped down off the platform of the chariot, and two slaves grasped the reins. Her height made her stoop to enter her tent, where both Camorra and Tasca were waiting for her. She loved to look at them. They were her normality. And before the battle, she again saw them as though for the first time. She saw how young and beautiful they were, growing as tall as their mother. She sighed and thought, *If only their father could see how beautiful they have become.*

And they were still proud of who they were, despite the savagery they had endured. To look at them, only Boudica would have known how badly damaged they had been. Oh, so badly damaged. And that was something for which the Romans would pay dearly. In the morning. With their lives.

"Girls, fetch me some food and drink. I must rest before tomorrow."

Camorra and Tasca left their mother's tent and went to the cooks to get a bowl of lamb in a stew of oats and some bread. And they knew also to bring a beaker of hot wine with spices and honey, which their mother loved.

Boudica lay upon her bed and allowed her slave to unstrap her armor, then her tunic, her shoes and her undergarments until she was naked. Another slave brought her a bowl of water and a flannel for her to wash her face and body. It was good to feel the cold water against her skin. She allowed the cooling water from the flannel to wash over her neck, her breasts and her stomach. Her breasts were still firm, despite having given birth to two children. Her stomach was hard and taut after weeks and weeks of fighting. Oh, how soft and indulgent she and her husband had become as friends of the Romans.

The slave soaked another flannel, and washed her legs, her feet and then, without waiting for approval, her woman's parts. Boudica turned over and allowed the slave to wash her back, her buttocks and her legs. She stood, and her second slave brought over a long dress for her to wear while she went to sleep.

What was it about water which was so refreshing? She remembered back to her childhood, when she would run down a bank and fling herself into the air, crashing into the slow-running river and feeling her mind suddenly wake up as the cold exhilarating water titillated her body. Even better were the times when her parents would take her to their forests on the east coast of Britain, and she would swim for the best part of the midday in the grasping clutches of the sea. She was a strong swimmer, so she was never in danger of the gods of the sea telling their currents to grab her and pull her forever into their depths.

Camorra and Tasca reentered her tent with a steaming bowl of food, and drink. Boudica thanked them and asked them to leave her so that she could rest. Alone at last, blissfully alone, she began to eat the camp food. Lumpy, hard, overcooked meat and evil-tasting oatmeal that it was, it was welcome and satisfying. She could have taken her cooks from her home but it would have soon got round that Queen Boudica was eating better than her army, and that was something she didn't want said of her. So she suffered from bad food, but suffered willingly.

She ate half the food, and drank the beaker of mulled wine. Then she lay down on her bunk and closed her eyes, trying to shut out the noise of her army's revelries prior to the battle. Her thoughts drifted from the many things she'd forgotten or hadn't had time to do, to the coming final conflict with the Romans in the morning. And the last thing she heard was the laughter of her people, drinking and enjoying themselves on the last night of their slavery.

Manduessendum, in the Middle Lands of Britain

Suetonius heard the noise, and wondered what it could be. It sounded like a thousand flocks of birds suddenly cawing and screaming over a wheat field. Others heard it, and looked at the general. But the noise died down, and the Romans continued their preparations for the coming battle.

Suetonius had visited every centurion, and every *centuria*, and paid them his compliments and wished them the fortune of Mars Ultor, who would protect them in the morning and ensure their victory. All of his men realized that they were heavily outnumbered, and all were fearful of the Britons' reputation for torturing captives, for cutting up their bodies and dismembering their victims while they were still alive.

But all had complete confidence in General Suetonius, and they knew with absolute certainty that when he addressed them in the dark hours of the following morning, he would tell them how they were going to be victorious, why they were going to win, and what rewards they could expect from their battle.

He checked the perimeter fence, despite the fact that he knew Fabius and the centurions would have checked the defenses a number of times during the evening, and when he was satisfied, he reined his horse and began to return to his tent. He knew he should eat, but his appetite had left him during the evening, as it always seemed to do whenever he faced a battle in the morning.

Suetonius dismounted and handed the reins of his horse to a sentry. He entered his tent, and a slave immediately began to remove his chest armor, leggings, greaves and tunic. When the general was seminaked, another slave brought him a bowl of water, and washed his face, chest and legs. He was then dressed in a toga, and a meal was served at his table. He had ordered a first course of oysters brought from the seas near to Camulodunum. It was a gesture of respect for so many fine Romans from that city who had been put to death by the Fury he would be fighting in the morning. Then he was served a bowl of poached sea fish, which was spiced with fennel; and finally, he enjoyed a plate of lamb and deer meat, served with olives, parsley and mint. He always ate alone. It was the privilege and the drawback of his exalted rank. In his younger days, he had enjoyed eating outdoors with his fellow officers, but as a general, and especially as governor of Britain, it was important for him to be aloof, to show no favor by dining with an army man of lesser rank, and to retain his own counsel.

When the meal was concluded, a slave washed his hands and face, and brought him a minted twig for his teeth, and left him alone to read the latest dispatches from Rome, as well as to write the orders for the night and to determine the password for the sentries for the night. He smiled as he wrote the evening's watchword, "Furies Retreat."

There was a cough outside the flap of his tent. "Enter, Fabius," he said, knowing the cough and the reason for the visit of his second in command.

The young man walked in and stood before the general's desk. "Forgive me for disturbing you, sir, but can I do anything before the General retires for the night?"

"Yes, Fabius, you can discuss with me the tone and nature of the speech I am to give to the men at sunrise. My view is that they are nervous because we are so vastly outnumbered, and because many of them fear facing the Celts again. These rumors of torture and desecration of dead bodies have spread through the ranks, and the men are frightened. I thought that when I address them, I might say something like this . . ."

It was still dark when the Roman army gathered on the large plain at the base of the hill where, in a few hours, they would fight off a vast horde of Britons. And it was cold. They shivered in the chilly hours before sunrise, and waited in eager anticipation both for their general, and for the warming light of the sun.

Conscious of the effect of cold and low spirits on a fighting force, Suetonius rode quickly from his tent to the base of the hill where his men had gathered. It was a large assembly, two whole legions, but still tiny compared to the sea of faces they would soon be facing.

Suetonius sat on his mount so that, when torches were splayed around him, he could easily be seen by all of the men in his army.

"Soldiers of Rome," he shouted. "I, your general, am proud to be fighting by your side this morning. You are the finest soldiers in the finest legions in the finest army the world has ever known. Neither the Assyrians, nor the Egyptians, nor the Spartans, nor the Athenians, nor even great Alexander of Macedon himself, could take to the field against you and survive. Never in the history of warfare has a greater army been gathered for the good of those they have come to conquer. And why are we here? Why do we leave our homes and our loved ones to tread on barbarian soil? Because we bring our knowledge, our arts, our sciences, our philosophies, our gods, and our way of life to savages who live in mud huts, who paint their faces like women, who wear the skins of animals, and whose language is the grunting of dogs and the bleating of goats."

His soldiers roared with laughter. It was just what they needed to hear. Those at the front were warmed by the illuminating fires; those at the rear were now relaxed and comfortable enough to breach the rigidity of military discipline and move their bodies to get warm.

"When the sun rises on this morning, you will climb to the top of this hill in front of me, and you will assume the positions of which your commanders instructed you last night. There you will wait until the Britons appear. They will be in vast numbers, but you have no reason to fear, because every Roman soldier who defends his position is worth ten Britons who attempt to climb up to kill him.

"I, like you, have fought against the fiercest of armies, and I have won. I, like you, have fought against brigands and thieves, against desert-dwelling tribesmen and tall dark-skinned fearless men from Syria, and have won. And this morning, I, with you, will fight against an undisciplined rabble, and we will win."

Again, his words were met with cheers and shouts of approval. He turned and saw that the eastern sky was beginning, just beginning, to illumine the tops of the nearby hills as though beacons had suddenly been lit. It was time to send the men to their positions.

"When you see them coming along the road, you men of Rome will despise the savages who scream at you; you will despise their yells and shouts, for they are undisciplined barbarians. In that mixed multitude, the women outnumber the men, and women, by their nature, are weak and valueless. These men who come against you are devoid of courage and have few weapons, and those they do carry are used on their farms to shovel the shit which their horses leave behind. Ignore the noises and empty threats made by these savages. Ignore their naked bodies painted in blue and red. Think of the beauty and gentleness of Roman women, and you will feel disgust at these hideous crones who bare themselves and come to fight you. Their ranks will shatter like a dropped plate when they feel your steel and they will turn to water when they meet the courage of a Roman army which has already beaten them so many times.

"They are not soldiers who come to do battle, but they're bastards, run-aways, refuse for your swords. These are the surviving brothers and sisters of the men we met in Wales, the men who fled whenever you Romans showed your-selves, and will flee again when they see our warlike ranks. Remember, men, that in any and all engagements with an enemy, it is the valor of the few which turns the fortunes of the day. It will be your immortal glory that with so few of us, we will win against so many of them. Keep your rank orderly and compact; throw your javelins accurately; charge forward in close attack as though you were a bar of iron; slash and hew a path with your swords, and when they turn and try to escape, pursue them until you kill every single one, and never think of spoil or plunder. Conquest and victory will give you everything you want. The gods walk beside you and give you strength for the honor and glory of Rome."

He gently urged his horse forward and rode into their midst. He was sur-rounded by thousands of men who only wanted the good luck of touching their general.

With a final check, he knew that everything was as ordered as it could be. Now he could only rely on his experience in a dozen fierce battles, on the skill, courage and discipline of his men, on the battle order into which he had placed his two legions, and on the tactics which he and his commanders had developed on the previous evening.

He heard them before he saw them. He felt them through the ground. Thou-sands and thousands of them. He shuddered, but was careful not to show his men any fear.

Suetonius had sent Fabius to the other side of the hill on which his men were stationed. His second in command would act as his eyes and ears on the right flank. As the first Britons slowly came into view over the rise along Watling Street and the numbers grew like weeds in a field on the distant horizon, Sueto-nius felt a murmur of horror from the rigidly still men in his army. Even far away, he could see that the British advanced toward his army as an unruly rabble; they walked all over the road; they sauntered through the woods and over the plains and in the fields. There was no line of men, no rank, no row, no column, no phalanx; it was more of a procession of half the population of Britain than an army marching into glory. It was a vast horde walking toward them, covering every part of the countryside as though they were a huge herd of cows being gathered by their cowman for milking.

As they drew nearer, their features became more and more distinct. Like their brothers in distant Wales, most of these men and women were naked. They had painted their faces and bodies in blue, drawn red circles around their breasts and sexual parts, and had caked their hair in mud.

The clothes that a few were wearing looked like they had been torn from the backs of animals. Even from a distance, Suetonius could see that their weapons were crude and valueless. But even the general was stunned by the numbers. For they kept on appearing over the hills, until it seemed as though the entire countryside was no longer made of trees and bushes and blades of grass, but was now composed of Britons.

And in among them were wagons carrying women and children and the elderly. When his intelligencers had reported that family relations had joined Boadicea's army as onlookers, he at first dismissed the information as an ill judgment at best, inaccurate at worst. But now he saw for himself that the soldiers of Boadicea's army were interspersed with family wagons, trundling along the path as though they were going to a feast and frolic in the countryside instead of a war. Suetonius looked in utter amazement. Didn't they realize how dangerous it would be to have wagons at the site of a battle? And noncombatant members of a family? Was this madness, or some kind of crazed tactic he'd not previously met?

Fascinated, he looked at the hordes coming across the fields and along the road toward his position. Naked men and women, wagons, children skipping along . . . it was the strangest army he'd ever encountered. But it was the naked women Suetonius simply couldn't get used to. Nowhere had he come across an army which was composed of as many women as men. Yet these women warriors were easily as good and competent with weapons as were the men alongside whom they fought; not as strong, but as tenacious, as determined, and certainly as vicious. In the battles he'd fought since becoming governor, he'd seen women round upon a hapless Roman soldier and hack him to pieces, then cut his head from his shoulders and lift it by the hair as a trophy, encouraged by their sisters, and tie it by the hair to their belts. He'd even seen some women warriors with three or four Roman heads on their belts. No wonder his men were frightened.

As more and more Britons appeared, spreading themselves over the hills and roadside in no military disciplined order, Suetonius knew that he had to do something immediately to stop his troops from panicking. His men were too disciplined to run away—a certain death sentence—but panic could freeze their arms and demoralize their hearts. He turned to his army, and shouted, "I have a bag of gold coins in my tent. I was going to use it to buy grain and wine for the coming winter for my family, but I think we would all be better served if, instead, I gave it to the soldier who manages to spear two of these barbarians with one thrust of his javelin. Remember, men, a bag of gold for two with one."

It was precisely what the troops needed. The men looked at their stern general in amazement, and then saw that he was grinning from ear to ear. And they smiled and nodded and felt suddenly confident again.

Boudica rode in her chariot at the front of her army, searching for the Romans' position. She ascended the rise in the road and as she breasted it, the country was arrayed before her. And then she saw their tents far away in the valley beside the river: hundreds of tents with the smoke of their smoldering fires rising in straight columns into the still air of the early morning. But the campsite was devoid of men.

She scanned the territory, and then she saw them. They were stationed far to the right, away from the valley, standing in straight lines on a hill. She first saw their standards, high on poles, daring her to attack. Then she saw their ranks, arrayed in precise military order. They were just standing there, waiting for her, almost beckoning her to attack.

Boudica judged the position of the Romans carefully. They had taken the position on the top of the hill, which was clever, and which meant that she and her army would have to ascend along the plain in front and then climb up the hill in order to attack. No matter, she thought. While they had the tactical advantage of height, she would overwhelm them by numbers.

But then, as her chariot drew nearer and nearer to the Romans, she looked more closely and saw the cliff at their rear and the woods at their right and left flank. *Yes,* she thought, *Suetonius has chosen a good location.* There's only one way for us to attack, and that's from the front. She scoured the terrain and contemplated sending a force around the hill to see if they could ascend the cliff. From up top, they could drop stones and rocks on the Romans. But the rock face looked solid into the distance, and she realized that her initial thoughts would lead to nothing.

The closer she drew to them, the more doubt began to grow within her as the morning light grew stronger. Her spy had told her that the Romans would be in the valley; she had planned to swoop down on them from the height of the road. But unexpectedly, Suetonius had positioned them on a hilltop, which would make Boudica's assault much more difficult. And her dismay grew as she neared, and saw that even to get to the Roman army, her men and women would have to cross a flat plain of ground on which there was no protection, and then ascend the hill through a fairly narrow gap in between the forests and rises in the landscape. At first sight, she doubted that any more than fifty of her men and women could fit side by side through the gap which led upwards to the hill.

This was a serious tactical problem, and she needed to rethink the strategy she and her advisors had planned the previous night when they assumed that they would have the advantage of surprise and they would sweep down like eagles and falcons on the river camp.

She looked around at the tens of thousands of men and women in her army. Hundreds and hundreds of wagons were lumbering beside them; people were riding on the wagons and talking to their family members. Memories of how she and her parents had trudged the long road from their Iceni homeland in the east of Britain to the shores of the south to celebrate a Druid ceremony came back to her. Those were days of sunshine and freedom and youth. She shuddered when she thought of who she had become. Now she was a warrior wearing a bronze helmet and breastplate, carrying a javelin and a sword, riding in a chariot and leading a vast army into the final battle. How far along the road of womanhood had she traveled since she was a girl!

But thoughts of her childhood evaporated like the morning mist as she tried to concentrate her mind on the new dangers which presented themselves. Last night, she had built up her warriors with a rousing speech about how they would have a tactical advantage of surprise; of how they would bear down on the Romans, running and screaming and throwing their lances and javelins and spears downhill, cutting and slashing with their swords and pushing the enemies into the sacred river.

But what confronted her was as bad as it could be, even though the numbers were on her side. She realized that she must regroup and delay the assault until she, Mandubracus and Cassivellaunus had had a chance to reassess their tactics. She shouted at her seconds in command to race ahead and try to prevent her army from running forward, and watched in dismay as they were utterly ignored by the mob; for that was what they were—a mob, no longer an army.

Wheeling her horse and chariot around, she looked over the thousands of heads of her people to try to spy her comrades, but all she saw was masses of clay-covered hair interwoven with straw and a sea of woad-blue faces. Slowly, Boudica began to rein her horses into the throng, shouting for people to beware of the knives on her chariot wheels.

She had to find Mandubracus and Cassivellaunus quickly so that they could prevent their tribes from attacking until they had regrouped and were ready. But the wagons of the soldiers' families were in the way, and Boudica found it difficult, indeed almost impossible, to impel her horses back into the army to find her comrades. How could she stop her army from walking forward? There was no time to find Mandubracus or Cassivellaunus; she had to turn around and ride to the very front of her army, and prevent them marching ahead. She needed time to reassess the situation, to work out a way to draw the Romans down from their positions onto the plain.

She was desperately struggling with the reins of the chariot to turn her horses around in the crush of people, when she heard the noise which made her heart nearly stop in fear. The front ranks of her soldiers had suddenly spotted the

Romans. The feelings of tiredness and apathy from the revels of the previous night evaporated, and she could sense a charge of energy and anger surge through her men and women. They were pointing up the hill. They were taking swords from their belts. They were beginning to walk faster and faster; some were beginning to run to the plain which led up to the hill. Instead of sauntering past her, giving her a friendly grin, the Britons were now streaming around and beyond her like a swift and angry river.

"No!" she commanded. "No! Stay; remain here. You're not ready. I have to —"

But as more and more Britons walked along Waechlinga Straet and spied the Romans, arrogantly straddling their holy hill, beneath their holy cliff, bounded by their holy forests, they suddenly and irrevocably became furious, and joined the forward thrust running toward the enemy.

"No!" Boudica screamed. "No! Stop. You must wait! Stop!"

She tried to wheel her chariot around to reach the head of the ferocious river of Britons flooding over the roadway and onto the plain. It was accelerating at breakneck speed toward the hill. But she was locked in to her position. She couldn't turn her chariot around because of all the carts and wagons which had surrounded her. She struggled and barked aggressive orders for people to move their wagons, but the rushing river of humanity was running to engage with the Romans and prevented her movement in any direction.

The entire army knew that the Romans were up ahead and was reacting as though the order to attack had been given; her army had a mind of its own, and was of a mind to kill and loot and destroy as it had done in Londinium and Verulamium.

And Boudica had utterly lost control.

CHAPTER SEVENTEEN

Manduessendum

General Suetonius watched them in amazement as they spread out upon entering the wide plain which led up to the hill. He was stupefied by their total lack of discipline. Where were their leaders? he wondered. Where were their commanders? Where was Boadicea?

The image which flashed into his mind when he'd seen the Britons streaming along the road and walking out of the forests, an image he couldn't get out of his thoughts, was a sight he'd witnessed in Egypt when a plague of locusts had first appeared as a black storm cloud on the horizon, and had then landed and wiped out an entire grain crop. But here came the Britons, spreading all over the field which fronted the hill, attacking without any order, any ranks, or any precision. It was as if his elite legion were about to be attacked by a herd of marauding schoolchildren. He shook his head in amazement. So this was Boadicea's army!

"Stand ready!" he shouted. "Make no move until my signal! Front rank, raise javelins; second rank, present javelins; third rank, draw swords and raise javelins! Remain in your positions. Make no move!" he ordered. "Bearers, raise your standards. Drummers, begin to sound the voice of battle."

As one, all of his front row raised their shields to protect themselves, and their lances to waist height to stab the first Britons who emerged through the narrow defile. The second rank hoisted their javelins to their shoulders in order to throw them at the next wave of Britons and delay the onslaught of the followers. And the third rank raised their javelins to waist height, ready to step forward beyond the front ranks in order to stab and cut and strike down Britons who were still standing.

"Drummers!" the general shouted, signaling them to begin.

The martial drumbeats sent a surge of courage through the ranks of his army. It always did. He called it the heartbeat of a battle, for without it, the men would not have known the rhythms to which they should thrust and parry, to which they should aim and throw their javelins. He nodded. He was as prepared as he possibly could be. Now it was in the hands of his army, his commanders, but most especially in the hands of Mars Ultor, the god of vengeance.

He turned in his saddle to look at the rear ranks of his army. Row upon row of soldiers arrayed up the hill. And at their flanks were his archers.

"Trumpeters!" he shouted. "Be ready to announce the next order." He gave a further instruction, and delighted in the voices of the trumpets rising above the war cries of the Britons as they neared his position.

"Archers!" he shouted. "Be ready to fire your arrows at the rear ranks of the Britons as they begin to ascend the hill. Remember, not one missile will leave your bows until my command. And remember the prize . . . a bag of gold for the angler who catches two fish with one hook."

Too disciplined to laugh, his soldiers acknowledged his remark by grim smiles.

Suetonius now had a moment to study Boadicea's formation. He knew that he had the advantage of terrain, but the overwhelming danger of being so outnumbered was still his greatest concern. He and Fabius knew the dangers of facing a good army, well led by an intelligent commander, who would compensate for the terrain disadvantage by fielding a tight formation. If he'd been in

Boadicea's shoes, he would concentrate on wearing down the Roman front line by distant archers, and then demolishing his middle-line troops with ballistae and long lances. And as a final act, a good commander would attack his rear by the use of fire arrows and all his other war machines. Suetonius knew that the Britons had none of the machinery of war, but everybody said that they were a fearsome race of warriors. Despite the way in which they were attacking him, he still feared what unknown devices or stratagems they might use against him. Nor had he forgotten Boadicea's destruction of five thousand of Rome's best warriors outside Camulodunum.

He waited impatiently as the Britons crossed the plain and began their ascent on the hillside. Never in his wildest dreams did he imagine that he would see what he now saw. Indeed, when he'd first seen Boadicea's army scamper over the ground, it had given him cause for wonder whether this was a diversionary tactic and perhaps her main body was coming somehow over the cliff face and down behind him.

Instead of an army marching up to the defile, thousands and thousands of wild undisciplined naked men and women were streaming across the landscape, screaming out war cries and shouting barbaric oaths; those who weren't naked were exposing their manhoods and taunting his men. The women were tearing off their bodices and exposing their breasts. Almost all were gesticulating wildly as they ran, their bodies unprotected, their sword arms looking as though they were scything a field of grain. They looked more like children than adults. It would be so easy for him to alter his tactics and order the archers to fire on the mob running toward him; in that way, he'd kill hundreds with the first flight and give the men an inexpensive victory; but that would possibly confuse his army and cause them to wonder about the rest of the orders they had to follow to the letter.

He looked over to Fabius, who was also frowning. Sensing that he was being looked at, Fabius glanced over to the general, and shrugged his shoulders. The general gave a sign that the Roman formation was to be held tight, regardless of the provocation.

He turned, and nodded to his orderly. The man ran quickly to the flank of the army, and ordered Cassus to attend upon the general.

"Is this how the Britons conduct their warfare?" he asked Cassus.

"I told you what they'd do," the Briton answered. "I said that they weren't like the Romans. That they didn't march like soldiers. I told you all these things, but you wouldn't listen. You have to send your men forward, or we'll all be killed. They have to go out of here and fight her. You'll win for sure, but you have to do it now." The young man was in increasing distress, patently terrified by the numbers of Britons and the hideous war cries they were making. Suetonius decided that as soon as the battle was decided, whether he won or lost, Cassus would become a casualty on his own sword. He detested the youth, and would be glad to see the back of him.

Now the field in front of the hill was crowded with tens of thousands of Boadicea's men and women; hardly a piece of ground was visible. It looked like a capacity crowd in the forum, all surging forward as though they were going to jump into the arena and participate in the competition. With a certainty built on decades of military experience, Suetonius knew that if he were to release his men now, they would march forward and slaughter thousands and thousands of Britons. But that would lose him the hill and the defile, and give Boadicea the advantage: a costly advantage to be sure, but with so many soldiers, it was too large an advantage to concede. No, he had to keep to his plan.

By now, most of Boadicea's army was already on the plain, surging over it toward the far hill on which the Romans were stationed. And in awe of the stupidity of the Britons, Suetonius saw something which at first he refused to believe. He glanced over to Fabius, and saw that the young man was also looking toward the rear of the Britons. For as the army was racing over the plain, the hundreds of wagons which had trundled along Watling Street were lining up off the road and halfway along the plain in order to gain a better view of the coming battle. Wagon upon wagon, cart upon cart, had positioned itself along the full length of the plain, effectively blocking off the ability of the Britons to retreat. It was madness on a grand scale. The defile was blocking the ability of Boadicea's army to advance, and now the wagons and carts were blocking the ability of the army to retreat. What idiocy was this? Suetonius wondered.

But he had no time for further speculation on Boadicea's motives, for the first of the Britons had reached the part of the plain where it began to ascend toward the hill, and where the terrain caused a bottleneck, concentrating thousands of her soldiers into a narrow line of relatively few who would be able to get through the defile and meet the Romans face-to-face.

Suetonius turned to his men, and barked an order. . . .

"Stop! Return! Come back here!" she screamed.

Boudica spurred her chariot toward the plain, negotiating her way through the massive throng as best she could, and shouted out orders to her army. But nobody was listening. They had the look of wild beasts on their faces. For days, they had been talking about slaughtering the Romans; now, spurred on by constant drinking and bravado, they were about to consummate the act. Their ears were closed to her entreaties; their eyes were closed to her anger.

"Return! Don't go forward. Can't you see it's a trap? Stop! For the sake of the gods, stop!"

She tried to ride toward the hill, whipping her horses to try to head off the bulk of her army. But she couldn't go forward because of the massive crush of men and women who were bounding across the plain like animals in heat, crazed with their desire to ascend the hill and fight the Romans. Her horses reared in fear at the press of people.

But as they neared the hill, her army found that they had to bunch closer and closer because of the lay of the land until only a few hundred at a time could run through the wide channel which ran between the wooded hillocks leading up to the hill. And then she saw in the distance that the first of her soldiers had emerged on the opposite side of the defile and were about to attack the Romans. She prayed to the god Teutates to protect her brothers and sisters, and not to allow the god Lugh anywhere near the battlefield.

General Suetonius saw the first hundred or so of the Britons emerge from the defile, and run like wild beasts, shouting and screaming at his front row of troops. There was no need for him to give orders, for his front line had already fixed their javelins and were ready to stab at the chests of any man or woman who approached. Suetonius still couldn't believe the unpreparedness and naïvety of the British advance. Hadn't the Britons been told that swords were useless against a line of men holding javelins? Didn't they realize that by rushing forward, dozens, more likely hundreds, would be impaled as the experienced lancers thrust, withdrew, and then thrust again?

But to give his men courage in the face of the attacking mob, he shouted out, "A bag of gold to the best fisherman. Now, Romans, skewer your prey for blood and honor."

And skewer them they did. The first to arrive exposed their chests as they raised their swords to slash down at the legionaries' heads. But swift jabs to the chest and stomach by the points of javelins felled one, then five, then fifty of the Britons. Falling short of the Roman line, the next Britons through the defile had to clamber over their fallen comrades, and as they were negotiating the twisting and flailing bodies, screams of pain filled the air and the vicious spearheads of the second row jabbed these men and women and they, too, fell at the feet of the Romans.

Breasts naked, chests bared, the Britons kept on coming through the defile, screaming and yelling war cries and bloodcurdling oaths. But it was like the children's game of spearing fish in a barrel. As the Britons kept advancing and falling, the front row of Roman soldiers had barely moved forward a step. Indeed, in the third row the swordsmen were now beginning to lower their swords, realizing there was little work for them to do.

"Raise your swords!" shouted General Suetonius in fury. "Prepare to attack!"

The general turned to his archers, and wondered if now would be the right time to let them fire their flights of arrows. But the British soldiers—he thought of them as victims rather than soldiers—were still pushing through the defile, concentrating their numbers in such a way that they were in greater danger of being crushed to death than being slashed by a Roman sword or skewered by a Roman lance.

Above the screams of the Britons and the yells of hatred and oaths of the Romans, Suetonius heard his name called. It was faint above the melee, but distinct. He looked over and saw Fabius gesturing to him. "Do we march forward,

General?" he shouted. "This is a slaughter. If the bottleneck continues, our troops might lose the ability to storm down the hill."

It was a valid point, and something which the general was already considering. He gestured to his second in command, that first he would release the arrows, and then he would order his swordsmen to advance.

Turning to them, he gave the signal for the archers to do their worst.

Boudica stood in her chariot, trying to discern what was happening. Clouds of dust and fury hid the front rank of the assault, but the Britons had suddenly come to a stop at the beginning of the ascent of the hill, and the entire army was banking up beneath the defile like a river about to breach its shore. Since the engagement had begun, Boudica had remained stationary in her chariot, praying that Teutates would protect her men and women, and give them victory over the Romans. But her sight was dimmed by the confrontation and she couldn't make out who was in the ascendancy and who was failing. These first few moments of battle were crucial. Morale would be gained if the Britons had an early success. Boudica was praying that she would see the rows of Roman soldiers being pushed back up the hillside and against the cliff face, and destroyed.

But as she looked, the air was suddenly full of swarms of insects: nasty vicious biting insects which seemed to fly at an impossible speed—faster than a plummeting sea eagle—from the hillside where the Romans were standing, down onto the heads of the Britons who were clambering to get past the defile and up the hill.

The Britons began to scream and drop down and fall. More and more flights came, and still more, until her men and women were falling in vast numbers, hundreds and hundreds screaming and clutching their heads and throats and chests. And then the long lances came flying through the air and more of her Britons fell and died screaming, until the ground was littered with British dead.

She slapped her horses on their flanks to drive them forward. She had to tell her men and women to retreat, to fall back and regroup so that they could fight the Romans on more even ground. But as she approached the bulk of her army, she stopped before the thousands and thousands of men and women who were waiting to ascend the hill and avenge themselves against the Romans. The huge bottleneck seemed to have stopped trying to move forward, and was now falling over itself, tripping up on its dead comrades, flailing helplessly, dropping down and rolling on the ground. And as the fallen soldiers tried to get up, more fell upon them, as though this were some deadly kind of children's game.

"Front section, forward. Middle section, advance ten paces. Move forward!" Suetonius ordered. "Infantry advance at double pace, swordsmen at single pace. Climb over the bodies. Swordsmen, file past and beyond lancers. Infantry, station yourselves at the neck of the defile. Move!"

He looked over to Fabius and nodded. The young commander turned and said to a messenger, "Order the cavalry to ride around the hill now."

"Both flanks, *Legatus?*"

"Both flanks! They are to meet up in a pincer in the middle of the plain. Immediately!"

The man saluted, and lit an arrow wrapped in oil-soaked rags. The messenger raised his bow and, flaming with black smoke, one arrow flew to the east, then another arrow to the west. Seeing the signal at the same moment, the cavalry commanders instructed their men forward, and rounded the forests and the hills until the plain came into view.

The Roman infantrymen continued to push their way through the lancers and climbed over the mass of quivering, dying and dead bodies arrayed before them. It was a slaughter on a scale of that which had been conducted on the isle of Mona. Only a handful of Romans had fallen casualty, yet the Britons numbered their dead in the hundreds—maybe even the thousands. And the battle had only just begun.

The infantry stabbed, thrust and pushed its way forward, using shields and swords to dismember and cut down any Briton resisted. The occasional British swordsman who managed to find enough room to strike against a Roman in the crowded throng invariably struck a shield, and his sword bounced harmlessly off.

In a sudden panic at seeing the Romans moving forward, some of the men and women tried to turn and go back down the hill, but they were met by enraged Britons trying to ascend and join in the fray.

Immobile, and in many cases unable to turn to defend themselves, they were slaughtered. Swords dug deep into shoulders and necks, severing blood vessels and tendons; bloody arms and heads were severed; the points of swords pierced naked flesh and tore vital organs and destroyed body cavities, killing men and women instantly in equal measure. The once emerald ground was now a mat of gory tissue, slippery with blood and innards. The press of men and women was now so great that many of the slaughtered remained upright and were swept along by the waves of people.

Still the archers shot volley after volley of arrows into the air; they hissed and whistled downward, wounding and killing all whom they struck. The hair-raising oaths and bloodcurdling war cries of the Britons were now changing in tone to frantic screams of pain and shrieks of panic. It infected the mass of Britons who were still running across the plain, eager to climb the hill and participate in the massacre and the victory over the Romans.

As they still tried to surge forward, they were met by increasing numbers of terrified people who were running back away from the hill and the defile. But as they ran, the earth of the plain suddenly shook with the pounding of the hooves of horsemen. The cavalry rounded on the plain from both sides of the hill and in a pincer movement attacked the middle of the British advance. The dozens of huge horses and the infantry which ran alongside them thundered into the center of the British army, sending the men and women scurrying in every direction. The horsemen cut swathes through the crowd of Britons; the infantry of the cavalry slashed with their swords at the fallen and numbed men and women.

General Suetonius moved his position so that his horse was standing on a mound, which gave him a better view of the entire battle. The plain down below was now an orgy of writhing confusion. His archers had wreaked havoc on the British warriors: His infantry had thrown their javelins, and many Britons were lying dead nearer to the bottleneck of the defile; men and women who were un-injured were looking around for leadership. They were lost, utterly lost and abandoned by their commanders. Yet still the rear troops surged forward, not realizing that their front lines were being slaughtered. And all the while, Suetonius asked himself, *Where are the commanders of the Britons?*

But there was nobody in control or command, and as a military man, Suetonius sneered in contempt for the value of a British king or queen. But now wasn't the time for him to be a judge of tactics. Now it was time for him to assess the value of his different fighting assets. When he saw that the horsemen and the infantry who ran alongside the mounts had cut a vicious swathe through the middle ranks of the Britons, effectively dividing them in two, he was satisfied that he could now advance.

The question was whether to push forward with the entire army and risk losing their strategic advantage of the heights on which they were standing, or whether potentially to allow Boadicea to regroup her still vast numbers, and try another tactic other than a suicidal head-on assault on the hill.

And then he remembered his greatest weapon. In the urgency of the battle, he'd not given sufficient thought to the Britons' families who had come in their thousands in carts and wagons to witness the humiliation of Rome. He smiled to himself, and then signaled Fabius for an immediate advance.

The young man looked over the breadth of the hill at his commander, his face not daring to question the order, but asking why risk a full frontal attack at a stage where Rome still held all the advantages of terrain strategy. The general pointed to the wagons which were stationary in a long line at the end of the plain. They were a barrier to the Britons' retreat. Fabius immediately realized how the general was going to use the wagons to his advantage, and saluted him, a sign of respect for his tactics and admiration for spotting an advantage which ordinary men would not have realized.

Fabius ordered the trumpets to sound the advance, and as one, his two huge legions began to push forward: The archers slung their bows over their shoulders and drew their swords; the lancers repositioned their weapons so that they shortened them for infantry combat and stabbing; and the swordsmen merely marched forward in lines, slashing and cutting anything which appeared before them.

Climbing over the bodies which blocked the exit of the defile, the Romans pushed their way to the front, causing Britons to fall over themselves. Death and mutilation followed in their wake. It took the better part of an hour for the entire Roman force to leave the hill, and to form up in three rows along the breadth of the plain at the base of their impregnable hillside.

When most of the Roman forces had left their positions and were marching and slaughtering the Britons as they pushed them into the wagons, General Suetonius heard a noise behind him. He turned and saw that Cassus was standing there. He felt sullied by the very presence of a Briton who would turn, not just against his own people, but against his own family.

"It looks like a great victory, General," the young man said.

Suetonius nodded.

"As I've been such a help to you, I wonder if my reward could be Boadicea. She's of no use to you now that she's been defeated, and I only want her for the night. In chains. That's fair, isn't it, General? I should enjoy the spoils of war, just like you and your soldiers will enjoy them."

Suetonius couldn't bear even to turn and look at Cassus. "Be assured, Briton, that you will enjoy all the spoils of war to which you're entitled. That is Suetonius' promise."

Boudica was in a state of abject fear and panic. More than any other on the field, she had full understanding of what was happening. She knew that her men and women were being massacred, cut down by horsemen and swordsmen, and the arrows and lances flying through the air.

Ever since her first soldiers had run up the hill like madmen, she had been desperately trying to get them to withdraw, to assemble near to the river, to retreat regardless of the consequences so that the next day, or the day after, they could fight the Romans on equal ground.

Nobody would listen to their queen. The Britons had hurtled forward and were now standing around as though in a daze, waiting for their gods to intervene. Even now, when there was some space on the plain and she could drive her chariot around, even now they wouldn't follow her orders to retreat. Some were merely standing there, unsure about what was happening on the hill; others had retreated from the hill and were looking around as though they were in the middle of a nightmare; but most were still trying to move past their comrades in order to ascend the hill to meet and fight against the Romans.

Again she shouted to her soldiers to retreat, but it was as though she didn't exist. Boudica was only queen while her people were victorious; when they were losing against Rome, they became a leaderless rabble. She shook her head, and pondered how she was going to win the day.

And then a trumpet sounded, and movement on the hill caught her eye. She looked upward, and saw that the Romans had begun their advance over the bodies of the fallen, through the narrow defile, and onto the plain. As they marched down and outward in military precision, she was in awe of how the enemy retained such discipline.

At a signal from somebody on the hill, the Romans, now in three long lines, began to move forward, pushing the Britons backward along the plain toward the road. She whipped her horses forward in order to beg her army to retreat, screaming at her troops to get out of the way, but again, the throng prevented her chariot from moving ahead more than a short distance. The mass of people again threatened to overwhelm any order and discipline.

Her only hope was to stand firm, and order everybody who passed her to stand still and regroup; but the frustration of trying to be heard, to get her men and women to follow orders, was moving her to the point of fury.

Boudica drove her horses onward to confront the Romans as they moved down the hill and onto the plain. She looked up at the hill, trying to determine whether she could see General Suetonius. Through the dust, she thought she saw a man on a horse, standing as still as a statue, looking over the field of fallen like some god. And beside him was a smaller figure. One not dressed as a Roman, but as a Celt. She thought she recognized him, and stared. But the frantic rush of Britons who were trying to escape frightened her horses, and she reined them in and turned away.

It took the better part of the morning for the Britons to be pushed back by Roman soldiers to the midpoint of the plain. And when so many had fallen, and exhaustion began to set in, the Britons, almost as one, decided to retreat and regroup. There was no order from Boudica or their kings or queens; there was no command—just an understanding by the exhausted warriors that the day was lost, and they had to withdraw.

In huge numbers, they turned and started to run back down the hill to the road. But as they ran, they found their retreat was blocked by their carts and wagons. Their families, realizing that the day was a disaster, tried to leave, but there were too many carts to suddenly turn around, and the roadway became jammed with hundreds of wagons and carts, traffic in a state of disarray.

And as the terrified Britons began to climb on board to rescue their families, the press of thousands of others overturned many of the wagons, causing further mayhem.

Again Suetonius, knowing the retreat was blocked and the vehicles were causing turmoil and confusion, sent in the cavalry, who drove more and more Britons into the wagons and carts. His archers used arrows, and his infantry used their lances and swords to kill vast numbers. It was a wholesale bloodbath. During the afternoon, Suetonius and Fabius directed their legions into killing any Britons who remained standing in the plain. Those who could had run away; those who couldn't were slaughtered by the swordsmen, archers and lancers of Rome.

The rulers of two of the largest tribes in Britain, King Mandubracus of the Trinovantes and King Cassivellaunus of the Catuvellauni, were killed on the battlefield, along with thousands of their subjects. The sons and daughters, sisters and brothers, mothers and fathers, of the Britons who had fought on the slaughterfields were killed, even though they hadn't been combatants. And Fabius sent parties of Roman soldiers to follow any fleeing Britons and to kill them also.

At the end of the exhausting day, as the sun was beginning to sink into the western sky, as the fields were no longer able to absorb any more blood and became a lake of gore, Suetonius realized that it would be impossible for him to accurately estimate how many Britons he had killed. But he knew that it numbered in the tens of thousands—maybe even seventy or eighty thousand. His own number of legionaries dead was a mere couple of hundred, a number so ridiculously small compared to the number of enemy dead that Rome would simply not believe it.

Yet despite the overwhelming victory, despite the satisfaction of knowing what his tactics had achieved, he took no pleasure in what he had done that day, just as he took no satisfaction in entering a piggery and slaughtering dozens of helpless pigs. These were valiant warriors. Stupid and misguided, maybe, but they had been badly served by amateur and disgraceful leadership. And they had all paid the ultimate price.

His last order to Fabius before returning to his tent on the river's bank was to have a detachment of his men go through the mass of bodies and to put anyone still barely alive out of their misery. No prisoners, no slaves were to be taken; no wounded were to be aided. All Britons who had raised their hands against Rome were to die. It would be a lesson for everyone.

Fabius nodded in understanding. It was harsh, but a necessary part of the way in which Rome maintained control over its empire.

"Oh, and one more thing, Fabius," Suetonius said. "I want you to take the Briton Cassus with you onto the battlefield. He is to identify the leaders of the revolt. When he's done so, have their bodies brought to my tent."

"Yes, General," he said, turning and walking away.

But Suetonius called him back. "And when Cassus has identified Boadicea and the other kings and queens who led this revolt, you are to execute him. Ensure that just before you strike the final blow, you explain to him very carefully that men like him, men who are traitors to their family and their people, have no place in a Roman world. He wanted a reward from us for helping us to fight Boadicea. He wanted to ravish her. Well, let a Roman sword put an end to a life such as his. Nobody will mourn him; nobody will remember him after this day. Men like Cassus are of no use to us," Suetonius told Fabius. "Rome needs no client kings in Britain after this day. There is no fight in these people. They need to be led by Romans, not by Britons."

His final command was that when all soldiers and their families were dead, everybody was to be doused with oil and set alight. "Let this flame light up the night sky of this barbaric land and be seen by all who look, so that they'll know the price of raising a rebellion against the might of Rome," he said. "And have ten bags of gold distributed between the two legions."

Fabius saluted and turned to leave. But as an afterthought, Suetonius said, "Oh, and send a message of our victory to Poenius Postumus, and tell him to put my sword to good use."

They knew that the battle was lost the moment they saw their mother. Her face was haggard. She looked like an old woman. Her clothes were dusty, her hair was wild, her eyes red-rimmed, and she wore the exhausted look of someone who hadn't slept in many nights. Camorra and Tasca helped her from her chariot, and supported her as they entered her tent. Neither girl spoke.

Camorra held her as she walked slowly, painfully into the tent. The girl thought that her mother had been wounded, but there was no blood on her armor, and her sword was still sheathed. Tasca drew back in consternation, watching her elder sister and her mother disappear into the tent. She stood alone, bereft, knowing that something horrible had happened, but not understanding its import.

Something in the sky caught the young girl's eye. About to enter the tent, she was momentarily distracted and looked upward. It was a bird, flying high in the sky. Impossibly high. Almost invisible. Yet it seemed to be hovering, motionless. She looked carefully, and tried to discern what kind of a bird it was. Perhaps it was an eagle, perhaps a falcon or an osprey. Maybe it was a bird of prey, waiting until the end of the battle so that it could swoop down and eat the dead Romans.

Normally, Tasca would run excitedly to her mother and tell her what she'd seen. But not now. Not having just seen the way her normally robust and hearty mother had returned from the field of battle. When Boudica had left in the dark hours of the morning, she had been exultant, telling the girls that this would be the greatest day of their lives; that this day, Britain would be forever freed from the heel of the oppressor. Tasca had watched her climb onto her chariot surrounded by hundreds of her cheering supporters. Even in the flickering lights of the fires, the child could see that her mother radiated glory.

Entering the tent, she remembered that before Boudica had ridden off to victory and grandeur, she had turned, and blessed both of the girls in the name of the goddess Brigantia, who looked after flocks and water, crops and healing and especially after fertility. Then she smiled and kissed her children, and was gone.

Tasca and Camorra had debated whether to run after her in secret, and look at the battle from a distance; but their mother had forbidden them to leave the camp, and because she was Britannia, they knew that they must obey her.

The entire day had been spent in games by the river, and wondering how the battle fared. As the day wore on, a few men and women started to return from the battlefield. The girls went up to the road and asked about their mother and the victory; but they were met by horrified stares, by shaking heads and tales of woe and disaster.

So when Boudica returned late in the afternoon as the sun was settling over trees in the west, they knew that things had not gone well for Britain. Still, their mother could deal with anything, for she was Boudica, and she was Britannia, and she was the queen.

"Come here, my darling girls," she said. Camorra was surprised by her voice, which was deeper and sterner than it had been when she had left this morning. It was the voice of somebody who had been shouting a lot. "Listen to me carefully. Our gods have deserted us, and we have lost the victory which was all but certain. The Romans have won, and are coming after us. Now, children, we have three choices. The first choice is that we stay here and allow ourselves to be captured; that means that we will be enslaved, humiliated, and what happened to you in Camulodunum will happen a thousandfold when you are slaves of Rome. We will be taken to Rome, and paraded like animals in the arenas and punished until we die a miserable death.

"Our second choice is to run away, and hide in fields and huts, and hope that the Romans will never find us. But this is not the life of a queen and her daughters, and the Romans will hunt us forever. And it is certain that Queen Cartimandua will find us and hand us over to the Romans, as she betrayed Caratacus.

"And our third choice, which I want you to agree with, is that we take poison, and in a few moments, we ascend into the heavens as great British heroes, and we meet with your father Prasutagus, and there we look down on the Romans, and laugh at their silliness."

She remained silent, hoping that her daughters realized that there was no option other than for her to kill them.

"We want to stay with you, Mother," said Tasca.

"We will die with you," agreed Camorra.

Boudica nodded, and kissed her children fondly on their foreheads.

Their bodies were found by a centurion and reported to Fabius. He rode swiftly and found the queen of the Britons, Boadicea, lying on her cot, rigidly and protectively clutching her two young daughters in her arms. They were recently dead, probably not more than a couple of hours.

He ordered that they were to be covered, as befitted their rank, and their bodies carried to the Roman encampment for disposal according to the wishes of General Suetonius.

Out of curiosity, and despite his exhaustion, Suetonius left his tent and uncovered the three bodies. He spent a long time looking at them, Fabius standing behind him, unable to see the look on his face.

In the darkness, the governor of Britain covered them up and breathed deeply. "So this is our enemy? I wonder how I'll look when I lose my last battle. Like her, I wonder, full of youth and vitality and inexperience? Or as I feel now, an old man who should be kissing his grandchildren, rather than presiding over the slaughter of countless men and women?"

"What shall we do with the bodies, General?" asked Fabius.

"The children will be buried by this river, so that they may rest in eternity and listen to its gentle rhythm. The mother, however, has dared to raise a rebellion against Rome. For this, she must be dealt with properly. Her body will be taken to the city of Londinium. To the north of the city, beyond the walls, there is a refuse tip. Her body is to be dumped there, and is to remain untouched until it rots and festers and returns to the earth. The crows of the skies will circle around her and will eat of her flesh, and all who pass by will smell the stench of her putrefaction, and will be revolted by her. This is a suitable burial place for a woman such as Boadicea. She was heroine to her people, but she led them to disaster.

"This is my decision. I have spoken."

And General Suetonius turned and entered his tent. Now that the revolt of the British had been put down, he was looking forward to his first proper night's sleep in days.

EPILOGUE

Rome—The Palace of the Emperor Nero

The emperor turned puce with fury. "I want to!" he screamed, "and what I want, I'll have. Understand me, philosopher. The emperor will have his way."

"What you want, and what you can have, are two different things," said Seneca, trying to remain calm. They had been arguing these points for hours, and each time he had produced a convincing argument and won the debate on logic, Nero had begun screaming and shouting again, and saying that he really didn't care what the people of Rome or the senate thought—he wanted to.

"I shall have what I want, and if anybody tries to stand against me, I'll end their lives. I'll have them thrown to lions in the arena. I'll send them to the galley ships. I don't care who they are." He rounded on Seneca, and screamed, "I want to!"

"Caesar, I'm begging of you to understand. The Lady Poppaea is very nice and pleasant and desirable. You've had her as your mistress for the past two years. Isn't that enough? Continue to bed her, take her to your villa in Neapolis and spend the afternoons with her in a boat. Set her up in apartments in the palace. Do what you want. But you cannot marry the wife of Senator Otho. The scandal would be overwhelming. The people would howl, especially when they find out that she's a Jewess; you know the feeling in the city these days about the Jews and the Chrestians."

"But why can't I marry her?" Nero screamed. "I want to marry Poppaea."

"You are already married to the Empress Octavia."

"So?"

"So to marry Poppaea, she would have to divorce Senator Otho and you would have to divorce the Empress Octavia."

"So?"

"So the Empress Octavia is the daughter of the god Claudius, the sister of the late Britannicus, the niece of the late Germanicus, and the great-granddaughter of Augustus' sister Octavia. There's no more venerable Roman lady alive than Octavia. And she's the empress of Rome. Divorce Octavia, and the entire palace will crash around your head. The people won't stand for it, the Senate won't stand for it, the army won't stand for it, Otho won't stand for it, and Octavia certainly won't stand for it."

"But I want to marry Poppaea!" Nero shouted.

"Then you will risk the army rising up in revolt against you, Caesar, and nothing can protect you."

"I have the Praetorian Guard. They're Germans. They don't give a fig for Octavia and Augustus and the rest of them. They'll fight the army to protect their emperor if it revolts."

In amazement, Seneca looked at the emperor. "You would cause a civil war?"

Nero realized that he'd gone too far, and shrugged his shoulders. His sullen expression told Seneca not to persist, but to allow the emperor the face-saving device of retiring from the argument gracefully. But it also showed how much the emperor was losing his grip on reality. It was probably at that moment that Seneca decided to begin the process of retiring from the emperor's service, liquidating all of his funds, and removing himself from Rome forevermore.

Both men sat like exhausted gladiators after their bouts, and sipped their wine.

WARRIOR QUEEN • 365

"Will I ever be able to marry Poppaea?" Nero asked quietly.

Saying yes would result in Octavia's poisoning. Saying no would result in his own. Seneca thought carefully for a moment, and said, "The circumstances could be arranged, but it would have to be a very gradual process, Caesar. You would have to appoint Senator Otho to some distant governorship. Then the Empress Octavia would probably have to seek a divorce from you for the sake of the empire. She would tell the Senate that she was unable to supply you with an heir, and she would have to apologize to the people of Rome for her failure. In return, you would have to give her a massive settlement, and a villa and a retinue. It would cost a fortune, but only under those circumstances would it be possible to prevent a civil war." He stressed the last two words to ensure Nero understood the full consequences of any attempted poisoning of Octavia.

"She hasn't given me an heir because I never sleep with her. I can't bear to look at her. She's so ugly and gross and hideous," Nero muttered.

"You have many beautiful young men and women in your entourage, Caesar. You're never short of admirers to sleep with you."

They were disturbed by a knock on the door, and a cough. A messenger walked into the room, bowed low to Nero, and handed Seneca a dispatch.

The philosopher begged permission from Nero to open the dispatch, and when it was granted, he read it quickly. Then he put it on his table to continue wrestling with the problem of Nero's lust for Poppaea.

Curious, Nero said, "What was the dispatch about?"

Seneca shrugged, and said, "Just word from General Gaius Suetonius Paulinus in Britain. There was a revolt by the Britons, which he has put down."

"Revolt?"

Seneca picked up the dispatch and found the relevant passage. "The general says that while he was in Wales dealing with the Druid priests on the island of Mona, some local chieftain called Boadicea rose up and destroyed three of our cities."

"Boadicea? That's a woman's name."

Seneca laughed. "Yes. In Britain, apparently, they send their women to fight their battles."

"What happened?" asked the emperor.

Seneca shrugged. "He met her and her armies in battle, and destroyed them. He reports that Boadicea lost eighty thousand of her warriors for a loss of four hundred of ours."

"Only four hundred?" asked Nero in surprise.

"So it seems, Caesar. But can we get back to the far more important topic of Poppaea? I beg of you to understand the dangers to the empire of continuing to insist upon marriage."

Tired of arguing, Nero rose, and said, "Alright. For now, I'll give up thoughts of marriage. But I won't stop seeing her. Is that understood?"

Seneca smiled and stood as Nero left the apartment.

Alone at last, he picked up Suetonius' dispatch and reread it. He shook his head, and thought about the problems he was suffering in Germania and Armenia. And then there was Syria and the perennial problem of Judea.

He sighed, and thought about the prospect of retirement. A life lived in the south, where the waters of the sea were azure and warm all year round, and where the tempers of Rome were distant, sounded very tempting. He'd made his fortune. Now that Britain was free of rebels, he would get his forty million sesterces back, plus his ten million in interest. With the rest of his money, he would look forward to a long and restful life with his scrolls, his friends, and his thoughts.

Yes, a gentleman's retirement sounded like a very good idea.

Acknowledgments

To misquote John Donne, no author is an island entire of itself. This is especially true of a novelist working in the largely uncharted waters of ancient history.

I have received unstinting help in bringing *Warrior Queen* to life from a number of people whom I wish to thank. First and foremost my wife **Eva**, whose incisive mind and judgment shines through every page; **Laura Cifelli**, my editor at Penguin has a keenness of vision and a perception which is remarkable and gratifying, but mainly inspirational. And my agent, **Allan Lang** of International Book Marketing of Princeton, New Jersey has been a wise, motivating and truly supportive friend.

I have drawn upon numerous authoritative texts and other media to assist me in the writing of this novel.

Readers who may be interested in further details of the historical aspects of Boudica might find much of merit in the following books:

The Annals, Publius Cornelius Tacitus
A History of Rome, Dio Cassius
A History of Civilizations, Fernand Braudel, Penguin
A History of Warfare, John Keegan, Pimlico
Technology in the Ancient World, Henry Hodges, Michael O'Mara
Women in Prehistory, Margaret Ehrenberg, British Museum Press
Fire and Civilization, Johan Goudsblom, Penguin
Ancient Greece, Utopia and Reality, Pierre Leveque, Thames and Hudson
The Ancient Mediterranean, Michael Grant, Meridian
The End of the Bronze Age, Robert Drews, Princeton University Press
Forbidden Knowledge, Roger Shattuck, St. Martin's Press
Hall's Dictionary of Subjects & Symbols in Art, John Murry Press
Sacred Architecture, A.T. Mann, Element
Strange Landscapes, Christopher Frayling, BBC Books
Sex in History, Reay Tannahill, Abacus Books
Writing, The Story of Alphabets and Scripts, Georges Jean, Thames and Hudson
The Creators, Daniel J. Boorstin, Vintage Books

I would also recommend the following internet sites which are truly excellent . . .
www.roman-britain.org/timeline.htm
www.roman-britain.org/
www.forumromanum.org/index2.html
www.sacred-texts.com/neu/celt/rac/

WARRIOR QUEEN

The Story of Boudica, Celtic Queen

Alan Gold

DISCUSSION QUESTIONS

✖

1. Boadicea (Boudica) was a noble woman who lived to defend her people from the invasion of the Romans. In *Warrior Queen,* she is portrayed very differently from the women of Rome, especially Messalina and Agrippina. Consider the differences between the Celtic women and the Roman women, and think about how their personalities determined the ways in which they reacted to the situations in which they found themselves. To what extent did the Celtic and Roman women determine their own destinies?

2. The Roman Empire was the arch colonizer of the ancient world. Thinking about the benefits and the detriments which colonization brought to an occupied people, consider ways in which a partnership could have been forged with British tribes which resisted Roman might; how might this approach be applied today to the many civil wars and conquests which abound in our world?

3. Romans worshipped many gods and goddesses; the Celts also worshipped gods and goddesses, but they also worshipped the spirits in the natural world. Despite the Druids formidable reputation for human sacrifice, consider the benefits of worshipping gods which have complete control over human actions, as opposed to a natural spirit which is present in all things.

4. Boadicea (Boudica) had a major impact on British history, but only a minor impact on Roman history because of her defeat. How different would things have been had she won? Imagine that General Suetonius had lost and the Roman army had been destroyed. What effect do you think that Boadicea's triumph might have had on the rest of the Roman Empire?

5. Boadicea is considered to be a great leader, as well as a fearsome warrior. To what extent do you think this is true? Think about how differently a modern military man or woman, trained in modern tactics of warfare, might have prosecuted a guerrilla war

against the vastly superior Roman army. Had you been leader of the ancient Celts, what steps would you have taken to ensure your victory?

6. Although most great women have been completely written out of history, except as wives and daughters of great men, a few have survived that we know of today. What qualities do you think great women needed to have over and above those qualities which we know were possessed by the great men of history? Women leaders in Celtic society are thought to have played as important a role in its governance as did the men. What lessons do you think that modern governments could learn from the way in which ancient Britain was ruled? What do you think they should avoid?

7. You are one of the defeated Celts marching back from the destruction of Boudica's army following the battle with the Roman General Suetonius. What mementos of the battle and the long march home would you collect in order to explain the significance of this event to your grandchildren?

8. One of the most difficult tasks of an author is to include or omit facts, events and characters for reasons of length and pace. If you had written *Warrior Queen*, what scene would you have liked to see included in *Warrior Queen*, and why? What scene would you omit?